FALL OF ICARUS

Brink of Distinction Book #2

By: Jon Messenger

Crimson Tree Publishing

This is a work of fiction. The characters, incidents, and dialogues are products of the author's imagination and are not to be construed as real. Any resemblance to actual events or persons, living or dead, is entirely coincidental.

Fall of Icarus

Copyright © 2012 by: Jon Messenger

Edited by: Cynthia Shepp

Cover Design by: Marya Heiman

Typography by: Courtney Nuckels

Crimson Tree Publishing
PO Box 561326
The Colony, TX 75056

www.crimsontreepublishing.com

PROLOGUE

"Captain on the deck!" the navigator yelled, as the small crew on the bridge of the *Liberator* leapt to their feet. Captain Hallith stepped off the lift and ran a hand along the bony ridges near his thinning hairline. Sweat beaded on his pudgy face from the exertion of walking down the long halls of the Alliance Cruiser. Where the sweat droplets fell, they pooled in rivulets along the sharp bone protrusions that ran along his jaw, cheeks, brows, and the base of his hairline. The Uligart smiled at the disciplined crew manning his bridge.

"At ease," he said softly.

The cramped bridge of the Alliance Cruiser was small enough that his nasally voice carried clearly across the room.

The crew took their places as the Captain took his at the top of the tiered rows of seats. "What's our status, Mr. Paporus?"

The ship's tactical officer, a large Oterian, reviewed the day's logs as he spoke. The tactical officer stood well over seven-feet tall. His tan, fur-covered body seemed grossly disproportionate on the small bridge, so much so that his jutting horns nearly scrapped the low ceiling as he moved. Captain Hallith only half listened, knowing that today's review would be dreadfully similar to yesterday's, and the day's before that, and the day's before that. The *Liberator*, an archaic vessel that was refurbished for its current mission, was assigned the duty of

1

patrolling the Demilitarized Zone between Alliance and Empire space. Established in the Taisa Accord nearly one hundred and fifty years previously, the Demilitarized Zone became a virtual barrier, existing of nothing more than sparse star systems and open space, but an invisible knife's edge through which ships from neither side would cross. The captain only accepted the position as a means for promotion, knowing that during a time of peace between the two organizations, job opportunities along the Demilitarized Zone held great potential for further advancement within the Fleet.

Until two days ago, Captain Hallith's job consisted of little more excitement than intercepting merchant vessels that travelled too close to the Demilitarized Zone. His crew boarded only one ship suspected of smuggling and, even after only a miniscule amount of illegal contraband was found, he threw the entire crew of that ship in the brig. Two days ago, however, Captain Hallith received a Top Secret communication from High Command. The blanket message, sent to all Captains patrolling the Demilitarized Zone, notified them of a potential new threat. Intel reported that a small fleet of deadly Terran Destroyers left Earth's orbit and had been spotted in Alliance occupied space. If that were the case, Hallith realized with a small amount of excitement, a direct engagement with the Terran Empire would catapult his career. He would be guaranteed a Fleet command position, instead of being delegated to a small, refurbished vessel like the *Liberator*.

Shaking free his fantasies of command, Captain Hallith noticed a worrisome expression on his navigator's face. "I'm sorry, Mr. Ninarath. What was that you asked?"

"I was merely asking what you thought about the rumors of a Terran invasion, sir," the Avalon asked in a soft, musical voice as he adjusted his white, feathery wings.

2

Captain Hallith always thought the Avalons looked like a sickly race, with their deathly pale skin and anemically thin bodies. He tried to avoid looking for too long at the navigator's slightly sunken cheeks.

"Do you really think there's a possibility that there are Terran Destroyers in Alliance space?"

"Well, I think about it quite a bit, to be honest," the captain replied, shifting his weight into his comfortable chair. The chair had been one of the few items Captain Hallith was able to specifically request during the rebuilding of his old ship. "But it's really hard to say how much truth there is to rumors about Terran attacks. Need I remind all of you that this isn't the first time the *Liberator* has been put on alert for a potential Terran threat? You're all too young to remember, but there was a time when everyone thought the Empire would attack at any moment. During those days, we were almost always on alert."

The captain settled into his chair, sliding down until he was able to rest his head against the back cushion and rested his hand on his full belly. "I think it would be a great opportunity to put the Empire in its place for violating the Taisa Accord, but I don't really put much stock in there actually being Destroyers out there."

"Sir, I have a contact," the communications officer chimed in. "It looks like multiple ships."

"Probably merchants off course," the captain replied dismissively. "Send them the verification code."

"And what if it's not a drill, sir?" Ninarath asked.

"What's that?"

"I'm just wondering what would happen if we later found out that there really were Destroyers in Alliance space. What if all this isn't a drill?"

Captain Hallith chuckled to himself. "Son, there hasn't

been a major conflict between the Alliance and the Empire in one hundred and fifty years. However, you've all trained extensively on how to conduct ship-to-ship combat. I think the Terrans might just be a little surprised if they were to go toe-to-toe with the *Liberator*."

"Sir?" the communications officer interrupted again.

"What is it, Mr. Chenowitt?" the captain asked of the Uligart.

"Sir, the ships aren't responding with any friendly frequencies."

The captain furrowed his brow. "What are they replying with then?"

"Nothing, sir," Chenowitt replied, a hint of nervousness on the edge of his voice. "I've hailed them repeatedly on the major communications bands and have received no response."

"And the FIS?" the captain asked, referring to the Friendly Identification System, a computer system that automatically sends a ship's designation when probed by Alliance Fleet requests.

"Nothing at all, sir. They're flying in complete blackout and radio silence."

"Smugglers," the captain muttered. He brought a microphone to his lips as he turned on the internal ship's radio channel. "Attention on the ship. This is Captain Hallith. We have unidentified ships rapidly approaching our positions. All hands, report to battle stations."

Captain Hallith pushed the microphone away and turned to his navigator. "Helm, bring us about and give me full forward view." The wall in the front of the bridge flickered to life, revealing a wide expanse of empty space. Slowly, as the ship maneuvered, distant dots swung into view.

"Give me magnification on those vessels."

The image of the ships grew closer in bursts as the camera magnified in stages. They grew from distant dots to sleek, aerodynamic silver bullets. As the image grew closer and crisper, the captain was able to see the shiny silver hulls of the six large ships. Along their sides, thin colorful pinstripes painted in overlapping patterns on the silver armored exterior of the vessels finally gave him their identity. Behind each of the six ships, the stars shimmered from the hot exhaust as their engines burned at their absolutely hottest, propelling the Destroyers toward the lone Alliance Cruiser.

His jaw dropping in surprise, Captain Hallith began barking orders to his crew. "Helm, bring us fully around and give me full speed! Tactics, arm all weapon systems!" He tugged hastily at the microphone beside him, nearly pulling it free from the wall. "All hands to battle stations! Terran Destroyers have crossed the Demilitarized Zone! This is not a drill!"

The Captain shook visibly as the *Liberator* accelerated, slowly building forward momentum from their worn engines. The forward view screen spun to reveal the space behind, showing the six Terran Destroyers growing steadily closer. No longer magnified, Captain Hallith could see the bristling weapons ports on the fronts of each ship. As the six ships got within range, the lead Destroyer fired a single rocket. On the front wall of the bridge, the Captain saw the launch and traced the streaking missile.

"Evasive maneuvers! Brace for impact!"

Quickly covering the distance between the ships, the plasma rocket's internal computer activated, directing the missile toward the leftmost engine on the *Liberator*. The antiquated ship was unable to move quickly enough to get out of range before the rocket drove into the massive rear exhaust, plunging into the superheated liquid plasma fueling the engines.

Everyone on board the *Liberator* felt the jarring shake as the missile struck the engine. Though Captain Hallith gritted his teeth tightly together, anticipating a ship–shattering explosion, it never came. Slowly, he released his death grip on the captain's chair.

"Give me a status report!"

The communications officer activated the internal ship's communications. A myriad of yells and screams could be heard from the engine room. As he listened, however, the captain was taken aback to find that they were yells of surprise, not pain.

Within the two–story engine, the metal cone tip of the rocket crumpled as it struck the burning liquid fuel, exposing a resilient dark canister within. Small explosives detonated around the perimeter of the internal canister, spilling forth gallons of dark fluid. The viscous, oily substance sloshed into the superheated plasma, where it began bubbling violently. Slowly, the black fluid turned tar–like, spreading into the engine. Everywhere it touched, the substance converted the molten plasma into a thick tar, jamming the engine.

Captain Hallith heard all this as it was yelled by a sea of frightened engineers and mechanics within the engine room. He felt the vibrations roll through the ship as it started to lose speed. On the view screen, the Terran Destroyers closed the distance even quicker than before.

"Sir, we're losing speed!" navigation yelled. "The left engine is completely unresponsive."

The Avalon navigator's voice faded into muted oblivion as Captain Hallith watched the weapon ports open on all six Terran ships simultaneously. Dozens of rockets launched from each ship, their smoking trails filling the screen with crisscrossing pathways. In their own hidden language, the smoky trails spelled inevitable death for the *Liberator*.

"Gods save us," the captain muttered as the first of the rockets slammed into the limping Alliance Cruiser. Metal plates buckled as blue and purple plasma explosions blossomed across the length of the ship. Burning oxygen vented into empty space as the hull was breached. Fire roared through the corridors, burning crewmen alive as they fled one explosion only to be caught in another.

The captain watched in dismay as missile after missile struck the *Liberator* until, gratefully, one ended his consternation by splitting the hull above the bridge. Captain Hallith and his crew on the bridge were obliterated by the subsequent plasma explosion, which saved them the more arduous death as their bodies were sucked through the gaping hull and into the void of space.

As the plasma blossoms cooled, debris of the former Alliance Cruiser drifted aimlessly in space. The Terran Destroyers flew by with barely a backward glance as they sought out their next target.

CHAPTER 1

Yen Xiao tapped his foot impatiently as the squadron commander continued the mission brief for the upcoming training exercise. Glancing down at his watch, he knew he was going to be cutting it close if the commander didn't stop talking. After all his hard work and political positioning, he refused to believe he might miss her arrival. He ran an irritated hand through his jet–black hair. Red splotches appeared on his yellowed skin as he gritted his teeth.

"Settle down," Adam Decker whispered from beside Yen. "You're starting to make me uncomfortable."

"I'm fine," Yen whispered harshly. "There's nothing wrong. I just wish he would quit talking already."

"Oh, you're fine?" Adam asked. "Then the fact that your spikes are flickering is just a coincidence?"

Yen turned sharply on his Pilgrim friend. True to Adam's word, Yen knew that the spikes that ran along his spine were rising and falling in rhythm with his quick breathing. Adam shrugged his massive shoulders before brushing his blond hair off his forehead. When Yen had first met Adam, the Pilgrim had always kept himself immaculately groomed. After the disaster of their first mission together, Adam had cared less and less about Alliance regulations on appearance standards. Even his strong Terran features were sometimes masked by fine stubble on his cheeks.

Much like the few other Pilgrims on board the *Revolution*, Adam was a conundrum. Born of Terran heritage, the Pilgrims were the original colonists for the Terran Empire, sent from their home world of Earth to the farthest star systems to discover new worlds full of easily exploitable natural resources. The Pilgrims, however, found much more: aliens. Making first contact with previously undiscovered alien races, the Pilgrims established trade treaties and, eventually, friendships. However, war between the Empire and the other alien species was inevitable. An unknowing incursion into Lithid space left an entire colony fleet annihilated and hundreds of thousands dead. In retaliation, the Empire declared martial law and attempted to eradicate the other species. To the surprise of the Terran politicians on Earth, the Pilgrims chose to side with the new Interstellar Alliance, fighting against the Terran threat. One hundred and fifty years had passed since the Taisa Accord was signed, establishing Alliance occupied space from Terran, but the Terran–descended Pilgrims were still an uncomfortable sight for some.

Yen frowned and looked down at his watch again. "I just don't want to be late."

"I'm about to take that watch away from you if you don't quit staring at it."

"Is there something you two would like to share?" Squadron Commander Garrix asked from the front of the room, his gravelly voice carrying obvious annoyance.

Both Yen and Adam looked up to see the Lithid squadron commander's featureless black, oval face staring directly at them, his barbed tail flickering in irritation. As natural shape shifters, the Lithids were able to transfigure their features into any humanoid shape. It was their natural state –

the faceless, glossy, and barbed exoskeleton – that Yen found most unsettling.

"If there's somewhere else you'd rather be, please let me know. The *Revolution* is leading a dozen other ships from the Alliance Fleet against the Terran Destroyers. You're getting the chance to take part in this battle because I say so. If either of you wants out, just let me know and I'll sign your transfer. Otherwise, you *will* pay attention during our pre-combat training exercises."

They both dropped their eyes, slightly embarrassed. "Sorry, sir" they muttered in unison.

Yen sank lower into his chair. Though he appeared to be listening, his eyes were barely focused on the Lithid squadron commander. As Garrix pointed his glossy, clawed hands at another of the targets on the holographic display and droned on in his gravelly voice, Yen thought about all he still needed to accomplish before she arrived. First and foremost, he needed to lose the coveralls. After wearing his body armor all day during training rehearsals, he could trace the salt stains on the dark fabric. Secondly, he realized, as a waft of sweaty body odor rolled across his nostrils, he needed to take a shower. Secretively glancing down at his watch, Yen started to seriously doubt he would have time to do it all and still make it to the airlock.

"I saw that," Adam whispered. "Quit looking at your damn watch. You're going to get us into trouble again."

Yen resolved himself to silent displeasure for the rest of the brief. He knew his role better than most of the other warrants and officers in the briefing room. Aside from Adam and Yen, no one else had any true combat experience, including the squadron commander. They held their positions and preached tactics based off historical records and simulated combat. It made it difficult to remain focused during briefings, knowing that none of them were truly tested against a real opponent when death was a viable result.

Yen looked up when he noted a shift in Garrax's tone, signaling that an end to the monotonous brief was nearing. He leaned over excitedly to Adam who, though he had chided Yen for not paying attention, wore a frown fraught with impatience.

"Are you coming or not?" Yen asked.

Adam stole a glance at his own watch. "You're going to be killing yourself to try to make it in time."

"Yes or no?"

"I'm out. There's no way I'm going to sprint the length of the *Revolution* just to go meet a woman, especially one who actually seems to find you attractive!"

He smiled as the squadron commander concluded his summary. "Your loss. I'll tell you all about her later tonight."

Yen was out of his chair and walking brusquely toward the rear exit to the briefing room before Garrix had finished saying "dismissed". Once out the door, he broke into a sprint, hurrying toward the lift that would take him down to the living quarters. There were some advantages to being a combat veteran, as Yen had found. Although he was only an insertion team leader onboard one of the *Cair* transport ships, Yen was given his own room on the *Revolution*, an honor normally reserved for a more senior officer. The door to his room slid open and he rushed inside, slipping past the small dining room table and flicking on the bedroom lights. His pristine dress uniform was already laid out on the bed, having been positioned earlier that morning. Stripping off the soiled uniform, Yen retained enough sense to carry the dirty clothes into the bathroom with him, knowing there was still a chance that he would not be coming home alone tonight.

Yen stepped into the shower and made quick work of scrubbing his body clean. It seemed that no sooner had the soap been washed from his skin and out of his hair, then the water was turned off and he was toweling dry. He realized just how rough he looked when he glanced in the mirror. Even against his yellow skin, the faint outlines of a bruise could be seen spreading across his left cheek, a gift from an overzealous Oterian during the training practice today. During their rehearsed incursion on an enemy ship, the Oterian had been too eager to exit the *Cair* mock-up. His thrown elbow, as he shoved his way to the front of the line, caught Yen on the side of the face, snapping his head backward from the force of the blow. Yen already had an adequate punishment planned for the soldier, but seeing the bruise reignited his anger.

Yen glanced down at his watch and jumped as he realized how much time had already passed. Running a brush through his long, black hair, Yen gave one final, cursory glance in the mirror before hurrying back into the bedroom and slipping into his uniform. No marks or lint stained the crisp Infantry uniform. Yen readjusted the series of medals that hung heavily on the left side of his chest; medals he had won during the multiple missions conducted while he served with the covert operations division of the Infantry. Dominating the rack of medals, hanging above the others, Yen caught sight of the Alliance Service Cross, one of the highest awards offered in the military. He earned it during his final mission with the covert operations, one which pained him to relive.

Yen had been one of seven soldiers assigned to his covert operations team a year before. They had been a close team, spending nearly every moment together, both on and off work. Though they were relatively junior based on their time in the military, the team was also the best in the Alliance. Many of the stories about his missions were impressive and made for great conversations at the bar. Many of his missions, though, he couldn't speak about now, nor did he think they would ever be declassified enough for him to share with even his closest friends.

His last mission had been a disaster. Betrayed by the Captain of their ship, a Pilgrim who harbored secret loyalties to the Terran Empire, Yen, Adam Decker, and over one hundred other soldiers were left for dead in a city full of mutated monsters; one final gift from the already overly generous Empire. For two days, the soldiers had fought against the ravenous Seques, but in the war of attrition, the Seques were destined to win. In the end, Yen's team leader sacrificed himself to kill the rogue Captain. Yen, Adam, and an Uligart named Buren, were all that survived. They brought word of the betrayal to the High Council and told them the other information they had gleaned during their conflict: that the Terran Empire had sent a small fleet into Alliance space. All three were awarded the Alliance Service Cross for their bravery and heroism.

Yen fingered the medal idly as he rode the lift up to the main airlock. He hoped he wasn't too late, though he knew the size of the crowds that would already be gathered around the airlock. The arrival of newly assigned soldiers was always a reason for a celebration. Though the Fleet and Infantry both covered missions throughout known space, it seemed that the military was a small world. It was inevitable that you ran into long lost friends and counterparts with whom you served years before. Yen wasn't looking for a long lost friend, even if some of his fellow comrades were going to be arriving today. His focus would be entirely on finding a single woman from the throng of new arrivals. He realized the daunting task ahead. Not only did he have to contend with fighting his way to the front of the crowd, he also had to contend with spotting Keryn amidst the sea of uniformed crewmen.

Yen's heart sank as the doors to the lift opened. The cheers of a massive crowd, along with the swell of dozens of overlapping conversations, washed over him, overwhelming his senses. Because of the droning squadron commander's brief, and his own daydreaming while getting ready, Yen was late. They'd already arrived.

Yen barely had any space to stand as he pushed his way off the elevator. Craning his neck, he tried to see over the crowd. He was fighting against a raging torrent of bodies, many of which were already heading toward his now empty lift, on their way to a hundred different points of interest throughout the ship. Still undeterred, Yen pushed his way further upstream; working his way toward the large iris through which the new recruits arrived. Yen caught sight of a few promising sights: a flash of silver hair, blazing violet eyes, deeply tanned skin. But each time Yen thought he saw something that reminded him of Keryn, the person turned and he realized it wasn't her. His emotions were cresting waves, first reaching a peak of anticipation only to be crushed in the wake.

Yen started to lose hope as the crowd began to thin. Had he arrived too late? Had she been one of the first to pass through the airlock, only to be snatched up by her pilot sponsor and whisked away? Fewer and fewer new arrivals trickled through the airlock as they finished exiting the transport docked outside. Looking down the tunnel, Yen didn't see her anywhere. Disheartened, Yen turned away and stepped toward the lift.

"Yen Xiao?" a familiar feminine voice called from behind him.

Yen, smiling broadly, turned to see Keryn Riddell

emerge from the gathered crowd. Her fine silver hair was pulled back into a professional ponytail, exposing her naturally deeply tanned Wyndgaart skin and the red and purple tattoos – identifying characteristics of her race – that traced the curves of her cheeks and disappeared beneath the high necked collar of her uniform. Intensely violet eyes sparkled maddeningly in the halogen light. Her image was burned permanently into his memory, though he met her only once before. She truly was just as beautiful as he remembered.

Sighing with relief, Yen spoke. "I was so worried I'd already missed you."

"I didn't see you at first, but I had faith that you'd be here eventually."

Yen served with Keryn's older brother, Eza, during his time on the covert operations team. On the same mission for which he received the Alliance Service Cross, Eza was killed trying to afford the rest of them time to escape the planet. Had it not been for the sacrifice of Yen's best friend, he would have died on the planet himself. That moment had not been lost in the passage of time and Yen felt obligated to look after Keryn, to ensure she stayed safe during her service as a *Cair* pilot. Yen, though, found his task of watching after Keryn more of a boon and less of a professional obligation.

"Are you going to show me around," Keryn asked, "or are we going to sit here all day in awkward silence?"

Yen shook his head as he realized he'd been staring. "I'm sorry. Come on, I'll show you the highlights."

They walked past the lift, choosing instead to walk the length of the ship. Their tour lasted for hours, though most of their time was spent examining the *Duun* and *Cair* ships that lined the enormous hangar bay. The hangar would be Keryn's second home once she got settled into her normal routine. She asked a ridiculous amount of questions as they finished their tour and made their way toward the housing area where Keryn would be living. Though Keryn was curious about much of the ship's day-to-day operations, most of their conversation remained solely on small talk: about Keryn's experiences in the Fleet Academy, her temporary position in the replacement center as she awaited permanent orders onboard an Alliance Cruiser, and how she felt after receiving her orders assigning her to the *Revolution*.

"I meant to ask you about that," Keryn said as they discussed her current assignment. "I was assigned to the Farimas Space Station while I was waiting for orders. All my fellow classmates were there. We were getting settled in for the long haul, since we were all told it would be up to six months before permanent positions opened up in any of the Cruiser Squadrons. Yet, miraculously, I suddenly get orders assigning me to the *Revolution*. No one else seemed to have received any orders except me."

"I guess you're just lucky that way," Yen said with a smile.

"You wouldn't have had anything to do with that, would you?" Keryn asked coyly.

Yen smiled mischievously. "Using my rank and position in such a way would've been unethical. Hypothetically, however, being one of the only war veterans onboard would allow me quite a bit of influence on a decision like that."

Though Keryn's smile still lingered, Yen could sense the pain behind her eyes at the mention of previous wars in which Keryn had lost a close loved one. Cursing himself silently at making such an obvious gaff, Yen casually tried to change the subject.

"It looks like this is your room."

Keryn nodded softly as she looked at the nondescript

door sitting amidst a dozen others on a very nondescript hall. As Yen entered the access code and the door slid open, revealing the rather barren kitchen and dining room areas. Two bedrooms extended from the main common room. Keryn's roommate, Yen already knew, had not yet arrived on board. Essentially, Keryn had her own room; another perk that Yen had coordinated specifically for her.

"It's everything I could have hoped for," Keryn joked, her sense of humor returning as she observed the empty room.

The air around Yen began to shimmer and dance, as though he were surrounding himself with a desert mirage. The cabinets in the kitchen opened and a pair of plates, glasses, and utensils floated out. Drifting across the room, they set down in their proper places on either side of the dining room table.

"Oh, yes," Keryn laughed. "That makes it much better." She turned toward Yen, arching an eyebrow. "You really have gotten better at controlling your abilities. What else can you do with that power of yours?"

"That'll have to be a discussion for another time," Yen chuckled, not letting Keryn know about the sharp pain he felt behind his eyes after using his powers. Ever since pushing his powers beyond their limit during his escape from the Seques, Yen suffered from headaches nearly every time he used his powers for anything more than mundane activities.

"So what do I have on my agenda for the near future?" Keryn asked.

"I wish I could give you a few weeks to really get comfortable with your new Squadron and find all the hidden nooks of the *Revolution*, but you're coming in at a bad time."

Keryn nodded, suddenly serious. "I had heard that we're going to be going to war with the Terrans. I'm glad you got me this assignment, Yen. I want my chance at revenge."

"Before you get your shot at the Terran Fleet, you have to go through the more mundane pre-combat training exercises," Yen explained. "We have another rehearsal tomorrow, then a real time ship-on-ship combat scheduled for the day after. If the squadron commander blesses off on it, I'd like to put you in control of a *Cair* for that exercise."

Keryn seemed surprised. "You have a *Cair* ship available for me already? I heard it usually takes weeks before a new pilot's attached to a specific ship."

"Normally, you're right. However, this ship happens to be special. Don't worry; you'll get to meet the *Cair Ilmun* tomorrow. You'll have plenty on your plate over the next few days."

Yen turned and started walking toward the door, not eager to overstay his welcome. Before he could leave, however, he had to try one last gambit. "Speaking of plates. I know you're still getting settled, but once you're comfortably established on the *Revolution*, I'd love the chance to take you out to dinner. My treat, of course," he hastily added.

Keryn smiled warmly. "I think I'd like that."

"Thank you for showing me around," she said as she followed him to the door. As they reached the hallway, Keryn placed a gentle hand on his arm. "I know you put your neck on the line to get me this assignment, get me into a *Cair* ship right away, and really help get me settled. It hasn't gone unnoticed. I won't let you down during the next few days' training exercises."

"Believe me, Keryn. It was nothing."

"Whether or not you think it was 'nothing', thanks again, for everything."

"You're welcome."

"Goodnight, Yen," Keryn said, giving his arm a gentle squeeze before stepping back inside her quarters.

"Goodnight, Keryn. Sleep well."

The door slid shut between the two. Yen smiled broadly, feeling exuberant as he walked down the winding halls toward his own room.

CHAPTER 2

Keryn's head no sooner hit the pillow than she was awake again, going through the next day's training scenarios on a ship simulator. Introductions to the rest of the Squadron had been rushed, leaving Keryn nervous about her first tactical outing with the other pilots. She had performed remarkably, though, and received accolades from Garrix on her piloting skills. Not all of the praise was hers alone, however. Yen sat in the copilot's seat during the entire simulation, giving her pointers and advice. In the end, though, it was her own piloting abilities that helped her stand out.

"You did great today," Yen praised as they walked back to their quarters. "I think you surprised a whole lot of the senior pilots."

"Yourself included?" she asked.

Yen laughed. "Yes, me too."

"It wasn't really that hard," Keryn explained. "The simulator here isn't much different from the one at the Academy, and I was top of my class when I graduated."

Yen's smile disappeared, her words acting like a trigger for a more serious conversation. "Don't start getting too arrogant. One of the reasons you did so well was because you were willing to take some uncalculated risks today. In a simulation, that's fine because you can fly fearlessly, knowing that the worst that could happen to you is a flashing sign telling you that your game is over. The same risks that you took today may not work when your opponent is a flesh and blood Terran, one who might be just as crazy as you are."

"I didn't mean anything by it," Keryn replied softly. Her tough demeanor transformed, revealing the younger girl that Keryn truly was. "I'm just trying to do my best."

Yen stared at her, unsure if her new attitude was a ruse to make him feel sympathy or if she truly hid a more sensitive personality behind her strong, abrasive exterior. As they stared at each other – Yen wondering if she were acting and Keryn longing for understanding – Yen finally smiled and slipped an arm around her shoulder.

"I made a promise to your brother that I would do everything in my power to keep you safe. I may come across a little harsh at times, but everything I tell you will keep you alive in the long run."

Keryn smiled, the confidence reasserting itself. "I'm not going to let you down."

"We'll see tomorrow," Yen replied. "Get some sleep tonight because tomorrow we'll be pitting our pilots against another Alliance Squadron."

Visibly relaxed as they walked, Keryn latched onto the new conversation, eager to help Yen forget about her moment of weakness. "Do you know who we drew to fly against?"

"We're taking on the *Defiant*. Both their pilots and their crewman are tough, so even if we make it to their Cruiser, we'll have a tough fight during the boarding."

Keryn elbowed Yen hard in the ribs. "What do you mean *if* we make it? I'll get you there. Whether or not you can manage to make it as far as the first hallway before getting your team slaughtered is a different story."

21

Yen, smiling broadly, shoved Keryn playfully. "You talk a big game, little girl. We'll see how well you do tomorrow." He paused, realizing they had already reached Keryn's room. "Get some good sleep tonight. I need you on your toes come tomorrow."

"Goodnight, Yen," she said coyly over her shoulder as she slipped into her room. Yen waited a couple moments after the door had closed behind her. Shaking his head in amazement at the strange Wyndgaart woman, Yen turned and walked to his own room. He had teased her incessantly, but he knew that she was right. Even if she could get them to the *Defiant*, the harder job was boarding a ship full of volatile enemies.

Keryn entered the massive hangar amidst a buzz of activity. Pilots and crews moved with mechanical precision around their craft, checking hull integrity and weapon systems. The noise of the room – tires squealing on the smooth floor, the din of a hundred different conversations, and the whir of machine guns running through practice fires – enveloped Keryn. She smiled softly, feeling at home amongst the droning sounds. This was the reason she became a pilot instead of going through the Ritual of Initiation, as did so many of her race. Keryn found her peace and tranquility here, among the technology and ballet of space combat.

Across the room, Keryn caught sight of Yen as he performed the preflight check on the *Cair Ilmun*. The sleek gunmetal grey ship glistened in the stark lighting of the hangar bay. Its wings drooped heavily from the weight of the two missile launchers and pair of machine guns. Though the *Cair* ships were not intended to be direct combat fighters like the *Duun* ships, they carried an arsenal large enough to defend themselves if necessary. Keryn hurried over, knowing that much of the work Yen now did was actually her responsibility.

Yen looked up as she approached. "Good morning, sleepy head."

Keryn rolled her eyes. "I'm not exactly late, you know."

"If you're early, you're on time. If you're on time, you're late. And…"

"If you're late, you're wrong," Keryn finished, having heard the same phrase repeated numerous times during her training at the Academy. "Why do I believe you could quote the textbook if asked?"

"Funny, but not far from the truth," Yen joked. "Now get over here and help me out."

Keryn joined Yen as he continued checking the hull integrity. In the void of space, even the most miniscule break in the armored plating would cause a deadly decompression. Keryn knew the importance of the check, but still paused as she ran an affectionate hand over the hull of the ship. Most of the *Cair Ilmun's* hull was immaculate, having been tended with great care since being assigned to the *Revolution*. Still, along its side, Keryn could still see long scratches that had never been mended. Slipping to the side of the ship, she ran her fingers along the grooves.

"We thought about patching those up," a gruff voice said from behind her, "but we think it's important that every ship have a story to tell."

Keryn turned and came face to face with a muscular Pilgrim. His blond hair hung over his forehead and he smiled disarmingly as he leaned against the wall.

"Adam!" Keryn exclaimed, hurrying over to his side. "Yen told me you were around. I was wondering how long it would be before you showed up."

Much as Yen had done for the months since the memorial

23

service, Adam had written Keryn as well at her request, telling the few stories he had of her brother prior to his death. "Sorry, Keryn. We Infantry grunts don't get a lot of chances to mingle with the right and proper Fleet people."

Keryn caught him unaware as she punched him hard in the gut. "Right and proper? You take that back right now," Keryn scolded while, simultaneously, smiling mischievously.

"Break it up, you two," Yen called, stepping around the nose of the ship. "We have work to do here."

"Sir, yes, sir," Adam muttered under his breath. He reached down and hoisted a heavy box full of equipment; supplies that the insurgent team would need once they breached the *Defiant*'s hull.

Keryn turned away from Adam and stepped over to Yen's side. She quickly changed the subject. "How does the *Cair Ilmun* look? We ready to put her in the air?"

"She's perfect," Yen said, though his eyes were no longer on the ship. "I think she'll do you proud."

"I only hope I can return the favor."

Yen heard voices behind him and turned as the rest of the Infantry soldiers approached the ship. Wearing their heavy body armor and carrying a full complement of weapons, all modified to fire nonlethal shots, the Infantry looked significantly deadlier than did Keryn, who wore only her piloting coveralls.

Whispering, so as not to be heard by the rough soldiers, Yen gave Keryn some advice. "Remember: confidence. That should be your watchword while you're flying. No matter how tough these guys are and how much they may intimidate you, you are still in charge of this ship. Never forget it."

The insurgent team pulled up short, eyeing their new pilot. Though Yen's words were still fresh in Keryn's mind, their meaning seemed lost on her. She raised her hand in a sheepish wave. "Hi," was all she managed to say.

The soldiers walked past her with barely a hint of recognition, climbing aboard the ship. Keryn cursed herself silently.

Hi? the Voice said condescendingly in her head. *These are experienced soldiers and all you could manage was a weak hello? We are definitely going to have to work on that.*

"Oh yes, that was the confidence I was referring to," Yen added, echoing the Voice's sentiments as he walked past her and climbed aboard.

Keryn frowned, feeling her own irritation. The Voice had been remarkably silent for so long; it was frustrating to hear it resurface. All Wyndgaarts were born with the Voice, a mental culmination of generations of fighting skills passed down genetically to each future warrior. When reaching maturity, it was commonly accepted that a Wyndgaart would merge with their Voice, thereby accessing all the contained memories of their ancestors. The merging, called Initiation, was what allowed skilled students to become the universe-renown Wyndgaart warriors. But, Keryn knew, that knowledge came with a price. With the merger came a loss of individual personality. Instead of the person you were, you became an overlapping personification of hundreds of your ancestors. Keryn had fought against the Voice, often ignoring it, so that she could follow her own path to the Fleet Academy. She was proud of her decision, but while the Voice seemed to find interest in building her confidence, it was also one of the biggest reasons she suffered from indecision. It was difficult to make a proper decision when your own mind was constantly contradicting you.

She turned and followed the others on board. As she entered the crew compartment, most of the Infantry were already seated, their large weapons stored beside them and their bags locked into place above. Already frustrated, Keryn shoved her way past the couple soldiers still standing in the middle of the compartment. She expected a muttered insult or two, but heard nothing in response. If the only thing they would respond to is violence, then Keryn was pretty sure she could give them more than they could handle.

Keryn slipped into the forward cockpit and found Yen already seated in the copilot's chair. Without sparing him a word, Keryn sat in her own seat and strapped the throat microphone around her neck. She flipped a series of switches above her and started the initial sequence to ignite the plasma engines.

"Forget about them," Yen said as he checked the gauges and computer display. "You want to impress them, show them what you can do at the controls of a ship. Get them where they need to be and they'll be yours forever."

Keryn, managing little more than a grunt in recognition, pressed a button and the exterior doors to the ship slid shut. The radio crackled as the squadron commander activated the internal ship channel.

"*Revolution* Squadron, this is Squadron Commander Garrix," the gravelly voice called to the ships as they all began preflight warm ups. "Have all ships in position in three mikes. We will decompress the hangar at that time and begin the combat scenario."

Piloting one of the *Cair* ships, Keryn knew that she had a while before she would be required to pull her ship out of its alcove and get on line. Through the thick window of the cockpit, Keryn could barely make out the dozens of *Duun* fighters as they rolled into their start positions.

"We have a couple minutes before you have to move,"

Yen said, "so let's go over everything one more time."

Keryn nodded and began reciting the training Yen had been drilling into her since her arrival onboard. "Hang back. Let the *Duun*'s engage. Look for an opening. Stop for nothing." She knew that *Cair Ilmun* wasn't made for head-to-head combat. As she had learned in the Academy, her role in combat was to keep her crew alive long enough to board an enemy ship. Once the *Duun* fighters had the enemy ships sufficiently engaged in combat, she would fly through any gaps in the sea of machine gun and missile fire until finally docking with the enemy vessel. Tapping her nails impatiently on the console in front of her, Keryn ran through the multitude of things that could go wrong in those four simple steps.

"You forgot the most important one," Yen added. "Relax! You're making me nervous."

Keryn smiled weakly. "I just want to make sure I do this right. I'm the most junior pilot in the Squadron. I've got a lot to prove."

"Then go out there and do what you do best." Yen looked down and watched until the blinking red light turn a solid green. "It's time to get into position."

Rolling the *Cair Ilmun* forward, she took her place at the back of one of five lines of ships. The sheer volume of fighters and transport ships filling the hangar was staggering. The thought of all those ships, and an equal number from the *Defiant,* all weaving through one another in open space seemed overwhelming. The Academy had put her through a litany of simulations and shown her video of space combats during the Great War between the Alliance and Empire, but it was nerve-wracking to know that she would soon be fully engaged in a similar combat.

The lights in the hangar dimmed, replaced by a harsh

red illumination. A dull roar filled the room as the breathable oxygen was vented from the hangar bay. As the massive door on the far end of the bay cracked open, the sea of stars and distant galaxies glowed against the inky curtain of empty space.

"We are a go!" Garrix called over the radio. "Launch in sequence!"

As the ships fired their plasma engines, they launched from the hangar bay, exiting into the void beyond. In Keryn's eyes, having never seen an assault on such a grand scale, it reminded her of angry insects swarming from a disturbed hive. The ships flew from the *Revolution*, spreading as they exited, and filling the space beyond.

Turning her ship and taking her place near the top right of the *Revolution*'s hull, Keryn was able to see the distant *Defiant* moving into position. As the hangar doors on their rival ship opened, distant specks poured from the ship's underbelly, filling the area in front of the large Cruiser. For a moment, though Keryn knew it to be false, there was an illusion that time had stopped. The two forces seemed to hang in empty space, staring at one another in eager anticipation for the other side to make a move. But Keryn knew that more was happening than she could perceive. Though there was no sound and no true sense of motion, Keryn's gauges said otherwise. The two forces were hurtling forward at incredible speeds, covering the distance between the Cruisers, eventually crashing violently into one another.

The *Duun* fighters from both ships disappeared into a sea of exchanged laser fire and faux rocket launches. Red lights on their hulls instantaneously illuminated many of the ships', a signal that they had been incapacitated or destroyed. Shutting down the engines, the pilots drifted as no more than obstacles around which the other *Duun* fighters danced in their brutal

28

ballet.

To Keryn's left and right, a few of the other *Cair* ships launched forward. She had to assume that they saw openings that she did not. In honesty, though, Keryn found it difficult to believe there would ever be a sufficient gap through which she could fly the *Cair Ilmun*. The *Duun* fighters created a wall of armored hulls and exchanged gunfire that seemed nearly impenetrable.

Yen noticed her hand twitching near the controls. "Not yet," he said calmly. "Wait for an opening."

More and more of the *Cair* ships moved, though she already saw a number of them disabled in the cloud of dodging ships. Keryn remembered Yen's words about winning over the Infantry by keeping them alive. She couldn't imagine the irritation the other insertion groups must be feeling, drifting in a lifeless ship, knowing that they had been killed without ever being able to lift a weapon in their own defense.

"All *Cair* ships, move forward," Garrix ordered over the radio.

"Not yet, Keryn," Yen said sternly.

She looked left and right, realizing that she was the only ship not moving forward. Her hands itched, jumping at the opportunity to fire the plasma engines and finally engage in combat. What did all the other pilots see that she did not? They were all moving confidently, as though they stood a chance of making it through the hail of gunfire between the two Cruisers. Maybe the squadron commander was right.

"*Cair Ilmun*," Garrix called. "Why have you not moved forward? Move out now."

"Don't do it," Yen warned.

Listen to him, the Voice agreed. *It's not time, not yet.*

"*Cair Ilmun*, you will engage."

Keryn saw over half of the other *Cair* ships floating, already destroyed during their mock combat. Fear rose in her throat as she realized the technique they had adopted. It was a war of attrition. No matter how many *Cair* ships were destroyed, always enough slipped through to invade the opponent's vessel. More than anything, Keryn didn't want to wind up like all the others that hadn't made it through. Fighting a war of attrition just didn't make sense to her.

"What is the problem, Magistrate Riddell?" the squadron commander barked over the radio, his gravelly voice full of irritation.

"Hold your position," Yen said over the aggravated commander. "Don't listen to him."

Keryn's hand moved to the console, but her fingers remained hovering above the keys to engage the engine. She didn't know who was right and who to trust. She believed Yen and knew that he had her best interest at heart, but he had been serving in the covert operations during all his combat experience. He didn't have any combat experience as a pilot. On the other hand, Keryn seriously doubted Garrix had any experience either.

"Magistrate Riddell, I am ordering you to move out!"

He's wrong, the Voice replied. *He's going to get you killed.*

Conflicted, Keryn let her hand drop and activated the engine. The *Cair Ilmun* shot forward and dove toward the weaving *Duun* fighters. Scanning side to side, Keryn searched eagerly for any opening in the sea of ships, some miraculously obvious pathway through the throng of fighters that would lead her to the *Defiant*. Though she searched, nothing became apparent.

"Watch on your left!" Yen called out.

Keryn saw the *Duun* fighter breaking contact and diving

30

toward her ship. She saw the fire leap from the spinning machine guns as she dipped her own wings, sending the *Cair Ilmun* into a roll. Though she saw numerous flashes of near missed shots, she moved out of range without being shot down. She smiled slightly and sighed, but her relief was quickly washed away as two more *Duun* fighters moved toward her ship. The *Duun* fighters, aside from eliminating one another, were tasked with the sole responsibility of destroying missiles or boarding ships that threatened their Cruiser. Even a single boarding party had the capability to completely destroy a Cruiser with a well-placed series of explosives. The *Duun* fighters would do all they could to destroy Keryn long before she could reach the *Defiant*.

Dodging left and right, Keryn saw the streak of a mock missile nearly miss their right wing. Tilting the ship upward, Keryn opened fire. With great satisfaction, she saw red lights flare on the leftmost *Duun* as she eliminated it from combat. In her celebration, however, she failed to notice the other *Duun* drop from behind the first, using its destroyed hull as cover. The flashes of machine gun fire glared through the thick cockpit window. Red lights lit up across the console, warning of multiple strikes to their hull. A warning claxon sounded loudly throughout the ship moments before her engines began to shut down.

Across the console before her, a single word replaced the gauges and screens: Destroyed.

Dead in the water, the *Cair Ilmun* drifted in space as the battle raged on. The only sounds Keryn could hear were the disappointed cursing of the Infantry now trapped in the back of her ship, dead without ever being able to lift a weapon in their own defense.

Keryn walked down the hall towards her living quarters,

biting back tears of frustration at her loss during the battle. After landing, none of the Infantry had bothered to spare her a second glance as they disembarked and walked back toward the debriefing room. Only Yen and Adam had stayed behind, though conversation was minimal and terse.

She didn't turn as she heard a hurried set of running footfalls behind her. A hand closed over her arm and spun her around. Yen stared at her, the jovial smile gone from his face. She matched his intensity with an angry look of her own.

"You here to tell me how much I screwed up?" Keryn growled. "Believe me, I can take care of reliving my failure all on my own." Jerking, she broke free from his grip.

"That's not why I'm here," Yen replied sternly. "Yes, you screwed up, but you screwed up because you didn't listen. If you do something like that when we finally face the Terrans, there won't be another chance to beat yourself up. We'll all be dead."

"Don't you think I already know that?" Keryn yelled at him. "And I did listen. I was ordered by the squadron commander to engage, and I engaged. I *follow* orders, Yen."

"You're right, you do. But that's the one thing that you did wrong. The one thing you need to remember above all else is that when you're in the cockpit, flying the *Cair Ilmun*, there is no one else that has a better view of the combat than you. Not Garrix, not the *Revolution*, not even me. When we're in combat, you are the captain of the ship. You answer to no one else. If it looks wrong, you disobey orders because, deep down, you know that it will save lives. You listened to someone who thought they knew better than you did. But up there, no one knows better than you."

Keryn sighed heavily. "And what do you propose I do next time?" she asked flatly.

"You want to find out? Then I propose you go out to dinner with me tomorrow," Yen said. Keryn arched an eyebrow in confusion. "I have some ideas that I think will help us out next time we fly. If you're interested, come to dinner with me tomorrow night and we can talk tactics."

Feeling some of her animosity flood from her body, Keryn allowed herself a little smile. "When you asked me out to dinner, this isn't exactly what I expected."

"Business first, fun later," Yen explained with a broad smile.

"Fine," Keryn conceded. "Tomorrow night. It's a date."

She turned before Yen could figure out a quick-witted retort and stepped onto one of the lifts. She gave him a playful wave as the doors closed. Yen shook his head in wonderment as he took the next lift down to his own room, still not sure if Keryn was the single most brilliant pilot he had ever encountered or the single craziest. In the end, he realized he really didn't care one way or the other.

CHAPTER 3

The twelve Alliance Cruisers orbited the bloated gas giant, each in their own elliptical path, pacing the empty space like caged animals hungry for their next meal. Captain Hodge, sitting in the captain's chair onboard the *Revolution*, looked nearly as agitated and feral. Her feathery white wings shook in irritation as she frowned, unhappy with the current situation.

"Anything yet?" she asked Magistrate Young, the Uligart communications officer.

Young looked nervous as he replied. "Sorry, ma'am. Nothing yet."

Captain Hodge sighed as she sunk deeper into her chair. For weeks, the *Revolution* and her sister ships had been on high alert, knowing that they could be called to duty at any time; called to hunt down and eliminate the Terran Destroyers. Yet, for all their bluster and repetitive training, no assignment had been forthcoming. She could nearly sense the tension seeping through the ship. Small fights had broken out, mainly between Infantry and Fleet soldiers. In garrison, such rivalries were ignored, often times welcomed, since the competitive nature drove both sides to excel. In a time of war, especially the first major public confrontation between the Alliance and the Empire in nearly one hundred and fifty years, Captain Hodge had neither the latitude nor the patience to deal with any disagreement that left a member of her crew in the infirmary.

A gentle cough woke Captain Hodge from her meditation. Looking over, her head leaning heavily on her hand in a show of discontent, the Captain noticed Young's patient look. "Yes, Magistrate Young?"

"Ma'am, there's a call for you."

Captain Hodge sat upright in her chair, her wings unfurling and stretching. Perhaps their time of waiting was finally over. "Forward the message to my console," she ordered.

As soon as the light at the base of her console flashed red, she reached out a shaking hand and pressed the button to receive. "This is Captain Hodge of the *Revolution*."

Another Avalon face appeared on the screen. Unlike Captain Hodge's more approachable and welcoming personality, the woman that looked back at her exuded a dour and gloomy visage. Narrow, arching eyebrows that gave her a constantly angry appearance hooded her pencil thin lips and narrow eyes. Adding those characteristics to her naturally gaunt face and pale skin, and Captain Nitella looked every part the villainess of a long forgotten fairy tale.

"You look disappointed to see me, Hodge," Captain Nitella said, her musical voice sounding harshly with sharp notes. Captain of the *Defiant*, Nitella and Hodge traced a professional, if not personal, competitive friendship back for years during their concurrent years of service in the Fleet.

"The disappointment is not because of you, Nitella," Hodge replied, slumping back into her chair. "I just grow so bored of flying around the same planet. I want action. I want intrigue. I want... something different."

"We could always do another practice exercise," Nitella offered, arching one of her angry brows.

Hodge sighed heavily. "No, I think we all had enough fun with the last one." The last training exercise had been a stalemate, ending with most of the smaller *Duun* and *Cair* ships destroyed in the space between the two Cruisers and little true damage done to either ship. The end of the battle had wound up as little more than two ships sitting miles apart launching mock rocket after mock rocket at one another, all of which were destroyed long before reaching their target.

Though no real answer had been decided and no winner declared, the training exercise had been a disaster to Hodge. Not only was she unable to destroy the rival ship, the exercise showed a great weakness in both her pilots and her weapons teams on board the *Revolution*. With war potentially days away, she feared that her crew was grossly inadequate for such a determined enemy as the Terran Empire.

"You look tired," Nitella stated. Hodge winced at the words. Even the most harmless of gestures seemed condescending when coming from her fellow Avalon. "I hope the stresses of captaining the Fleet are not getting to you, Hodge."

Captain Hodge frowned, refusing to be pulled into an argument with her rival. "Unfortunately, Nitella, I can't continue this conversation. I want to make sure the lines are clear in case a more important call comes through. I'll talk to you later."

Hodge ended the call before the other Avalon realized her backhanded insult. Rubbing the palm of her hand over her eyes, Captain Hodge realized that Nitella might have been right. She had been manning the helm on and off for days, anticipating a call that had yet to come. Yearning for a distraction, she turned to her tactical officer and second in command.

"Eminent Merric," she said, "come and discuss the last training exercise with me." She hoped that he had seen something she hadn't; that maybe, somewhere in their failed venture, there had been salvageable piloting.

Merric walked quickly to her side. The tall Pilgrim had immaculately trimmed dark hair, offset by pale skin and a permanent frown. Always displeased, Merric was a stickler for regulations, often able to quote the most obscure Fleet rule when it suited him. Though Hodge found him abrasive, she also knew that the crew feared his almost weekly inspections, which allowed her to run the ship without fear of mechanical or technical failures.

"Yes, ma'am," Merric said as he snapped to attention before her.

"Relax, Eminent Merric," she said, though she saw only the slightest shift in his position. Shaking her head softly, she realized that he was relaxed. "I want to discuss the training exercise against the *Defiant*."

If it were possible, Merric's frown deepened. "It was a despicable display, ma'am."

Captain Hodge tried not to shoot him a disapproving look that would have matched his expression. "I realize the failures of this ship and its crew. What I am looking for is anything positive that came from our exercise."

Merric paused, searching for a proper response. "The ship defenses worked admirably, as did the *Duun* pilots as they repeatedly destroyed both the invading *Cair* ships and incoming missiles."

"And our own *Cair* pilots? How did they do?" Captain Hodge already knew the answer, but strove to develop Merric as a leader. Though he was callous when dealing with subordinates, he was a brilliant Fleet officer and held a lot of potential for future advancement and, if fate was in his favor, command of his own Cruiser some day. Prior to then, however, he still required positive grooming.

"They struggled to find any opening in open space. One of our pilots even hesitated when ordered to advance. Only two of the *Cair* ships actually made it to the *Defiant*, and those were immediately destroyed by Captain Nitella's quickly responding ship defense forces. None of our Infantry ever got close enough to place an explosive that would have caused any serious damage, nor were they able to locate any officers of significant rank to take as prisoners of war."

Captain Hodge had already heard about Magistrate Riddell and her disobeying of a direct order by the squadron commander. Riddell was young, Hodge knew, and fresh from the Academy. She had taken a great risk recruiting Keryn as a replacement *Cair* pilot, succumbing against her better wishes only when nearly begged by Magistrate Xiao. Captain Hodge hoped that she found her confidence soon. It would be a great disappointment to lose so young a pilot in the heat of battle because she was unable to follow orders.

"Ma'am," the Communications Officer interrupted. Merric shot him a disapproving stare, but Captain Hodge brushed aside his rebuttal.

"What is it, Magistrate Young?" she asked.

"You have another call, ma'am."

Captain Hodge rolled her eyes. She was sure that Nitella had finally realized the double–edged sword of her departing words. It was just like her to call immediately back, eager to offer the last retaliating words of the conversation. "Please tell Captain Nitella that I'm indisposed, being right in the middle of a tactical briefing."

Turning back to Merric, the captain was surprised when

Young cleared his throat loudly. It was an annoying habit of Young's, one she would have to address later. "What is it, Magistrate Young?"

"It's..." he paused, clearly nervous. "It's not Captain Nitella, ma'am."

"Then who is it?" Merric interceded. "Out with it, man!"

"It's a message from the High Council," Young replied meekly.

Both Captain Hodge and Eminent Merric paused, their terse replies forgotten. "You've confirmed the signature?" Hodge asked.

"The message is authentic, ma'am," Young answered. "Would you like me to transfer the message to your console?"

"No!" Hodge replied quickly. "No, Magistrate Young. Please transfer it to the conference room. I'll take it there shortly." Captain Hodge met Merric's stare of wonderment. Behind his eyes, though, she noticed disappointment that she did not invite him to listen. A message from the High Council, however, was not meant for prying eyes. "Eminent Merric, alert me at once of any changes while I'm away. Magistrate Vargus," she said to the ship's navigator, "keep us on course."

"Yes, ma'am," the Wyndgaart navigator replied.

"Give me two minutes, Magistrate Young, and then transfer the message."

Captain Hodge climbed quickly from her seat, tucking her wings in tightly to her body as she hurried to the lift. As the doors closed, she allowed her knees to shake slightly in the cooling darkness of the elevator. There could be no confusion as to why the High Council was contacting her. As commander of the Alliance Fleet assigned to eliminating the Terran threat, this would be their declaration of war. Captain Hodge smiled, knowing that they would soon be embroiled in the single greatest conflict of their generation.

As the lift doors opened, she offered only absently acknowledged greetings to the crewmen she passed, intent, instead, on the door at the end of the hall. Captain Hodge entered her captain's code and heard the doors hiss open. The lights began to flicker to life, but the captain was seated in her chair before they could fully illuminate the dark conference room. She activated her console and noticed the already blinking red light at the base of the screen. Nervously, she reached out and pressed the button, receiving the message. Though she knew the call was previously recorded and she would not speak personally to the High Council, it was still a nerve-wracking experience as the dark screen was filled with the bright red Council symbol.

On the screen, the symbol melted away, revealing six shadowy figures sitting around a semi-circular table. Though the lighting in the room did little to reveal details of each of the six individuals, their identities were unmistakable as they spoke in turn.

"Captain Hodge," a gravelly-voiced councilmember began. "You have been tasked with the single greatest responsibility ever offered to a member of the Alliance Fleet in recent history. It has fallen on your shoulders to hunt down and eliminate a Terran threat."

A massive and gruff councilmember, clearly dwarfing the others in sheer size, spoke next. "As you already know, the Terran Destroyers invaded our space a few months ago and have since assaulted and destroyed five Alliance Cruisers. This atrocity, in itself, cannot go unpunished."

The Avalon councilmember spoke next, his musical voice wavering with age. "But this is not the only atrocity they have committed. The Terran Fleet has also attacked an Alliance outpost, eliminating one of the only communication nodes we had for that sector of space. Without it, it was difficult to identify their exact location. However, that situation has now been rectified as well."

"We have a ship in pursuit of the Terran Fleet," a new councilmember added. The three remaining councilmembers looked too similar in the gloomy darkness to discern one from another, though Captain Hodge placed the strange accent of the speaker as coming from a distant rural star system, one predominantly occupied by Pilgrims. "Our spy has been sending updates about the Terran activities, including their whereabouts, any new assaults on Alliance vessels, and projected course."

One of the two remaining councilmembers spoke up next. "It is this information that we are forwarding to you now. With it, we expect you to move your Fleet to engage the Terran threat. Updates from our spy will continue during your travels to ensure that you are provided all pertinent information when planning your assault. We don't need to remind you how much hinges on your actions in the next few weeks, Captain Hodge. Should you fail, the Alliance will be left in an awkward position, one easily exploitable by the Terran Empire."

The last councilmember finally spoke. "Captain Hodge, this is our declaration of war against the Terran Empire. They have committed an atrocity by invading our space, and yet another by attacking ships patrolling the Demilitarized Zone. You are to use all resources available to ensure that our response is swift and decisive. Much rests on your shoulders. Do not fail us."

With those haunting last words, the screen once again flashed the brilliant red High Council symbol before leaving her staring at the black, silent console. Captain Hodge sat unmoving for quite a few minutes, her eyes not moving from the screen for fear there was more to the message. Though this was what she had been waiting for over the past few weeks, to suddenly be ordered to war was daunting, and frightened Captain Hodge more than she wanted to admit. Repeatedly, her mind kept wandering back to the engagement with the *Defiant*. Neither ship had performed well. Even with superior numbers – her twelve ships to their reported six – the Terrans had the experience of multiple combat engagements on their side. Mirroring the Council's last message, she was scared they would fail.

Finally, on legs that felt like lead, Captain Hodge climbed from her chair and walked back toward the hall. As she walked, the worries washed away, pulled free of her by the air that brushed past. She left the room, walking steadily toward the lift that would return her to the bridge. Behind her, the lights went dark in the room and the door slid shut. The nervousness of the captain was left behind, there in the darkness. Presented to the crewmen she passed was a determined and bold captain, driven by a single purpose: the destruction of the invading Terran Fleet.

She was calling orders to her crew before she fully departed the lift, catching them all by surprise. "Magistrate Vargus, take us out of orbit. Put us on a course that I will send to you shortly. Magistrate Young, broadcast a message to all the captains. Tell them to break orbit and follow our lead. Eminent Merric, please notify all officers and warrants on board the *Revolution* that we are having a mandatory formal dinner tomorrow night. I will make all necessary announcements about the High Council's message then. Before you ask, yes, we are going to war."

CHAPTER 4

Yen entered the ballroom with Keryn on his arm. She looked stunning, with her tanned skin highlighted by a silver sequined dress. The plunging neckline accentuated the curves of her body and left nearly every man in the room staring as the pair was announced to the crowd. Yen understood their surprise. He had been equally amazed when he picked her up from her quarters and found her so stunningly dressed. She had flashed him a warm smile then, the same warm smile that she now gave him as they entered the ballroom. Yen's heart melted at the sight of that smile. He couldn't deny that there was a distinct spark of chemistry between the two. Since she arrived on board the *Revolution*, there had been coy smiles, affectionate touches exchanged between the two, and endearing glances. Yet neither openly admitted their feelings, nor had either of them been brazen enough to broach the subject. Still, it stroked his ego to have the most attractive woman on the ship on his arm tonight.

Standing at the doorway as their names were called, Yen scanned the crowd of gathered faces. To him, they all seemed so young and naïve. Many wore expressions of deep-seated anticipation, mired in a burning desire to be heroes. Almost none of the hundreds of warrants and officers in the ballroom had ever experienced war, death, and loss. They had graduated from the Academy, or Field Officer Training, during a time of peace, never with an expectation of having to prove themselves during real combat. For too many, Yen noticed, that had translated into a yearning to make a name for themselves. Yen had seen that attitude too many times before as well. He had attended their memorial services after they died doing something foolish.

The other emotion that Yen noticed was that of surprise. Many were eager to begin the night's festivities if only to answer their building litany of questions. Both Yen and Keryn had been surprised by the announcement of the formal dinner. For so many weeks, even before Keryn arrived, there had been a monotonous droning of repetitive days. Yen, Adam, and the rest of the insertion team trained repeatedly on breaching tactics on a Terran vessel, but it had amounted to little since they had no orders to attack the Terran Fleet. Now, though, the rumors circulated like wild fire. Gossipers spread stories of High Council orders and impending battle. Yen had to admit that at least some of the rumors were founded. The Alliance Fleet had broken orbit and were now speeding toward an unknown location. He had to assume it somehow coincided with the dinner they were now forced to attend.

Yen, tugging on his stiff collar, directed Keryn toward a designated table, around which Adam and some of the other Infantry warrants and officers were sitting. Adam's date, a tall, dark haired Uligart warrant that Yen didn't immediately recognize, smiled invitingly as they took their seats. Yen conducted the formal introductions of everyone at the table, though most were familiar to Yen. As both a pilot and the leader of his Infantry insertion team, Yen had befriended most officers and warrants on both sides, Fleet and Infantry. As such, he became an important liaison and mediator during the many disagreements. Lately, that aspect of his job had taken most of his time; at least the time he wasn't spending with Keryn.

"So," Adam interjected, wasting no time with formalities before getting to the crux of the conversation. "What do you think this is all about? My money is on deployment orders."

"I don't know, Adam," Yen replied. "I'm as much in the dark as you are."

"That's a load of crap," Adam quickly responded. "You're never in the dark. You always know more than you let on. Read someone's mind, for crying out loud."

Yen frowned, but his sentiment wasn't shared with the rest of the table. Many laughed. Keryn, however, raised an eyebrow in surprise. "You can do that?" she asked.

"Trust me, sister," Adam's date chimed in, "there are few things Yen Xiao can't do with that crazy power of his."

Keryn leaned in close. Yen could smell the intoxicating perfume she wore. It was very distracting in the midst of a conversation. "You ever read my mind, and you'll never live to regret it." She winked at him as she leaned away and rejoined the rest of the table's conversation.

Aside from her beauty and intelligence, Yen admired her social relaxation. Keryn easily slipped into nearly any conversation, having a multitude of stories to share on nearly any topic. Though she had been on the ship less than a week, she added people daily to her growing circle of friends.

Their conversation was interrupted, however, by the chiming of silverware off a crystal glass. Keryn and Yen had to shift their chairs to see the rear doors to the ballroom, where Captain Hodge and her small entourage entered before taking their seats at the head table. Only Captain Hodge remained standing, obviously planning to speak before sitting with Eminent Merric and Squadron Commander Garrix.

"Good evening, everyone," she began with simple formalities. "I'm glad that you were all able to make time in your busy schedules in order to join us for this dinner, though I do realize I didn't truly leave you much of an option in the matter." She paused while flittered laughter rolled through the room. "There is much that we need to discuss tonight; many rumors that either need to be confirmed or stifled before they get out of hand. Right now, however, is not the time for long–winded speeches. I find it's upsetting to be the bearer of important news and then try to eat a heavy meal. Therefore, I will leave you with only this acknowledgement of your questions: we have broken orbit and are currently flying toward an undisclosed location. You can speculate amongst yourselves as we eat. Following dinner, I will tell you everything I know and give you as many answers to your questions as I can offer. For now, please enjoy both the food and one another's company."

The room erupted in chatters of conversation as she took her seat. For many, Captain Hodge's teasing speech added fuel to an already hotly burning fire of speculation. For others, there was a worrisome expression on their faces. Yen not only understood their concern, but also was happy to see the reality of the situation finally sinking in for the new pilots and soldiers. Maybe, if they could understand the dangers associated with real combat, some of them might survive to see how the war develops. Yen had spent quite a bit of time thinking about what was to come and had come to a realization. Their attack against the Terran Fleet would be brutal, but would be far from the end of the war. If anything, he knew that their attack would only ignite the fervor of the Terran Empire. The single attack could lead to years of open warfare, the likes of which hadn't been experienced in a century and a half. The stories of those brutal battles, leaving millions dead on both sides, had never been forgotten. Yen cringed at the idea of another war like that, in which so many were left dead. No, Yen had realized that the assault on the Terran Fleet could not be the end of the Alliance assault, but rather the tip of a long and deadly spear. He only hoped those in power, the High Council in particular, thought much the same.

Dinner was served, though conversations took precedence over eating. For many in the room, their food was barely touched by the time their plates were taken away, having only shifted their entrées from one side of the plate to another while discussing their theories in hushed tones with those they shared their table. Thankfully, Yen, Adam, and Keryn had avoided most of the gossiping, spending their time lost in small talk and pleasantries. Having served together for over a year, Yen and Adam had many stories about one another, which kept Keryn laughing throughout the meal. By the time dinner was over, their table's jovial attitude still remained. They still joked between one another as Captain Hodge finished her meal and stood once more. A silence fell over the room as she gained everyone's undivided attention. Cameras in the room turned and began recording. Yen had a suspicion that her speech would be replayed on all ships in the attack Fleet simultaneously.

"Over the past few months," Captain Hodge began, "a new and dangerous threat has emerged from the Terran Empire. A small invasion Fleet of six Terran Destroyers slipped into Alliance space, in clear violation of the Taisa Accord. This is the first major incursion in violation of the Accord in one hundred and fifty years. If that were their only transgression, it would be grounds enough for us to go to war. However, as you are all aware, invading our sovereign space was not the only atrocity they committed, nor was it the most recent. Almost a year ago, direct actions of the Terran Empire resulted in the deaths of over one hundred Infantry soldiers on Perseus II. More recently, however, this invading Fleet has attacked and destroyed five Alliance Cruisers."

Yen felt the ache in his chest at the mention of Perseus. From the corner of his eyes, he could see the same sorrow-filled expression on Keryn's face at the mention of her brother's loss.

"The Terrans have done more than just invade our space. They have made an open declaration of war, a declaration that has not been lost on the High Council. In response, the High Council contacted me yesterday with new orders; orders to break orbit and make haste toward the Terran Fleet's location. Our orders are simple: destroy the Terran Fleet at all costs!"

A raucous cheer erupted from the crowd as the rumors were validated. To Yen's surprise, he felt a hand fall on top of his. Keryn squeezed his hand hard as he looked at her. Her violet eyes burned with an agitated fervor and he could see her breasts rise and fall with excitable breaths. Turning his hand, he laced his fingers with hers and held her hand as Captain Hodge continued.

"Your enthusiasm is a direct reflection of what I felt when I heard their message. To know that all of our training and all of our waiting has finally come to fruition, it was nearly more than I could bear. However, I encourage you to continue your diligent training and rehearsals during the next few weeks of transit. We face a dangerous and determined enemy in the Terran Fleet. I don't need to remind you that they have already destroyed five ships just like the one we now crew. The enemy ships are filled with combat veterans who know that a retaliatory strike is inevitable." Captain Hodge's musical voice grew louder as she continued, her cheeks flushed with emotion. "They will be expecting us, so when we attack, we will have to attack with reckless abandon. We cannot be afraid! We cannot be unsure! But most importantly, we cannot be deterred! In less than a month, there will not be a single citizen in either the Alliance or the Empire that doesn't know the incredible exploits of this battle fleet!"

The roar of the audience was deafening as the captain harped on the chords they all wanted to hear. They could be heroes, faces and names that the Alliance would remember forever. Though Yen still had his reservations about catering to the youthful exuberance of the crowd, he couldn't deny that he was beginning to feel his own heart race at the thought of being the hero of the Alliance. His smile was infectious as he turned to Keryn and tightly squeezed her hand. He could see the fire burning behind her eyes and knew that she was as eager to go to war as any of the other pilots and soldiers in the crowd. It was reassuring to know that soon they would all have their chance.

Following the captain's speech, the formal dinner evolved into a more social event. Music full of heavy beats and minor chords played over the intercom and many of the officers and warrants cleared the center of the room to dance. Alcohol flowed freely and it wasn't long before a red-faced Adam and his date bid Yen and Keryn adieu and left, leaning heavily on one another to make sure neither collapsed on the way back to his quarters. Adam and his date were not the only couples who slipped away nonchalantly to spend more personal time together. Soon, the densely packed room thinned until less than half of the original crowd remained.

As Yen watched the dancing, writhing crowd in the middle of the room, he felt warm breath on the side of his neck. "Would you like to go for a walk with me?" Keryn whispered into his ear.

Yen could feel a yearning passion twisting in his stomach. Without saying a word, for fear that his voice would betray his excitement, Yen nodded and pushed away from the table. Keryn stood and joined him and, still hand in hand, they walked out of the ballroom. He had intended to lead her back toward his quarters, but once they were free of the ballroom, Keryn took charge and pulled him along toward one of the lifts. Unsure of where they were going but feeling strongly sexually aroused, Yen fought little, figuring she had something mischievous in mind.

To Yen's surprise, once inside the elevator Keryn pushed a button that would take them to one of the observation decks.

As soon as the lift doors opened, Keryn playfully slipped away and hurried ahead, taking a place near the thick windows. As he strode forward, she gave him barely a second glance as she lost herself in the distant stars. He slipped his arms around her slender waist and followed her gaze out the window.

"They're beautiful," Keryn said cryptically.

Yen followed her gaze, but saw only the stars beyond the window. "They're great," he said, trying to understand the awe he heard in her voice. "No matter where you go, though, they change very little."

"Maybe you're right," Keryn said softly, "but they're the reason I joined the Academy. I looked up at the stars every night when I was growing up and wondered what it would be like to fly among them. I could have gone through Initiation and became a warrior, but then I would have been doomed to spend each mission on a different planet, always looking at the stars but knowing that they would be out of reach."

Nudging him backward, she turned and faced him. They coy glances he had received before had been replaced by a stern seriousness. "You're not the first guy I've had feelings for, Yen. I've met my share of both boys and men as I've grown, but none of them truly understood my passion. They've come and gone from my life because they couldn't see past the physical me and truly appreciate my deeper commitment to being a pilot." She placed a gently hand on his chest, feeling his pounding heartbeat. "With you, I finally am friends with someone who shares my passion for being a pilot in the Fleet. It's important that you truly understand me, Yen."

Yen was caught off guard by the depth of her concern. Simultaneously, he felt a small ache in his chest. "Just friends?" he asked.

Keryn's smile was sympathetic. "It's not that I don't have feelings for you. But right now we both have a mission to do and a war to prepare for. The last thing either of us needs is messy emotions getting in the way of our common sense and tactical decision-making. For the next few weeks, we focus on preparing for the Terrans."

She reached out and ran an affectionate hand over his chest. "If we both make it through this next fight alive, then I promise we'll talk about the you and I. Do we have a deal?"

"I don't think I have a choice in this."

Keryn laughed. "You don't. Anyway, we can't sleep together yet."

"No?" Yen asked, finally starting to regain his composure.

"No. You still haven't taken me out to the dinner you've been promising."

CHAPTER 5

A single dinner between Yen and Keryn turned into dinner nearly every night as the *Revolution* traveled toward the inevitable conflict with the Terran Fleet. Regardless of where they wound up – be it at the ship's mess hall, one of the few restaurants on board, or even a home cooked meal within one of their two quarters – they were rarely seen together without a console between them, displaying previous battle plans and going over both traditional and non-conventional strategies. For Keryn, she seemed to glean quite a bit more from the non-conventional warfare than she did from standard attack patterns. Much as she had been trained from a young age during her warrior training, she had been taught to always be on your opponent's blind side, striking at his weaknesses. She saw no reason to approach space combat any differently.

Though she absorbed all she could from the training sessions, simulations, and console explanations that Yen offered, she couldn't deny a strong desire to spend time with him. Yen was remarkable in nearly every way. He told countless war stories from his time in covert operations, which included both Infantry and some minor Fleet encounters. She also found that they thought very much alike, with Yen offering his insight on abnormal strategies that Keryn yearned to implement into real combat scenarios.

After weeks of training and tactics, Keryn's confidence had grown exponentially, though she still had trouble shaking her memory of the abysmal loss during the *Defiant* training exercise. Aside from Yen and Adam, she talked to few of the Infantry soldiers assigned to the *Cair Ilmun*. She didn't know what they thought of her or if they had any confidence in her abilities when they faced the Terran Fleet, but she knew that she wouldn't let them down. Still, the nervous recognition of her own failure hovered over her like a storm cloud.

Keryn quickly realized that a lot of her brooding came from the fact that all she and Yen had done together for nearly two weeks was study and train. She knew that they both needed a break.

As they sat together in Yen's quarters one night, Keryn set down her console and rubbed tired eyes. "Can you really read minds?" she asked.

Yen smiled and flicked the switch that would turn off his own console. "So I take it we're done studying for the night?"

"Yes," Keryn conceded, "we're done studying. Now answer the question."

"I can read minds, though it's spotty at best. It's not so much that I get clear words from the other person. More accurately, I get senses and feelings; sort of a kaleidoscope of emotions that paint a picture in my mind. I see what they see via their thought patterns more than their actual words."

"Sounds complicated."

"Not really. Take right now for instance," Yen said, leaning forward and narrowing his eyes as though in deep conversation. "I'm getting the impression that you long to have sex with me."

Keryn laughed. "I guess that power of yours really is spotty, superhero."

Yen shrugged. "I didn't have to use powers to figure that

53

one out."

Keryn's blushed. She grasped for a change of subject. "What else can you do, aside from embarrass innocent women?"

Yen leaned back in his chair and rubbed his chin thoughtfully. He obviously wanted to find something to do that would definitely impress Keryn. Finally finding his answer, he leaned forward, placing his right hand on the table, palm skyward. "This is something that I've been working on for over a year now and only recently perfected. Prepare to be amazed."

The air around Yen began to shimmer, wavering as though heat was rolling from his skin. The wavering air flickered angrily as he concentrated. In the palm of his hand, a single blue tendril began to extend toward the ceiling. It shook unsteadily for a moment before settling. The top of the tendril tipped forward like a serpent's head, glancing side to side as though examining its new surroundings. The head of the tendril turned around and looked at Yen before tilting to the side inquisitively, awaiting its next orders.

"That's amazing," Keryn said, laughing at the amount of personality present in such an inanimate object. "It's almost like it's alive."

Yen's smile was weak as he strained to maintain his psychic projection. "Sometimes it feels alive," Yen explained. "I may be the one manifesting it, but it comes with its own personality, like it's less an extension of me and more a self-aware servant of mine."

Keryn's eyes narrowed. "So you don't control it? What if it gets out of control and starts doing real damage?"

Yen shook his head, his eyes never leaving the tendril. His voice seemed to come from far away, as he spoke through the shimmering air around him. "Think of it like your Voice. It's a part of you, but clearly doesn't control you. I can dismiss it with a thought if it gets out of control, but that's never happened. It may seem to have its own mind, but it still shares mine as well, which means that it knows my intent and ambitions."

"I think it's cute, but what can you use it for?" Keryn asked, watching the tendril twist around itself in Yen's palm like a young animal searching for something to do out of boredom.

"It's a physical manifestation of my power, but it's still incorporeal. I can pass it through any armor, clothing, or skin. In addition, because it's made of psychic energy, I can use it to lash out at an opponent and disrupt his nervous system. Send one of these against a Terran in a full battle suit and it will disable him without ever firing a shot."

"Useful," Keryn said as a statement more than a question. "I like it."

"That's not all it can do, you know," Yen said cryptically as a smile crept across his face. "These little tendrils can have quite a few other uses."

"Like what..." Keryn began before stopping in mid-sentence, her breath frozen in her throat.

Beneath the table, from Yen's other palm, a second tendril extended toward Keryn. The tendril passed insubstantially through the thin uniform pants Keryn wore. As it brushed across the skin beneath, the tendril activated nerve clusters and pleasure receptors. The pleasurable signal was carried to Keryn's brain, instantaneously driving her hormones wild and causing her entire body to flush.

Gasping for air, she finally managed to speak. "Stop," she said, her lips quivering.

Though obviously strained from the effort of maintaining two tendrils, Yen still managed a strong laugh as he withdrew both tendrils. The air around him stopped moving and the room settled back into its former self.

"I told you," Yen said as he continued laughing, "it has many, many other uses."

"Don't..." Keryn managed, her eyes closed as she tried to settle her wayward emotions. "Don't ever do that without warning me first!" Her breath was still ragged as she tried to control her pounding heartbeat.

They sat in silence for quite some time as Keryn regained control of herself. She fought against the obvious desire to act on her spiked lust knowing that her acting on it was exactly what Yen had intended when he sent the tendril her way. Finally, her body calmed though she still felt a stirring of desire burning in her belly. She also didn't dare stand, knowing that her legs were probably unstable.

"You're an ass," Keryn said, opening her eyes slowly and staring at the still smiling Yen.

"I have my moments," Yen joked.

"It makes me wonder how many women have been exposed to your little tendrils." In one swift moment, she had shifted the balance of power out of Yen's hands and into her own.

Yen was caught with his mouth open, unsure of how to reply. She had deftly turned the tables on him, leaving him wondering if he could talk his way out of the situation. Of course, Keryn had not been the first woman exposed to his powers like that, though he wouldn't have expected her sharp mind to connect those dots quite that quickly. He stammered, hoping that he could find the right thing to say, but was finally saved when the transponders they both wore crackled to life, broadcasting a message to everyone on board the *Revolution*.

"All hands to battle stations," Captain Hodge's voice called over the ship-wide intercom channel. "This is not a drill. We are approaching the Terran Fleet. I say again, all hands to their battle stations."

Keryn and Yen looked at one another in surprise as the message began to replay, their previous encounter already forgotten. They both leapt to their feet, knocking over their respective chairs in their hurry. Reaching the door, Keryn glanced over her shoulder.

"I'll see you at the *Cair Ilmun*," she said, before disappearing into the hall.

The rush through the ship was difficult, with everyone running one way or the other as they tried to get into uniform and man their respective battle stations. Keryn shoved her way past the slower movers, intent on reaching her quarters, slipping into her flight suit, and getting to her ship before the rest of her team. The message had been unclear about how long they had until the Terran Fleet came into range, but Keryn wasn't willing to take the chance of being late. Once she reached her quarters, she inputted her code and moved quickly into the cool darkness beyond. Before the overhead lights had fully flickered to life, she was in the bedroom pulling her flight suit free from its hangar. She dropped her clothes to the ground, not worrying about putting them away as she slipped into her one-piece suit. Clipping her belt around her waist, she drew both her pistol and long knife from the cabinet and attached them to her belt. Feeling ready, she turned and hurried toward the hangar bay.

Within the bay, pilots and crews ran madly from one end to the other, conducting pre-flight checks and arming the multitude of weapons tubes hanging heavily under the wings of their respective ships. At the far end of the bay, Keryn saw a large group of pilots prepping a ship she hadn't truly been exposed to before: the Weapons Platform. Consisting of little more than a dozen large bore plasma missile tubes surrounding a single cockpit and engine, the Weapons Platform was capable of maneuvering closer to the enemy Destroyers before launching a dozen Cruiser–grade plasma rockets toward its target. Though slow and bulky, the Weapons Platform offered yet another resource for surprising, and ultimately destroying, the Terran Fleet.

No surprise to Keryn, by the time she arrived at the *Cair Ilmun* Yen was already examining the outer hull. He offered her only the briefest of acknowledgements before going back to his examination. Adam placed a comforting hand on her shoulder as he passed, carrying a large arsenal of weapons before dropping them in the crew compartment. Keryn felt nervous; because not only they were going to war but also because this time, as she recalled from Yen telling her repeatedly, there would be no room for mistakes. If she screwed up this time as she had before, she would not only lose her own life but that of Yen and Adam as well. While she would mourn her own death, she refused to be responsible for the deaths of those she cared so much about.

The rest of her insertion team rushed over to the ship, decked in full battle armor and carrying their own collection of weapons. Each carried a pistol and rifle and had a knife and a series of grenades strapped to their hip. To her surprise, as they passed, they all offered words of encouragement and confident smiles. Keryn smiled in return, feeling bolstered by their confidence in her.

Before she was even able to slip into the *Cair Ilmun*, she saw some of the *Duun* fighters rolling forward, pre–positioning for launch. Though the message had been cryptic, Keryn quickly realized that someone knew the timeline and, judging from everyone else's actions, they would soon be launching against the Terrans. She hurried inside the *Cair Ilmun*, letting the door slide closed and seal behind her. In the cool darkness of the crew compartment, she met the stern stares of the Infantry soldiers, already strapped into their seats. Though no one said as much, she knew something needed to be said.

"I'm not the best at motivational speeches," Keryn admitted. "I've never had a lot of opportunities to try to motivate someone else. However, I don't think I need to tell you what's about to happen. I know a lot is riding on me. Hell, all of our lives are riding on my ability to fly us to one of the Terran Destroyers. I may not have given you many reasons to trust me before, but I promise you that I will not let you down. You will get to one of the Destroyers, even if it kills me."

The silence that ensued was finally broken by a gruff Pilgrim voice. "We trust you, Keryn," Adam said. "Make us proud."

A chorus of support broke from the rest of the team. Keryn, smiling, walked up to the cockpit. Sitting in the copilot's chair, Yen nodded to her as she entered. "They believe in you," he said. "We all do."

"I need you to do me a favor, Yen," Keryn said a little sheepishly, hoping not to offend him.

"Name it."

"I need you to go back to the back and join the rest of the team. If I'm going to do this, then it's something I need to do alone. You won't always be there to support me and give me advice, so I need to learn to succeed entirely on my own."

To her surprise, Yen smiled as he unbuckled his restraints. He stood and placed his hand on her shoulder. "Good luck, Keryn," he whispered. He walked into the crew compartment and Keryn slid the door separating the two sections of the ship closed. Alone in the cockpit, she took a deep breath before taking her seat. She turned the series of switches that would start up the engine and complete the pre–flight checks. As the engine warmed up, a familiar Voice spoke in her mind.

I know you said you want to do this alone, the Voice said, *but I want you to know that I'm here to support you. No matter the differences we've had in the past, you and I are eternally one mind. Without you, I can't exist. Whether you want me here or not, I will do everything I can to help. I won't let us die today.*

Surprising even herself, Keryn smiled. "For once, I'm glad to have you here."

Pushing forward on the controls, the *Cair Ilmun* rolled out of its alcove and took its place amongst the other ships preparing for launch.

As the *Revolution* entered the galaxy, the dozen ships in its Fleet spread out in a two ship tall line and advanced on the central planets of the system. Having already detected the Cruisers on radar, the Terran Destroyers were similarly aligned in anticipation of the grueling battle to come.

"All Cruisers, this is Captain Hodge," the message proclaimed from the *Revolution*'s bridge. "The enemy has decided to stand and fight, which will lessen the work that we will have to do in pursuing them. Hold your line until my order. Arm all plasma warheads, load all rail guns, and await my orders. On my mark, prepare to deploy the Squadrons. And, for everyone, Gods' speed."

CHAPTER 6

Both ranks of ships fired their initial volleys before the fighters had the opportunity to launch from their underbellies. Across the inky void, plasma rockets streamed, their smoky exhausts filling space with intricate weaves of overlapping trajectories. Near the center of the battlefield, blue and purple plasma explosions blossomed soundlessly, turning the front view screens of the Cruisers into brilliant, colorful displays while, simultaneously, masking the movements of the enemy ships.

With their actions blocked from the Terran Fleet, the Alliance Cruisers began firing massive barrages of rail gun slugs. Though a bit archaic when compared to the complexities of the plasma warheads, the rail guns were some of the most effective weapons in the Fleet's arsenal. Built of three parallel metal bars, set in a triangle pattern, the rails of the guns were heavily magnetized. Large metal slugs, oppositely polarized from the rails, hovered in between the rails until propelled forward, where small grooves in the metal rails projected the magnetic fields forward, launching the slugs from the Cruisers at high velocities. In the frictionless space, the slugs never lost their kinetic energy until striking a solid object, like a planet or, in this case, a Terran Destroyer.

The slugs from both sides raced through the darkness,

their matte coatings leaving them nearly invisible against the backdrop of distant space. On the *Cair Ilmun*, Keryn gritted her teeth as the *Revolution* shook from impacts. Her view blinded by the hangar bay door that still remained closed, she could only imagine the damage being done to the ship and hope that they would soon have the opportunity to launch, preferably before the *Revolution* was destroyed from counter fire. Keryn had never been fully engaged in space combat like this before, which left her irritable and scared. Though she didn't know what she would face beyond the confines of the *Revolution*, she finally began to understand how the Infantry in the crew compartment behind her must feel. She would rather take her chances against an armada of Terran ships than sit in the belly of a Cruiser with her fingers crossed that she wouldn't be obliterated without every launching.

Keryn released an audible sigh of relief when the bright red light above the hangar door finally shifted to green. She released fists that had been clenched until her knuckles had turned white. Shortly thereafter, the roar of venting gas filled the massive hangar as they prepped for launch. Keryn switched on the internal communications channel and took a deep breath before speaking.

"We're getting ready to launch," she said, hoping her voice sounded confident to those relying on her piloting skills for survival. "Sit tight and I'll get you to a Terran Destroyer shortly."

As the bay doors slid open, the first of the *Duun* fighters launched, spilling free of the ship and hurtling toward the enemy Destroyers. Keryn followed as quickly as possible, clearing the *Revolution* and finding her position off its right flank. Her heart pounding, she was glad to be clear of the Cruiser and in open space. She felt as though she stood a chance relying solely on her own piloting abilities instead of relying on the piloting skills of someone maneuvering a few million tons of alloy girders and armored plating. Though the *Cair Ilmun* was free of her Cruiser, not all ships were so lucky. Debris from a number of ships torn apart by metal slugs floated near the hangar bays of the nearby Cruisers; ships that were destroyed before making it more than a few hundred feet from the hangar bay. Three ships down the line, blue and purple flames jutted from the hangar of the Cruiser. From the midst of the superheated inferno, a few ships limped free of the hangar, tumbling end over end as they fell into the zero gravity of space. Looking around, Keryn couldn't tell how many pilots had been fortunate enough to clear the hangar bay before a missile struck it. She hoped several, for the sake of the ship's entire Squadron. The reality of war quickly settled over Keryn as she realized that hundreds of pilots and insertion teams could have their lives simultaneously ended in the briefest of moments.

Focus, Keryn, the Voice whispered. *You can't help them, but you can stay focused enough to make sure something similar doesn't happen to you.*

Across the empty space, Keryn watched the enormous hangar bay doors opening on the Terran Destroyers. From their undersides, the Destroyers disgorged their own Squadrons. Keryn realized that from the perspective of an opponent, her earlier assessment of Squadrons looking like swarms of angry insects was incorrect. It wasn't insects that she saw spilling from the Terran ships, charging across the space toward the Alliance Squadrons. Sitting above the *Revolution*, Keryn saw the ships merge into a single sea of flowing fighters, rolling like waves in the ocean, until they slammed violently together. Their momentum built as more and more fighters entered the fray until they were less of crashing waves within a sea and more like a destructive tsunami. As the tsunami crested, slamming against one another, it was punctuated by a brilliant splash of plasma detonations.

Keryn watched, mouth agape. When the *Revolution* and *Defiant* had faced one another, she had struggled to find a clear opening through the net of two fighting Squadrons. Before her, filling every inch of available space as far as she could see, over a dozen Squadrons clashed together, filling the spaces not occupied by flying fighters with the wreckage of those already destroyed. Keryn shook her head in amazement and fear, unsure if she would ever be able to pilot through the insanity before her.

To her surprise, the *Revolution* below her began to move. Down the line, the other Cruisers broke from their positions and began individual maneuvers, leaving more difficult targets for the Terran Destroyers to attack. In response, the Terrans began similar maneuvers. Keryn sat amazed by the sheer quantity of rockets fired from each of the Cruisers and Destroyers. Engaging her engines, Keryn remained in position above the *Revolution*, along with the majority of other *Cair* ships. As they began shifting, a single *Cair* broke from its position and began traversing the chaos on the battlefield, eager to reach to Destroyers on the far side. Keryn found her breath caught in her throat as she watched the pilot weave past a group of Terran fighters. To the pilot's credit, he outmaneuvered some of the more agile fighters as he streamed onward, passing into the middle of the battlefield. Just when she thought he stood a chance at making it, the wing tore free of the *Cair* ship, struck by a wayward rail gun slug. Spinning, the *Cair* ship was helpless as a Terran fighter launched its rockets. Keryn's heart lurched in time with the exploding *Cair* and left her feeling empty. Just as quickly as hope had filled her, the realization that over a dozen

Alliance soldiers were instantly killed weighed heavily on her.

"I can't do this," Keryn whispered as she watched more and more fighters and transports destroyed in the ensuing melee. "There's no way through that."

You can do this, the Voice replied. *Don't get overwhelmed and don't get excited. Remember what we learned before. You are the captain of this ship, which means we don't move until you're completely confident that you can get us from one side to the other safely.*

"What if I never get that confident?"

Then you let everyone in the back of this ship die, eternally disappointed in your failure as a pilot.

Keryn frowned, biting back the tears of frustration. She hated the Voice's blatant honesty, but couldn't deny the wisdom of its words. More than anything, the Voice knew which of Keryn's buttons to push to spur her into action. Taking a deep breath, Keryn looked back over the battle. She slowly let her eyes slip out of focus. When training to be a Wyndgaart warrior in the schoolhouse, Keryn had used a similar technique when facing a very agile opponent. Try to focus on each individual strike, and you miss the more subtle secondary attack. By taking in her opponent's movements as a whole, she was able to map their strategy and find holes in their defenses. Looking back at the battlefield, Keryn tried the same thing here. Instead of focusing on a single ship and watching its inevitable demise, she took in the full scene. Slowly, the ships flowed into a single, seamless mass, writhing against one another. In this perspective, Keryn began to see that the battling ships did not fully cover the whole area of space. Small gaps appeared, though they closed almost as quickly as they appeared. Keryn believed, given enough time and a bit of patience, that she could exploit one of those openings enough to get them through.

Though Keryn now felt more confident, she wasn't sure how to explain her strategy to the other *Cair* pilots, and she cringed as more and more of them grew impatient and attempted their flights. Each ship covered more and more distance than the one before, but the result was always invariably the same. Over a dozen lives lost every time, for nothing more than a few hundred feet of ground gained. Without some distracter, Keryn feared that too many of the *Cair* ships would be destroyed before a sufficient opening presented itself.

Keryn quickly switched her radio channel to the Squadron's *Cair*-specific net. Overlapping voices filled the channel, making it difficult to distinguish true orders and strategy from mind-numbing chatter. Some of the voices were from wounded or destroyed ships, their pilots barely alive enough to call repeatedly for help, though they knew in their hearts that there was no system in place to retrieve a downed pilot until the war was over. Some of the chatter was a play-by-play narration of the *Duun* fighters, cheering and jeering alternately, depending on how the Alliance pilots were performing. They debated between one another about which *Duun* would survive and which would fail. They watched their own shipmates destroyed by a malicious Terran enemy and they mocked the loss. Anger built within her. The young pilots around her treated this war like it was a game. A loss of a fighter translated to little more for them than a piece on a board game, moved incorrectly into an ill-advised location. They lost the piece, but it was quickly brushed aside as they moved on to the next. Having no more true combat experience than they did, she couldn't fathom why she took this more seriously. Could they not hear the calls of the wounded and dying pilots?

"Shut up!" Keryn screamed into the radio, overwhelming even the most raucous conversations. Only the meek calls from the wounded could be heard on the otherwise silent net. "What is wrong with you people? Our pilots – friends and people with whom many of us graduated from the Academy with – are out there fighting and dying and you're treating it like it's a game!"

The stretching silence told Keryn that no one was strong enough to oppose her push for a leadership role. It had come surprisingly naturally for her at the Academy to take on the role of leader, once she had identified the tactics necessary to compete in the daily competitions. Her leadership abilities had led her to graduate at the top of her class, earning her commission as an officer in the Fleet instead of just a warrant. Now, whether they liked it or not, she would force her newly assumed role on them all.

"I know that some of you are scared right now. I can accept that. When I saw the Terrans pouring out of their ships, I got a little scared too. Nevertheless, every one of you needs to realize that you have a ship full of Infantry soldiers that are relying on you for their very survival. Do something foolish like the other *Cair* pilots that launched before us, and you not only sacrifice yourself, but you sacrifice all of their lives. I, for one, wouldn't be able to go on knowing that I was so careless with someone else's life."

"What are you trying to say?" an anonymous gruff voice replied. The tone of his voice, though, told Keryn that he had not meant the words to be confrontational.

"When the time is right, and it isn't yet, I need all of you to be ready to move. As soon as an opening presents itself, we're going to latch on to the closest Terran Destroyer and let our Infantry counterparts do their job. I know you don't know me very well. You haven't served with me that long and many of you are already questioning as to why you're bothering to listen to me at all. The truth is, as the most junior pilot, I don't have the authority to order you to follow me. What I do have, though, is the confidence to tell you now that most of us will make it out of this alive if you're willing to listen to me."

"But not all of us," someone replied over the radio. "Not all of us will survive, is what you're saying."

"I'm not one to lie to you," Keryn answered. "This is war, and people always die in wartime. All I can promise you is that you stand a much better chance at living if you follow me than what you would if you go at this alone."

The silence that ensued left Keryn worried that no one took her seriously. She knew that, had the tables been turned and someone else had given the same speech, she would be hesitant to trust her life to someone she barely knew. What Keryn did know, however, was that she was right. Of all the pilots she had worked with over the past few weeks, none took their job or previous training serious enough to perform at the level they needed. Trust her or not, Keryn had a plan that she believed in and would take anyone with her that volunteered. *If* anyone volunteered.

Either they join you or they don't, the Voice said. *You know you're doing the right thing.* Surprising to Keryn, it was reassuring to hear the Voice's words of encouragement.

"I'm with you," the gruff voice finally replied, breaking the tense silence. "So, what's the plan?"

Keryn smiled as other pilots chimed in, throwing their support behind her.

"For right now, we hold tight and wait for an opening. How many of you have ever flown in a cone formation?"

Over the next few minutes, Keryn went on to explain her plan in painful detail. The cone formation had been something she had worked on with Iana Morven, her Pilgrim roommate and best friend at the Academy, at great length during some of the aerial training exercises. Though only practiced using individuals wearing jet packs, Keryn had confidence that the same techniques could be applied in their current situation. As Keryn spoke, she truly regretted spending so much time with Yen and so little time with her fellow pilots over the past few weeks. Strategies like the one they were now conducting would have been much better suited for an environment where they could have practiced. She had entered the *Revolution* with the mentality of being an outsider, having known only Yen and Adam previously. If she survived this battle, she would do all she could to better incorporate the rest of the pilots into her newly formed clique.

Once Keryn was confident that the rest of the *Cair* pilots understood her plan, Keryn began searching for the other thing she required: a distraction. Without a distraction to thin the ranks of the swarming fighters, even her strategy didn't stand a chance of success. In the end, she got her distraction. However, when it finally did come, it was nothing like Keryn had expected.

CHAPTER 7

Captain Hodge cringed as the *Revolution* shook from another blast. Sparks flew from some of the consoles on the bridge, showering the area in flickering lights that cast deep shadows across the room. The front view screen wavered unsteadily as the power to the bridge fluctuated.

"Can you please get me some defenses before we are blown out of the air?" she yelled over the automated voice announcing fires throughout the ship.

"We're working on it, ma'am," Eminent Merric called back as his hands flew quickly over the console before him. His eyes darted from side to side, reading inbound trajectories of rockets and slugs. He inputted more data that was forwarded directly to the weapons bays, who worked feverishly to defend the *Revolution* from the attacks of both the Terran fighters and long–range assaults from the Destroyers.

"Magistrate Vargus," Captain Hodge ordered. "Change our heading. Bring us twelve degrees to port."

"Yes, ma'am," the Wyndgaart Navigator replied as he wiped the beading sweat from his brow. The tattoos along his jawline danced as he clenched and unclenched his teeth.

On the view screen, the *Revolution* fell into line a respectable distance behind the *Vindicator*, which led the small contingent of Cruisers around the right side of the battle. As had been rehearsed, the Alliance Fleet intended to flank the Terran Destroyers on both sides, pummeling them both from the heavy weapons on the Cruisers, and the smaller rockets loaded on the *Duun* fighters. Their tactical strategy was still going as planned, though Captain Hodge had greatly underestimated the Terran's tenacity. From her vantage point, she could already see deep scoring along the *Vindicator*'s hull and had no reason to believe that her own Cruiser looked any better.

She pulled her command console in front of her and activated the area radar. The red and blue markers indicating enemy and friendly forces nearly filled the screen. Though most of the activity remained focused near the empty middle of the galaxy, small red targets occasionally broke free of the swarm to attack the larger Cruisers skirting the sides of the battle. The exchanging fire had already cost her one of the Cruisers, the ship having been completely destroyed by an unfortunately lucky plasma missile strike that ignited one of its fuel stores. The resulting explosion had buckled the majority of the hull. Externally, the ship hung in the air, listing only slightly to one side. Behind the armored plating, however, Captain Hodge knew that the raging inferno of exploding plasma had gutted the ship, leaving few survivors. Two more Cruisers were badly damaged and mostly inoperable, though their engines still operated well enough for them to limp weakly from the battle.

The Alliance had claimed its own victories so far as well. Two Destroyers had been left in ruin, one of which was little more now than chunks of debris floating in space. Another of the six Destroyers was severely damaged, a large chasm having been opened along the top of its hull after a ruined *Duun* fighter slammed into the Terran vessel. Breathable gases still leaked from the open gash on the ship and its returning fire had greatly diminished over the past few minutes. There was a chance, though Captain Hodge refused to put faith in long shots, that the Destroyer crew was slowly suffocating and would soon be completely out of the fight. Still, the captain knew that they were a long way from ending this conflict.

A group of Terran fighters dove from behind a nearby planet and began attacking the *Vindicator*. The captain had anticipated such an attack, knowing that no trained Fleet would leave their flanks as undefended as the Terran flanks had appeared. A number of the fighters exploded in the air as they approached, having been struck by defensive rail guns. Against such a small target, the large bore rockets were overkill and grossly inaccurate. Much like the *Revolution*, however, its remaining Cair ships were circling the Vindicator, awaiting the opportunity to accelerate toward one of the remaining Destroyers. The fighters targeted these ships first, and an unfortunate series of explosions marked the destruction of the majority of remaining *Cair* ships around the *Vindicator*. With most mobile defenses eliminated, the fighters began firing their rockets directly at the Cruiser. Another pair of explosions erupted on the side of the *Vindicator*, rocking the ship as it flew around the battle. Captain Hodge could see the oxygen leaking from the newest wounds to the ship.

"Magistrate Young," Captain Hodge called, her melodic voice strained from stress. "Contact the *Vindicator* and get a status report from their most recent damage."

After only a brief pause, Young replied. "Captain Rochelle reports that the *Vindicator* is still capable of flight, though they need any assistance they can get to remove the rest of the Terran fighters."

Captain Hodge nodded. Captain Rochelle was a strong commander and wouldn't quit unless completely destroyed.

"Call back some of our *Duun* fighters in order to defend the advancing Fleet. If we don't get rid of those fighters, we're as good as dead. And let the *Vindicator* know that help is on the way."

Though things were going as well as could be expected with the battle, Hodge still hated to see so many Fleet crews being killed while under her command. Even with the *Revolution* pulling up a secondary position and, therefore, not the main target of the Terran attacks, she had received a number of reports of deaths throughout her ship, results of sudden decompressions after rocket or slug attacks.

The call had gone out to the Squadron, recalling some of the *Duun* fighters for protection. Before they could arrive, however, Captain Hodge saw something on the view screen that made her heart drop. Moving mostly unnoticed by the rest of the Fleet, a small group of Terran fighters flew toward the *Vindicator*. A pair of large plasma rockets rotated in carefully rehearsed orbits around the cockpits of the ships. Captain Hodge knew the tactic well, her own *Duun* fighters being capable of the same technique. The computers on board the fighters were capable of linking to the computer systems within the rockets. Assuming control of their trajectories, the fighters were able to better maneuver the missiles through the din of war and strategically place their launches with surgical precision. Normally, such rocket attacks were thwarted long before reaching a Cruiser. With the Fleet skimming the side of the battlefield, however, they had left themselves exposed to an effective Terran counterattack.

"Merric!" the Captain warned. She knew the danger of letting those fighters slip unchallenged as they approached the *Vindicator*. "Target those fighters and destroy them quickly!"

Merric followed her view and saw the fighters. The

Revolution launched volley after volley at the small ships, but their skilled pilots kept them mostly out of harm's way. It was only due to the superior quantity of fire launched in their direction that deadly rail gun slugs destroyed two of the three fighters. As the ships were destroyed, their missiles drifting away unguided. The last fighter, however, having avoided the same fate as his counterparts, glided along the hull of the *Vindicator* until it reached the rear of the ship, where the exposed engines burned brightly during its acceleration.

Captain Hodge watched in horror, knowing that she could no longer fire on it with the fighter so close to the *Vindicator*, as the small ship turned and launched a single rocket into each of the Cruiser's two–story tall engine exhausts. From the deck of the *Revolution*, the bridge crew waited for the inevitable explosion that would nearly decimate the *Vindicator*. Though the plasma engines were difficult targets under normal conditions, a well–placed rocket attack would be devastating as it ignited the volatile plasma fuel cells in the rear of the ship.

To everyone's surprise, there was no damning explosion in the rear of the *Vindicator*. Two insignificant explosions erupted in each of the engines. To Captain Hodge, it seemed incredibly anticlimactic, though she had trouble believing that such well–rehearsed and well–placed rocket attacks could have faltered as these apparently had. She couldn't help but to believe that there was more going on than meets the eye. Moments later, her suspicions were validated.

The engines, usually burning brightly with alternating swirls of blue and purple plasma, began to dim as the engines onboard the *Vindicator* faltered. Beginning to lose speed, the *Vindicator* grew steadily closer to the *Revolution*. Captain Hodge watched in confusion as the superheated plasma in the engines cooled, dimming until only a pinprick of light still emerged from the damaged exhausts. Eventually, even that narrow light faded away and the *Vindicator* floated helplessly in the space without any hope of maneuverability.

"Ma'am," Young called from the Communications console. "I've got a lot of activity on the radio waves."

"Put it on the intercom."

The yells of surprise and outrage could be heard clearly as the *Vindicator* called for help. The garbled mess of voices made distinguishing a single report from the multitude nearly impossible. However, it wasn't long before a clear voice overwhelmed the others, cutting off their transmissions so he could be heard.

"*Revolution*, this is Captain Rochelle of the *Vindicator*," the stern, heavily accented voice called as the captain slowly silenced the rest of the emotionally charged reports.

"Open a channel and patch his video through to my console," Captain Hodge ordered. Her previously dark screen flickered to life, revealing a surprisingly calm, but visibly upset, Pilgrim male. Rochelle's styled hair and thick, handlebar moustache offset his deep blue eyes, which pierced Captain Hodge from the console.

"Captain Rochelle, this is Captain Hodge. What's your status?"

"My status?" Rochelle asked caustically. "Both my engines have died for no apparent reason. I'm getting reports from my engine room that the plasma in both engines has been converted into some unknown, black, tar–like substance." Leaning forward, Rochelle dropped his stern persona as a look of genuine concern crossed his face. "You have to help me, Hodge. I can't maneuver any more. They're going to attack any moment and I have no way to avoid their missiles. Help me!"

Before Captain Hodge could manage a reply, the bridge

of the *Vindicator* filled with warning claxons the same time that Eminent Merric began yelling his own report.

"I have multiple launches from the nearest Destroyer," Merric yelled to be heard over the concerned calls for help. "I'm counting..." He paused as he rechecked his numbers, not believing the first report. "I'm counting over a hundred slug and rocket launches." Merric looked up, disbelief cast on his face.

Captain Hodge looked back at Rochelle. The Pilgrim's face revealed that he knew his death was imminent. His stoic visage quickly replaced his look of dread as his eyes locked firmly onto Hodge.

"Goodbye, Captain Hodge, and good luck," Rochelle said, his accent thickened with the raw emotion in his voice.

Observing both the console picture of Captain Rochelle and the forward view screen, Captain Hodge watched in horror as missiles detonated along the port side of the *Vindicator* while thick metal slugs tore holes clean through the ship. A stream of exploding plasma rockets blossomed along the hull in a clean line from bow to stern, splitting the *Vindicator* in two. Slowly, the two halves of the Alliance Cruiser drifted apart, separated by a growing sea of debris and bodies torn free from the interior of the ship. Looking down, Captain Hodge saw only her own reflection on the now dark console monitor.

Biting back her tears, Captain Hodge knew that there wasn't time to mourn their loss, not with three more fully capable Terran Destroyers still in the fight. Still, she couldn't erase the memory of the Terran's secret weapon. Something had been in the warheads of those rockets, something capable of shutting down the massive engines of a Cruiser. There was no way to know how many of those rockets the Terrans had in their arsenals on board each Destroyer. with that sort of technology in the hands of their enemy Captain Hodge suddenly worried about more attacks by the smaller Terran fighters. A few more well targeted assaults like the one on the *Vindicator* and the Alliance Fleet may lose this battle after all, regardless of their superior numbers. Though she hated to pull her own *Duun* fighters away from the main dog fights out on the battlefield, Captain Hodge made a command decision that she felt was right if the Fleet stood any chance of surviving.

"Magistrate Young," Captain Hodge said, her voice flooded with weariness. "Contact all Squadrons and tell them to pull back to their respective Cruisers. Order them to provide covering fire to the larger vessels while we engage the last of the Terran Destroyers."

As the message went out both to the fighters and the rest of the surviving Cruisers, Captain Hodge hoped she had made the right decision. In all the years of training and combat maneuvers since the Taisa Accord was signed, no commander had ever ordered their fighters to withdraw. And, though she knew that the scenarios during training were nothing like what she was seeing now, she couldn't help but feel that she would eternally be judged for making such a rash decision.

CHAPTER 8

Keryn watched with dismay as the *Vindicator* was destroyed. She listened intently as Captain Hodge recalled the *Duun* fighters back to their respective Cruisers. To her surprise, the devastation of one of the Cruisers gave her the opening and distraction she had required. As she watched from the cockpit of the *Cair Ilmun*, the *Duun* fighters broke contact with their Terran counterparts and split down the middle, flying toward both the two flanking groups of Cruisers. Sensing weakness, the Terran fighters gave chase, splitting along similar lines. The result was instantaneous. Keryn was able to see open space in the middle of the battlefield, an area that only moments before had been filled with swarming fighters More importantly, just beyond the open space the three remaining Destroyers came into view, no longer concealed behind a screen of smaller ships.

Though every other ship was moving toward the Cruisers, Keryn broke from her position, switching on the *Cair*-specific channel as she moved. "All *Cair* ships, follow me. I'll take the tip of the cone. Everyone else, fall into position behind."

Slowly the other pilots shook off their surprise at seeing a Cruiser so easily destroyed and followed the *Cair Ilmun*. Though some of the pilots opted for the more protected interior of the cone, many pilots surprised Keryn by taking up flanking spots around her ship. Keryn had studied long enough and made enough mistakes during her time at the Academy to understand the effectiveness of three-dimensional combat. On the ground, the Wyndgaarts trained using a similar technique called a wedge. By having a single person at the point of the wedge, it allowed the other members to have overlapping fields of fire on all sides, making it both dangerous and effective at penetrating enemy defensive lines. In space, similar rules applied, though they added another axis to the grid. In a cone, the three-dimensional equivalent of the wedge formation, Keryn's lightly armed *Cair* ships were able to not only fire in all directions, but were also able to overlap their fire for greater effectiveness.

The cone launched and quickly moved as far away as possible from the returning *Duun* fighters. Though she had confidence in their new formation, Keryn didn't want to tempt fate by facing a Squadron of Terran fighters before they were clear of the Cruisers. Skirting the sides of the dogfight, Keryn was able to observe the feverish pursuit by the Terran fighters. She doubted they truly understood the Alliance technique of bringing the *Duun* fighters back to the Cruisers. In the eyes of the pursuing Terrans, all they saw was a full retreat by the one threat still remaining to their own Destroyers. However, Keryn knew better. Pulling the *Duun* fighters back to the Cruisers not only protected the Cruisers from any more of the mysterious attacks that Keryn had watched the Terrans use on the *Vindicator*, but also allowed the Cruisers to add their own firepower when defending against the gnat-like Terran fighters.

Keryn's group was nearly clear of the swarm of ships and into the open void between both forces before a group of Terran fighters spotted the odd formation and turned around, moving on an intercept path that would bring the two groups face to face. The only thing that surprised Keryn was the length of time it took for them to spot her force. Still, the Terrans had grown overly confident in their pursuit of what they assumed was a retreating enemy. They didn't send a large group to intercept and destroy Keryn's *Cair* strike force. They saw a group of lightly armed transports and sent only the minimal force they thought they needed to eliminate the new threat. The Terrans greatly underestimated Keryn's resolve and tactical ingenuity, a mistake she would gladly shove back down their throats.

"We've got company," Keryn warned to her insertion crew still strapped into their seats in the rear of the *Cair Ilmun*. By now, Keryn could only imagine the frustration they must be feeling. "Hold on for a couple more minutes and I'll get you to a Destroyer."

As the Terran fighters entered range, both sides opened fire. The *Cair* formation rolled independently of one another, dodging a lot of the incoming fire. Still, Keryn felt the *Cair Ilmun* jerk as a spray of machine gun fire struck one of the wings. Luckily for her, the wings were not a necessary part of space flight operations, only truly being used for stabilization once the *Cair* ship entered an atmosphere. Though it would have to be repaired, the injury to the ship wouldn't keep her from the fight. In retaliation, the *Cair* cone returned fire. The overlapping machine gun fire filled the space in front of their formation with a nearly impenetrable wall of gunfire. Too late, the Terrans saw the effectiveness of their opponents and tried to evade, but there was no space within range that wasn't being filled with the roaring machine gun bullets. Metal peeled away from the hulls of the fighters as they exposed bellies, wings, and cockpits to the deadly barrage. Wings tore free. Sparks lit the dark space around the ships. Fires filled and consumed the cockpits. By the time Keryn and her team quit firing, only debris filled the area before them. Though Keryn had lost nearly a third of her *Cair* ships to the fighters, they had opened a gaping hole through the Terran defenses, leaving the Destroyers to fend for themselves.

"We're on a short timeline," Keryn called over the radio. "It won't take the Terrans long to realize that we're attacking one of their flagships. Watch for fighters coming in from behind, and tell your insertion teams good luck. On my mark, break formation. Three, two, one, mark."

On her command, the cone broke apart with *Cair* ships heading off in nearly every direction. Though the tighter formation was effective against the Terran fighters, sitting too close to one another was a death sentence when facing the slugs and rockets of a Destroyer. As individual ships, they became small and difficult vessels to target by the slower, yet dominating, Destroyer weapon systems.

Karen, dodging the dark metal slugs and massive rockets, led the *Cair* ships as they descended on the nearest Destroyer. Skimming the hull, Keryn watched the other ships fall on the Destroyer like leaches, extending and attaching their flexible boarding tubes onto the hull of the large ship. Extending like the proboscis of a butterfly, the tubes allowed Infantry soldiers access to the interior of the Destroyer.

Keryn chose a spot further down the hull in order to make her landing. Judging by the lack of weaponry in this section, she thought it closer to crew compartments, areas that would be unmanned during a fully involved space battle. The less resistance Yen and his team had to face getting onto the ship, the better the chance of their survival. And, to Keryn's surprise, she was truly afraid of Yen getting hurt. As she set down on the hull, another *Cair* ship latched on just ahead of her, obviously sharing her ideology about keeping the team safe. The *Cair Ilmun* rocked gently as the boarding tube affixed to the hull, stopping the *Cair Ilmun*'s forward momentum. Keryn unhooked from her seat quickly and opened the door to the crew compartment. Already free from their seats and locking magazines into their weapons, Yen and his team wore stern visages as they focused on the dangerous task at hand.

With a nod from Yen, Keryn pulled open the floor hatch near the cockpit, revealing the tube running to the solid hull beneath. One of the Infantry soldiers broke free from the group and wordlessly dropped into the hole. Though there was breathable air in the tube, he still dropped weightlessly to the Destroyer's exterior. Reaching into his pack, he withdrew and began assembling a series of explosives in a circular pattern near the edge of the tunnel. Satisfied that everything was in place, the soldier pushed off from the ground, extending his arms upward as he flew back to the *Cair Ilmun*. Yen and Adam grabbed him when he got in range, and pulled him back within the safety of the ship.

With a smile, the Infantry soldier looked at Keryn. "Fire in the hole," he said softly as he pressed the detonator in his hand.

A series of muffled explosions detonated on the hull beneath them, shaking the *Cair Ilmun* slightly. Thick dust and smoke rose through the hole, but the insertion team barely seemed to notice. One at a time, they dropped into the hole, drifting completely between the *Cair Ilmun* and the dark interior of the Destroyer below. The group disappeared until only Keryn, Yen, and Adam were left on board.

Reaching out with his large hands, Adam rested a hand on Keryn's shoulder and gave her an affectionate squeeze. "You've done good so far," he said reassuringly. "Be careful and we'll see you soon." Smiling one last time, Adam lifted his machine gun and dropped into the hole. Keryn watched him drop until his shaggy blond hair disappeared into the darkness below. Finally, it was just Yen and Keryn remaining on board.

"I want you to promise me that you'll stay on the *Cair Ilmun*," Yen said.

Keryn knew the wisdom behind his words. If they needed to evacuate quickly, which was always a possibility in their dangerous line of work, they needed her on board and ready to fly. However, Keryn also knew that most pilots ignored that rule and went into the ship as well. Especially in Keryn's case, she was as skilled a fighter as anyone on the insertion team was and Yen knew it.

"I can see the gears turning in your mind," he said a little more sternly, "and I'm asking you not to go into the ship. No one knows what we're going to face inside the Destroyer. They could have automated systems that are going to tear us apart as soon as we step foot on board. If that's the case, then all you'll do by following us is get yourself killed too. I care about you, Keryn, and I couldn't do my job if I thought your life was in danger."

Keryn was surprised at his honesty. "Be safe and I won't have to come after you."

Yen stepped toward the edge of the causeway. Before he could enter the connecting passage, Keryn grabbed him by the arm and pulled him toward her. Leaning in, she kissed him deeply.

"What was that for?" Yen asked, as they broke their embrace.

"In case you do something stupid and I don't get to see you again," she whispered.

Without a reply, Yen stepped over the edge and dropped toward the Destroyer below. Keryn's smile quickly faded, replaced by a deep frown. She didn't like being relegated to a support role, not when she was so capable in hand–to–hand combat. Still, she understood his concern, since she felt the same gnawing of worry in her belly knowing that Yen, Adam, and the rest of the team were now facing the unknown.

Closing the floor hatch behind her, Keryn walked back to the cockpit and began manning the two separate radars: one scanning the space around the Destroyer for any aerial threats and another scanning the interior of the hull. She only hoped they managed to complete their mission before either the Terran fighters outside, or the Terran soldiers inside, figured out what they were doing.

CHAPTER 9

As Yen cleared the hole blasted into the hull of the Terran Destroyer, the artificial gravity tugged at his legs, pulling him into the darkness below. Landing in a crouch, Yen stood slowly, taking in the scene. Around him, their faces cast in dark shadows, his team had already spread out, taking up positions near the only door exiting the room. Yen checked his rifle and examined the determined and anxious faces of his team. Though the masks of their faces remained stoic, he could see the shine of nervousness behind their eyes. He felt it too, though he would never admit it. His team had breached the hull of a Terran warship, one of the first teams of Alliance soldiers to do so in over a century and a half. The layout of the ship was unfamiliar, as were the hazards they would face. They were blundering into the unknown wielding only their martial abilities and the weapons by their side. Everything about the operation had the potential to end in disaster. Glancing up, peering through the hole above him, Yen looked to the hovering *Cair Ilmun* some thirty feet above him. Above him, Keryn sat at the controls of the ship, monitoring his team. Did she wonder what they were doing, sitting in the dark room below? Did she worry about his safety and long to see him when this was over nearly as much as he longed to see her? Yen didn't know, and he shook his head trying to dislodge the distractions.

One of the soldiers broke from the shadows and stood by Yen's side. Yen looked up and stared into Adam's blue eyes. Shouldering one of the team's two heavy machine guns, Adam towered over Yen; his muscles bulging from holding the heavy weapon, though he offered no complaints. Shaking his head one final time, he brushed aside any further thoughts of Keryn and focused on the mission ahead.

"What's the plan," Adam said, echoing Yen's thoughts. His deep voice sounded muffled in the tight confines of the room. The other teammates turned, eager to hear Yen's reply.

"Keryn was able to dock us near the rear of the ship," Yen explained. "I figure that even though we're quite a few floors above it, the engine room would be our best bet. Take out the engines on this Destroyer, make it dead in space, and let the *Duun* fighters finish it off."

"They're going to expect that," Penchant said in his gravelly voice. The Lithid carried few visible weapons, though Yen had been training with him long enough to know that any part of Penchant's body could be transformed into a deadly instrument. "We're going to run into a lot of resistance."

"I expected a lot of resistance when we came aboard," Yen interjected. "You can't tell me you expected to have an easy time raiding a Terran Destroyer."

"Why not just go straight for the bridge, if we're already dead set on running into trouble?" Janus asked, stretching his wings as much as he could in the cramped space.

"Because we're not the only team on board," Yen said, "though we are the most experienced. Every team that doesn't have their heads on straight will be heading straight for either the bridge or the control center. Yes, we'll run into trouble trying to reach the engine room, but it's less likely to be as heavily guarded as one of those other two locations."

"We're burning sunlight, people," Adam said, his former platoon leader mentality reasserting itself. "We've made the decision to go after the engine room, so we stick to the plan. Anyone have any more questions?"

Though Yen could see more questions just below the surface, no one spoke up. Pulling weapons tightly into the crooks of their shoulders, the team gathered around the door. Karanath, a beastly Oterian, jammed a metal pole in between the seams of the door and pulled. Slowly, light began to seep through the growing crack until finally, with one last surge, the door slid open. The team members on either side of the door crossed their fields of fire as they scanned opposite directions down the hall. Using only hand and arm gestures, they signaled that the path ahead was clear. Filing out, the team took up positions in the hall, Adam watching the team's rear while the rest began moving slowly down the eerily quiet hallway. Yen led the way, constantly expecting a danger that didn't seem forthcoming.

The halls of the ship were immaculately clean. The bright silver walls fell just short of being mirrored, though they were disorienting for Yen as he constantly caught his own reflected movement out of the corners of his eyes. Along the walls, signifying either the Empire or the specific ship designation, a series of multi-colored pinstripes ran parallel to the ground. They passed a series of doors inset in their individual alcoves, all closed and sealed. Above each, numerical designators identified each room. Though Yen had no idea what the designators meant, whether these rooms were living quarters or storage bays, he quickly dismissed the idea of searching each one individually. Their time onboard the Terran Destroyer was limited and the longer they sat in one place, the sooner they would face overwhelming odds in a Terran counterattack.

Instead, Yen signaled his team to warily watch the doors, but to press on toward the rear of the ship.

Through Penchant's featureless, glossy black face, Yen could tell the Lithid was irritated. The lust for war had been pumped directly into his team's veins like a psychotropic drug, driving them until they yearned for Terran bloodshed. His entire team, Yen included, had boarded the Destroyer expecting defensive positions and extensive fighting, making his team earn every inch of ground they covered between the *Cair Ilmun* and the engine room. To this point, they had found nothing but pristine hallways and unopened doorways hiding mysterious contents. It had to be a trap, Yen thought, or else the other *Cair* transports had lured the defensive forces away from this sector. Keryn had landed close to only one other ship and far from the rest, so he realized it could be a possibility. On the other hand, it could be a trap, he knew with just as much certainty.

Yen slowed his pace, letting Penchant take the lead as they walked cautiously down the hall. Ahead, he noticed the first hallway leading off from the main passageway into which they had entered. Raising his hand in a tight fist, the team froze in place. As he opened his hand, extending his fingers skyward, the soldiers moved quietly to the side of the hall, taking up defensive positions in any of the nearby alcoves. Penchant flattened himself against the wall as Yen slid up beside him.

"Tell me what you can see," Yen whispered, his voice barely audible even to Penchant.

Nodding, Penchant relaxed. The glossy exoskeleton on his face began to swirl and flow as though made of a viscous liquid. Slowly, from the left side of his face, a small swirling cone began to extend, like the reaching arm of a newly formed tornado. Stretching outward, the tornado grew wider until it reached a uniform width before it stopped moving. The faintest of lines formed across the end of the now cylindrical appendage before it popped suddenly open, revealing an eyeball. Yen smiled to himself, both impressed and simultaneously disgusted. The new eyestalk stretched around the corner, allowing Penchant to observe the length of the hallway while revealing almost no part of his body. Turning the eyestalk side to side, Penchant looked for anything out of the ordinary, but instead found himself staring down a morbidly similar hall to the one they were already walking. Retracting the eye, it fused back into his featureless face, leaving no mark that would have told an outside observer that the stalk had ever existed at all. Penchant turned his head toward Yen and shook it slowly.

"Nothing at all," he hissed.

Yen barely heard him as the air around him began to shimmer. He had the utmost trust in Penchant, but couldn't shake a nervous feeling as though they were overlooking something obvious. Yen expanded his consciousness and searched the area nearby for any hint of sentient life, knowing that a positive search would reveal any Terran ambushes waiting to be sprung. At first, he received only feedback from his own team. Slowly filtering familiar brain patterns from his search, Yen sought Terran thought patterns instead. The pain built slowly in his temple, distracting his focus. Shaking his head, he saw Penchant preparing to step around the corner. Concentrating once more, Yen was visibly stunned as the echoes from two distinct minds rolled back from down the hall they were getting ready to pass. His hand shooting out, Yen grabbed a hold of Penchant's weapons bandolier, jerking him back to safety less than a second before the Terran soldiers opened fire.

Gunfire split the uncomfortable silence as rounds

slammed into the wall across from the opening to the new hallway. Rounds ricocheted, peppering Yen's team with flying debris and molten metal. Dropping to the ground in order to avoid the sprays of gunfire, Yen and Penchant eased backward into the relative safety of the main hall.

"I didn't see them, sir," Penchant growled over the din of gunfire. "I swear I didn't."

Yen nodded, understanding. "They were in the alcoves. They're using the thick walls as cover."

"That's going to make it almost impossible to get to them," Penchant said.

"Nothing's impossible," Yen said, his dark eyes glowing excitedly. Yen began to coalesce a thin blue tendril in his open palm, similar to the one with which he had teased Keryn after dinner. Not stopping at a mere foot long serpentine tendril, however, Yen pushed himself as the blue psychic manifestation grew increasingly longer. As it extended past four feet, it began wrapping back around his arm, making more room in the spacious hallway as it continued to extend. While Yen worked on creating his weapon, the rest of the team moved closer to the entrance to the hallway, positions from which they could lean out and fire at the newest threat. Yen hardly noticed their movements. His brain felt as though it were on fire as the tendril cleared ten feet and continued to grow. Not much more, Yen knew, before it would be ready. At nearly fifteen feet, the tendril now wrapped fully around his arm and wound around his shoulders and chest. Yen relaxed and smiled softly.

Stepping gingerly over his prone teammates, Yen took one more opportunity to scan the area, marking the location of the nearest Terran soldier. The gunfire had fallen silent as the Terrans eagerly awaited their next target. Yen gave them credit for their patience, but mocked their ignorance, thinking they were safe around something as insubstantial as a metal wall. Extending his upper body just far enough to see down the hall, Yen jerked his arm forward. The psychic whip passed through his body with no effect, but launched forward, extending fifteen feet down the hall. The blue tendril struck the wall behind which one of the two Terrans was hiding and passed through it unobstructed. Protruding out the other side of the seemingly solid wall, the glowing blue tip of the tendril surprised the Terran soldier, who was unable to move as it passed undeterred through his armor and into his body. His nerves felt as though they had caught fire and boiling magma pumped through his veins. Screaming in agony, the Terran stumbled backward, exposing himself for the rest of Yen's insertion team. Opening fire, rounds tore through the thick armor of the soldier. His body danced and jerked as more and more bullets penetrated his body before, in a heap of gore, he fell to the floor. The remaining Terran returned fire, though it seemed weak in comparison. Leaning back around the corner, the team hid safely away from the Terran's barrage.

Yen's temples pulsed, sending shockwaves of pain down his neck and radiating through his shoulders. Though the whip had been effective, he felt drained and struggled to maintain his control. As the pain washed over his forehead and took root in the deepest recesses of his brain, the blue tendril flickered before dissipating, as though caught in a strong wind. The dim glow it had offered disappeared and, gratefully, the pressure within Yen's head eased.

Noticing the furrowed brow and beads of sweat forming on Yen's brow, Adam approached from the back of the group. "Need me to take care of this last one?" he offered.

Without speaking and afraid to move his head more than a little, Yen nodded gently. He could feel the bile churning in his stomach and was more focused on suppressing his urge to vomit than eliminating the remaining Terran. Smiling, Adam tightened his grip on the top hand guards on his heavy machine gun before stepping around the corner.

Adam knew which alcove the Terran hid behind, though he was unable to see any exposed flesh, as he would have hoped. Moving slightly to his right, Adam knew that it barely mattered where the Terran hid. There was a reason he had brought so large a weapon. As he squeezed the trigger, the jerk of the first round leaving the barrel nearly drove Adam backward. Pressing down on the front grip to keep the barrel from rising too much, Adam poured hundreds of rounds per minute into the thick metal wall. Shreds of metal and the polymer beneath flew into the air, filling the space between Adam and the Terran with a haze of white snow and glistening metal flakes. The armor piercing rounds tore quickly through the remaining corner of the alcove before finding the softer flesh beneath. As a round finally pierced through the metal plating against which the Terran leaned, the wall panel jerked, as the round slammed into the soldier's shoulder. Ripping through body armor, flesh, and bone alike, the wall beyond him was splashed with streaks of red as the Terran's arm was nearly torn free of his body. His howls of pain were cut short as a second and third round struck him in the lower back. Shredding internal organs and soft skin, the large caliber rounds shattered the front plates of his body armor as the exiting bullets left massive, gaping holes in the Terran's stomach. Gurgling softly, he looked down before a final round lifted him from his feet, throwing him headfirst into the wall. Crumpling, the Terran slid to the ground without even so much as a twitch as his mind accepted the fact that he was now dead. With a gentle whir, Adam released the trigger, letting the glowing barrel cool in the softly recycled air of the

Destroyer's circulation system.

Yen, his headache receding despite the noise, looked down the hall at the destruction beyond. Blood and gore could be seen just beyond the sheet of falling debris. Large holes scored the wall beyond the decimated alcove. The bodies, or at least what remained of them, were strewn in awkward positions, both on top and buried beneath the rubble. Shaking his head and rubbing his ear in an attempt to remove the ringing, Yen smirked.

"Well," Yen conceded, "at least they know we're here."

"I was never much for stealth anyway," Adam admitted, smiling to himself.

Yen turned to the rest of the team. "Check your ammunition and equipment. If you're short, let someone know so we can cross-level supplies. Give me the thumbs up once you're ready and we'll move out."

His own weapon still hung unused at his side, so Yen pulled free a magazine and handed it to one of his teammates. As the rest collected their gear – supplies they had dropped during the gunfight – Penchant approached Yen.

"I almost got myself shot, sir," the Lithid admitted with what seemed almost a tinge of embarrassment. "You saved my life."

"You're right," Yen replied, shutting off any hope of sympathy. Turning toward Penchant, he glared at the Lithid. Behind his dark eyes, Penchant swore he saw a flicker of soft blue light. "Which means you now owe me your life. If it ever comes down to it, I will expect to be able to collect on that debt."

Though the Lithid was used to the traditional stern officers within the Infantry, something about Yen's tone caught him off guard. Flinching, Penchant wanted to shrink away from the half-crazed psychic. Then, almost as quickly as it had appeared, the look in his eyes was gone and the soft smile returned.

"Alright team," Yen called out as though nothing had happened. "Let's get ready to move out."

CHAPTER 10

Keryn watched the radar with her stomach twisting in knots. Drumming her fingers on the console in front of her, Keryn tried to quell the rising nausea, an unfortunate side effect of her nervousness. Nothing would have made her happier than fighting alongside the team as they raided the Terran Destroyer. Instead, she was relegated to the *Cair Ilmun*, watching a screen of glowing blue dots signifying the members of the team. Her heart had stopped when she saw the two red dots appear on the screen, though they were quickly eliminated by Yen and his team. Frustrated, Keryn sank deeper into the pilot's chair. The radar was a direct update recorded by some of the equipment the team was carrying. As it detected foreign contacts on the ship, Keryn's screen updated. As a result, she often didn't receive an update until the group was fully entrenched in a battle against the Terrans. It was like watching a sporting event two to three seconds after the action happened. She could hear the explosions and yells long before the radar showed her any danger. Though Keryn knew that wouldn't always be the case, that the radar could detect enemies well in advance of the team engaging the Terrans in combat, it hadn't been the case thus far.

By tracking their movements, Keryn had surmised that Yen was leading the team toward the engine room. She had smiled at his decision, taking his team far from the chaos that would surround the Destroyer's bridge and control center. The infiltration team was comprised of some of the best Keryn had come across. They were hardly glory-hounds, and the thought of charging the bridge in a suicidal attempt at martyrdom had not appealed to the team. The way they were moving now allowed them to do the most damage possible while engaging the fewest Terrans. Yen was smart, and Keryn felt a swell of pride in her chest knowing that they stood a good chance of survival under his leadership.

The radar image flickered briefly on the console's screen. Keryn, brow furrowed, leaned forward and watched the monitor closely. Again, for the briefest moment, the image wavered. Slamming her palm into the side of the console, she expended the extent of her technical proficiency. Beyond that, there wouldn't be much she could do to fix the malfunctioning console. To her dismay, the flickering continued, picking up a quicker pace as it continued to waver unsteadily.

Frowning, Keryn reached to her throat and activated her microphone. "Yen, this is Keryn. Do you copy?"

A fine veil of static was all the radio offered in response. Her frown deepening, she spoke again. "Yen, this is Keryn. Are you there?"

"Keryn, this..." Yen answered, though his voice was distant and faint even over the radio. Between the clearly understood words, the rest were obscured by a rain of static. "...moving toward... contact soon..."

The console wasn't malfunctioning, Keryn realized. The signal was being broadcast from the team itself. The further into the Destroyer they ventured, the more interference the signal received. Much like the broken radio signal, the radar was only working intermittently as the steadily rarer signals broke through the external disturbances and slipped through the heavy metal plating surrounding the hull of the Terran ship.

"Great," Keryn muttered. "Not only was I left behind, but now I can't contact them even if I wanted to." Nothing frustrated Keryn more than feeling helpless. Stuck on board the *Cair Ilmun*, receiving only sparse radar and radio updates, she could do little more than wait and hope that Yen came out okay.

That was what truly bothered her, Keryn realized. It wasn't that she wasn't involved in the combat, though she would gladly take that opportunity should it arise. What bothered her was that she was trained to be a warrior. Both in her school training as she grew up and during her time at the Fleet Academy, she had learned to rely on others and support them in times of danger. Now, when someone she cared about was thrust into danger, she wasn't there to help. Should they run into trouble, Keryn could do little other than fly away, firing her meager weapons toward the thick hull of the Destroyer. Slamming her fist onto the console, she cursed loudly to herself, her voice echoing through the cockpit.

Moving her hand aside, Keryn saw the blue dots held in a state of suspended animation as she waited for the next update to arrive. The signals from the radar that did slip through the hull were frozen moments in time, no longer displayed as an up to date real time analysis. As she watched, the screen flickered again as another signal burst was uploaded to her computer system. Keryn exclaimed as the blue dots ceased to be the only images on the screen. Hugging the north end of the screen, in the direction that the team had been moving, nearly a dozen red dots had appeared. More disturbing to Keryn was the image that appeared between the *Cair Ilmun* and the boarding team. Doing a quick mental count as the image shifted again, Keryn counted over thirty red dots, signifying Terran soldiers, moving into a flanking position behind Yen's team. She reached so quickly to the microphone at her throat that she had to cough roughly from the trauma to her neck as she violently pressed the microphone activation button.

"Yen, this is Keryn!" she yelled anxiously into the microphone. "Yen, come in!"

She waited, but the only response was the white noise of building static. Either they had moved too far away to get a clear signal or they were too engaged in a battle to answer the radio. Either way, they had no way to know that they were in trouble.

You could warn them, the Voice offered.

"The hull is blocking the signal," Keryn said aloud, her voice sounding fretful in the empty cockpit.

The hull *is. However, there isn't a hull in your way if you go onto the Destroyer.*

Keryn's eyes drifted back to the sealed hatch just inside the crew compartment. The boarding tube was still attached and granted access inside the Destroyer. The radar hadn't shown any signals close by yet, which meant she would have time to warn Yen before they triangulated her signal and began moving in her direction. It could be done, but she'd have to move now.

With little more than a thought, Keryn leapt from the pilot's chair and rushed back to the hatch. Flipping the locking switches to the side, she pulled back on the large door. As the hatch finally opened and locked into the upright position, Keryn was able to peer into the darkness beyond the flexible tube keeping the *Cair Ilmun* attached like a parasite to the Terran ship. She knew that the radar could have been wrong. The Terrans could be waiting in the dark room below, ready to ambush her as she recovered from disorientation after dropping into their artificial gravity. Still, the ache in her chest reminded her that Yen was in trouble. With only the briefest pause to pull her pistol, Keryn stepped over the ledge and dropped into the hole.

As she became weightless, her braid of silver hair floated behind her as she dropped. The change from gravity to weightlessness was disorienting, as though she had plunged from a dock and was now submerged in frigid water. For a moment, she struggled to take a breath as she was overwhelmed by the sensation of drowning. As quickly as the feeling began, however, it disappeared as her lower half entered the Terran's atmosphere. The artificial gravity within the Destroyer yanked her downward, where she fell and took her first full gulp of breath. As her heart slowed its erratic beating, she keyed the microphone.

"Yen," she whispered, fearful of disrupting the still silence around her. "This is Keryn, do you copy?"

The reply was more than the harsh static she had been hearing. His reply, though still broken, was also punctuated by sporadic gunfire. "... read you," Yen yelled over the radio. "... busy... now."

Frustrated, Keryn moved into the hall, trying to get a better reception. With the *Cair Ilmun* unguarded, she didn't want to wander too far for fear of it being destroyed or, worse, boarded by Terrans. Still, her priority remained warning Yen and the rest of his team of the danger maneuvering behind them. She moved stealthily down the silver-walled hallway, slipping from alcove to alcove as she headed deeper into the heart of the Destroyer.

"Yen, do you read me?" Keryn tried again over the microphone.

This time his reply was only slightly distorted, though she could sense the irritation in his voice. "I read you, Keryn, but we're a little busy right now. I don't really have time to talk..." The rest of his sentence was drowned out by nearby gunfire. "We've run into some stiff resistance."

"I know, damn it!" Keryn yelled, her own irritation growing. "But you've got more heading your way!"

"Say again?" Yen replied, his voice finally reaching some semblance of clarity.

"There are nearly thirty Terran soldiers moving around to flank you while you're busy with the group in front of you. You need to get your team out of there now."

There was a pause over the radio; a nerve-wracking silence that stretched longer than Keryn would have liked. She hoped she hadn't waited too long before notifying Yen. Finally, to her relief, he replied. "How long do we have?" Keryn noted a gratifying lack of weapons fire in the background.

"A few minutes," she answered as she approached a hallway intersecting the passage she moved down. "Maybe less depending –"

She was interrupted as two Terrans stepped around the corner, as surprised to see her as she was to see them. Their weapons still hung at their side as both sides stared at one another.

"Keryn," Yen's worrisome voice called over her radio. "Are you there? Are you okay?"

In a surprisingly calm voice, Keryn replied. "I'll be with you in a second."

As the front most Terran began to raise his weapon, Keryn lashed out with the pistol in her hand, stabbing forward with the barrel as though it were a knife. The heavy barrel struck him between the upper plates on his body armor and the visor on his helmet. She felt the muscles in his neck tighten as he exhaled loudly and began gasping for breath. The Terran's eyes widened as he noticed the calm, calculated look in Keryn's eyes as she squeezed the trigger. Leaving the barrel at point blank range, the bullet tore into the soldier's neck, shredding through muscle and trachea. It passed unabashed through his carotid artery before ripping out the back of his neck, only barely missing his spine. Gurgling as blood poured into his crushed throat, the Terran clutched in a steadily weakening attempt to stop the jet of blood that smeared across the silver wall.

Before the front Terran could collapse to his knees, Keryn launched a roundhouse kick that knocked aside the second soldier's rifle, jarring it free from his hands. Disarmed, he reached forward, his thick hands closing around her neck. Shifting her weight backward, she drove the heel of her left foot into the Terran's kneecap. With a satisfying snap, she heard the bone break. Howling, the Terran dropped to his knees, his leg no longer able to support his weight. Keryn broke free of his grip and leapt in the air, bringing her heel around in a spinning kick that landed solidly on the Terrans plastic visor. As it shattered, shards of the visor flew into the Terran's eyes and bit into his flesh. Keryn watched him only momentarily, reveling in the blood seeping from his ruined face and running between his fingers, before drawing her knife and driving it into his chest. Twitching once, the Terran laid still. She didn't have to bother turning toward the other soldier. His destroyed windpipe had allowed blood to pool in the depths of his lungs. The amount of blood that had poured from his body coated the ground, leaving it tacky. Looking down, Keryn wasn't sure if the soldier had asphyxiated before dying of blood loss. In the end, his means of death mattered little.

Keryn leaned down and rolled the bloody Terran over so she could see his face. A deep seeded curiosity filled her as she knelt beside his body, running her hand over his strong features. Though she had spent enough time around Adam, her former roommate Iana, and the other Pilgrims onboard the *Revolution* to not be surprised by the appearance of the Terran soldier, it felt different to stare into the face of an enemy. She had never seen a Terran so close before, though she had heard more than her fair share of stories of the atrocities they committed during the Great War. She couldn't help but associate the ideal of the Empire with violence and aggression. Growing up, the Terran Empire was the antagonist in all her childhood bedtime stories. However, the face before her didn't seem as demonic as the stories had always described. In his death, the Terran almost looked at peace.

"Keryn, are you there?" The radio broke her from her meditations. "Talk to me. What's going on?"

Keryn keyed her microphone. "I'm fine," she said calmly, before remembering why she came aboard in the first place. "You need to get your group out of there now, Yen. They know where you are and are closing in on your position."

Suddenly, the lights went out, casting the interior of the Destroyer into impenetrable darkness.

CHAPTER 11

Yen frowned in the darkness. The inky blackness was so encompassing that he couldn't even see his hand in front of his face. "Everyone switch to thermals," he ordered.

The world slowly came back into focus, bathed in the cool blue hues of the ship's interior, contrasted sharply by the vibrant reds and oranges of body heat being emanated from his team. Under the scrutiny of thermal imaging, Yen could see the quickly cooling puddles of heat, pools of blood that had poured from the bodies of his injured men. Already three of his men were injured, one severely. Though they had broken through the Terran ambush, the enemy had taken their toll on Yen's small strike force.

Yen looked down the hall, where shades of increasingly deep blue stared back. The view was unnerving. While using the thermal goggles, Yen lost his depth perception. Objects that were dozens of feet away looked no further than Yen's own men, who stood less than ten from him. At first, Yen felt a sense of vertigo wash over him. He remembered feeling the same way during his first trip into space. He had seen planets on the front view screen of the ship and they had appeared as massive orbs hanging in the night sky. But as they flew closer, at speeds rivaling the speed of light, the orbs grew no closer. With no sense of depth, it was nearly impossible to tell how near or far an object truly was.

Straining to look down the hall, Yen could see no sign of the pursuing Terran force, but Yen wasn't fooled. It would only be a matter of time before the wide hallway was filled in an angry yellow glow as nearly thirty Terrans reached Yen's position. Turning back toward his team, Yen watched as they loaded the wounded onto collapsible litters. Though his soldiers needed medical care, Yen refused to leave until they had completed their mission. Still, their mission would have been unfortunately brief had Keryn not risked her own life to warn Yen.

Keying his microphone, he called to Keryn. "You okay?"

"I'm fine," she replied. "I lit a glow stick, so at least I can see again."

"I need you to go back to the ship," Yen said sternly, eager to cut off any argument before she could make foolish recommendations about coming to his rescue. "There are too many Terrans between you and my team. You'd never make it if you tried to come get us."

"So what about you? I just leave you all here to die?"

Yen looked around the darkness. "We'll find another way."

"How?" Keryn asked defiantly.

"I don't know," Yen replied harshly. He didn't want to argue with Keryn right now, not when he had so much more to contend with. They were finishing loading the wounded soldiers onto the litters and were almost ready to move. Yen wasn't happy about the arrangement, however. Three soldiers were wounded and unable to fight, but six more would be slow to react since their hands were full with the litters. Until they escaped the ship, Yen knew that his team would be moving slowly, which put them at a greater risk of the Terrans surrounding them before they could escape. All the more reason, Yen realized, to complete their mission, find a way to escape, and put some space between his team and the Terran Destroyer. Without speaking, Yen gestured for his team to move out. Yen felt his frustration build as they moved deeper into the aft of the ship. Logic and emotion battled within him. He knew Keryn was just concerned about him and wanted him to be safe, but in a time of war emotion was a detriment. She needed to think less about keeping him safe and worry more about self-preservation.

When his radio clicked back on and he heard Keryn's voice again, Yen realized how long the uncomfortable silence had stretched between the two. Is this what it would be like to date Keryn? Uncomfortable silences as both played their passive aggressive roles? Yen shook his head and pushed aside thoughts of a future relationship with her. It was a distraction he didn't need right now.

"I think I might know a way out," Keryn said excitedly, snapping Yen free of his wandering mind.

"How?" Yen asked.

"When we docked, there was another *Cair* ship that docked near the far end of the Destroyer, just above where the hull swells to compensate for the engine room. It was still there when I left the *Cair Ilmun*, which means that the infiltration team may still be somewhere around your location. You'll need to head up one floor, but you should be able to evacuate the Destroyer on their *Cair*."

"We'll head that way," Yen said. Though they were speaking on a private channel, Yen still lowered his voice so as to not let others hear what he said next. "Be careful, Keryn. I mean it."

"Always," Keryn replied confidently before turning off

her microphone.

Yen looked over his shoulder at the blue shades of hallway behind them. There was still no sign of the Terrans, though that barely put him at ease. They knew the ship significantly better than did Yen's team. They also knew where Yen and his team were headed. From their current position, it left little doubt that the engine room would be their target. Even now, they could be moving parallel to his position, taking shortcuts in order to cut them off. The more Yen thought about it, the more real the possibility became. This was their ship, after all. It made sense that they would be flanking Yen, trying to destroy him before he could complete his mission. He glanced nervously left and right. Though there were no shadows in the blue glow of the thermal goggles, Yen could *feel* the presence of Terrans all around him. It had been over a century since the last Alliance soldier was on board a Terran ship. No one knew what technology they had in their possession. Maybe they were able to cloak themselves from heat signatures.

Yen raised his fist, calling the team to a halt. Penchant, from the point position, and Adam, from the rear of the group, came to Yen's side to find out what made them stop. They both looked at Yen inquisitively, though the psychic's focus seemed a million miles away.

"We need to keep moving," Penchant said quietly.

"We're almost above the engines," Adam added. Yen knew he was right. He could feel the gentle vibrations in the floor. "Let's get this mission done and get out of here."

"No," Yen said sternly, his eyes slowly coming back into focus. "No, they're waiting for us."

"You can't know that," Penchant replied impatiently.

Yen frowned. Through the goggles, Penchant couldn't see the stern look Yen gave, though the intent was obvious. "I *can* know it. I can feel it in the walls, under my feet, in the air. They're all around us, even now."

Adam looked around nervously. Gesturing, the team spread out further, hiding as well as possible in the surrounding alcoves. "I hope you're not right, Yen," Adam whispered. "We're too close to the back of the Destroyer to suddenly run into a small army of Terrans."

Yen closed his eyes, letting the contrasting blue and red heat signatures disappear into an open field of black. There was a use of his psychic power that Yen had used before, when he served as a spotter on a sniper team. Then, he had used his abilities to look through solid walls to find Terran soldiers before his team entered a building. Breathing deeply, Yen let that same power saturate his mind.

Adam took a step back as waves of heat patterns danced in the air around Yen. The patterns swirled as though Yen were caught in the center of a raging inferno. A stab of pain bit into Yen's forehead above his right eye, but he shook it away without a second thought, concentrating instead on finding his focus. As he opened his eyes, the walls around him melted away. His thermal–enhanced vision pierced the solid structures of the ship, revealing a gentle glow of heat from a short distance ahead, near the rear of the Destroyer. Pushing his second sight deeper into the ship, the glow consolidated into individual heat signatures. Yen had been right. Not only had the Terrans flanked his position and cut him off from the engine room, they had already set up defensive positions around the stairwell and elevator lifts that would grant access to the lower engines. If they were to complete their mission, Yen and his team would have to find a way through the Terran defenders.

Walls slowly reformed in his vision as Yen retracted his

psychic powers until, finally, he found himself standing back with his team. Grimacing, his head pounding, Yen rested his hands on his knees as he waited for the nausea to subside. "They've set up another ambush for us."

"Where?" Penchant asked. "How many?"

Yen took a deep breath and stood upright. The world swam before his eyes for a moment before settling. "There are about thirty or so Terrans dug in around the stairs and elevators at the rear of the ship. They're set up around some sort of open foyer."

"Then we go another way," Adam stated.

Yen shook his head. "There is no other way. By now, the Terrans have cut us off from behind too."

"So we just go forward," Penchant said, his tone implying that it was not a question. Yen smiled weakly, knowing that if anyone would be eager for a fight, it would be the Lithid.

"Yes," Yen confirmed. "We go forward and we finish the mission we started."

"I'm assuming you have a plan," Adam said, shrugging his shoulders in defeat.

"More or less."

"That isn't very convincing," Adam frowned.

"Well, I have less of a plan and more of a good idea," Yen said, smiling mischievously. "Adam, I want you to take a team over one hall and then turn toward the back of the ship. I'll take the other team and continue on ahead. This still won't be an easy fight and our only real chance is to hit them from multiple angles to keep them guessing."

"What about them?" Adam asked, pointing at the three wounded.

Oradine, one of Yen's Avalon soldiers, was still bleeding from an abdominal wound in spite of the coagulants applied to the gunshot. They would be a liability during the battle. He really only had one choice.

"We leave them here for now," Yen said, regretfully. "Once we make a hole through the Terrans, we gather them up before we move to the *Cair*."

Adam's brow furrowed in disapproval. "What if the hole we make through the Terran ambush is only temporary? What if we don't have time to come back and get them?"

Yen frowned, already foreseeing Adam's line of questioning. He had wondered the same things before making the difficult decision. "We can say 'what if' all day, but in the end it has to be my decision. If I'm wrong about this and we have to leave them, then I'll be the one that has to live with it."

He could see Adam's disappointment, but the Pilgrim said nothing else. Yen and Adam split the team down the middle, the Oterian remaining with Yen so that each group carried a heavy machine gun. As the others checked their weapons and any explosives they carried, Yen pulled Adam aside.

"This isn't going to be an easy fight," Yen explained. "Stay on your toes."

"What do you want to use as the signal to engage?" Adam's tone was completely professional, betraying nothing of his previous dissatisfaction.

"The Terrans will be on thermals too, but we're going to try to minimize their effectiveness in this fight. Stay out of sight with your team until I initiate contact. If all goes well, I'll be able to open a small window where the Terrans will be distracted. You move when that happens."

Adam nodded in agreement. "In that case, I should be wishing you luck. Sounds like you're just suicidal enough to need it!"

Reaching out, they shook hands before Adam turned

away. Gathering his team, he jogged back down the hall, the way they had already come. Shortly thereafter, he found the side hallway and disappeared from sight. Yen watched a moment longer, making sure he wasn't surprised by gunfire. When he was confident that Adam was on his way, Yen gathered his own men and moved down the hall.

After only a brief walk, Yen slowed his group. Ahead, an open doorway emitted a steady glow of heat. Yen slipped forward until he could peer around the corner of the alcove and examine the source of the glow. Beyond the open doorway, the room opened into a metal shop, which glowed with its own red aura of warmth. Yen stepped inside and felt the heat rolling off of the majority of tools within the shop. When the Alliance had attacked, the shop must have been in full use, repairing and fortifying the Destroyer. Though evacuated quickly, the ambient warmth remained long after the Terrans were gone. Yen held his hand above a set of welding torches, the tips of which still glowed a brilliant white. The flame when lit, Yen realized, would have to burn incredibly hot leave such a high residual heat after being turned off for quite some time. Slowly, a plan began formulating in his mind. Yen smiled and picked up the nearest torch, examining the searing tip. This would be just the distraction Adam would need to make his attack. Picking up a second torch, Yen rejoined his team. No one made a comment about his new weapons as he moved them further down the hall. Eventually, the hallway ended in a sharp turn, one that Yen knew would lead to the open foyer beyond.

Leading the way, Yen flattened himself against the corner. He dared not peek around, knowing that even the faintest sliver of his face would give off a telltale heat signature. Instead, he lined up the rest of his team behind him before opening the valves on both the welding torches. A faint hiss was released, followed by the sharp smell of gaseous fuel. Opening his hands, the two torches floated weightless in the air, encapsulated in the soft blue glow of his psychic energy. Yen pushed the pair around the corner, hanging in the air at nearly head level. He could only imagine how the white-tipped torches would appear to the Terran soldiers. Side by side, they would have looked like the eyes of a demon, emerging from the cool blue of the surrounding walls. A demon was a fitting image, Yen realized, as he snapped his fingers. On the torches, flint and steel struck together on his command, showering the front of the torches with sparks. The burning embers ignited the leaking gas, erupting into jets of flames that burned scorching white.

Under the view of the thermal goggles, the light burned the Terrans' pupils as it overloaded their goggles, casting them into a thick darkness. Yen could hear their screams of both surprise and pain as he suddenly released the valves and shut off the flames. Stepping around the corner, his men moving quickly with him, they began firing into the front of the Terran ranks.

The Terrans had taken cover behind barricades, but many had stood in agony as the flames left permanent lights dancing in their vision. Exposed to the still goggled Alliance team, the Terrans dropped as rounds tore through flesh and shattered bone. Taking advantage of the distraction, Yen charged forward, the rest of his team close behind. Yen hurdled the low barricade and fired directly into the faces of the stunned Terran soldiers. Blood splashed across the floor as the Terrans fell and Yen tucked into a roll on the far side, narrowly avoiding their blinded counter fire. Turning to follow Yen's attack, the Terrans were woefully unprepared as Penchant led the rest of the team through the barricade. His face elongated into a snout with razor–sharp incisors, Penchant clamped his powerful jaws down on the head of a nearby Terran. Shaking his head from side to side, the Lithid reveled in the coppery taste of the blood that filled his mouth. Penchant dropped the limp and mangled body to the floor as Karanath smashed into the barricade, shattering its weak foundation and sending wood, metal, and Terrans sprawling onto the floor of the foyer.

At the same time, he could hear Adam leading his team against the eastern barrier, his heavy machine gun tearing through the sheets of metal and the tender flesh behind it. As they tried to regroup to face the new threat, Yen flicked his hand toward the Terran defenses. Panes of metal sheeting and wooden slivers flew from the ground, tearing through the air like makeshift projectiles. The wood and metal sliced through flesh, peppering the Terran soldiers. Collapsing to the ground in pain, the Terrans were easy targets for Adam's team as they broke through the far barricade.

The Terrans that had survived thus far broke ranks as they tried to flee the combined assault, but found there was nowhere to go. With both major exits cut off by Yen's team, they tried to run across the open foyer and charge up the stairs. Left in the open with no cover, however, Yen's men made quick work of the last of the soldiers.

They stood in silence around the corpses of the Terrans, taking in the scene. As far as they knew this was one of the first major engagements against the Terrans and, through two ambushes, Yen's team had decimated their ranks. He felt virtually invincible, ready to take on the entire Empire. However, he had enough wits about him to know that it was time for them to move on. Giving commands, Yen ordered some of the team to go retrieve the wounded soldiers. Adam joined him as he stood in the gap between the staircase and the elevator.

"What are you thinking?" Adam asked.

"Up or down. I can't decide which way I want to go."

Adam turned toward Yen. The Pilgrim's face was flushed from the exertion and he was smeared with blood, though Yen couldn't tell how much of that, if any, was his. "I appreciate what we've been doing here as much as anyone, Yen. We've done some damn incredible things with a fairly small group. But this is just one floor. They know we're going for the engine room, so we can expect this to get worse every step of the way. Let's take the stairs up and get on that *Cair* and get the hell out of here."

Yen nodded as though agreeing, but didn't move. His eyes remained fixated on the elevator. "Where do you think it leads?" he asked cryptically.

Adam had started to turn away, but now followed Yen's gaze. "The elevator?"

Yen nodded.

"Down, would be my guess," Adam replied sarcastically.

Behind the pair, Yen's team returned carrying the wounded. Still, he kept his eyes on the sealed elevator doors. "I know that. How far down, do you suppose?"

"All the way down," Adam answered, his voice full of irritation and impatience. "We're wasting time. Let's go."

Yen gestured toward Karanath, waving the Oterian over as he continued his conversation with Adam. "I came here for a reason, and that was to blow up the engines of this ship. I'm not leaving until that's done."

Adam leaned in so that others couldn't hear. "So you're willing to jeopardize all our lives just to fulfill your twisted sense of duty?" he hissed.

Yen turned toward the Pilgrim, a sardonic smile cast upon his lips. "My dear Adam," Yen said, his voice taking on a dangerous edge that Adam hadn't heard before. Behind him, Karanath began prying open the elevator doors. "The Terrans shut off the power, which left the elevator stranded. I couldn't take it even if I wanted to."

Adam arched an eyebrow. "Then why are you…" Adam stopped in midsentence before cursing himself for his short sightedness. Smiling himself, Adam turned to the rest of the team. "We're going to need everyone's explosives."

Yen was right. The elevator was frozen in place three floors below them. As Adam packed pound after pound of explosive clay into one of the larger packs, Penchant slid agilely down the cable and onto the lift's roof. Adam tossed the bag into the elevator shaft and Penchant caught it easily, lowering it down and onto the roof. Activating the sensors throughout the bag, Penchant climbed back out of the shaft and joined the others. Yen laughed softly as he handed Adam his pistol.

"Would you care to do the honors?" Yen asked.

Adam gladly took the pistol and aimed it at the cables. They had packed enough explosives into the bag to level a building. Even protected, the engine would suffer irreparable damage from the shockwave alone; more if Yen and his team were lucky enough to set up a secondary fuel explosion. Adam smiled at the possibilities as he squeezed the trigger. The pistol went off like a cannon blast, shearing the metal cable and reverberating loudly up and down the elevator shaft. As the elevator car plummeted away with a screech of grinding metal, Yen and his team began running up the stairs, trying to put as much distance as possible between themselves and the upcoming explosion. They had just made the landing on the floor above when the entire Terran Destroyer lurched violently.

Yen was tossed from his feet, as was the rest of the team. Splayed out across the floor, they gripped the worn carpet for support as secondary explosions bucked the floor beneath them. The ground started growing warm seconds before the elevator doors on this level blew outward and purple and blue plasma flames rolled out, licking the ceiling above and scorching the thick metal. Waves of unbearable heat rolled over the team, stealing the breath from their throats and leaving their skin tender and reddened. Yen laughed maniacally throughout it all. As the ship finally settled, the team climbed cautiously to their feet. Though it was impossible to tell motion on a moving ship of this size, Yen knew that the Destroyer was no longer moving; that their assault had completely destroyed the engine.

With Yen lost in his own malicious thoughts, Adam called out to the rest of the team. "Everyone up! Let's get to the *Cair*!"

Secrecy was no longer a concern, so the group ran with reckless abandon. They came across the bodies of an infiltration team, not far from the entry point of the *Cair* ship. At the base of the vestibule leading into the *Cair*, Yen found the pilot, still wearing her jumpsuit, her pistol hanging limply in her hand. His thoughts were immediately ripped back to Keryn and the sadistic energy fled from his body. Yen felt weak and sickened; a hollow pit was left in his chest, only to be filled immediately after by a sharp stab of guilt. He had truly enjoyed the slaughter of so many Terrans.

Activating his throat microphone, Yen called to Keryn. "Keryn, this is Yen. We've reached the other *Cair* and are getting ready to board. Get out of here and regroup with the *Revolution*."

———

Relief washed over Keryn when she heard Yen's voice. She had sworn that the ship was shaking itself apart as she saw the plasma explosion tear through the back of the ship.

"I am so glad to hear your voice," she admitted breathlessly.

Her heart had sunk when she assumed the worst and she was relieved to hear that they were still alive. With them now boarding the *Cair* closer to the rear of the Destroyer, Yen was right. It was time to detach from the Terran ship and return to the relative safety of the Alliance Cruiser. Throwing the locks on the hatch, Keryn returned to the pilot's chair and flipped a switch, which blew all the bolts holding the boarding tunnel in place. The flexible tunnel drifted away from the *Cair Ilmun* as Keryn turned her ship around, intent on heading back to the *Revolution*. Though the Destroyer was disabled, it still had full weapons. Keryn hoped she could make it free of the Terran warship before they started firing on her.

As she turned back to the Alliance Cruisers, though, she realized that the Destroyer was the least of her problems. Between her and the Cruisers, hovering in space and waiting for her, was a squadron of Terran fighters.

CHAPTER 12

The Terran fighters fell upon the *Cair Ilmun* as soon as it left berth on the Destroyer. Keryn flew like a woman possessed, weaving and diving in seemingly random and hypnotic patterns, but for every fighter she evaded, another took its place in pursuit. A nearby rocket explosion rocked the cockpit of the ship, nearly jarring Keryn from her seat. Growling in frustration, she pulled herself back into place and pulled the controls hard to the right, turning in a tight circle in order to avoid the next missile launch. She had already stopped looking at the radar for help. All she had learned in the Academy had gone out the window when she found herself alone in space, assaulted by a swarming Squadron of enemy ships. The combination of their ship signatures, missile launches, and suppressing machine gun fire left the radar console screen filled with indistinguishable dots of red; the one blue dot signifying the *Cair Ilmun* looking lost amidst the swarm.

At first, Keryn thought she stood a chance of escape. The Terran fighters had split into separate groups. Only a small handful of ships had pursued Keryn while the others set about systematically destroying all the *Cair* ships still attached to the Destroyer, thereby stranding all the infiltration teams still onboard. It was with relief that Keryn had noted that the *Cair* ship Yen and his team were moving toward had been, so far, spared from the Terran counterattack. Their attention split between the litanies of *Cair* ships, the Terrans were surprised when Keryn shot down two of the Terran fighters, using the substandard weapon systems on board the *Cair Ilmun*. Realizing that she posed a larger threat than previously assumed, other fighters pulled back and joined the chase. Now, Keryn was badly embroiled in a space battle she didn't think she could win alone.

You're not alone, the Voice said. *Let me help you.*

Keryn scowled. She was hardly in the mood to argue with the Voice, not when her life was hanging in the balance.

"Not now," she hissed. "Not ever."

In between her reminiscing and her debate with the Voice, a fighter slipped into place above her. Keryn heard the warning of her radar only moments before the fighter opened fire with its forward machine guns. Bright red tracer rounds split the dark space between the two maneuvering ships. Keryn cut the controls hard into a climb and managed to avoid the majority of deadly gunfire. A few stray rounds, however, punched through the rear hull of the ship. Keryn could hear the screeching of metal as the heavy bullets shredded large holes in ship, tearing through the wiring and pipes hidden between the armored plating and crew compartments. Their momentum waning, the bullets slammed into the floor of the crew compartments, leaving wide holes throughout the back end of the *Cair Ilmun*.

The *Cair Ilmun* shook violently as the crew compartment began to decompress. Warning claxons roared throughout the ship, their sound drowned out only by the whooshing of air being sucked out of the punctures. The lights dimmed and were replaced by brilliant red auxiliary lights. The sudden vacuum ripped bags and unhooked seat webbing from their place. The smaller items were instantly torn through the hole, left to drift free in space. Larger items, like the heavy weapons bag that Adam had left behind, jerked against the metal hooks holding them in place like a rabid animal.

In the cockpit, Keryn was nearly pulled from her seat as the rounds struck. The sudden vacuum pulled her taunt against the padded seat, her silver hair hanging rigidly behind her. She could feel the strong tug at her scalp as she feared the vacuum would pull her hair straight from her head. Hanging at her sides, Keryn's arms felt like lead weights, pulled invariably toward the rear of the ship.

Fear lodged in Keryn's chest. With her arms held at her sides and the suction drawing her body further from the ship's controls, the *Cair Ilmun* was incapable of maneuvering out of the way of the Terran's next attack. Unless she was able to move – and soon – she would be destroyed with no hope of rescue.

Merge with me, the Voice said insistently. Though the *Cair Ilmun* was close to destruction, the Voice still spoke with a calm clarity that cut through the din of warning sirens. *We can get out of this together.*

Keryn couldn't manage a retort, even had she wanted to. The pull of the vacuum felt as though an Oterian were kneeling on her sternum, collapsing the ribcage and making it impossible to draw more than a painfully shallow breath. She could feel her heart pounding in her temples as it tried to keep blood flowing to her extremities. Despite the driving beat of her heart, Keryn's limbs began to grow cold as the veins were constricted, cutting off a clear flow of blood. Her tanned skin was taunt and paled and her pupils widely dilated. Along the edges of her vision, darkness began to creep. As she gasped for air against the weight, the console in front of her began to waver unsteadily. She was losing consciousness and no matter how much she cursed at herself, Keryn was unable to raise a hand to close off the cockpit from the rest of the ship.

Decide, Keryn, the Voice said sternly. *Either you let yourself die here or you let me help you!*

Over the roaring of escaping oxygen, Keryn heard the soft rattling as the larger items in the crew compartment strained against their restraints, pulling inexorably toward the gaping holes above them. Consciousness was ebbing quickly for Keryn. Even the Voice sounded distant as it continued to berate her; it grew murky and unclear as more flashes of light danced in Keryn's vision. From what sounded like a million miles away, Keryn heard a sharp snap. Adam's weapons bag broke from its mooring and was launched toward the roof. Slamming into two separate bullet holes, the contents of the bag were pulled into both. Inflexible, they jammed the punctures, temporarily blocking the vacuum and the escaping oxygen.

Feeling as though a thousand pound had been lifted from her body, Keryn took a sharp breath. The dancing lights receded and the darkness slid uncomfortably back toward her periphery. As blood poured back into her body, her extremities tingled as a painful headache spread behind her eyes. Keryn, though not completely clear of the pulling vacuum, was able to reach up weakly and push the command button on the console. Behind her, the heavy door slid shut, cutting off the crew compartment from the cockpit. With the door in place, the rest of the weight left Keryn's body. She nearly pitched forward from the exertion and relief. Leaning forward, however, she could see the pursuing Terran fighters, sweeping back around for another pass of gunfire and missile launches.

Keryn's thoughts came slowly, as though being passed through a thick mud before reaching her limbs for action. The

Terrans would be on her in a second and the *Cair Ilmun*, with its entire rear compartment now trapped in weightlessness and many of its systems damaged by flying debris from the machine gun fire, was limping slowly through space with an incapacitated pilot. There was little Keryn could do but watch the fighters advance on her position while she tried to regain her wits.

Swallow your pride, the Voice chided. *Merge with me so we can both live! Quit being so damned stubborn!*

Keryn noted the hint of hysteria creeping into the edges of the Voice's tone. She knew the Voice was tied to the same fate as Keryn. Should Keryn die, the Voice died with her. Even in her stupor, Keryn shook her head, refusing to give in to the Voice's demands.

This isn't about me, it yelled. *This is about survival, for both of us. Are you truly so petty that you would be willing to let yourself die just to spite me?*

Keryn shook her head again, her lungs burning badly enough that she still didn't trust herself to speak. Was she really just trying to spite the Voice? Was her stubbornness really born out of a pettiness to be right? Difficult answers slipped away as the pounding in her temples and behind her eyes worsened.

The red dots grew closer on the monitor before her. From the larger red dots of the Terran fighters, small missile launches were detected. Keryn bit back the tears of frustration. She had worked so hard to stay separated from the Voice, only to find herself in a position of helplessness, faced with the real choice of merging or dying.

They've launched, the Voice screamed. *It's now or never! Merge with me! Merge, damn you!*

Tears slid from the corners of Keryn's eyes. "Yes," she whispered. Taking a deep breath, she screamed into the empty cockpit. "Yes!"

The console before her blurred and twisted as the floor beneath her pitched wildly. Keryn focused on a single star, glowing in the far distance. Slowly, the white light of the star grew, expanding until it filled her vision. The brilliant, blinding white light of the star passed into the cockpit before washing over Keryn and washing away her consciousness.

All around Keryn, the world was a dusty brown rock quarry. Narrow fissures split the rock beneath her feet into tall spires of isolated stone, cutting like open sores over the landscape as far as she could see. Between the towers, the fissures dropped away into dark nothingness. Having been enveloped moments before by the imminent impact siren of the radar and the blaring warning claxon, the world in which Keryn found herself was a stark contrast. The silence was deafening. Her ragged breath sounded like a charging train as it passed her ears.

Turning in place, Keryn found herself utterly alone. The world didn't curve slightly away on the horizon. The new world was flat and infinite, leaving only a blurred line where the split landscape met the dull tan of the midday sky. No rock formation broke the monotony of the landscape, save the narrow fissures that dropped implausibly deep into the core of the alien world.

"Hello?" Keryn yelled, cupping her hands around her mouth. The words fell from her lips, swollen with the dense air, and carried barely any distance from her before dissipating away into silence. No echo rolled back to her ears, nor was there a sound of other life on the desolate plain.

Frustrated, Keryn began walking in a random direction. She found that it didn't matter which way she walked; there were no identifying markers that told her north from south or east from west. At first, her steps were slow and cautious, moving carefully from one stone spire to another, though the fissures were much too small for her to fall through. Slowly, though, she began picking up her pace as panic settled into her awareness. There was nothing to be found in this world; no person to whom she could talk and ask questions and no distinct markings that explained why she was here. She only remembered giving into the Voice and then finding herself here in the broken desert. Keryn feared that she had been right all along; that merging with the Voice stole your own personality and replaced it with one of the Voice's devising. Unable to accept such defeat, Keryn began running, searching wildly for a way to escape the desert and retract her decision to merge.

"I was wrong," Keryn yelled as she ran, her lungs once again burning for air. "I don't want this!"

Her quick run became a sprint, her feet kicking up clouds of acrid brown dust behind her. Sweat beaded on her brow but quickly evaporated in the dry, stagnant air. Tears were already burning in her eyes as Keryn was overwhelmed with fear and anger.

"Take it back! I made a mistake!"

Keryn's foot caught on a protruding rock spire and the pitched forward, catching herself with her hands. She slid to a stop on the stone, her knees skinned and her palms bruised from her fall. She let her head hang down, her hair cascading over her face, as she sobbed quietly.

"I didn't want this," Keryn whispered between her large tears.

You did want this, Keryn, an androgynous voice said from beside her. Startled, Keryn jerked to the side. Trying to put her hand down for support, the bruised and bloodied palm gave way and she pitched onto her back. Keryn squinted to see the person standing above her.

You asked for us to come, and we answered your call. Keryn stared up at her own face. Above her, a perfect replica of herself stood, her silver hair sparkling even in the meager sunlight on the brown world. A gentle and caring smile was cast upon the doppelganger's lips and she batted her eyes with a seemingly infinite patience. Keryn knew the doppelganger; had seen it before. During her time at the Academy, the replica had appeared to Keryn in a dream. Now, however, the dream had found a physical form. When it spoke, it sounded neither male nor female, but speaking instead with either masculine femininity or effeminate masculinity. The doppelganger reached out her hand to help Keryn to her feet.

Scowling, her mind still reeling from her double's sudden appearance, Keryn batted aside the outstretched hand and pushed herself to her feet unaided. The warm, welcoming smile of the doppelganger never faded as she stood calmly by and let Keryn regain her thoughts.

"If you're who I think you are, then I don't want your help. I made a mistake."

And just who do you think we are?

Keryn arched an eyebrow toward her double. Something tugged at Keryn's consciousness, just beyond the realm of her understanding. "You're the Voice."

Yes, we are.

It was then that Keryn realized what had struck her as unusual about the doppelganger, what set it apart from the similar vision in her dream during her time at the Academy. It wasn't that the Voice sounded androgynous. Instead, Keryn realized, it spoke as though a hundred individual male and female voices were overlapping, drowning out any individual inflection until all that remained was a droning tone that was neither male nor female.

"We?" Keryn asked nervously.

Still smiling its infallible smile, the Voice gestured behind itself. Stepping one step to the side, Keryn was stunned to see a line of more than a hundred Wyndgaarts queued behind her doppelganger. They all smiled the same cordial smile. Keryn recognized her mother and father standing in line behind her replica, as well as her grandparents behind that. Familiarity, either from personal interactions or through apparent physical family similarities – living and dead – stretched back as far as Keryn could follow until, near the end of the line, she was unable to make out more than the general shape of the Wyndgaarts.

"What is this?" Keryn whispered in disbelief.

The genetic memory of all your ancestors, the Wyndgaart all replied at once. *Every one of your ancestors who ever merged with the Voice are immortalized within you.*

Disoriented after watching over one hundred Wyndgaart all speaking simultaneously, Keryn stepped back in front of her doppelganger. To her amazement, the rest of the Wyndgaart disappeared behind her double as though they never existed.

We understand that you weren't ready for us when your friends all went through the Ritual of Initiation. You only called out to us when placed in a position of utter helplessness, when there was no one left to turn to. We have answered your call.

Keryn shivered despite the warmth in the air. "I don't think I can do this," she said weakly.

You face death without us. We came to you only when you were ready, in your heart, to merge with us. There is no turning back now.

Tears welled in Keryn's eyes and spilled unabated down her cheeks. Turning her head aside, she tried to focus on anything else in the desolate, rocky plain. She had turned to the Voice in desperation and, as she knew it would be, the Voice had been there to answer her call. Regardless of whether or not she now thought it was a mistake, she had set in motion events that could no longer be stopped. Keryn was now left with little choice than to accept her new fate.

Taking a deep breath and feeling slightly more resolved, Keryn turned back to her doppelganger and wiped away the streaking tears on her face. She asked the only question that she thought mattered now.

"Will it hurt?"

No, it won't. Nor will we ever let anything else hurt you again.

The doppelganger lunged forward, its arms extended toward Keryn's abdomen. Instinctively, Keryn tried to move backward, out of the Voice's reach, but the doppelganger lifted into the air and flew at her. As its outstretched arms touched Keryn's skin, they passed into her as though her body were insubstantial.

Keryn's breath caught in her throat as the arms, head and shoulders of the doppelganger disappeared into her body. Still moving forward, her double slid deeper inside of her. Keryn could feel a warmth spreading through her torso and limbs as the legs finally slid into her body and the doppelganger passed completely within Keryn. Gasping, Keryn looked up to see the entire line of Wyndgaart moving toward her. One at a time, they passed into her body, the line speeding forward until the individual bodies became little more than blurs as they slammed into her exposed torso. Keryn tilted her head backward and screamed as the never–ending line continued.

The scream subsided as Keryn sat upright in the pilot's chair of the *Cair Ilmun*. Less than a second had passed since she had muttered an acceptance to the Voice's insistence. The missiles from the Terran fighters still advanced, the radar still blaring its imminent impact warning. Stretching slightly, like a feral tiger would once finally released from its cage, Keryn let her hands close over the ship's controls.

Smiling sadistically, Keryn easily maneuvered the *Cair Ilmun* out of the way of the incoming rockets before driving the ship directly toward the Terran fighters.

CHAPTER 13

Moving the wounded from the Destroyer and into the *Cair* was exhausting. By the time Yen collapsed behind the controls, sweat was beaded along his brow and his breathing was labored. Adam slipped through the cockpit doorway moments before Yen detached the boarding causeway and the *Cair* ship broke free of its moorings.

Yen, with his fingers moving adeptly across the ship's controls, turned the *Cair* so that they were facing the rest of the Alliance Fleet. Yen felt drained. The adrenaline that had kept his reflexes so keenly empowered was starting to wane. There were limits to how much a body could remain in a heightened state before the exhaustion of battle began to settle into its bones. Unfortunately, Yen knew, there was still far too much to be done before he could earn a good night's rest.

Accelerating forward, Yen skimmed the hull of the Terran Destroyer. Missile strikes and rail gun slugs had scarred the once gleaming hull, which now had unflattering streaks along the armored plating. Slipping left and right, Yen avoided the protruding radar arrays and weapon ports that jutted from the otherwise sleek surface. At such a low altitude, the Terran warship would have difficulty pinpointing their position. Aside from any defending fighters, Yen could fly virtually invisible until it was time to break from his position and fly at high speed toward the *Revolution*.

On both sides of their speeding *Cair* ship, Yen and Adam were able to see other *Cair* transports still docked to the Destroyer. Over a dozen teams had attacked the Terran Destroyer en mass and many of those teams were still inside, fighting and dying to complete their mission. Yen frowned, feeling cowardly for flying away from the Terran ship while so many of his brethren were still fighting. Still, they had come to complete a mission and, as far as he knew, they were the only team to succeed. Guilty as he might feel, he had no reason to feel as though they did an inadequate job.

His worries about the other teams were interrupted as one of the *Cair* ships to the right side of the cockpit erupted in flames. Though soundless in the void of space, Yen flinched as the core of the ship collapsed in a ball of flame. The wings crumpled, tilting toward the hull of the Destroyer before breaking free and floating into space.

"We got fighters coming in fast," Adam cried out.

Against the black backdrop of the starlit night, Terran fighters dove toward the Destroyer. They fired volleys of missiles as they approached, the trails leading unwaveringly toward the helpless *Cair* ships. Long plumes of smoke trailed behind the rockets as they covered the distance. Slamming into the *Cair* transports, the Alliance ships were consumed in flames one after another. Of all the ships that were destroyed in the fighters' first pass, Yen only saw one try to break from its position and run. Unfortunately, it too was destroyed by a well-placed rocket attack. For the rest of the ships, however, Yen knew that either the teams were obliterated onboard or they were now trapped within the Destroyer, greatly outnumbered and now hunted with no hope of escape.

"They're targeting the *Cair*s," Yen said, giving voice to

the obvious atrocities of war.

"It's their job," Adam replied. "All the more reason for us to get the hell out of here."

Yen nodded in agreement as he began entering commands into the console. Though the gravitational inhibitors worked effectively to lessen the force of the acceleration, Yen pushed the engine hard enough that he even felt the pressure on his chest as they broke free from the hull of the Destroyer and began flying toward the *Revolution*.

As they crested the nose of the Destroyer and once again entered open space, Yen heard Adam share his gasp of surprise. What had been a relatively empty void between the two lines of opposing ships when they had boarded the Destroyer was now filled with an embattled squadron of Terran fighters. Aside from the fighters designated to destroy the *Cair* ships, the squadron moved as one, circling in a tight turn and charging back toward the Destroyer. Squinting against the darkness, Yen could barely make out the faintest shimmer of metallic hull against the background of space. Typing onto the controls, the console monitor zoomed in on the glistening ship standing between the Terran fighters and the Destroyer. Yen groaned as details began to clarify on the screen. He could clearly make out the markings of the *Cair Ilmun*.

One wing was twisted, mangled from gunfire. Large puncture holes were visible on the magnified display. From his angle, he could see the last hitched gasps of breathable oxygen venting from the holes. Though a low fire still burned in the *Cair Ilmun*'s engines, all around the ship was littered debris, contents jettisoned from the crew compartment. Though Yen watched for a few heartbeats, the *Cair Ilmun* didn't move from its position. He wanted to believe that Keryn was okay, but he had no way to know if she was even still alive. The damage to the

Cair Ilmun was extensive and it showed no sign of maneuvering out of the way, even when the Terran fighters fired a barrage of rockets in her direction. The smoke–trailing missiles streaked toward the *Cair Ilmun*, but it remained stoically defiant in their path.

"Move," Yen whispered into the quiet cockpit. Adam flinched beside him at the sound. They both watched as the rockets grew closer, the onboard computers locking onto the small ship.

"Come on, Keryn," Yen said a little sterner. "Get out of the way."

The missiles broke from their tight formation, spreading out in order to strike the *Cair Ilmun* from converging angles. Yen's heart ached at the thought that the woman he loved was only moments away from dying and he was helpless to stop it.

"Move, damn you!" Yen hissed.

At the last possible moment, the *Cair Ilmun*'s engines flared to life and it dropped into a steep dive. The missiles were unable to maneuver quickly enough. As the first few slammed into one another, they erupted into a growing blossom of superheated plasma. The ball of flames expanded as the heat consumed the other rockets until the entire dark space was lit up from the blast. Squinting against the sudden bright light, Yen searched the area for any sign of the *Cair Ilmun*. The explosion had been both massive and devastating. Even with Keryn flying quickly away, Yen found it hard to believe that she had avoided that blast completely unscathed.

"I don't believe it," Adam said breathlessly as he pointed to an unassuming stretch of empty space. Following his gaze, Yen saw it as well. A small glistening ship burst from the cooling cloud of plasma and flew not away from the Terrans, but right at them. "She's suicidal!"

"No," Yen corrected, "I'm pretty sure she's homicidal. And she's going to need our help."

Accelerating quickly forward, Yen knew that it would be precious seconds before he joined the fray. Already, he could see the combined tracer rounds of more than a dozen fighters firing toward Keryn's position. To his amazement, she deftly avoided their gunfire. Flames leapt from the front of her barrels as she returned fire, scoring nearly perfect shots straight through the cockpit of one of the charging fighters. There was no explosion marking the ship's demise. Instead, the fighter tilted one wing and drifted away at an odd angle, the ship no longer manned by a living pilot.

As he flew forward, Yen marveled at the aerial acrobatics that Keryn showed. She shot through the midst of the Terran fighters, her gunfire clipping the wings of two of the ships as she rocketed past. Splitting, the fighters circled around on different paths trying to cut her off. The *Cair Ilmun* quickly eluded any potential trap they set, regardless of their angle of approach. To Yen's wonderment, yet another fighter was destroyed as Keryn returned fire, pulling the *Cair Ilmun* into such a tight loop that Yen found it hard to believe that a maneuver like that was possible.

Yen could tell that the fighters were equally surprised, though they began to regroup quickly. Keryn had the advantage for a short while as the Terrans underestimated her abilities, but Yen doubted that would last much longer. Accelerating faster, Yen could hear Adam's quick breathing as the excitement built within the cockpit.

Yen activated the radio system and spoke into his throat microphone. "Keryn, we're coming to help."

"It's appreciated," her voice called back. Yen was taken aback by Keryn's calm and collected tone, despite putting the

Cair Ilmun into a tight pirouette in order to avoid another hail of gunfire. Something about her sounded different, almost as though she were taking pleasure in her near death experience.

"Are you okay?" Yen asked hesitantly.

"I've never been better," was Keryn's complete reply. Yen knew they didn't have time for formalities, but something seemed greatly wrong with Keryn's behavior. With all the damage to the *Cair Ilmun*, it was possible that she had lost a lot of breathable air and was suffering from dementia. Still, her lightning quick reflexes and inhuman maneuvers left Yen doubting that she was flying with a lack of oxygen.

"Keryn!" Adam interrupted. "You've got a fighter behind you!"

Yen noticed it too late to yell a warning. He cursed himself loudly in the cockpit for letting his concern for Keryn distract him from watching the fighters. Even with Adam's warning, though, the Terran pilot was closing quickly on the tail of the *Cair Ilmun*. A missile launch would be moments away, Yen knew, and there would be little Keryn could do to avoid it at that range. Instead of weaving from side to side in order to lose her pursuer, Keryn cut the engine on the *Cair Ilmun*. Launching a rocket forward toward empty space, she used the recoil from the rocket launcher to drive her ship backward in the frictionless space. The Terran fighter dipped slightly as it realized what Keryn was doing, but its cockpit still scraped along the bottom of the *Cair Ilmun*. Sparks flew as the armor on both ships grazed one another until, finally, Keryn was behind the Terran. Igniting her engines, she fired her machine gun, tearing apart the hull of the fighter.

Yen's worry deepened as he entered the combat. Keryn was a youthful and inexperienced pilot, yet she was flying as though piloting through a dogfight was as natural as breathing.

She had already made short work of three of the fighters and Yen had no doubt that she would quickly dispatch the rest. Still, what she was doing should have been impossible for even one of the most seasoned pilots onboard the *Revolution*. Something had happened, something Yen couldn't just yet fathom.

Opening fire, Yen's tracer rounds tore into the cockpit of a surprised Terran fighter. The remaining fighters immediately broke from their current formation and attempted to readjust to face two determined and deadly pilots. Pressing their advantage, however, Yen pulled up beside Keryn and gave chase to the unorganized Terrans. Though the radio remained silent, the two *Cair* ships began maneuvering around one another like professionals. As they engaged the Terran fighters, one would draw the enemy's fire as the other moved into a flanking position. The fighters carried a heavier arsenal and outnumbered Yen and Keryn, but they seemed to stand little chance against the unstoppable team. Though his concern was not abated, Yen had to admit that he was very impressed with Keryn's piloting skills.

Using a disabled fighter for cover, Keryn dropped toward the exposed underbelly of one of the remaining Terrans. Most had already broken ranks as the once organized dogfight degraded into a chaotic battle during which only the two Alliance ships seemed to understand the rules. The Terrans, by comparison, seemed always to be two steps behind the flanking and dodging *Cair* transports. The fighter that Keryn now attacked had been one such ship. As his remaining comrades broke to the left in order to avoid her and Yen's latest assault, he had unfortunately turned right. Skimming past the debris that now filled the space around them, Keryn opened fire on the strong metal on the bottom of the fighter. Her rounds tore through the armored plating, piercing the bottom of the pilot's chair and vaporizing the Terran within the cockpit. Another fighter drifted free, a victim of Yen and Keryn's daunting attack.

Within minutes, the last of the fighters were destroyed. Yen checked his stores and realized that he was running low on both machine gun ammunition and the meager supply of rockets loaded on the *Cair* ships. Keryn, having started the battle before him, couldn't be in much better shape. They had pulled off a miracle by defeating an entire squadron of Terran fighters with just the two *Cair* ships, but they had now reached a point where luck ended and common sense reasserted itself. Yen turned his ship back toward the *Revolution,* ready to return to the safety of the much larger Alliance Cruiser. It took him a few moments to realize that Keryn wasn't following his lead. Checking his radar, he saw her still hovering in space, watching the Destroyer that they had both just left.

"Keryn, this is Yen," he called over the radio. Only static answered his call. Yen frowned, the deep sense of wrongness seeping back into his mind. He activated his throat microphone again. "Keryn, this is Yen. Answer me."

"They deserve to die," she replied, her voice low and cool, but carrying a razor's edge of anger. "All the other teams that went with us are now dead or captured. The Empire caused way too much damage for us to simply fly away."

Yen's brow furrowed. "We're not just flying away. The Destroyer is disabled. I made sure of that before I left. Leave it to someone else to finish. Let one of the Cruisers do the dirty work."

"And let someone else take the glory?" Keryn retorted sharply. "We did the hard work, Yen. I fought through the Terran fighters to get you there. You took the risks of losing your own life and that of your team just to follow through on something as mundane as destroying the engine of the Destroyer. I'm

135

telling you that we can do so much more. We can not only disable the warship, we can decimate it."

Anger burned in Yen's chest. The sacrifice and danger that he and his team had gone through was hardly mundane. They had done what no other team had accomplished in over a century. He had struck a decisive blow against an arrogant enemy. Who was she to downplay his accomplishment?

"I don't know what's going on with you," Yen barked back, "but I'm ordering you to turn the *Cair Ilmun* around and return to the *Revolution!*"

"'When we're in combat, I am the captain of the ship. I answer to no one else.' Sound familiar, Yen?" Keryn growled. "And you sure as hell can't tell me what to... cut hard right!"

The tactical command thrown in at the end of her sentence confused Yen and his hesitation almost resulted in the death of him and his team. Tilting the wings of his *Cair* hard to the right, a heavy metal slug nearly half the length of his ship went flying by. Painted dark colors, it virtually vanished into empty space as soon as it had gone a few hundred feet beyond him. On the console, the radar was blinking wildly. The Destroyer, though unable to fly, still had a full complement of weapons. Dozens of rail gun slugs were filling the space behind Yen.

"We need to get out of here, now!" Adam yelled as another slug narrowly missed their ship.

"Keryn, get out of there," Yen called into the radio. On the radar, however, Yen saw the blue dot signifying the *Cair Ilmun* growing further away rather than closer. Instead of retreating with him, Keryn was actually charging the Destroyer.

"What are you doing?" he yelled into his microphone.

"No one fires at me," Keryn hissed. "I'm going to make sure they never do it again!"

CHAPTER 14

There was a pattern to the rail gun slugs and plasma missiles. It pounded like a heartbeat. Fifteen seconds between each volley of eight metal slugs. Seventy-one seconds to load and launch a new plasma rocket. Keryn couldn't believe that she had never seen it before. It was so simple and predictable. Realizing the pattern, Keryn was able to find the surprisingly wide gaps in the Destroyer's defensive fire. Rolling to the right, she easily avoided the next round of rail gunfire. Keryn accelerated quickly, knowing she had fifteen seconds to close the gap on the Destroyer before it was able to fire again. By then, she knew, she'd be ready to skirt their next assault.

She had been surprised to find a similar pattern amongst the Terran fighters. Behind each of the fighters, Keryn had traced their trajectory, drawing imaginary lines through the empty space. The numbers danced across her vision as the fighters wove around one another in seemingly random patterns. Tracking their movements, Keryn had computed the complex mathematical equations in her mind, revealing a simple and predictable pattern in their intricate weave. The numbers made order of their seeming chaos. After that, it had been a simple matter of pulling at the loose threads in their weave, eliminating one fighter after another until nothing remained.

Undaunted by now facing a full Destroyer, Keryn found herself giggling in the cockpit of the *Cair Ilmun*. Had someone asked her if she thought it were possible for a transport ship to bring down a Terran warship, Keryn would have called them crazy. Yet maybe she was the crazy one. Here she was, diving toward a Destroyer easily a hundred times the length of her own ship. Yet she knew that it was all too possible, if the pilot only had the knowledge she possessed. Knowing that she was going to succeed on what should have been a suicidal mission just deepened her laughter. With a sharp realization, Keryn recognized the strange emotion brewing in her chest. It wasn't hysteria like she first believed, it was merriment. She was enjoying herself.

Keryn was stunned by her overwhelming sense of glee. She was getting ready to obliterate a Destroyer, potentially killing thousands of Terrans on board. While she felt no sense of guilt at their deaths since they were her enemy, happiness seemed like the wrong emotion to feel at a time like this. Keryn shook her head to try to break free of the weird sensation, but the sadistic joy remained like a shell encasing her mind.

As Keryn sat confused, her lips started to move though the words were not her own. "Stop fighting me," her own voice filled the cockpit. "You made your choice, now accept it."

Though it sounded odd to hear it speak outside of her own mind, Keryn knew the Voice as soon as it began. She fought for control, pulling back hands that yearned to fly the ship in spite of her mental orders. Her body struggled against her commands, leaving her fingers curling inward like claws, but never fully leaving the console.

"Stop this!" Keryn heard herself yell. "You're going to get us killed!"

The warning claxon sounded from the radar screen. From eyes she didn't control, Keryn saw the next barrage of rail gun slugs being fired from the Terran warship. Relinquishing control momentarily, Keryn's fingers flew over the controls, turning the *Cair Ilmun* aside at the last possible moment to avoid the metal projectiles. Once they were clear and Keryn knew she had another fifteen seconds to spare, she made a move for control of her body.

A grunt escaped her lips as she tried to force them to move. "Give me back my body," she muttered through a nearly paralyzed mouth.

"It's not yours anymore," the Voice replied. "You chose to merge. Now unless you intend for us to die out here, then leave me alone so that I can finish what we came here to do!"

Keryn maintained a symbiotic control only moments longer before conceding to the Voice. She felt sickened by the thought of no longer being in control. She had been relegated to an outside observer for her own actions. It made her stomach turn, a feeling that was personified by the nausea she now felt. In all aspects, she was still firmly entrenched in her own body. All sensations were hers to share. To a degree, she assumed, so were the decisions they made. But the Voice was now driving and Keryn was little more than a passenger, navigating the road.

She felt drained. Even the meager fight for her hands and lips had taken its toll. Mentally, Keryn felt exhausted. Internally though, hidden from the prying eyes of the Voice, Keryn smiled. Their roles were now reversed, with Keryn acting as the conscience to the sadistic ideations of the Voice. But, more than just being able to speak her mind, Keryn knew that her personality that had existed before had not been completely erased. For the other Wyndgaart who were willing participants in the merger, Keryn surmised, the eradication of their previous personality was probably the case. But Keryn still existed. No matter how suppressed, she could now bide her time until the Voice gave her an opening.

Dodging easily out of the way of even the computer controlled plasma rockets, the *Cair Ilmun* descended further toward the Destroyer. The mathematical projections of rates of fire remained etched across her vision, but deep in the recesses of her mind, another memory began to surface. Overlaid on the massive Terran warship, a secondary image coalesced. In all respects, the ghost image looked very much like the Destroyer it mimicked, though subtle differences could be found. The nose of the ship was less defined, leaving the appearance of an unfinished vessel. Many of the gun ports that existed on the true Destroyer were missing in the overlapping picture. Even the length of the ship was smaller in the reflective image. Realization of what she was seeing came unbidden to Keryn's mind, as though images and pictures that she had never seen were now readily accessed. It wasn't just a ghost image Keryn saw. It was a memory.

Somewhere in the confines of the Voice, there existed a Wyndgaart who had fought in the Great War, the first time the Alliance and the Terrans had faced one another in combat. The Terrans had made some impressive improvements to the Destroyers since that time, but the adage remained the same: the more things change, the more they stay the same. Delving into that memory, Keryn replayed the other's experiences of approaching a Destroyer nearly a hundred and fifty years before. That long lost Wyndgaart had boarded the Destroyer and found her way through the ship, fighting toward the weapons bay that was housed in the front of the Terran vessel. In her memory, Keryn saw the piles of metal slugs being lifted by the heavy mechanical forklifts. To each side, she also saw rows upon rows of the powerful plasma rockets queued in preparation for launch. And as the ghost image began to evaporate, dispersed like a fine vapor as the modern day Destroyer launched another volley of plasma rockets, Keryn realized why that memory had been pulled to the forefront by the Voice. Sinking deeper within her own mind, Keryn smiled at the plan that was formulating.

The seconds ticked by in her mind like a pounding metronome as the *Cair Ilmun* wove through the suppressive fire.

Twenty.

They slid past the next series of metal slugs.

Thirty-five.

They had less time to maneuver out of the way of the slugs the closer they got to the Destroyer.

Fifty.

Were it not for the lightning quick reflexes of the Voice, Keryn was sure they would have been destroyed long ago. However, she knew there would only be one more volley.

Sixty-five.

The Destroyer consumed most of the view from the cockpit as the *Cair Ilmun* flew straight for the front of the warship. The rail gun launches were dangerously close, though the Voice kept the ship skimming past their attacks. Keryn felt the excitement and bliss building inside of her again and it sickened her. Still, she knew the math as well as the Voice. It would be fifteen seconds until the next rail gun launch, but this would all be over in less than six.

Keryn felt the *Cair Ilmun* jerk as it fired one of the few plasma rockets in its reserve. The shot was perfect, as she knew it would be. When it came to combat, everything the

Voice did was perfect. The small plasma rocket sailed toward the front of the Destroyer as the *Cair Ilmun* banked and began accelerating away. Behind her, the missile sped forward, taking nearly five seconds to cover the remaining distance between the two ships. Just as the sixth second ticked by, seventy-one seconds since the last missile launch from the Destroyer, the *Cair Ilmun*'s perfectly fired rocket entered the rightmost missile port on the Terran warship, just as the Terrans fired their own rocket volley. The two missiles struck one another inside the tube connecting open space to the weapons bay. The resulting explosion ripped open the side of the Destroyer as superheated plasma roared back down the missile port, filling the weapons bay with a deadly inferno. Consuming the rows of awaiting plasma rockets, the *Cair Ilmun*'s shot set off a chain reaction of explosions. One concussive blast after another ripped the front of the Destroyer apart, peeling back the metal plating on the nose of the ship, splitting the hull and exposing over half the ship to the vacuum of space.

The Voice quite vocally cheered their success as the *Cair Ilmun* shook from the shockwave as the Terran Destroyer was annihilated, filling the cockpit with the laughter Keryn had already come to despise. Her hands were now free from the controls as the Voice reclined in the pilot's chair, reveling in her victory. Unassuming, the Voice didn't notice the faint smile that was cast upon Keryn's lips. Moments too late, she felt the adrenaline pumping through her body and her heart rate increasing.

Pulled from underneath Keryn's head, her hands closed around her throat. Choking in surprise, the Voice lost control of her mouth as Keryn's words poured through it. "I want my body back, you bitch!"

Growling, the Voice quickly reasserted itself, though it

still struggled to pull free the suffocating hands. "You made your choice. It's not your body any longer."

As the hands constricted around Keryn's throat, the cockpit started to grow dark. Her vision narrowed until it was little more than a tunnel as the darkness closed in around her. Slowly, the darkness slipped further inward until her vision was little more than a pinprick before darkness consumed it all.

The blackness melted quickly away, replaced with a desolate brown world of cracked clay ground and an undistinguishable horizon. Keryn was standing before a mirror, the reflection of which sneered angrily at her.

"What do you think you are doing?" the Voice yelled from the mirror. "You could have killed us! Right now we're floating unconscious in the middle of a warzone! What were you thinking?"

"I was thinking that I can't live like this," Keryn said calmly, in a tone that seemed to surprise the Voice. "I thought merging was the right decision at the time, but I've quickly learned that it was a mistake. You don't deserve my body."

The reflection smiled maliciously. "That is a great speech, Keryn. I respect the sentiment. However, I'm a much bigger part of you than ever before. Exactly how do you intend to get rid of me?"

"I want you out of my body," Keryn whispered, her voice carrying over the empty terrain.

"Excuse me?" the Voice asked, arching an eyebrow.

Keryn looked up, locking her gaze with that of her reflection. More sternly, she repeated herself. "I want you out of my body."

"It doesn't work that way," the Voice said, though her tone had lost some of its luster. "I'm inside of you now. You can't just…"

144

"I want you out of my body," Keryn interrupted. She could feel the strength welling inside of her.

"Stop saying that," the Voice demanded.

"I want you out of my body."

"Shut up!" the Voice yelled. It looked nervously left and right. Reaching out, it tested the confines of the mirror, but found it to be a prison.

Keryn took a step forward. The Voice fell silent, watching her every move. For seemingly an eternity, the pair just stared at one another until finally Keryn broke the silence.

"I want you out of my body."

Though the words were whispered softly, the effect was dramatic. Keryn's body was wracked with pain as her arms flew out wide. Internally, it felt as though she were being ripped in half. She struggled against the pain, biting down on her bottom lip until she felt blood spill into her mouth and a coppery taste coated the back of her throat. Before her, the mirror cracked down the middle. Spider webs extended from the image of the Voice, who howled in anguish. Focusing her attention inward, Keryn clutched the two halves of herself, the parts that had begun to separate and tear apart, torn in opposite directions. The mirror before her shattered, spraying shards of glass into the air. Keryn's body swelled as hands and faces pressed against her skin from inside her body, as though in response to the breaking of the mirror. Keryn tilted her head back and screamed in pain as she felt the hands break free from her body, exploding outward. A hundred Wyndgaart were flung from her body in all directions, filling the air with limp forms that flew vast distances away.

Keryn's eyes flew open and she let out a blood-curdling scream that filled the cramped cockpit. Back in reality, she groaned from the ache in her chest and the pain throbbing in her lower lip. She reached up and her fingers came away bloody where she had bitten nearly clean through the flesh. Pausing momentarily, she waited for the telltale sound of the complaining Voice, but it never came.

Keryn sat upright and found herself feeling strangely hollow. There was a vast emptiness, one that had been filled for so long that she never knew the extent of the bottomless pit that existed within her. Strangely, it saddened her immensely, yet scared her at the same time. The Voice was gone; silent regardless of Keryn's internal search for some glimmer of its existence. Keryn, shaking softly, knew that a part of her heritage and genetics had been wiped away in a single act of self-preservation.

Though the loss of the Voice pained her, it wasn't the most frightening thing to Keryn. She had succumbed to the Voice because she had been caught in a moment of weakness. Ever since she was a young child, Keryn had always assumed she was strong-willed. Yet when faced with adversity, she had caved and fled to the Voice for protection and comfort. It made her feel weak, as though she would always be reliant on others for her protection. Anger welled within her at the thought.

Keryn was so deep in her introspection that the suddenly blaring radio scared her enough that she let out another cry of surprise.

"Magistrate Riddell, this is Magistrate Xiao. Are you okay?"

Keryn frowned. The Voice had left her feeling weak and vulnerable. Keryn realized as Yen called over the radio that this wasn't the first time she had felt vulnerable. Try as she might, Keryn couldn't deny the fact that she was falling in love with Yen. Every time she was around him, she reveled in the comfort he offered. He filled her with a confidence that she couldn't manage on her own. For that reason, if for no other, it frightened Keryn to know that she would soon have to be around him again. Her merger with the Voice in no way had lessened her love for the psychic warrior. But it was that love, and the weakness that accompanied it, that Keryn feared would leave her too vulnerable once again. With great trepidation, she activated the microphone.

"This is Riddell," she said curtly. "I'm fine."

"Thank the Gods!" Keryn cringed at the evident relief that she knew was coming. Yen continued, "Follow us back to the *Revolution*. I am so glad to hear…"

Keryn reached up and turned off the radio. Though she felt bad for Yen, she felt her sympathy quickly turn to irritation. She had put herself in this situation by relying too heavily on the help of others. First the Voice and now, she realized, the help of Yen. Had he not flown all the way to come to her brother's memorial? Was he not responsible for her assignment aboard the *Revolution*? He had even provided the *Cair Ilmun* for her. Until Keryn could reconnect with her own internal strength, she didn't want to feel as though any of her accomplishments were the direct result of her reliance on others. She didn't want to feel weak, no matter how much she hated herself for that thought.

Until she could find the strength of will she had somehow lost, she needed to distance herself from everyone she knew. Yen Xiao included.

CHAPTER 15

The heavy scars of battle marred the surface of the *Revolution* as it flew toward the Farimas Space Station. The rest of the Fleet, all at least as heavily damaged as the *Revolution*, flew in tow, surrounding and escorting a captured Terran Destroyer. Disabled from the battle, with its crew held in brigs throughout the Alliance ships, the Destroyer no longer posed the deadly threat it once had.

Though the *Revolution* was the least damaged of all the Cruisers, she proudly displayed her scored hull as they flew in formation. Plasma rockets had burned deep holes through the armored plating and the metal slugs of the rail guns had gouged chasms that exposed the interior of the ship to the void of space. Hundreds of crewmen had died during the battle and entire sections of the ship were now uninhabitable, having been automatically sealed once the atmosphere within the ship had been breached. One of the holes in the hull exposed the ruins of the former bridge, now undistinguishable aside from the twisted and melted girders that had made the framework of the room. A fire within the bridge had killed both the navigator and the communications officers and resulted in a shift of command to an alternate post deeper within the *Revolution*. Though the original bridge was now destroyed, much like the head being severed from the beast, the *Revolution* still flew on with Captain Hodge safely in command.

Within the hangar bay, the damage splayed across the surface of the Cruiser was echoed in the mass of damaged and destroyed *Duun* and *Cair* ships that littered the bay's open floor. Many ships, like the *Cair Ilmun*, had limped back to the *Revolution*. They had been held together solely by the strength of will and determination of their pilots. Upon their return, the ships had collapsed in the gravity of the hangar, their metallic forms too severely damaged to return to their berths within the alcoves of the bay. Crews worked feverishly to salvage what they could from those ships too damaged to fly, as well as to clean away the dark red stain of blood that streaked the floor the full length of the hangar bay. Many pilots had returned with little of their bodies left beyond their iron will. They had died still strapped in their ships or, to the dismay of the other pilots, drug themselves free of their cockpits only to die on the floor in a pool of their own blood. Lying unceremoniously on the hard, cold floor of a hangar, gurgling and choking on your own blood, was far detached from the romantic vision of how pilots expected to die.

Keryn knew that she should be there, among the workers clearing away the debris and remains of the pilots. It had been days since the end of the battle and nearly every other pilot had contributed to the cleanup efforts. A couple of times she had made it as far as one of the clear glass windows that overlooked the hangar bay before her heart lurched and a deep pain stung her in the emptiness in her chest. In the end, she had invariably turned around and returned to her quarters.

She had been hailed a hero, both for destroying an entire Terran Squadron and single-handedly decimating a Destroyer. But Keryn didn't feel much like a hero. She smiled amicably when others stopped her in the hall or asked to sit with her at the mess hall, but conversation was always light and she left them bewildered, unsure of how to take her aloof attitude. For Keryn, it was a time of soul searching, though she still remained unsure of what, exactly, she was searching for. Her soul was incomplete, having been torn apart by her own actions.

Mostly, though, Keryn spent her time avoiding Yen Xiao. She had changed her routine to avoid him; going to meals earlier or later and working out in the middle of the night. He had knocked on her door a few times and had called more times than she cared to count. Eventually, she had simply deactivated her messaging service so that she wouldn't have to listen to his concerned and upset messages. His messages had pained her as well, knowing that she was intentionally hurting him. Keryn knew that he loved her just as she loved him, but until she could find her own way and purpose, she couldn't imagine herself spending time with Yen.

The ache in her chest was from more than just the loss of the Voice and her distancing from Yen. Many of her fellow pilots were now dead, Squadron Commander Garrix among them. While leading the Squadron against the Terrans, his *Duun* fighter had been struck by a plasma rocket and obliterated. There was nothing left of Garrix to bury. His memorial had been one of dozens conducted over the past few days. Keryn had skipped most of them. There was nothing to say to all those soldiers and crewmen who had sacrificed their lives during the first real war between the Terran Empire and the Alliance in over one hundred years. They were the true heroes, Keryn knew. And it was that knowledge that made it difficult for her to accept when others called her a hero.

Keryn stood in front of her mirror, adjusted her dress uniform, and looked at her own reflection. She kept waiting for the reflection to move, to speak as the Voice had done in her vision. In some ways, Keryn wished it would move. Though she hated herself for admitting it, she felt a little lost without the constant criticisms and compliments of the Voice. However, her reflection never wavered; it was just her own image she saw. The bruising under her eyes from lack of sleep and deathly pallor that had settled over her tan skin were only the beginnings of the physical manifestations of her inner turmoil.

Taking a deep breath, Keryn looked at herself once more in the mirror. The medals she had been awarded for her actions during the battle gleamed upon her chest, though she found their sparkle a little depressing. Finally, she understood what a fellow pilot had told her after her brother's memorial service. After Eza had been posthumously awarded the Alliance Service Cross, Keryn had been telling the story of how he had earned the medal. A pilot had corrected her, letting her know that medals like that weren't awarded, they were received. She hadn't understood the difference then, but she found herself understanding now. A person was awarded a medal for performing admirably, either in combat or in peacetime. But what was admirable about killing thousands of Terrans in a single attack? No, Keryn hadn't been awarded her medals, she had simply received them.

Now, she realized, as she stood in front of the mirror, the list of decorations that she would receive would grow by one, though this one carried with it a much bigger burden. As she walked out of the room, Keryn tried to remember any vignettes of wisdom that Squadron Commander Garrix might have imparted before his untimely death. Frowning, she realized that she couldn't remember any. She hadn't known him long enough for him to impart his wisdom. Turning off the lights, Keryn knew that she would soon be struggling to figure out the job on her own as she assumed the mantle of Squadron Commander for the *Revolution*.

Almost none of the pilots on the *Revolution* had been battle tested prior to the conflict with the invading Terran Fleet. Through her actions, or rather through the actions of the Voice, Keryn had become a hero and established herself as the premier pilot on board. Had she thought about it earlier, she would have realized that she was a natural selection for the position. But she felt like a fraud. It hadn't been her that had performed those amazing feats of aerial acrobatics. They were assigning her to the role of Squadron Commander under false pretenses, yet she had never taken the time to correct their mistake. She would do her best to fill the role, though the threat of failure loomed ever–present over her shoulder.

The walk through the *Revolution* to the auditorium where her promotion ceremony would be held was a startling trip for Keryn. The interior of the ship had fared little better than the exterior. When she had first come aboard, the *Revolution* had been pristine. Now, the walls were buckled from unseen explosions. Black soot coated the walls from distant fires, spreading their dark marks across the walls like a drop of blood in water. In parts of the ship, electrical wires hung from the ceiling where workers slaved to restore power to damaged sections.

Entering one of the only operational lifts on the *Revolution*, Keryn pressed the button for the correct floor and leaned her head against the cool interior wall of the elevator. She had tried to come up with a memorable speech, but everything she wrote felt trite. Hoping to make up her speech in the heat of the moment, Keryn now worried that, possibly, that decision had been a mistake. Weariness crept into her thoughts, leaving them muddled and unclear. When it came time for her to speak, Keryn wasn't sure if she'd be able to say little more than a polite "thank you" before departing the stage as quickly as possible. Smiling softly, though the humor did not reach her eyes, Keryn thought that exiting the stage quickly might not be a bad idea. At least her promotion would be memorable.

As the lift doors opened, Keryn walked the short distance down the hall to the large double doors that would lead to the auditorium. An honor guard had been posted in the hall and they nodded politely as they opened the doors. Very little noise escaped the auditorium, though Keryn quickly surmised that it was due to a subdued mood in the room rather than a lack of audience members. In fact, Keryn realized with a start, the room was nearly packed with pilots, soldiers, and crewmen. In her mind, the ceremony was going to be a low-key event, attended only by those with directly vested interests in her promotion. Instead, a hundred sets of eyes turned to observe her entrance.

Keryn, feeling even more nervous than before, was escorted by a member of the honor guard down the aisle of the auditorium and to the stage, where she climbed the steps and took her seat facing the crowd. She couldn't help but feel exceptionally vulnerable sitting on the stage, with so many people watching her. Even the few meager conversations that had been going on when she entered had died away. Scanning the crowd, Keryn's eyes unintentionally fell on familiar faces. Sitting a few rows back, behind the rows of pilots – her future subordinates, Keryn had to remind herself – sat the former infiltration team of the *Cair Ilmun*. Yen and Adam sat side by side, talking to one another in low tones. Yen nodded to the comments the Pilgrim made, but his dark, unreadable eyes never left Keryn. Beside them, the rest of the team smiled comfortingly. Though she smiled weakly toward them, her eyes were drawn back to Yen and his piercing gaze. It felt as though his scrutiny was pulling her apart, peeling away her defensive layers until she was left exposed. Keryn wanted to find a place to hide, preferably far away from that critiquing look. Her concerns were quickly alleviated, though, as the doors opened once again at the back of the auditorium.

"*Revolution* Commander!" the guard yelled into the room.

As one, the people in the room rose to their feet and stood at the position of attention. They remained that way as the winged Captain Hodge made her way through the crowd. The Avalon captain exuded an aura of command, something Keryn instantly recognized and yearned to emulate. When she had the time, Keryn would have to sit down with the captain and learn her secrets.

Climbing the stairs, Captain Hodge called out to the audience in an authoritative tone. "Take your seats."

The Captain took her place behind the podium as the audience sat. "I would like to thank you all for taking the time to come to this ceremony during such difficult and trying times. I know that there remains much to be done within the *Revolution*, so it means that much more that you would be willing to be present for this promotion ceremony."

"Magistrate Riddell did not come to the *Revolution* that long ago. Going into the battle against the Empire, she was actually the most junior pilot in the Squadron. Nevertheless, in the face of war, we were all children. We were juvenile and immature to the difficulties that we would all confront. In those moments, when the horrors of war were cast before us, true leaders were forged from the flames of the plasma explosions erupting all around us."

Captain Hodge looked affectionately toward Keryn, her words no longer directed at the audience. "There is an old phrase that says that leaders are not born, they're made. Leaders learn from themselves, their superiors, their peers, and their subordinates. From conflict, they learn resolution. From pain, they learn compassion. From loss, love."

"For the first time since the signing of the Taisa Accord, you are taking control of a Squadron full of battle–tested pilots. You were selected because of the incredible accomplishments you have already performed. However, I encourage you to never become complacent. Learn both your fortes and liabilities. Without understanding your own strengths and weaknesses, you can never learn of the strengths and weaknesses of your subordinates."

Looking back at the audience, Captain Hodge continued. "My charge to Squadron Commander Riddell is to learn from all of you, but my charge to all of you is to envision yourself in her place. Understand and learn from her trials and tribulations. Once you realize the hardships that she must endure, you truly begin to appreciate the leaders appointed over you."

"Rarely have I met a more qualified, dedicated, and brave pilot as the one that I am promoting today. For that reason, along with a myriad of others, I am honored to be standing here, before you all, to promote Magistrate Riddell to the rank of Squadron Commander."

Moving to the position of attention, the captain's voice carried through the room. "Publish the orders!"

As everyone rose to their feet once more, a narrator began reading the official orders that would promote Keryn from Magistrate to Squadron Commander. The responsibility felt daunting; she felt detached from her own mind as Captain Hodge walked to her side and pulled off her former rank, replacing it with the glistening wreath and decorations that signified her new one. When the captain was done, she stepped to the side and the room erupted into clapping and cheers. Keryn, blushing slightly, walked sheepishly to the podium as the clapping died away and everyone took their seats.

Keryn cleared her throat as the room fell silent. "I struggled to find the words to express what this promotion meant to me. I thought of all those beside whom I fought during the battle. I thought of all those who sacrificed themselves so that we could be victorious against a determined and deadly enemy. I thought of Squadron Commander Garrix, my predecessor who was among those who died in the war. Somehow, words just didn't seem to capture the depth of what I wanted to say."

Scanning the crowd, she searched for the words to say. "I can't say that I'm going to be the best. I've been told that I fought well in the battle and that's why I'm standing here today. But fighting well when you're by yourself behind the controls of a ship does not necessarily translate well into being a leader. I researched leadership attributes before coming here today. One of the items on the list said that you should never downplay your potential in front of your subordinates. But the truth is, I don't know if I'm going to be a good leader. What I can guarantee is that I will do everything in my power to try to become the leader you all deserve. If I learned nothing else from this battle, it's that I'm willing to sacrifice almost anything to accomplish my goal. Even if it means…"

Keryn paused as she caught Yen's eye. She hadn't even intended to look at him as she spoke, but her gaze had fallen on him inadvertently. She felt the swell of her affection for him and knew immediately what she needed to say next.

"I will do whatever it takes, even if it means sacrificing

my personal relationships to ensure your safety. My job as Squadron Commander will always be my top priority and I will push aside any other trivial relationship to ensure that the relationship between Commander and pilot takes precedence."

Looking away from Yen, Keryn addressed the rest of the crowd. "I thank you for this opportunity and I look forward to serving you all. Thank you."

As she finished, the room once again filled with cheers. She shook Captain Hodge's hand as the clapping slackened and people began filing out the back door. Intentionally staying behind, Keryn struck up a conversation with the captain, though she remembered little of what they said to one another. From the corner of her eye, Keryn watched Yen leave with Adam and the last of the departing audience. When she was sure they were gone, Keryn thanked Captain Hodge for her time and made her way out of the auditorium.

She had only made it a few paces past the door when she heard a voice behind her. "What the hell was that all about?" Yen asked, his voice edged with anger.

"You heard what I had to say," Keryn replied without turning around. "I don't think I could have made it much clearer."

"No, it was quite clear. Everyone in the auditorium knew what you were talking about."

Keryn turned around. Yen's yellow skin was flushed with frustration. Saddened, Keryn regretted the obvious heartbreak she was putting Yen through, but she knew that she had to remain stoic in her decision.

"I have new priorities, Yen. I have pilots that are depending on me. I can't keep wasting my time with a sidebar relationship when I have so many people expecting me to lead."

Yen's jaw dropped. "Wasting your time? Is that what

you think we've been doing for the past few months? You think this has all been some big waste of time?"

Keryn kept her voice calm, despite the trembling she felt in her legs. "I'm sorry, but I made my decision."

"You're not sorry!" Yen yelled. "I'm looking you in the eyes and I don't see one bit of remorse!"

Other people looked at the arguing pair. Yen's temper had drawn the attention of the pilots and crewmenwho had remained behind, mingling in the hallway or waiting to congratulate the new Squadron Commander.

"Keep your voice down, Yen," Keryn replied sternly.

The red drained from Yen's cheeks and he took on a cold demeanor. "Is that a direct order, ma'am?"

"What is that supposed to mean?"

Yen shrugged. "You only put on that rank a couple minutes ago, but you already seem to be wearing your *superior* rank so well." His choice of words seemed to ooze sarcastic venom.

Keryn stepped closer to him until they were face to face. "Is that what this is about? Are you jealous? Well, let me tell you something, Magistrate Xiao. Grow up and get over yourself. Because I know I've already gotten over you."

She turned and stormed off before the startled Yen could manage a stinging retort. She didn't care who watched as she shoved her way past the gathering crowd and onto the nearby lift. When the doors closed and she was alone, Keryn let the tears spill down her cheeks. She hadn't meant to be so harsh, but she knew it was for the best. For the next month of travel, she wanted the chance to figure out her life and the best way to do that was to not have Yen around. And after that argument, she was pretty sure that Yen wouldn't speak to her before they arrived at the Farimas Space Station.

Keryn took a deep breath and wiped away the tears from her eyes. She was a Squadron Commander now and needed to start acting like it. By the time the elevator doors opened on her floor, Keryn emerged with a glowing confidence that betrayed no hint of the emotional woman who had entered the lift.

CHAPTER 16

The view from the lift was both amazing and disheartening as Yen, Adam, and Penchant rode the elevator from the outer ring to the core of the Farimas Space Station. The *Revolution* dominated their view, but numerous other Alliance Cruisers were docked in their berths around the ring. No sooner had they disembarked then repair teams had begun work both on the exterior and interior of the ships. Already, they could see sparks flashing from welding torches as new armored plates were welded over the gaping holes and scars on the hull of the *Revolution*.

"We took a real beating," Adam muttered as they stared through the glass window of the elevator. The trio was crammed into the normally spacious lift along with members of the *Revolution*'s crew, all of whom had been granted shore leave during repairs.

"Yes, but we won," Yen added. His mood remained dark, as it had for the past four weeks of transit.

Adam frowned at his friend's tone. Leaning in close to Yen's ear, Adam whispered so that only the psychic could hear him. "It's been four weeks. Let it go."

"Screw you," Yen growled, his gaze never leaving the damaged Cruisers.

Adam shrugged, accepting that his friend's mood was

not going to improve soon. Instead, he turned toward the stoic and unemotional Lithid. "What plans do you have during leave, Penchant?"

The featureless black, oval face turned toward Adam. Without eyes, Adam wasn't entirely sure if Penchant was looking at him directly or just in his general direction. Eventually, Penchant's shoulders shrugged in an unassuming gesture. "I thought I would spend a large portion of my shore leave studying Terran and Pilgrim anatomy. I know so little about your race's physiology. I need to know what you're made of if I'm ever required to shift into that form."

Adam rolled his eyes before placing a firm hand on both Yen and Penchant's shoulders. "No," Adam said to Penchant before turning to face Yen. "And especially 'no' to you. We're on shore leave. I'm not spending my first vacation in months with a Lithid studying textbooks and a self-absorbed psychic."

"Then what do you propose?" Yen asked in irritation.

"We drink, for starters," Adam replied.

"You know I can't get drunk," Penchant corrected.

Adam sighed. "Then immediately afterward we'll go dancing, or we'll take in a show, or we'll just find someone smaller than us and pick on them. I don't give a damn what we do, but I won't be cooped up with a pair of whining bitches for my entire vacation. So both of you, snap out of it!"

The trio lost themselves in other people's conversations as they finished the long ride toward the space station proper. Below them, the armored exterior of the station rose up to meet them, growing closer until the lift disappeared into the interior of the station. Immediately, the elevator was cast into darkness before the interior lights activated. They could feel the centrifugal forces growing steadily heavier from the rotation of the station as they neared the end of their trip. Passing beyond the dark walls of the station's interior, light flooded through the glass windows as the lift came to a stop in a vaulted hall and the doors slid open.

Immediately, the trio was assaulted by a myriad of sounds. Large liquid crystal billboards displayed the stern visage of the space station's commanding officer as he read through a series of enforced rules for personnel taking leave on the station.

"… fighting will be placed in the brig for a mandatory twenty-four hour recuperation period," the voice blared through a series of hidden speakers. "Those who will be consuming alcohol are reminded to drink in moderation. Public displays of indecency will not be tolerated. Any personnel entering off-limits establishments will…"

Adam gestured to the closest screen. "And here is *another* prime example of someone with a stick up their ass." He furrowed his brow until he had reached a similar impersonation of the commanding officer. "Fun will not be tolerated during your leave. Should you be found violating our policy, the Fun Police will quickly apprehend you and you will be beaten until the fun is excised."

Yen caught himself laughing in spite of his dour mood. Grabbing Adam by the arm, he pulled him away from the monitor. He glanced quickly to each side, ensuring that the Fun Police were not pursuing them for public displays of laughter. The trio scanned their identification cards as they passed through the kiosks, officially signing out on shore leave. Yen let the others get ahead of him before turning back and accessing one of the monitors on the kiosk. Typing quickly, he entered her name onto the screen. The search quickly came back with no one matching that name. It didn't surprise Yen that Keryn hadn't taken her leave. Since their argument, she had handily avoided him at all costs. Consumed fully in her work, she had put her pilots through a series of flight simulations, much to the dismay of her already weary Squadron.

Feeling a strong hand on his shoulder, Yen stepped away from the kiosk and let Adam lead him toward the two-story archway that led into the actual city of Farimas. As they cleared the kiosk area and moved across the open courtyard between the disembarkation area and the city entrance, civilians began standing and applauding the crewmen, soldiers, and pilots of the *Revolution*. At first, the cheering civilians were small, isolated groups, but the clapping spread virally until, before long, the entire crowd was applauding and clapping wildly.

Penchant slid between Adam and Yen, hiding himself from public eye. "This is a little awkward."

Adam raised an eyebrow at the concealed Lithid. "We're the first crew to fight and defeat the Terran Empire in a long time. We are heroes to these people. So quit cowering, give them a smile, and thank them for their support." Confidently, Adam flashed a broad smile and waved to some of the gathered crowd.

"I'd prefer to stay a little more under the radar, Adam," Yen muttered, his voice barely carrying over the clapping. "Why are you drawing more attention to us?"

"I'm doing it for them," Adam said, the smile never leaving his face. Yen followed his gaze and found Adam waving and winking toward a group of Academy-aged girls who giggled from Adam's blatant attention.

"You're impossible," Yen sighed, grabbing Adam's arm. "Let's go, lover boy."

Together, the trio made their way past the crowd and under the massive archway before entering into the first floor of Farimas City. The ceiling of the city's first floor rose thirty feet above the three as they cleared the archway. The walls of the surrounding buildings brushed the ceiling, acting both as edifices for the stores and supports for the heavy ceiling above. The smooth streets and alleyways that interconnected the main thoroughfares of the city were pristinely kept, as were the storefronts themselves.

Yen, Adam, and Penchant found themselves in the business district of the city. All around them, merchants hawked their wares to throngs of recently disembarked Fleet personnel. Despite being confined to the interior of a massive space station, the sprawling city was full of lush greenery, which recycled the oxygen throughout the ship. Hanging plants draped their lazy vines down the sides of the buildings as ivy and other climbing plants clung to the lower structures. Trees lined the streets, accentuated by smaller shrubs and open parks with lush green grasses. Yen tilted his head skyward and let the warmth of the artificial sunlight soak into his skin. It had been a long time since his body had felt anything even remotely close to sunlight and it seemed to instantly brighten his mood.

"So where to?" Penchant asked, wasting little time absorbing the noises and subtleties of the city around him.

Adam motioned toward a series of lifts and stairwells that led both up into the ceiling and disappearing into the floor below. "The city is split into three levels. This one is the main level of the city and the most sprawling. Above us is mostly the residential area. We'll have to head up there eventually to check into a hotel. Below us is where we really want to go, though. That's the entertainment district of the city. It's more heavily patrolled by the guard force, but it's also where we'll find the bars, clubs, and theaters."

Yen stared at the stairwells and shifted the weight of the

overnight bag from one shoulder to the other. "We'll head up first. I want to drop my bag and get cleaned up before we go exploring."

"Do my ears deceive me?" Adam asked curiously. "Does it sound like Yen Xiao might actually be interested in enjoying himself during this leave?"

Yen's arm shot out, punching Adam in the ribs. "Kicking your ass is step one to having a good time."

"Come on, children," Penchant said dryly as he led the way upstairs.

Riding the escalator, the trio passed through the thick ceiling of Farimas City's main level before entering through the floor of the upper level. For Yen, it was a little disorienting. The artificial sunlight of the main floor faded away during the transition, only to be replaced by a second level of artificial sunlight above them. The streets themselves also added to Yen's disorientation. Structured like an ancient floating city, the residential floor of the city had vast handcrafted rivers that flowed through the streets. Framed on either side by raised sidewalks, large bridges spanned the rivers and interconnected the city blocks. Even the architecture of the buildings was different, relying more on faux bricks to create a more archaic look to the city. It seemed hard to believe that so differently designed a city could exist just forty feet above the bustling business district below. A large glass dome was clearly visible near the center of the residential district,. At his query, Adam identified it as an observation deck, something he described as a romantic escape in the heart of the city.

Adam, being the only one of the three that had visited Farimas before, led the way over the sturdy bridges and along the winding rivers. Yen quickly found himself lost to the twists and turns. He was sure that, if left alone, he would never find his way back to their hotel. Eventually, Adam led them across a wide bridge and stopped before a pillared exterior. The tall pillars reached nearly to the ceiling and were capped by an extending balcony above. Draped from the balcony were both the Alliance and Fleet flags, proudly displaying their support for both organizations.

Yen looked at the mirrored glass windows and the intricate reliefs carved upon the brick exterior. Mentally calculating, Yen was suddenly aware of how few credits remained in his account. "This place looks a little out of our price range," he muttered, slightly embarrassed.

Adam smiled broadly. "This is one of the forgotten gems of Farimas. It's off the beaten path and it offers discounts to active duty Fleet personnel on shore leave. With the three of us splitting the cost for the room, it won't be that expensive."

Yen wasn't convinced as he entered the hotel. A small fountain bubbled happily in the center of the large, open foyer. To either side, artistically upholstered couches and chairs offered plush relaxation for weary travelers. The countertops, behind which the concierge waited with a patient smile, were crafted from artificial marble. Though lightweight compared to its contemporary cousin, the false marble was still significantly more expensive then most other substances available for architects and shipbuilders. Yen swallowed hard, his eyes tracing the carvings and small statues set into alcoves along the walls.

"Welcome to the *Infinturius*," the manager said politely as the trio approached the marble countertop, "the finest hotel to be found in Farimas City."

Adam handed over his identification card, which the manager swiped through the system. The computer beeped loudly and a soft green light glowed form its monitor. The manager looked up with a warm and inviting smile.

"Welcome back, Mr. Decker," he said, significantly more cordial then he had been upon their arrival. "I'm glad to see that you could stay with us again."

"Thank you," Adam replied. "Can you give us my normal room?"

The manager typed furiously on the computer before looking up, the broad smile having never left his face. "Absolutely, sir. I'll have someone come around immediately to take your bags up to your room." Lifting a handheld console and setting it on the counter, the manager continued. "If you could please sign here and here, we will get you set up immediately."

Yen nearly choked on his own saliva when he saw the price for the room. Even split three ways, the room would cost him nearly all of his savings, leaving little money to use the rest of his leave. Though Yen tried to say something about it to Adam, the Pilgrim passively held up his index finger, stopping Yen in mid-thought. As the manager walked away to get the keys, Adam turned toward Yen.

"Are you crazy?" Yen hissed, not waiting to get to the heart of his complaint. "We barely have enough money to cover this room!"

"No," Adam replied, "*you* barely have enough money to cover this room. But I'm not going to ask either of you to pay for any of it. Consider this my treat to you; a friendly gesture to make sure we all have the best time possible during our leave."

"Adam," Penchant added. "We can't ask you to pay for this room. We can find somewhere cheaper."

"Of course we can," Adam said with a sigh, "but that's not the point. You have to understand that I'm an infantryman. I've been on active duty for a few years now. I've been assigned to Fleet duty during that entire time. When we're on the ship, how many times have you seen me spend lavishly? None. I just don't spend money when we're away on missions. During all that time in space, I just quietly collect my paycheck and keep to myself. But when I go on shore leave, that's my time to treat myself like a king. I take all the money that I've been saving up over the months and I stay at the best hotel possible. I eat the best food I can. I drink the most expensive drinks. And why, you ask? Because I'm an infantryman. My next mission is very possibly my last."

Adam's shoulder's drooped. "So yes, we could stay at a cheaper place, but I'm not going to. Leave if you want or stay if you want, but I'd prefer you enjoyed this time with me."

Yen arched an eyebrow and look at Penchant, who shrugged as well. "Well, Adam, I guess we're staying. After all, if we don't, who knows how much of an emotional sissy you'll turn into."

Penchant and Yen both laughed, the Lithid's gravelly laughter sounding coarse and grating. Adam smiled, despite himself. "Laugh it up," he said. "And remind me to shoot you later, when I get the chance."

The manager returned with three copies of their room key. "If you're both done having fun at my expense," Adam offered, "then let's go upstairs and get ready for a wild night on the town."

CHAPTER 17

Keryn walked the empty halls of the *Revolution*, glad to be away from the bustle of activity that accompanied their docking at the space station. Nearly everyone had left the ship, eager to begin their shore leave, leaving the ship a vacant ghost. Only the sounds of hammering and the distant sparking of the welders repairing the Cruiser broke the silence.

It was a welcomed change from the past four weeks. Keryn had thought that the hardest part of being promoted to Squadron Commander would have been planning new strategies and taking her pilots through the simulations. Instead, her hardest task had been finding creative ways to avoid Yen Xiao. He hadn't actively sought her company and she knew his blood still boiled at the thought of their argument. Still, against her own desires, she had refrained from apologizing. Though the time apart had been difficult, it had also been invigorating. Keryn found more and more time to examine her own interests and desires and, slowly, she grew more confident as a leader. Her Squadron still grumbled at the thought of more simulations, but they performed admirably, no matter how difficult the battlefield she envisioned.

Walking down one of the empty corridors, Keryn turned the corner and almost ran into Captain Hodge. Sliding quickly apart, the captain placed her hand on her chest in evident shock.

"Squadron Commander," she said breathlessly. "I hadn't expected anyone else to still be aboard." Slowly, Captain Hodge regained her composure. Her look of surprise was replaced by one of suspicion. "Why are you still on board?"

Keryn shrugged. "I had a lot of work to do, ma'am. I figured I could take some quiet time while everyone in the Squadron is enjoying their shore leave to catch up on some of the projects I'd been procrastinating to finish for the past four weeks."

Shaking her head in disapproval, Captain Hodge replied. "You're exactly right, Keryn. Everyone under your command is enjoying their shore leave, except for you."

"There's nothing for me down there that I can't appreciate by remaining on board."

The Captain frowned. "You don't honestly believe that, do you?"

"I believe it enough, does that count?" Keryn asked, laughing slightly.

Captain Hodge sat on a bench nearby. Tapping the seat next to her, she invited Keryn to sit as well. "You know, it may sound like a bad cliché, but you remind me a lot of a younger me. When I was a young officer, I believed that I could change the world... if only there was one more hour in every day. I worked myself nearly to death to try to set myself apart from my peers. And I was successful. I was one of the youngest Avalon to ever be promoted to the rank of captain and be given command of my own Cruiser. It was a remarkable day, but you know who celebrated with me?"

Keryn knew where the story was going, and frowned at the realization. "No one, ma'am."

"Exactly. Against popular belief, there is no such thing

as being married to your work. At the end of the day, your work is a fickle lover. The job that you fill, the one that you're so attached to, can easily be filled by anyone else. So if you want something that's actually committed to you, you need to get your butt off this ship and go enjoy your shore leave."

Keryn smiled. "Is that an order, ma'am?"

"If it has to be," Captain Hodge laughed.

Keryn lowered her eyes, unsure if she would follow that order even if it was given. She didn't want to go through the grueling effort of trying to find a good man amongst the sea of horny crewmen all on their shore leave. If she was going to go through that much work, she might as well stay on the ship and do some work that would truly make a difference.

As though reading her mind, Captain Hodge interrupted. "I can see you're still not sold on the idea," she said in her musical tones. "Come with me, Keryn."

With no more directive than that, the Captain stood and began walking toward the front of the ship. Curious, Keryn climbed to her feet and followed. Leading her through winding halls and past dozens of work crews, Captain Hodge never looked back to ensure Keryn was still behind her. A strange sixth sense let her know that Keryn hadn't strayed far. The captain was cryptically quiet; something that only piqued Keryn's interest further. As they neared midship, Captain Hodge came to a stop in front of a bank of elevators. More than familiar with this particular lift, Keryn had taken this specific elevator down to the hangar bay many times before. As the doors opened, both women stepped inside.

Confined in a smaller space, Keryn couldn't resist asking questions. "Exactly what is it you need to show me in the hangar bay?"

"You'll see," the Avalon replied, adjusting her feathery

171

wings. "It's my final gift to you before I ship you down to the planet for your shore leave."

Keryn rolled her eyes, but was sure to do it in a way that the captain couldn't see.

As the doors slid open, Keryn was surprised to see that they were not on the hangar bay floor. Instead, the elevators opened onto the observation deck which overlooked the open bay. Keryn had come here many times since the battle with the Terran Fleet, often to check on the repair work being conducted on her ships. They had patched up the fighters and transport ships as much as possible, but some repairs could only be conducted once they reached a facility like the space station.

Captain Hodge stepped toward the glass and motioned for Keryn to join her at the window. Nonchalantly, Keryn stepped forward. She already knew what she would see. Welders and munitions specialists would be working diligently to repair and rearm the Squadron, making it space worthy for any eventuality. Once, Keryn would have thought them daft for spending so much effort preparing a Squadron of ships during peacetime operations. But now that they were at war with the Empire, the next battle could truly be only months away.

When she stepped to the glass, Keryn was floored by what she saw. The repairs were evidently completed long ago. The piles of scrap metal and worker's tools had long since been removed. Both the *Duun* fighters and *Cair* ships were stored in their alcoves, glistening in the halogen lights. From her vantage point, she could even see the *Cair Ilmun*, fully repaired as though no harm had ever come to her. But it wasn't the repairs that surprised Keryn. Around a large number of the *Cair* ships, men in jumpsuits swarmed over the vehicles, moving large engine–like machines into position near the rear of the crafts. The men in jumpsuits were completely unfamiliar. She had seen the work crews when they came aboard from the space station. Their uniforms looked nothing like these.

"Who are those men and what are they doing to my ships?" Keryn asked with a mixture of surprise and anger. Those ships were her direct responsibility as the Squadron Commander. She found it hard to believe that Captain Hodge would approve anyone to make modifications to her ships without her consent.

"Keep watching," Captain Hodge said calmly.

Looking closer, Keryn watched as one of the men turned around, his eyes cast toward the observation deck where they watched. Emblazoned upon his chest in stark red design was an emblem with which everyone in the Fleet was familiar. The men working on the *Cair* ships worked directly for the High Council.

As Keryn turned, the Captain shook her head, stopping her question before it could be asked. "I can't tell you why they're here or what they're doing to your ships. Everything they're doing is classified, though I'm sure you'll find out soon enough. I only brought you here because you need to realize that it would be better if you're not around while they're doing their work. Stumbling upon them in the middle of their operation and asking the wrong questions could damage your career."

Taking her gently by the arm, Captain Hodge turned Keryn away from the window. "Believe me when I tell you that I fully support what they're doing. But for the next few days, the best thing you could do is take my advice and enjoy your shore leave."

"I don't know what they're doing down there," Keryn said curtly, "but I won't be able to just forget about it and enjoy my leave."

"Then find something to take your mind off it," the Captain replied playfully.

Keryn frowned, knowing what she was alluding to. "No offense, ma'am, but I'm not exactly looking for a relationship right now."

"Who said anything about a relationship? Just find a cute guy down on the space station and let him help you relax."

Keryn couldn't help but let her mouth fall open. This was not the conversation she was expecting to have with her captain. "Ma'am, I just can't do that."

"Then you need to learn. Sometimes, when you're piloting a ship, it's not about reaching your final destination. When you're caught in a nebula, sometimes any port in the storm will do." The captain let her words hang in the air a moment longer before ushering Keryn back toward the lift. "Go pack your things. I'll expect you on the next lift heading down to the city. And yes, commander, that is an order."

The captain's smile vanished as the elevator doors closed and the lift carried Keryn back to the living quarters. She was stunned, by both her odd conversation and what she had seen in the hangar bay. She absently threw clothes into her bag and changed out of her uniform. The next lift would be leaving in less than an hour, granting her almost no time to consider everything before she had to depart. Keryn wondered if that wasn't part of the captain's plan all along.

Riding the lift to the city itself gave Keryn lots of time to think. The High Council wouldn't be involved in ship modifications unless something big was being planned. After the Fleet battle, though, Keryn had trouble imagining what could be so big that it would require their intervention. The thought of it both excited and scared Keryn to death. The Fleet encounter had been daunting and frightening. But this, she could guarantee, would be much bigger than anyone would believe.

Lost in her own thoughts, Keryn didn't pay attention to the cheering crowds as she walked under the arch and into the city. Turning a sharp left, she rode the lift up to the residential level and found the closest, cheapest hotel available. Not caring about the niceties that could have been found with a little more effort, Keryn dropped her bag on the bed and looked out her slightly dingy window toward the canals that wound through the street. Yen would have loved a place like this, she realized. Frowning, Keryn knew that it was thoughts like those that she had come here to escape. The upper level was beautiful, she had to admit, but she wasn't overly interested in admiring the city's architecture. Captain Hodge's parting words still ran through her mind. Smiling to herself, Keryn realized that maybe the captain was smarter than she even let on. No more thoughts of Yen, she promised herself. Maybe any port in the storm was exactly what she needed right now.

Switching the placard on the door to read "do not disturb" just in case she was too engrossed to remember to do so later, Keryn walked down to street level and made her way back to the lifts. She'd find the entertainment district two levels down and, somewhere, the perfect distraction to the stresses of command.

CHAPTER 18

Music from a dozen clubs spilled into the wide street as Yen, Adam, and Penchant made their way through the entertainment district. Neon lights flashed overhead, advertising musical acts and carnal pleasures. Scantily clad women and intoxicated men walked down the dimly lit streets, their bodies swaying to the beat of the music. The normally bright, artificial light had dimmed overhead, replaced with a soft ambient light like that of a nearby moon. False constellations sparkled in the ceiling overhead, giving the illusion of wandering the streets of a planet–side city.

Though Yen had been resistant to the idea of going out tonight, he was glad that he had finally caved to Adam's persistence. The heavy bass beats that pounded through open doorways drowned out the negative thoughts that had been filling his mind. Closing his eyes, Yen let himself get washed away in the competing music.

Adam led the trio toward a club on the far end of the street, though his eyes wandered constantly from side to side as he admired the passing women. Yen's eyes wandered as well, though he was too busy reading the passing marquees for movie theaters. A number of new films were being shown, but new was a very relative term for Yen. Even before joining the *Revolution* and fighting the Terrans, Yen had been with a covert operations team. Being cooped up on a Cruiser for months at a time as they transited from one mission to another had left him detached from popular culture. It wasn't just the movies that seemed foreign. Yen was very self-conscious of his clothing as well. The loose shirt and hide pants he wore had been fashionable once, but that was apparently years ago. He felt dated compared to the contemporary and revealing clothing that the younger crewmen and soldiers wore.

Reaching the club, the trio slipped through the door and was instantly awash in a sea of sensations. Loud music pulsed heavily enough that Yen could feel the beating drum in his chest, as though it had replaced his own heartbeat. The air was full of a mixture of smoke, sweat, and pheromones. Their mixture alluded to the dancing in the middle of the room. Half-naked bodies writhed together in barely concealed allusions to sexual acts. Watching the sweaty figures, Yen felt his pulse quicken beyond even that of the beating drum.

Adam led them around the edge of the dance floor until they reached the bar. He gestured for drinks, his own words decimated by the general din of noise. Soon, they were relaxing at a booth, enjoying both the view and their strong drinks. Yen had to admit that this sort of entertainment was exactly what he needed. The loud music and alcohol quickly obliterated his sour mood and he found himself smiling, not just at the ambiance but at the women whose eyes he caught from across the room. Adam, recognizing his improved attitude, leaned across the table to be heard.

Though his lips moved, Yen struggled to hear what he said. He frowned and leaned closer, but the words were still lost to the pounding music. Yen leaned back in his seat and shook his head, to which Adam scowled angrily. Holding up his hand to warn Adam, Yen closed his eyes. The air around him began to shimmer slightly and the loud noise slowly faded. Opening his eyes, Yen could hear Adam's thoughts clearly.

"Is this better?" Yen said, the words forming directly in Adam's mind. Though Adam heard Yen speak, the psychic never moved his lips.

Adam began to speak aloud, but Yen shook his head and pointed to his temple. Concentrating, Yen heard Adam's response.

"No, this is not better. This is actually really creepy."

Yen smiled. "But at least I can hear you now. What were you saying?"

"I was trying to tell you that you need to go find a girl. I'm glad you came out tonight, but if I don't find you some sort of entertainment by the time this night is over, I'm going to feel like I failed you as a wingman."

"Thanks, but no thanks. I'm just here to relax."

Adam winked at Yen. "So am I, but I've found the best way to relax is with a woman sitting on your..."

Yen didn't let him finish the sentence as he severed the psychic connection between the two, allowing the loud music to once again crash back into his ears. He could see Adam laughing at his obvious discomfort at the topic of conversation, but he didn't press the issue any further.

After an hour in the bar, the mixture of music and alcohol began to wear on Yen and his head began to ache. It had been exactly what Yen needed, getting away from the ship and enjoying time with his friends, but he could feel himself growing tired of the scene and eager to just get some good rest tonight. Despite both Adam and Penchant's urgings to stay, Yen stood and waved goodnight. Sliding past the dancing bodies and slipping along the wall toward the front door, Yen opened the door and reveled in the doorway as the blast of cool air struck his face. Though the recycled breeze was artificial, Yen didn't care as it quickly dried the glistening sweat on his skin.

Stepping out of the doorway, Yen turned down the street and inadvertently ran right into a woman walking the opposite direction. Though Yen staggered backward, the woman actually slipped and fell backwards, landing roughly on her bottom. Startled, Yen immediately rushed over and extended his hand to help her to her feet. He had expected a disgruntled scowl from the woman, but was surprised to find the Pilgrim actually smiling and laughing softly. As she took his hand and climbed to her feet, not an easy task in the tall heels she wore, Yen took a moment to admire her figure.

Though surprisingly shorter than he had expected, she was well proportioned. Her long blonde hair was hanging loose and it framed her youthful face. Her bright blue eyes sparkled in the night air and her smile was both relaxed and enchanting. As much as he tried to keep his gaze above her neck, she wore a low cut blouse that clearly left her ample cleavage on display. As he helped her to her feet, he let his eyes pass admiringly over her chest.

"I am so sorry," Yen gushed. "I didn't even see you there."

Standing her full height, the woman was still a head shorter than Yen. "It's okay. You'd be surprised how many times I get overlooked." The Pilgrim smiled broadly at her own personal joke. Even after being nearly trampled by Yen, she kept a surprisingly positive sense of humor.

Yen laughed despite himself. "I won't make that mistake twice, I promise. Listen, I feel terrible about knocking you down. Let me at least buy you a drink to make up for it."

The woman raised an eyebrow as though thinking over his offer before replying. "No."

"No?" Yen asked, surprised.

"No, you can't buy me a drink," she explained. "I just left a bar and I think I've had my fill for the night." Her tone changed, taking on a coy undertone. "However, there was a pretty nice outdoor café a little ways down the street. I'd be willing to let you buy me coffee. It seems like a pretty fair deal after nearly trampling me."

Yen's smile broadened. "How can I say no? I think I might be able to suffer through buying you coffee as a fair trade to almost killing you."

The woman turned and extended her elbow, which Yen slipped his hand through. Leading her down the street, they quickly found their way to the outdoor café and took a seat at a small table.

"This is much better than talking in the street," she remarked as she looked at the menu.

Sitting across from one another, she seemed remarkably at ease with a perfect stranger. "I just realized that I don't even know your name," Yen said with a sudden surprise. He extended his hand across the table. "I'm Yen Xiao."

"Iana Morven," the Pilgrim woman replied as she shook his hand. "You here on shore leave?"

"I am," Yen said, but paused immediately afterward. He knew her name from somewhere before, but couldn't quite place it. "You seem familiar somehow. Have we met before?"

Iana arched an eyebrow. "I don't think so. I've only been a few places since joining the Fleet, so it would be a very small circle that I would travel in."

"I didn't even realize you were Fleet. What ship are you assigned to?"

Iana frowned. The perky attitude faded quickly, replaced by a darker and saddened visage. Yen immediately regretted the question. "I'm sorry," he said. "You don't have to answer that."

"No, it's okay," Iana replied softly. "I was assigned to the *Vindicator* until…"

She left the statement hanging, but Yen knew how it ended. The *Vindicator* had been one of the Cruisers that was destroyed during the battle with the Empire. Everyone on board had been killed, leaving its Squadron stranded and homeless.

"I'm really sorry," Yen consoled.

"Don't be. I was only assigned to the *Vindicator* a few weeks before the battle. I hardly knew anyone on board, except for the members of the Squadron. Now we're all being split up and reassigned."

"Any idea where they're sending you?"

"I'm being reassigned to the *Revolution*," Iana answered.

His interest piqued, Yen smiled broadly. "Then I guess it's not just chance that brought us together. I'm from the *Revolution*."

Iana returned his broad smile as the waiter brought them both cups of coffee. She sipped her drink as she stared into Yen's dark eyes. "You know, my fortune told me I'd run into a nice guy today. I just didn't think to take it so literally. So what can you tell me about my future Squadron Commander?"

Yen's smile froze on his face, his cup equally frozen halfway to his lips. It felt as though a blast of cold air had struck him, cooling the burning emotions running through his veins. "She's a very well decorated pilot," Yen said a little flatly. "She's a little harsh at times, but all in all she's a good Commander."

"That's it?" Iana chided. "Just that she's a good Commander?"

Yen shook his head. "Forget about work. We're both on shore leave right now and shouldn't be talking about assignments and the leadership. We're here to enjoy ourselves." Though his earlier lust was cooled, he still enjoyed spending time with Iana and figured it was worth trying his hand at extending their evening together. "Listen, I hardly feel like buying you some coffee makes up for me trying to kill you. When was the last time you saw a good movie?"

"Are you asking me out on a date?" she asked matter-of-factly.

Yen blushed slightly. "I guess I am."

"Then I'd be delighted."

Signaling toward the waiter, Yen scanned his card and paid for their drinks. Pointing down the street toward one of the neon flashing marquees, Yen led her toward the movie theater as they resumed their pleasant conversation.

CHAPTER 19

When the lift doors opened on the entertainment level of Farimas City, a half dozen solicitors approached Keryn. Holding out flyers, coupons, and assorted necklaces, they nearly surrounded the small group who exited the elevator with her. Keryn pushed her way past and absently took one of the brochures from a solicitor, giving her something to read while she walked. She hadn't come to the entertainment district with a destination in mind. Instead, she had simply wanted a chance to walk and clear her mind while, simultaneously, looking for a bar that would catch her eye.

The brochure in her hand was full of bar listings for the lower city. Keryn read by the flashing neon lights as she strolled past the already intoxicated crewmen and soldiers who whistled suggestively. Brushing her flowing silver hair out of her face, she ignored their comments and continued reading. About halfway down the page, one of the advertised bars caught her eye.

The Frozen Nebula, it read, *is a bar that caters to the warrants and officers of the Fleet. Its well-kept interior and affordable drinks make it a premier establishment for the upper echelon of Fleet leadership.*

Keryn knew that anyone reading an advertisement like that would actually be less likely to search for the Frozen Nebula.

Even the write up sounded arrogant, meaning that it probably kept a rather short clientele list. Under normal circumstances, Keryn would continue looking for a more popular place. But currently, with everything weighing heavily on her mind, a bar with a sparse population was exactly what she needed. Reading the directions on the brochure, Keryn slipped through an alleyway and turned right, heading deeper into the center of the entertainment level.

Though she heard the loud music pouring from the nearby bars and was blinded by the flashing marquees, Keryn ignored these as she searched the row for the Nebula. Reading off the street numbers, she walked a few more blocks before finding the bar. Set slightly back from the rest of the garish bar facades, the Frozen Nebula was a rather unassuming building. Its clean white bricks reflected the brash lights of the more aggressive bars, though its own sign was severely subdued by comparison. Carrying only the bar's title in rather blockish letters, it lacked the neon glow of those nearby. A single, heavy wooden door led to the glowing interior. Through the window, Keryn could see a few patrons seated amongst the well-spaced tables. It seemed like the perfect place to escape reality for a few hours.

Keryn stepped through the door and let it swing closed behind her. As soon as it settled into its frame, the loud sounds of music and conversation disappeared. The entire room was soundproofed, blocking out the wild partying just outside its door. The interior of the Frozen Nebula was a mirror of its sterile exterior. Dark wooden tables were well spaced and seemed to absorb the dim light of the bar. Though a soft music played, no one danced. Instead, it seemed to be a communal area to which warrants and officers came for camaraderie and to hold intelligent conversations. It seemed like a far cry from the bars Keryn had frequented since joining the Fleet. Young herself, Keryn had grown accustomed to gyrating bodies and music so loud that her whole body vibrated in rhythm. Keryn, glad for the change, walked to the bar and ordered a drink.

Spinning in her stool until she faced the rest of the bar, Keryn leaned back against the brass railing and looked at the crowd. Couples occupied many of the tables. Hunkered over in obviously private conversations, they reached out toward one another with innocent touches of the hand and arm. Keryn frowned. She had hoped to come to the Frozen Nebula to escape thoughts of couples and romantic rendezvous. She should have known better. Shore leaves were notorious for starting physical relationships among lonely members of the Fleet.

"You don't look happy to be here," a strong male's voice said from beside her.

Keryn jumped, surprised to have not heard someone approach in such a quiet bar. Turning, she was even more surprised to see who it was. Jumping quickly down from her stool, she stood at the position of attention.

"Eminent Merric," Keryn said, still standing at attention. "I didn't realize it was you."

"Stop that," he said, aggravated. He waved his hand absently, telling her to relax. "If I wanted all the pomp and circumstance, I would have remained on the ship. Down here, we're just two single people enjoying our shore leave."

Keryn could smell the alcohol on his breath and could see the slightly red–rimmed eyes. She wasn't sure how much his drinking played a role in his blatant pick up line. Though he was probably far from being drunk, she was pretty sure that the alcohol was helping with his confidence.

"What makes you think I'm single?" Keryn asked, trying

to change the subject. Merric was a very handsome man, with a strong Pilgrim jawline and well-defined muscles that were evident through his tight shirt. His looks aside, he was still her superior officer and even contemplating a physical relationship with him was something she wanted to avoid.

"Come on now, Keryn," Merric said, leaning in closer. "Everyone in the Fleet heard about your lover's quarrel after your promotion. You and Magistrate Xiao have been avoiding each other like you're each carrying a plague. It's obvious you're not together." He ran a finger suggestively up her arm. "It's probably for the best anyway. You deserve a better man than that."

Keryn turned and looked Merric in the eye. She couldn't deny that she found him attractive, but she also couldn't deny that he was arrogant. As much as that might be true, she realized, he was no worse than Yen, and she had almost immediately fallen for him.

"Buy me a drink and I'll decide who the better man is," she said with a smile.

Ordering two drinks, Merric led Keryn to a back table where they would have more privacy. As they talked, Keryn was not surprised to find that Merric had graduated top of his class at both the Academy and Pre-Captain Course. The second-in-command of the *Revolution* had been promoted early all the way up the line, much like Keryn was doing now. In fact, professionally, they were very similar. It was pleasant for Keryn to find someone who nearly matched her own occupational ambitions, if not personal goals.

They talked for a couple hours, though when Keryn tried to figure out what, specifically, had been said, she found it all to be one big blur. In part, she blamed it on the strong alcoholic drinks that Merric had ordered throughout the night.

Part, though, was the fact that she hadn't truly been overly interested in the topic of conversation. She had taken her shore leave begrudgingly and at the command of Captain Hodge, but she had every intention of avoiding the topic of work while relaxing. Instead, she found herself deep in conversation with her immediate supervisor.

Draining the last of her glass, Keryn looked at her watch and was stunned to realize how much time had passed. Though there were no true days and nights on the space station, her body still aligned itself with the watch on her wrist, which told her it was now creeping into early morning.

"I'm sorry, Merric," Keryn said apologetically, "but I really need to get some sleep."

Merric dropped his hand onto her thigh and suggestively rubbed the inside of her leg. "You know, you don't have to go home alone tonight."

Keryn wondered what it would be like to be wrapped in his muscular arms. It had been quite some time since she'd been with someone and the blaring opportunity almost made her immediately agree to his proposal. Still, she felt uncomfortable with the thought of sleeping with someone she just got to know, even if she had known him as a supervisor for over a month.

"I can't," she said, shaking her head. "Not tonight at least. Sorry."

Merric nodded and withdrew his hand. "The invitation is open ended. Just give me a call if you change your mind."

"Thank you for the drinks and the company," Keryn said as she stood. Politely, Merric stood as well until she had turned toward the door.

Keryn exited completely and was surprised by the heat outside the Frozen Nebula. The scent of sweating bodies and other unnamed bodily fluids assaulted her and she suddenly remembered how distant a world the inside of the bar had been. For a moment, she turned around and looked back through the window to make sure the entire evening had not been a hallucination. Reassured by the still clean white bar front behind her, Keryn walked into the street and began heading back toward the lift that would take her to the residential level.

After making it nearly halfway down the street, she had to pause as one of the movie theaters opened its doors and the patrons of the late night film exited. Standing patiently, leaning against a nearby building, Keryn alternated between watching the crowd leave and remembering her enjoyable evening with Merric.

As the crowd thinned and Keryn prepared to step back into the street, she found herself frozen in place as an unusual couple exited the theater. Linked arm in arm and laughing at one another's jokes, Keryn couldn't believe her eyes as Yen and Iana walked out, oblivious to Keryn's presence, and turned away from her, heading back toward the stairs and elevators.

She seethed with anger as a deep seeded sense of betrayal settled over her. The sight of her best friend and former love walking so casually and, apparently, affectionately, together infuriated her. The feeling of a knife being plunged into her back made Keryn stagger backwards and lean even heavier against the stone fronted bar. Her lower lip quivering, Keryn bit back the tears that threatened to fall. Unable to stop them, she angrily wiped away the few tears that did stream down her face. Turning away, not eager to follow the new couple, Keryn looked back the way she came. A few blocks away, shining white against the other dark bars, the Frozen Nebula called to her. Wiping her face with the back of her hand once more, she regained her composure before walking back to the bar.

Opening the door, she immediately saw Merric, still seated at the table she had left him at a few minutes before. She walked over slowly, holding back her desire to rush over and simply sit in his lap, and stood beside his shoulder. Merric seemed genuinely surprised to see her, but found himself unable to misinterpret her sultry look.

"Does this mean you've changed your mind?" Merric asked smugly.

"Any port in the storm," Keryn whispered.

Merric furrowed his brow. "I didn't quite catch that."

"I said this means that I would like to go back to your place tonight," she said more confidently.

Merric smiled and stood, slipping an arm behind her back. Leading her out of the bar and back toward the lifts, they didn't say a word to one another. Keryn still brooded silently over what she had seen and savored the warm, strong hand gently caressing the small of her back. They rode the lift together up to the residential level and walked the short distance to his hotel that, as she had assumed, was significantly nicer than the one she had been staying at. Passing through the lobby, they entered one of the elevators. She smiled as he pushed the button for one of the top floors, the floors that contained the hotel's suites. No sooner had the elevator doors closed than he leaned over and kissed Keryn passionately. She responded quickly, pressing her body against his and wrapping her arms around his neck.

They entered his hotel room in a whirlwind of sexual activity. Clothing was quickly peeled away as his hands rolled over every inch of her body. Her own hands fumbled clumsily with his tight shirt, pulling it over his head hastily before his lips were able to find the side of her neck and shoulders.

That night, their bodies were twisted into a myriad

of positions well into the morning, until both of them finally collapsed into the bed from exhaustion. He was every bit the lover that Keryn expected him to be: he was a rough lover with wandering hands, but took care of her every need. After they were done and lay panting and sweaty in bed, Keryn realized that she was content but not satisfied. With her anger sedated and the adrenaline fleeing from her body, she immediately knew the reason why, and hated herself for thinking it.

Merric was a lot of things, but he was not Yen Xiao.

CHAPTER 20

Yen awoke and stretched, feeling the tension in his back and shoulders ease. Though rested, he had slept awkwardly on his side with his head unsupported and his arm pinned beneath him. Now, as blood flow returned to the limb, he could feel the pins and needles spread painfully from his elbow to his fingertips. Flexing the numb digits, Yen sat up on the couch.

He wasn't in his room. Yen doubted he was even in the same hotel. The layout of the room seemed somehow wrong. The curtains lacked a certain luster that he had found in the room Adam had rented for them. Even the material of the sofa on which he sat felt rougher and less refined. Slowly, as the cloud of weariness fled from his mind, Yen remembered where he was. The night before had been spent with Iana; first at the café, then at the movies. When she had offered to take him back to her hotel, he had readily accepted her invitation. Yet, he wasn't waking up in her bed, nor was she beside him.

"Good morning, sleepy head," a female called from behind him.

Yen turning stiffly, saw the short blonde Pilgrim exit from the bedroom. A large towel was wrapped firmly around her torso, hugging her breasts and hanging loosely over the rest of her body. She used a second towel to dry her still dripping hair.

Yen smiled at Iana. "How did you sleep last night?"

"Hmm," she said as she furrowed her brow in thought. "I was both cold and lonely last night. How about you?"

Yen scratched his head, feeling slightly uncomfortable. "I'm really sorry about that. I really didn't think that was how the evening was going to turn out. Not after I had such a good time with you all afternoon."

Iana walked around the couch and sat down next to him, throwing her naked legs over Yen's. The slit on the towel fell aside, opening dangerously far up her thighs. "Don't worry about it. I understand. I really do. I'm not going to lie to you though. I can't remember the last time I was so disappointed by someone not sleeping with me."

Yen caught his gaze falling to where the two sides of the towel, and subsequently both her legs, met. "It's not because I don't find you attractive, Iana. You really are beautiful. I just can't do this right now."

Iana sighed as she slid her legs off his and covered herself again. Looking straight ahead, she refused to meet his stare. "You really love her, don't you?"

"Honestly, I don't think I realized just how much until last night. I had an incredible time with you, but when we got back here and I saw you naked…"

Iana blushed at last night's memory. "We don't have to talk about that."

"Sorry," Yen apologized, blushing slightly himself. "You looked beautiful, but I couldn't stop thinking about Keryn. It was her I wanted to be standing in front of in a random hotel room. It just felt like I was betraying her by spending the night with you."

"Those are some pretty serious emotions."

Yen laughed slightly. "You're not kidding. It's just so invigorating to finally tell someone this. I don't think I knew how much I loved her. Now, all I want to do is go find her and tell her how I feel."

"Wow. I can't really think of another way to say it than that."

Though Iana seemed like she wanted to be happy for Yen, he could still see her pouting. Her full lips were pursed and her pale blue eyes twinkled mischievously. It was a look that Yen was sure she had practiced and used before, with great effect. Even now, he found himself wanting to reach out and console her.

Sensing the awkward tension between them, they both spoke at once.

"I should really get ready to go," Yen spoke while Iana said, "I really need to get dressed."

Iana stood quickly and walked back toward the bedroom. She tossed her body towel casually aside without closing the door to the bedroom, leaving a clear, tempting view for Yen. He suddenly found it hard to swallow as he, for the second time, found himself admiring her firm and well-proportioned body. Though he could feel his blood stirring, Yen knew it was just lust and not the full love that he felt for Keryn.

"I wasn't just feeding you lines last night, you know," Yen said over his shoulder as he turned away from the temping view. "I really do want to help you with your assignment on the *Revolution*."

"That's sweet," Iana replied as she exited the bedroom, having slipped on a bathrobe to cover her body. "But now that I know that Keryn is the new Squadron Commander, I think I might be able to do my own jockeying for a position. Thank you, though."

Yen turned toward her and put his hands on Iana's shoulders. "I hope this doesn't make things strange between us when we're working together."

"Are you kidding me?" Iana laughed. "You've seen me naked. There isn't much more comfort two people can have together than that." Smiling at one another, there was another pause before Iana spoke again. "Go, Yen. You know she's in the city and if you let her get back to the *Revolution* without telling her how you feel, I'm going to do it for you. And when I do it, it'll include a lot of really sickeningly sweet words that are going to make you look like a sissy."

Yen laughed heartily. "I'm going, I'm going. Thank you for putting up with me."

He let the door close behind him as he left Iana's hotel room. The elevators were directly ahead, but he stood in the doorway, his hand still clutching the doorknob. Part of him was proud of his fortitude and loyalty to Keryn. Another equally strong part of him was still kicking himself for not taking advantage of a beautiful woman when he had the chance. Finally, through a battle of wills, Yen let go of the door and walked to the lift.

The elevator doors slid closed and soft music began playing as he rode the lift down to the lobby. Though he knew she had to be staying somewhere, Yen didn't even know where to begin looking for Keryn. The Farimas Space Station was a sprawling construct, full of hundreds of streets and alleyways. Yen had no way of knowing if Keryn had stayed at a hotel or if she had splurged and rented a townhouse during shore leave. Hell, he realized, he still wasn't completely convinced Keryn had even bothered to take shore leave at all. Lately, she had become so married to her position that it seemed impossible to drive a wedge between her and the Squadron.

He was still grappling with his pending search when the elevator doors opened to the lobby and he stepped out. Moving around the corner, Yen nodded to the concierge before turning toward the front doors of the hotel. Looking up, he froze in his tracks. There, silhouetted against the bright morning sunlight, Keryn stood at the window watching the flowing river beyond. Yen's heart leapt in his chest, surprised both by her appearance and by fate bringing them so quickly together. Drawn forward, Yen stopped when he was only a body's length away.

"Keryn," he said, breathlessly.

She turned quickly, her violet eyes narrowed at the sound of her name. Seeing Yen, she seemed to hardly relax. If anything, she tensed further. Hesitantly, Keryn brushed her silver hair out of her face sheepishly, exposing the brilliant red and purple tattoos that framed her face.

Keryn glanced quickly over Yen's shoulder before speaking in a hushed tone. "Yen, what are you doing here?"

"It's a long story," Yen sighed. "But I'm really here looking for you. Is this where you're staying?"

Keryn frowned as she appeared to collect her thoughts. "I can't talk about this right now. Whatever we need to talk about, we can do it when we're back on board the *Revolution*."

Yen arched an eyebrow. Keryn seemed closed off and hesitant, a far cry from the reunion he had expected after finding her on the space station. He took a step closer, but she took a step away. "I don't think the *Revolution* is the right place to say what I need to say."

"You need to leave, Yen," Keryn said slightly angrily. "This is neither the time nor the place for the conversation that I want to have with you."

Yen could feel his own anger rising. "What has gotten into you?"

"I…" she began before pausing.

Before she could finish her sentence, a strong male voice called from behind Yen. "Is there a problem here?"

Yen turned to find himself face to face with Eminent Merric. At first, he simply stared at the Pilgrim, uncomprehending of why he would be getting involved in their personal conversation. Subtly, though, Yen caught Merric's stolen glances toward Keryn. Suddenly, it became painfully apparent, and Yen was suddenly aware that he was caught standing in between Merric and Keryn.

Turning quickly on Keryn, Yen's face betrayed his surprise and hurt. "You and Merric? How could you?"

Keryn's eyes flashed angrily. "Me? How could I do this? That's more than a little hypocritical, don't you think?"

"What are you talking about?" Yen said, his volume rising in reflection with his frustration.

"You need to keep your voice down," Merric threatened from behind Yen.

"Stay out of this," both Yen and Keryn replied simultaneously.

"What am I talking about?" Keryn asked. "I'm talking about you and Iana Morven!"

Yen stared dumbfounded at the Wyndgaart woman before him. He struggled to figure out how she could have known about them.

Misjudging Yen's confusion, Keryn continued with a sadistic smile. "That's right, Yen. I saw you two together, so much in love as you exited the movie theater last night. And somehow I don't think this is the hotel that you're staying in."

"That's what this is about?" Yen said, laughing despite his frustration. "This is all about me and Iana?"

Keryn flushed with anger at his laughter. "Don't try to

deny it!"

"Believe me, I'm not! But you're basing this entire argument on the fact that you saw me with another woman. Not kissing her. Not holding hands. Just with her. So all this anger and all this jealousy is based off the fact that you can't stand to see me with someone else. You don't want to be with me, but Gods forbid that I'm happy with anyone else." Yen's eyes narrowed and his voice dropped dangerously. "And because you saw me with another woman, that gives you the right to go have sex with your boss?"

Keryn's hand struck so quickly that Yen didn't have time to raise his own in defense. Her open strike caught Yen across the cheek, snapping his head to the side. Turning back toward her, Yen stared at her in disbelief. He could feel the marks on his face stinging strongly from where her firm slap had struck. Keryn looked back defiantly, though tears welled in her eyes and spilled down her cheeks. Without a word, she turned away and stormed out the door.

With her slap, the anger and irritation Yen had felt fled from his body. He hadn't intended to be so harsh and he felt guilty after seeing that his words had made her cry. A mixture of emotions drove him; conflicting urges to both pursue her out of love or out of betrayal and anger fought within him. Confounded, Yen stood in the lobby and stared at her departure.

His revelry was broken by a rough shoulder nudging him out of the way. Merric walked past arrogantly with a faint smile on his lips. Raising a hand, he waved as he reached the doors leading out into the street.

"So sorry, Xiao," Merric said haughtily as he held the door open. "I guess it's true what they say: you can't win them all. Best of luck next time around."

As the door swung shut behind Merric, Yen's emotional

turmoil disappeared. All his conflicting feelings of love and hurt toward Keryn were replaced by a yearning for revenge against Merric.

Common sense quickly reasserted itself as he stepped outside, into the blindingly bright artificial sunlight. Yen could see no sign of Keryn, though he looked up and down the street. He had no doubt that, once out of sight of the hotel, she had run back to wherever she was staying. Frustrated, Yen knew that he had to make things right with Keryn. Regardless of his feelings of betrayal, he still loved her. Now, though, Yen found himself facing a sprawling three-level city and hundreds of streets and alleyways. He would find her before shore leave was done and they returned to the *Revolution*; he was sure of that. Sighing, he knew that finding her would probably take all day. Pushing his plans of relaxation to the back of his mind, Yen set off to find the woman he loved.

CHAPTER 21

Keryn let her feet lead her through the city, oblivious to her final destination. In reality, it mattered little to her. Her mind whirled with dread, replaying the events at the hotel. She rubbed her eyes, still painfully aware of the hot tears that still leaked from their corners. She loved Yen; there was no denying it. But in her haste to find herself after separating from the Voice, she had unwittingly fallen into the arms of a man she truly didn't think she liked. Merric had been convenient, a distraction from the weight of leadership. He had understood her complaints and worries about being the Squadron Commander since he served in such an influential position on board the *Revolution*. She had been able to speak frankly about fellow officers and not only did he understand her dilemmas, he was able to add constructive criticism about the individuals, since he knew them personally. But is that what she really wanted in a relationship? Constructive criticism? Of course she knew the answer. Keryn wanted Yen, but her rash decision to bed Merric might have cost her the one chance she had with him.

Keryn looked up and wasn't at all surprised to find herself standing outside the Frozen Nebula. Even in her distraction, she had come somewhere familiar, and on an unknown space station, familiar areas were few and far between. Keryn pushed open the door and let the cool air and soft music wash over her, cleaning away the mental grime of the rest of the entertainment level. Glancing briefly at her from his task of cleaning the glasses with a spotless rag, the bartender nodded before resuming his task.

Being early afternoon, the bar was mostly deserted. Those who had come for lunch had already finished their meals and moved on. It was still too early for the nighttime festivities, and many who sat in the bar did so to drink away their problems. In sharp realization, Keryn wondered if that wasn't exactly why she was there as well. Away from the others, separated from any chance of running into crewmen from the *Revolution*, and in a bar that catered to a very small crowd, the Frozen Nebula had inadvertently become Keryn's escape from reality. Keryn slid up to the bar and dropped heavily into a barstool.

The bartender moved in her direction. Stopping in front of her, he gave a soft smile that spoke volumes on how much he understood her pain. "Rough day already?" he asked, ready to spill forth the sage wisdom that every bartender accumulated during their time serving drinks. "Let me get you a drink and you can tell me all about it."

"I'll take the drink," Keryn replied curtly, "but I'll keep my problems to myself."

"Suit yourself," the bartender said politely. She ordered the same drink Merric had bought for her the night before and cringed at her first sip.

She knew now that last night had been a terrible mistake. Seeing Yen and Iana together had made her angry and, in retaliation, she had turned to a friendly face for comfort. It had seemed an innocuous act the night before, but the ramifications were more than Keryn thought she could bear. Her one night of pleasure had brought immeasurable pain in her life. What if Yen never forgave her, either for sleeping with Merric or for publicly humiliating him by slapping him in the hotel lobby? She could clearly remember the look of sheer disbelief on his face and the four red lines of her fingers imprinted on his cheek. It had been a shortsighted reaction to his harsh words, but he hadn't been wrong to say those things. Still, she hadn't been the first to find comfort in the arms of another, had she?

Keryn could imagine Yen holding Iana in his arms. She would cradle her head in his chest as she pressed her small, curvy body against his. Iana's fingers would trace the outline of his stomach muscles as her hands sank lower. He would purr in pleasure as her hands caressed him...

"I thought I might find you here," a familiar male voice called from just behind her. In her daydreaming, Keryn hadn't even heard the door to the Frozen Nebula open. Turning, she frowned at the sight of Merric. His cocky smile was pasted across his face. Without an invitation, he sat in the stool next to her.

"Go away, Merric," she muttered. "I just want to be alone right now."

"I hear you say it, but I don't believe you mean it," he replied. Sliding closer, she could feel his warm breath on her cheek as he spoke. "I think you are just afraid."

Keryn leaned away and gave him a confused look. "Afraid of what?"

"You're afraid of what will happen if you give into temptation again like you did last night. You hurt Yen's feelings and now he's suffering through a strange sense of inadequacy. I feel his pain, I truly do. But he'll just have to understand that you found a better man now."

Rolling her eyes, Keryn responded. "You really are full of

yourself, aren't you?"

Merric shrugged. "Why shouldn't I be? I was the one you slept with last night, not Yen. Anyways, it seems like he's already found a replacement for you in that little blonde pilot. What's her name? Ivana?"

"Leave it alone, Merric," Keryn warned. "Don't start getting into things that don't involve you."

"But it does involve me," Merric replied. "I have to protect what's mine."

Keryn spun her chair so she was facing Merric. "What the hell is that supposed to mean?"

"It means exactly what it sounds like. Down here, we're all on shore leave. I'm just Merric. You're just Keryn. But once we get back to the *Revolution*, you all work for me. Since you're with me now, if Yen gets out of line again like he did today, I'll just have him moved to another ship."

"And you think that's what I want?" Keryn asked indignantly. "You think I got close to you just so that I could use your position for revenge on Yen? How childish do you think I am? And what happened to the man that I met last night?"

"The man you met last night is still sitting in front of you," Merric cooed. "And the one you had sex with all night is here, too, just waiting for an invitation."

Keryn felt nauseas. All of his kind words and seeming understanding was melting away, being revealed, in its core, as just a ploy to get her to sleep with him. Merric truly was a despicable man.

"Last night was a mistake," Keryn answered. "And it will never, ever happen again."

Merric flashed his warm smile, the one she had assumed to be compassionate when she saw it last night. "Don't be like that, Keryn. Why don't we go back to my place and talk about it."

"I don't think so," she replied flatly.

Merric reached out and grabbed a hold of her arm roughly. "There's no reason to be rude. Come on, baby."

"Let go of me," Keryn said, trying to pull away, but his grip remained strong. She could feel his fingertips biting into the inside of her arm, bruising the skin beneath her shirt. "You're hurting me."

"The lady asked you to let her go, Merric," Yen said from the doorway of the Nebula. The door was still open, allowing the warm air and chaotic sounds of the city to filter into the otherwise quiet bar. "I advise you to heed her advice."

Merric didn't bother to look at Yen, instead focusing all his attention on the cringing Keryn. "Mind your own business, Xiao. We were just talking, weren't we, Keryn?"

"No, we were done talking," Keryn said angrily. "Now let go of me!"

"Let go of her, now," Yen said, his voice stern as he stepped out of the doorway and toward the pair sitting at the bar.

Merric flung Keryn's arm aside, nearly knocking her from the stool. "I told you before, you little prick. Mind your own..."

Merric never got to finish his sentence. His eyes caught sight of the air shimmering and dancing angrily around Yen's body moments before Yen's power reached out and lifted Merric from his seat. Dangling like a rag doll a few feet above the bar, Merric struggled against the unsubstantial and invisible hands that gripped him firmly in place.

"You should have listened to me, Merric," Yen said, his eyes pulsing with blue power. "Someday you'll learn to listen to me when I speak."

Yen sent Merric flying through the air with a wave of his hand. Crashing into a table, Merric's body shattered the dark wood tabletop before he came to rest against the next table in line. Chairs scattered and were left overturned by the commotion and the few patrons of the bar were paralyzed, frozen in mid-drink or mid-sentence by the psychic attack.

"Yen," Keryn said with some relief.

Instantly, the shimmering faded away and Yen's dark eyes reasserted themselves against the flickering blue power. He walked closer, but stopped just shy of arm's reach away from her.

"I'm sorry," he stammered quickly, a much changed man from the assertive attacker she had seen walk through the doorway. "I shouldn't have said those things to you at the hotel."

Keryn was keenly aware of the eyes that watched Yen cautiously and the groggy moaning of Merric who was just beginning to regain consciousness. "Would you like to walk with me? I think I'd rather talk about this someplace else."

Yen looked around at the destruction he had caused, surprised as though seeing his handiwork for the first time. "That's probably a good idea."

Downing her drink, Keryn turned and led Yen from the bar. When they were clear of the Frozen Nebula and lost among the sea of afternoon crowds, they slowed their pace and walked for some time in silence. Both took deep breaths as though trying to start a sentence, but neither spoke. Finally, Yen broke the silence.

"You didn't deserve what I said," he muttered, as though haphazardly asking for forgiveness. "I was just surprised and hurt to see you with Merric."

"Merric was..." Keryn wasn't sure how to finish that

sentence. Finally she settled on telling him what had been going through her head at the bar. "Merric was a stupid, stupid mistake. I was looking for comfort and he was there."

Yen cringed at hearing Keryn so passively talk about her time with Merric. She immediately regretted the turn of the conversation, but couldn't find a more polite way to explain herself.

Yen looked down at his feet as they walked and shoved his hands deep in the pockets of his jacket. "Why did you have to turn to Merric at all? You've avoided me for so long; why couldn't you just come to me?"

Keryn stopped, forcing Yen to stop and turn toward her. "I wanted to come to you, I truly did, but when I left the bar last night, I saw you. I saw you and Iana walking together. And now today you leave her hotel room. What was I to think?"

"Nothing happened between me and Iana," Yen stated firmly.

"How can I believe that?"

Yen sighed. "Do you know what Iana and I did last night?"

Keryn shook her head and stepped away. "I don't want to hear what you two did. I'd rather not know."

"We talked about you," Yen interjected.

Keryn froze in place, staring at him with great skepticism. Yen smiled softly at her, trying to put her at ease.

"I didn't know that you and Iana were friends when I first met her. I'm not going to say that I went back to her place for an entirely platonic time, but once we were there, I couldn't go through with it. All I kept thinking about was you. I looked at her, but I saw you. We spent all night long analyzing every single feeling I've ever had for you; every single time we've spent together. Iana told me I had to find you to tell you how I feel. That's why I was coming to see you when we ran into each other in the hotel. I finally wanted to tell you that I love you."

"You two really didn't do anything together?" Keryn asked meekly.

"I promise. My entire evening last night, just like every night before for the past few months, was spent with thoughts of you filling my mind."

"I'm such an idiot," Keryn muttered. Stepping forward, she leaned heavily into Yen's chest and let him wrap his arms around her comfortingly. He kissed her on top of her head and ran his fingers through her hair.

"Don't worry," he whispered. "You're not alone. I'm the one that threw my boss through a couple of hardwood tables."

Keryn began laughing hysterically, letting out all the turmoil of emotions. Yen quickly joined in the laughing and by the time they were done, both were wiping tears from their eyes. Keryn pushed away from Yen so she could, once again, look him in the eyes.

"So where does this leave us?" she asked.

"I'm not going to lie to you," he replied. "It's going to take time to rebuild the trust between us. But I meant what I said. I love you, Keryn. I want to be with you."

She stepped forward again, this time wrapping her arms around his torso. "I want to be with you, too," she muttered softly, letting her stresses wash away with the rhythmic beating of his heart.

CHAPTER 22

The Uligart waiter led Yen through the maze of crowded tables to a secluded booth near the back of the restaurant. As he sat, the waiter politely dropped a napkin into his lap and stepped back.

"Is there anything else I can get for you right now?" the waiter asked with a faint accent. "A drink or appetizer, perhaps?"

Yen's gaze remained fixed on the doorway, but he reached forward and tapped the inverted drinking glass. "Just water right now, please."

As the waiter walked off to retrieve a pitcher of water, Yen glanced around the crowded, but subdued, restaurant. Gentle music, played by a string band, filled the expansive dining room of the Particle Accelerator, one of the more expensive restaurants in the Farimas Space Station. The far side of the room was lost in the gentle glow of candlelight, the only source of light for the large room. As Yen waited, he found himself hypnotized by the dancing flame of the small candelabra that acted as a centerpiece of his table. Beyond the flickering candlelight, in the center of the room, a few couples danced close together to the slow, soft music. Yen's heart beat a little quicker at the sight of loving couples pressed together, their bodies seemingly inseparable in the dim light.

The waiter returned and, after flipping Yen's glass over,

poured a nearly full cup of cold water. Nodding, Yen absently thanked him. Taking the cue, the waiter quickly turned and left, leaving Yen alone with his thoughts. Leaning back in his chair, he reached forward and twirled the full glass of water that sat before him, watching its fluid slosh upward, nearly cresting the lip of the crystal glass.

Yen was nervous and, frankly, had every right to be. He had every reason to assume that Keryn would stand him up; that even though she invited him to dinner and not the other way around, she just wouldn't show up and Yen would be left sitting alone for a large portion of the night. There were many shortcomings in their blossoming relationship, the worst of all right now being trust. Keryn had quickly accused Yen of sleeping with Iana, even when it wasn't the case. Even worse, she had slept with Merric as a retaliatory gesture, something that seemed more like a poorly written dramatic play than real life.

These thoughts weren't conducive to a true first date between them. Yen looked down and picked up the outermost fork, the smallest of the set, and spun it between his fingers. He tried to focus on the fork reflecting the dim candlelight and block out the invasive thoughts. She would come, he told himself. She had promised, and his trust in her had to be rebuilt somehow. Suddenly realizing how silly he looked fidgeting with a fork, Yen cleared his throat and set the fork back down in its spot beside his plate.

His impatience did not last much longer. As he looked up, he saw Keryn walking across the room, being led by their waiter. Yen climbed clumsily to his feet to welcome her to the table, but found himself at a loss for words. Keryn had pulled her hair up into a mound of loose curls, a few of which hung free of her hair clips and cascaded down her neck and shoulders.

She had adorned herself with a vibrant red, sleeveless dress, which not only accentuated the tan of her skin, but also ignited her red tattoos. Even her violet eyes seemed to sparkle deeper from the sequined dress. Keryn smiled broadly and wound her way past the remaining tables, pausing at Yen's booth. Gesturing, he invited her to sit before doing so himself.

Yen knew that there should be some witty repartee to begin their conversation, but somehow words eluded him as he stared at her confident beauty. He tried to keep his eyes from falling toward her exposed cleavage, but Yen was too eager to drink in the full sight of her. Noticing his look, Keryn laughed softly.

"It's okay to look," she remarked, "but maybe you should wait until after dinner for that."

"Sorry," Yen apologized. "You get so used to seeing women in their uniforms that, sometimes, you forget how amazing they look when they are away from the Fleet."

"You don't look so bad yourself."

Yen looked down at the clothes he wore. He shrugged as though to tell her that these were clothes he pulled straight out of his closet, but Yen knew better. The clothes were new, purchased earlier today after he received her phone call. Keryn didn't know it yet, but he had also spent a considerable amount of money both on dinner reservations and his own private hotel room, away from Adam and Penchant. Most of his savings were now gone, but to see Keryn in this dress with her hair so eloquently fixed, made the expenditures well worth it.

"I took the liberty of ordering for us in advance," Yen said, changing the subject. Looking across the room, he caught the eye of the waiter and signaled that they were ready to begin their meal. Throughout their four course meal, they talked and laughed as though nothing had transpired between them over the past couple days; as though the past events had never existed in their relationship. Yen felt at ease and laughed more naturally then he had in recent memory. Something about Keryn made him feel comfortable and at home. The knot of nervousness in his stomach slowly eased, replaced by the quick flittering of his heart every time she smiled or reached out during a story to touch his hand.

As they were finishing dinner, the band took a break and the restaurant was bathedin the subdued conversations of the restaurant patrons. Their conversation slowed as well as they both leaned back away from the table, feeling incredibly full from the phenomenal meal. Looking away from Yen for the first time since their dinner began; Keryn admired the fluted columns and mosaics painted across the walls. As her eyes fell on the dance floor, she turned back to Yen with a mischievous smile.

"Dance with me," she said.

Yen looked at the dance floor and, beyond, to the empty stage where the string band had been playing prior to their break. "Sure. The band should be back in just a second."

"I don't want to wait for the band," Keryn said, rising slowly from her seat. "I want you to dance with me now."

Yen furrowed his brow in confusion before chuckling softly. "But there's no music. What are we going to dance to?"

Keryn turned away from him and faced the dance floor. From over her shoulder, she called back. "One thing I've learned is that, sometimes, you have to make your own music in life. Are you willing to make music with me, Yen Xiao?"

Yen didn't miss the barely concealed allusion. He quickly left his seat and followed Keryn onto the dance floor. Placing a hand on her hip, he took her other hand in his as she slid closer to him, until their bodies were pressed firmly together. Other patrons turned and watched the unusual pair as they stood, motionless, on the dance floor.

Feeling the eyes on him, Yen tried to ignore them and instead focus on the woman in his arms. "So what now?"

"Make music for us," Keryn cooed.

Yen smiled softly and closed his eyes. He ran through a litany of songs that he knew, but each seemed wrong for the situation. Finally, from the deeper recesses of his mind, a song emerged that he hadn't heard in years. Letting his power course through his veins, a soft and gentle song began to emerge from the air around him. The song was from a lifetime ago, sung to him by his mother when he was just a young boy. Played entirely in a language that no one had heard in more than two dozen years, the words were not important and were, in fact, lost more to the melodic rhythm. The tones, minor and major chords intermixed, brought forth feelings and emotions from within all who heard it. Combining both the flowing harmony that portrayed love and the harsher flat notes and minor chords that symbolized loss, the song told a story that was unmistakable.

Keryn began moving her body in rhythm to the gentle music that saturated the air around the couple. She lost herself in the strange but familiar words, finally resting her head on Yen's shoulder. Kissing her gently on top of her head, Yen smiled and found himself focusing both on maintaining the song and reveling in the feel of her athletic body pressed against his. Slowly, Yen realized that others had joined them on the dance floor. Lured by the melodious song, they danced together, often with tears glistening in their eyes.

For nearly ten minutes, the song from Yen's childhood filled the dance floor and entranced those who heard it. Finally, sadly, the song reached its inevitable end and the music faded, leaving the dozen couples on the dance floor saddened by the sudden silence. Slowly, someone clapped, turning toward Yen and Keryn. Others quickly joined in until the pair blushed from the sudden attention.

Keryn turned toward Yen and looked him in the eyes. "Everything is going so well tonight, I don't want it to end. Let's go somewhere."

"Where?" Yen asked in eager anticipation. He could feel his blood beginning to churn.

"Anywhere that we can continue enjoying each other's company."

Thinking back to Adam's tour of the city, Yen knew where to take her. He smiled and slipped his hand into hers, interlacing their fingers. "I think I know just the place."

They seemed out of place as they walked together through the empty streets of the residential level of the Farimas Space Station. Dressed as they were for a formal dinner, they garnered strange looks from those who were heading toward the lifts, on their way to the entertainment district. Walking past the canals, Yen and Keryn walked toward the center of the level, where a large glass dome could be seen. Weaving through the last few streets, they emerged beneath the dome in an expansive park, full of blossoming trees and bushes. Above them, however, was the reason Yen had brought her here.

When Adam had been showing Penchant and Yen to their hotel, Yen had seen the dome and, later that day, asked Adam about it. Built in the center of the residential city, the dome was an escape for those who grew homesick and lonely for life planet–side. Sitting in the park on a bench, surrounded by the lush greenery and looking upward through the glass dome to the mass of perfectly visible stars above, Yen suddenly understood what Adam had meant. It was like being home;

an illusion of sitting in a park on a far distant planet, virtually alone with the woman he loved.

"This place is amazing," Keryn whispered, trying not to shatter the mood that seemed to saturate the area around them.

"Without you," Yen said, turning toward her, "this is just a seat in a park. It's being here with you that has made this place so much more to me."

Leaning forward, Keryn kissed Yen fully on the lips. Yen could taste the sweetness of her lips and felt her desire in her darting tongue and already heaving chest. As they pulled apart, Keryn sighed heavily and stared deep in Yen's eyes.

"I want you to take me home with you tonight," she said.

Her sultry tone caught Yen by surprise. He caught her stare and saw her violet eyes burn with a passion he had not seen before. Wordlessly, he nodded, unable to find the words that would properly convey his own smoldering lust.

They walked quickly back to Yen's hotel room, riding the elevator up to his floor with a palpable sexual tension between them. As the door to his room slid quietly closed behind them, Keryn turned toward him. No sooner had it latched firmly into place than their hands began groping at one another while their lips sought the subtle curves of one another's bodies. Keryn's dress fell quickly away, as did Yen's newly purchased jacket and pants. Eventually naked, they caressed one another as they made their way to the bedroom, a trail of forgotten clothing lost behind them.

Keryn pushed Yen down onto the bed and knelt above him. Her face and chest were flushed with passion and her hands shook slightly with anticipation. Though his eyes were open, Yen's focus was beyond the naked woman above him. As she lowered herself down, sliding downward until their hips pressed against each other, small blue tendrils protruded from Yen's back. Keryn's soft moans filled the room as the tendrils wrapped around her body. Everywhere they struck, they ignited waves of pleasure. For her, it was like a sea of uncompromising sexual enticement washing over her, crashing against her lithe frame over and over again.

As the night began for the two lovers, Keryn screamed out in pleasure for the first, but certainly not the last, time.

CHAPTER 23

They were inseparable over the next few days of their shore leave. Together, Yen and Keryn toured the restaurants of the space station. Yen accompanied Keryn on shopping excursions through the business level during the day and they spent each night wrapped in each other's embrace. Though they slept little, they awoke refreshed, beaming with happiness as they went about their day, hand in hand.

After a few days of total isolation, they agreed to join Adam and Penchant for a late lunch. By the time they arrived, the restaurant was busy, though Adam's towering Pilgrim frame was easy to spot from across the room. Pulling chairs up side–by–side, Keryn and Yen sat at the table.

"If you two don't stop, I'm going to be sick," Adam stated without allowing for so much as a hello.

"What are you talking about?" Yen asked.

"The smiles. The hand holding. The exuberant joy as though he just popped the question." Frightened by his own accusation, Adam lowered his voice. "He didn't pop the question, did he?"

"Oh, for crying out loud," Keryn exclaimed. "We've been dating for a couple days now. Give it some time."

"At least a week or so," Yen added.

Adam rolled his eyes and turned toward Penchant.

"Back me up on this, buddy."

Penchant turned his featureless oval face toward the adoring pair. "Lithids don't show a lot of public affection. If I had a mouth, I'd be frowning in displeasure."

"You're both insufferable," Keryn sighed. "Can't you just be happy for us?"

"No," Penchant said flatly.

"Probably not," Adam quickly added.

Their food arrived while they were still laughing. They ate slowly, engaging more in conversation than taking the time to finish their food. The early afternoon lunch crept into late afternoon and threatened early evening. Around them, the daily syndicated television shows gave way to news broadcasts. As had been the case for the past few weeks, stories of heroism and loss from the Alliance and Empire battle dominated the airwaves. During their conversation, they mostly ignored the news stories. Having lived through the experiences, the stories seemed somehow hollow and contrived. They were full of memories that not one of them wished to relive. Most importantly, the news insisted on showing photo montages of those who had perished in the battle. It was much too painful for survivors to experience day after day, so they had subsequently tuned out the news as a whole.

During their meal, though, with the news in the background, they suddenly became aware of a hushed silence in the room as all eyes were turned on the multitude of monitors that lined the walls of the restaurant. Turning, they saw that where normally a dozen or more programs would be playing simultaneously, now all the screens reflected the same image. An empty podium stood before a large banner bearing the blazing red emblem of the High Council. After what seemed like an eternity, a middle-aged Wyndgaart approached the podium and turned toward the cameras. His crimson eyes were flat and revealed nothing but somber composure as he spoke.

"Good evening," he said, his voice clear and strong. From within the folds of his robe, he pulled out a thin, flexible console. All four people around the table could see the image of the High Council shining through the thin console, a scrawl of words quickly rolling by. Reading directly from the vellum, the Wyndgaart read the High Council's message.

"One hundred and fifty years ago, the encroaching Terran Empire drove a juvenile Alliance to the brink of extinction. In response, the alien races banded together and faced this threat in one of the most brutal and deadly wars ever recorded in known history. As a result of that war, the Empire was driven back to its own space. The precepts of the Taisa Accord, signed that day a century and a half ago by both ruling parties, clearly defined the occupied territories of both the Empire and the Alliance. Though small intrusions in violation of the Accord have existed, never has either side been so brash as to directly contradict the precepts laid down by our forefathers."

"Nearly three months ago, the Terran Empire made the first move in violation of the Accord, by openly encroaching into Alliance space. Our response, as must be the case, was swift and aggressive. The Terran Fleet that was sent across the Demilitarized Zone was demolished, struck down by our superbly trained pilots, soldiers, and crewmen. The High Council extends its deepest thanks to all those who participated in the battle, both those who survived and those who paid the ultimate price in protection of our way of life."

The Wyndgaart looked up, no longer reading from the console. "Not all the Terrans were killed in the battle. Some were taken as prisoners and their technology salvaged from one of their Destroyers. The combination of the two revealed

217

some startling discoveries. We have discovered that the Terrans have been waging an underground war in Alliance space for decades, undermining the independence and sovereignty of our colonies. They have done everything short of openly declaring war between our two cultures. The extent of their offenses are so vast and disturbing, they cannot be shared in a forum such as this."

Keryn swallowed hard, knowing where course that his speech would soon take. The spokesman returned to his pre-written notes before reading the official declaration. "These atrocities cannot go unpunished. The High Council declared war on the Empire when they encroached on our sovereign space. At that time, we were a reactionary force, responding with violence to the intrusion of the Terran Fleet. Our time of being reactionary is now at an end. From this moment on, the Alliance will be on the offensive, pressing our advantage against the Empire until every last Terran soldier is defeated and every last Terran ship destroyed."

"One hundred and fifty years ago, the burgeoning Alliance fought the Terrans to a standstill. We are no longer a youthful conglomeration of races. Today, we are a unified front, powerful and deadly. There will be no stalemate this time. There will be no Accord signed when all this is completed. This time, we will bring the Empire to its knees before we take its head."

With no more pomp and circumstance, the Wyndgaart stepped off the podium and disappeared off the screen, leaving the audience staring in wonder. As quickly as it had happened, the screens turned back to the evening news anchors, who sat dumbfounded in front of the cameras. Clearly, they had not been briefed on the message beforehand, and now they scrambled to cover the news story as it unfolded.

As quickly as the monitors had gained their attention, the four now quickly ignored the telecasters. Turning to one another, they sat in silence, each lost in their own thoughts. Keryn glanced up once at the monitor, feeling a deep seeded hatred toward the Wyndgaart spokesman. It had been easy to stand before a camera and tell the known universe that there would be a second Great War. But the spokesman wasn't a soldier, nor were the High Councilmembers. They were politicians who made tactical and militaristic decisions based on anger, frustration, and intelligence passed along second or third hand. They weren't members of the Fleet or Infantry who would have to lay their lives on the line in order to succeed at their own aggressive plan. In that respect, Keryn realized just how alone the four people at the table truly were.

"It doesn't make any sense," Adam said, breaking the silence.

"Which part?" Yen asked sarcastically.

"How much more 'offensive' could we get? I mean, we were fighting for our lives against six Destroyers. What do they want from us now? Planet hopping? Wiping out one outpost after another until we finally reach Earth?"

"You joke," Penchant growled, "but this war won't be won until we reach Earth. You thought the Fleet was tough, just wait until you run headlong into the Earth defensive system."

"I heard about that," Adam added excitedly. "After the battle with the Lithids and the defeat of their Fleet, the Terrans were sure the Alliance would bring the fight to their doorstep. So the Terrans chose to hide on Earth, and built a grid system in orbit around their homeworld. That thing's supposed to be damn near impregnable."

"So we're just supposed to fly right into a satellite grid's laser defense system?" Yen asked angrily.

"I guess we'll find out soon enough," Keryn said, holding up her transponder. They could all hear the low humming tone that signaled a recall to the *Revolution*. Moments after Keryn held up her transponder, everyone else's began to vibrate and emit the same tone. "We're being recalled. Grab your stuff and meet me back at the ship."

Quickly parting ways with the other two, Keryn and Yen hurried back to their hotel. The streets were already packed with Fleet personnel all hastily checking out of their rooms. The signal they had received was not isolated to the *Revolution*. Every Fleet ship docked at the Farimas Space Station had sent out their general quarter's message, recalling all personnel.

Keryn packed exceptionally quickly, knowing that as the Squadron Commander, she would have more responsibility in the next couple of days then most on board the *Revolution*. Yen seemed lost, not quite certain how his infiltration team would fit into the grand scheme of an Alliance assault. The directive was surprising and would be attempted on a scale far surpassing anything else attempted since the days of the Empire's Manifest Destiny Directive. To Keryn, her feelings alternated between excitement and fright. She hardly paid attention as she finished packing and wasn't even sure if she had remembered everything before hurrying downstairs. Keryn sat by impatiently while Yen checked out of the room. As soon as he was done, they left the hotel and ran through the streets toward the lifts that would take them to the outer ring.

As expected, the lift was packed with returning personnel. As soon as she approached the kiosks that would scan them back off leave, Keryn swiped her card and was surprised to be met on the other side of the kiosks by a pair of burly Fleet security guards. Their shoulder patches identified them as belonging to the *Revolution*, though she didn't recognize their faces.

"Commander Riddell," one of the two said in a tone that made it more of a statement and less of a question. "You are to accompany us at once. Captain Hodge has a vital communication for you."

"What about Magistrate Xiao?" she asked, gesturing toward Yen.

"I'm sorry, ma'am," the other guard chimed in. "Our orders were for you alone."

Keryn turned toward Yen and shrugged apologetically. "Get on board and find the others. As soon as I get done with... whatever it is that I need to do, I'll find you."

Nodding, no longer showing the public affection for which they had quickly become renowned since they were once again in uniform, Yen turned toward the lift and was quickly lost in the sea of pressing bodies. Following the guards, Keryn was led to a private airlock, on the far side of which was docked a small transport ship. Motioning for her to step inside, Keryn found herself in the surprisingly spacious confines of a private transport. The entire ship was richly upholstered and, though it could have easily sat nearly two dozen soldiers, it had seats for only six. The rest of the space was filled with personal console tables.

As she looked around, both stunned and confused, the cockpit door slid open and Captain Hodge emerged into the crew compartment. Her smile seemed strained as she shared it briefly, but it was quickly replaced by her stoic demeanor. Wordlessly, Captain Hodge sat down heavily into one of the chairs, gesturing for Keryn to sit in a chair across a console table from her.

"I'm sure you're a little confused right now," the captain said in her melodic tones.

"That's an understatement, ma'am. I don't think I've had a chance to think straight since the news conference."

Captain Hodge nodded knowingly. "I understand, but I can't help you. I told you before that there were many things going on that I couldn't tell you about, simply because of their classified nature. Now, there are things going on that I can't tell you about because I simply don't know myself." She reached into the jacket pocket on her uniform and pulled out a small disk. "I was given this with direct orders to bring the disk straight to you. I was not allowed to view the contents, nor am I allowed to be in the room when you watch it. This is truly for your eyes only."

Keryn stared at the disk as it was placed in her hand. With no more words shared, Captain Hodge stood and exited the airlock at the back of the ship, disappearing into the throng of people still waiting for the elevator within the space station.

Hesitantly, Keryn turned back to the disk still resting in her hand and was suddenly very aware of the console built into the desk in front of her. Alone in the crew compartment, Keryn slid the disk into the slot on the side of the console and sat back in the plush chair.

The blue screen of the console flickered to life before turning an inky black with a vibrant red symbol in the middle. Slowly, that too faded away, leaving Keryn looking at a horseshoe shaped conference desk, behind which six wizened and cloaked figures stared back at her.

"Hello, Commander Riddell," the elderly Wyndgaart High Councilmember said. "We have a special mission for you…"

CHAPTER 24

The stage at the front of the auditorium had been converted until it was nearly unrecognizable. A large cylindrical container sat on one end, a series of cables and wires running from it before disappearing behind the thick curtains on either wing of the stage. A series of test tubes and small medical instruments lined tables that had been prepositioned along the back wall. On the far right of the stage a surprisingly empty table stood; a lonely piece of furniture amongst the bustle of the rest of the stage.

Yen, Adam, and Penchant took their seats in the front of the auditorium, with a clear view of the displayed science experiment. Yen was honestly surprised from his trip through the halls of the *Revolution*. In remarkable time, less than a week, the shipyard had repaired the majority of damage the Cruiser had sustained during the war. Though there were still entire hallways marked as off limits to non-essential personnel, the ship no longer appeared in distress as it had when it first made dock at the space station.

Yen looked over his shoulder and watched the lines of recalled Fleet personnel filter into the auditorium, but he didn't spot Keryn among them. Other familiar faces caught his eye as they entered, both previous friends from the *Revolution* and some newcomers, Iana included. As the crowd began to thin, the last of the people entering the auditorium and finding their seats, Yen began wondering if Keryn would arrive for this meeting at all. When he had just about given up hope of seeing her, he was stunned to see a ghostly figure enter the room. The Uligart male frowned at the gathered crowd as he searched for a seat. Yen turned back around and slumped heavily into his seat.

"What's gotten into you?" Adam asked from beside him.

Yen nodded toward the back of the room. "It's Buren," he said, still surprised.

Adam turned quickly to look and Yen could hear the Pilgrim's breath get caught in his throat. "I thought he got out of the service."

Yen turned around as well, looking again at the stern-looking Uligart. "I did too. Hell, we all almost did after Purseus II. You think it's just a coincidence he's on board?"

"Not in a million years," Adam replied. "Though I don't like the idea of the three of us being back together."

Yen felt the bad blood shared between them and the Uligart standing at the doorway to the auditorium. Buren, Adam, and Yen had been the only survivors of the slaughter on Purseus II, the same battle during which Keryn's brother had died. The three survivors had flown together for months in the cramped confines of the *Cair Ilmun* before being rescued. Buren had been in shock, barely speaking or interacting with the other two. When they were finally rescued, while Yen and Adam recounted their story to a multitude of ranking officials, Buren had been quietly whisked away. Diagnosed with severe post-traumatic stress disorder, Buren was admitted to a hospital. He should have been kicked from the service, Yen thought sourly. Instead, Buren stood proudly in the back of the auditorium, in full military regalia. On the shoulders of his uniform shone the brass rank of Magistrate. Despite his medical condition and inpatient care at a hospital, he had been inexplicably promoted to the rank of an officer. It was too convenient to be a coincidence.

Their pondering was interrupted as Captain Hodge climbed the steps leading to the stage. A general hush fell over the crowd as she stepped gingerly over the multitude of wires that coated the stage's floor. She walked to the center of the stage before turning to address the crowd.

"I'm sorry to have pulled you all from your shore leave. Rest assured, I wouldn't have done so if I didn't have a very good reason. By now you've all heard the message from the High Council. It's been decided that the Alliance will go on the offensive against the Terran Empire. For those of you who were engaged in the last battle, you've surely asked the same question of yourself that I have many times: how much more aggressive than the last battle do they expect us to be?"

A light laughter filled the room, though it was heavy with nervousness and sadness at the memory of the Fleet engagement.

"I joke, but the truth of the situation is staggering. Before this meeting began, I received a classified communication from the High Council, laying out their plan of attack against the Terran Empire. When they say that we are going on the offensive, they truly weren't kidding."

"I'll be honest with you all. The *Revolution* was the least damaged Cruiser in the Fleet following the last battle, and we are still a few weeks away from completing repairs. Other ships have received just enough repairs to remain space worthy. But our time is short; so short, in fact, that we don't have time to wait for the rest of the repairs before we begin flying toward our target. The remaining repairs will be conducted in midflight."

Captain Hodge tapped a series of buttons on the console imbedded in the podium. The lights in the auditorium dimmed and a holographic representation of Empire-occupied space appeared.

"Earlier this week, we received information that a massive Terran Fleet had left orbit around the Empire's home world of Earth." Small red dots appeared in the hologram, showing the large Fleet heading toward the Demilitarized Zone. "Based off our most recent battle, it is safe to assume that the Terran Fleet is heading toward Alliance space with the intent of conducting a full-fledged assault on our strongholds along this side of the Demilitarized Zone. From their angle of advance, the border stations near the Indara Nebula will be the first to fall. If not stopped, the Fleet will continue its advance until it reaches more inhabited planets."

The captain's voice dropped, though it still carried through the room. "I don't think I need to remind you of what happened during the Great War. If the Empire still has access to any Planet Killer weapons, then everyone we know could be in danger."

"So we're going to face the full Terran Fleet?" Yen asked loudly, his voice cutting through the silence in the room. "With a third of our ships damaged, we're going to face a Fleet that has numerical advantage?"

Captain Hodge smiled. "No, Magistrate Xiao. We are not going to attack the Fleet. The first thing I told you was that the Terran Fleet had left orbit around Earth. They left their home world defenseless. We're taking the war to Earth!"

Stunned chatter erupted throughout the room. Penchant and Adam both leaned in and the three talked amongst themselves, echoing the sentiments of those seated around them.

"This is suicide," Penchant growled. "The defense grid around Earth would decimate the Fleet as soon as we got in range."

"Something tells me that the Terrans would be ready for something like this," Adam added. "They wouldn't just leave Earth defenseless."

Yen sat in silence, trying to block out everyone's panicked conversations. There was something they were all missing, and Yen was patient enough to wait to find out what it was.

"Silence!" Captain Hodge yelled, her voice cutting through the conversations. As everyone turned back toward her, they found the Avalon glowering at them, her face flushed with anger. "Do you honestly think that the High Council doesn't know about the Terran defenses around Earth? Do you truly believe that they would knowingly send us all to our deaths without any sort of defenses of our own? Don't be fools!"

Captain Hodge took a deep breath and continued. "You've all heard the rumors of Earth's defenses." Pushing a control on the console, the holographic image changed to that of a blue-green planet. Around it, floating in a synchronous orbit, small metallic satellites could be seen. Their orbits ensured complete coverage above the atmosphere of Earth. "The fact is, they're true. The Terrans do have a satellite system in place capable of annihilating our Alliance Cruisers. But there's a plan to get around their defenses. To explain it further, I'd like to introduce Doctor Birand, a representative of the High Council."

A rail-thin Uligart took the stage, looking fragile in his oversized laboratory coat. A general hush fell over the audience as they watched the nervous man run a hand through his thinning hair and push his glasses up further on his face. Yen frowned. Surrounded by what Yen had to assume was his own technology, there was still something that seemed to keep the scientist on edge. He had learned long ago that when a man seemed nervous about his own plan, it was usually doomed to failure. Gingerly, not wanting to alert anyone to what he was doing, Yen began to probe the scientist's thoughts.

"Thank you, Captain, for allowing me to be here," Dr. Birand said softly, with a faint stutter. He glanced up at the holographic portrayal of Earth, hovering above his head. Smiling, he began pacing the stage as he talked, as though the movement helped him gather his thoughts. His speech came slower as he methodically selected his words for greatest effect. "You can all see the image hovering above the stage. Ever since the Great War, Earth has spent a small fortune building one of the most elaborate satellite systems in history, a system so complex that no ship stands a chance of passing through without being summarily destroyed. The access code changes every twenty–four hours with the new codes being shuttled to inbound crews only when they enter the solar system, and that only happens after a whole litany of authorization codes have been verified by Earth's central command. Even if we tried, we would stand no chance of gathering all those access codes from any of the captured Terran crews."

Yen saw the flicker of faint images, peeled unwillingly from the mind of the scientist. Broad golden lasers, the result of harnessed solar energy, fired from satellites surrounding a blue and green planet. His heart beat faster. To wield such power would make a man unstoppable.

The Uligart stopped pacing and faced the crowd, a look of confusion temporarily cast upon his face before he continued. "So what options do we have?"

"Don't attack Earth at all," someone yelled from the

back of audience. Nervous laughter sputtered through the crowd, though Yen was pretty sure the man wasn't joking.

Dr. Birand smiled softly. "No, unfortunately we will be attacking Earth. It does, however, still leave us with the problem of Earth's defenses. For the past few years, I have been heading a secret research project that would be invaluable in just such a situation. The results of those years of research are sitting on this very stage with me."

Yen's eyes fell back to the pedestal, covered with electronic wires as though wrapped in a cocoon. A disturbing series of images flashed in quick procession through Yen's mind. Flayed skin and exposed organs quickly overlapped with disgorged eyeballs and animals with missing limbs. Yen jerked his eyes back to Dr. Birand, but the Uligart's expression revealed nothing of the troubling thoughts flowing through his mind. Walking calmly across the stage, the doctor picked up a glass cylinder and carried it to the pedestal. Setting it down, he left his hand on top of the object as he addressed the audience.

"What we developed during the past few years will mark a change in the way the Alliance will travel through space. But for now, until it can be produced and implemented throughout the Alliance, it has been more locally installed for your use. Ladies and gentlemen, I give you warp technology!"

Yen narrowed his eyes as he watched the nervous man. Warp technology was a myth, something that had been speculated amongst the scientific elite for generations. The concept of moving at instantaneous travel between two points was a fairy tale, as far as Yen was concerned. Even the scientific community was unconvinced that using such technology wouldn't destabilize the region in which it was used, resulting in a black hole rather than passable portal. It was obvious that others shared Yen's mentality. There hadn't been the gasp of surprise that the doctor had obviously been expecting. The skepticism he now faced obviously made him even more nervous as Yen could see large droplets of sweat forming on his ridged brow.

Eager to move the presentation forward and see what proof he brought, Yen spoke up. "How does it work, doctor?"

Dr. Birand turned quickly to the new voice. He held up two fingers, which he drew together as he spoke. "Ah, well, it's a little complicated. The basic principle is that we found a way to fold space, so that point A and point B, which are normally millions of miles apart, are touching one another. The physics behind it are simple, so long as you understand…"

The doctor's mind had gone blank as the air around Yen wavered faintly. He tried his best to contain the shimmering, so as not to give himself away. He pushed the doctor forward, reveling in the twisting of a weak–willed mind. The doctor had no mental defenses against Yen's intrusion, so Yen began dropping psychic suggestions. The technical aspects of the technology bored Yen. If he were to be impressed, Yen demanded a demonstration. It was that thought that he psychically implanted in the doctor's mind.

"You know what?" Dr. Birand said slowly. "I'm sure the technical aspects of this are boring. I think this would just be easier if I demonstrated it for you."

Moving to the rear table, Birand picked up a handheld console and began typing feverishly. Around the pedestal, the wires began to glow as electricity coursed through them, powering an unseen engine within the center of the cocoon of wiring. The noise built until it filled the room and drowned out the muttering of the still skeptical audience members. From the side of the pedestal, a small two–prong fork emerged from the wires. Between its metal prongs, red electricity arced wildly, rolling from the base of the fork to its tips before sputtering out into the air above. Yen could feel the hairs on his neck stand on end as the entire room seemed charged both with tension and with an unknown energy. He leaned forward, mocking the moves of Adam and Penchant beside him. The entire room seemed to be leaning forward in anticipation, suddenly sharing the doctor's enthusiasm.

Don't screw up, not this time. The alien thought leapt to the forefront of the doctor's mind, stated over and over in a confident mantra that belied the doctor's seemingly innocuous personality. Something about the project scared the man to death and Yen was suddenly very worried about the outcome of this experiment.

A crack split the air before Yen had time to probe further. A shockwave fell over the crowd, throwing them back into their seats. Wind whipped Yen's hair into his face and, as he brushed it aside, his eyes fell on the center of the stage. Hovering above the split fork, a red whirlpool had formed. Its tapered end disappeared only a few inches beyond the event horizon and pointed toward the empty table across the stage. Just over the rushing roar of air being pulled into the wormhole, Yen could make out the doctor's gleeful laughter.

Stepping forward, the doctor stood behind the pedestal, just a few feet away from the angry, red wormhole. It flickered as though alive and aware of the scientist's presence. Yen could see the air pulling at the doctor's laboratory coat, drawing it closer to the event horizon. The doctor didn't seem to notice as he reached out and nudged the glass cylinder toward the glowing red disk, hovering in the air. As the cylinder drew near, Yen could see the forces pulling it into the wormhole. It teetered momentarily, as though unsure whether or not to enter, before the suction of the event horizon pulled the cylinder inward.

From Yen's point of view, he couldn't see the object as it entered the wormhole, nor as it was stretched into the finite funnel. He strained to see anything in the air that might betray the destruction of the object or its obliteration in the heart of the wormhole, but he could see nothing. A commotion drew Yen's attention away from the hovering wormhole. Adam pointed across Yen's body, toward the previously empty table on the far side of the stage. Following his gaze, Yen saw the completely intact cylinder resting unassumingly on the table, as though it had been there all along.

A hush fell over the crowd as they watched Dr. Birand reach over and throw a switch, effectively shutting off the power to the wormhole. The red circle shimmered unstably before dissipating into the air. Yen looked back and forth from the cylinder to the cocoon of wiring around the pedestal.

"And this technology," Yen said, sitting upright in his chair. "It will safely get us past the satellite grid around Earth? We'll be able to warp a Cruiser right past their satellites and into their atmosphere?"

"Not quite," Birand stammered. "The technology hasn't been perfected for moving so great a mass as a Cruiser. However, while repairs were being made on the *Revolution*, many of your *Cair* and *Duun* ships were outfitted with the new warp engines. You'll be able to fly the smaller transports safely past the Terran defenses."

Yen frowned, not convinced. He kept remembering the distorted images that had flashed through the doctor's mind just before activating the warp engine. Yen was sure that he and the doctor had differing definitions of the word "safely".

CHAPTER 25

"Why are you doing this to me?" Keryn bemoaned. "This isn't fair!"

"This isn't about equality and fairness," the elder Wyndgaart of the High Council said, his voice coming from the speakers within the furnished crew compartment of the transport ship. "This is about you finding Cardax and locating the information we seek. The Oterian is a threat that must be eliminated before he can do any more harm."

Keryn crossed her arms and sulked, leaning back heavily against the upholstered chair. "You've just told me that we're going to attack Earth, one of the greatest assaults that will ever be recorded in history. But instead of me leading my Squadron, you're asking me to give that up to pursue some Oterian smuggler? I don't give a damn about this Cardax person or what he knows. I care about my team and I want to stay in command. I want to lead my Squadron during the assault!"

"This isn't about what you want, Commander Riddell," the Oterian Councilmember interceded. "You have repeatedly reiterated that you are genuinely concerned about your pilots and members of your Squadron. You act as though your concern for the Fleet is your top priority."

"That is my priority," Keryn replied curtly.

"You watched the *Vindicator* be destroyed, did you not?"

the Avalon Councilmember interrupted, her musical voice soothing Keryn's raw nerves. "The Terran Fleet used rockets filled with the same Deplitoxide that Cardax sold them. It ruined the engines and left them helpless to the Terran attack. Thousands of Alliance crew, pilots, and soldiers died in that attack. Cardax will not stop, and neither will the Empire. If we do not find this smuggler, thousands more will die from his betrayal."

Keryn ground her teeth together. She understood the concept of betrayal. It was the same emotion she felt burning inside her. There had never been a time when Keryn had not strove to be the best. Now, she was watching the culmination of all her hard work disappearing as she was stripped of her command in order to lead a different mission. Looking at the console's monitor, she stared into the eyes of the wizened Councilmembers, sitting around the semi-circle table. Their stern visages let her know that she truly did not have an option of whether or not to accept her new mission. Against her better judgment, Keryn knew that defying the will of the High Council simply wasn't a choice she could make.

Sighing, Keryn responded. "Explain the mission to me again."

"Interrogations of the surviving Terrans revealed the startling information," the Lithid Councilmember answered in a gravelly voice. "Nearly a year ago, the Oterian smuggler named Cardax had a fairly insignificant organization, mainly moving equipment, supplies, and weapons around the Demilitarized Zone. His operation was supplying armaments to dissidents living around or on the contested planets. Though he ran a fairly small organization, his group grew in popularity almost overnight after he began advertising a new chemical weapon. The weapon, the same Deplitoxide that was used against us, brought him too far into the spotlight for him to continue working in the shadows."

"Once we were aware of his operation," the elder Pilgrim continued, "we had no choice but to send a team after him. If half of what he claimed was true, then the Deplitoxide was too dangerous to remain on the open market. Unfortunately, Cardax discovered our plans before we had a chance to apprehend him. He fled, hiding among his clientele and remaining off our radar. We continued to pursue him, but to no avail."

Keryn furrowed her brow in confusion. "If that's the case, then how did the Terran Empire wind up with the Deplitoxide?"

"Cardax became careless," the Uligart responded. "In his overzealousness to elude capture by Alliance forces, he was driven too far into the Demilitarized Zone. A Terran patrol came upon his ship and captured him. For the next few months, Cardax was tortured by the Terrans while the small samples of Deplitoxide were examined by a Terran scientist named Doctor Solomon. In the end, the Empire realized the limitless potential of the chemical and demanded more from Cardax. In a moment of cowardice, Cardax agreed to become the supplier for the Terran Empire."

"The Terrans have made Cardax both very wealthy and very dangerous," the Wyndgaart said. "He is openly supplying the Empire with Deplitoxide now, though neither the Empire nor the Alliance knows his source for the unusual chemical. We would require you to discover the source by any means necessary."

"What is this Deplitoxide?" Keryn asked, feeling the weight of helplessness settling over her.

"We were able to analyze some of the chemical that was retrieved from the captured Terran Destroyer, though there was too little to do any in depth research," the Lithid explained.

"It's an organic compound that absorbs large amounts of heat. The individual cell membranes allow heat to be trapped within its nucleus and, as a result, created a thick, black byproduct. The internal heat also causes cellular mitosis, resulting in an exponentially expanding number of the organic cells."

Keryn remembered the engines on the *Vindicator* sputtering and dying. "So fire a rocket full of this Deplitoxide into a plasma engine, and these little buggers won't quit multiplying until they've absorbed all the fuel cells?"

"A crude but effective description," the Avalon replied.

Keryn clenched her fist and looked away from the monitor. She felt split, her anger focused on two separate targets. On one hand, she hated being used. The High Council knew her skills would be invaluable against the Earth defenses. But instead of leading her Squadron, she'd be relegated to a lesser mission. She felt as though, inadvertently, she had done something wrong; that she had somehow wronged the High Council and this was her punishment. Cardax, however, infuriated Keryn. Not only was he a traitor to his own kind, to all of the Alliance, he was also directly responsible for the destruction of the *Vindicator*. The buckling hull and the screams of the dying that had echoed across her radio channel had haunted Keryn ever since. If there was a way to bring retribution for all their deaths, Keryn wanted to be the harbinger of his death.

"I have more questions," she stated flatly.

"We have answers," the Pilgrim stated.

"Where do I find Cardax?"

The Pilgrim smiled, his face cracking into a web of wrinkles. "So you've accepted our mission?"

Keryn frowned. "I don't see that I have much choice in the matter."

"There's always a choice," the Oterian explained. "You just wouldn't like the alternative. Cardax has already established a neutral meeting location in the Demilitarized Zone. It was from this planet that he made the delivery to his Terran agents. The small, desert planet is called Pteraxis. Go there, and bring back the information."

"And Cardax?" Keryn asked.

"He is of little consequence once you have the information," the Uligart said coldly.

Keryn smiled softly at the news, though it did little to warm her feeling of being punished. "When do I get my team?"

"They are being assigned to you as we speak," said the Avalon. "They will be joining you on the *Revolution* tomorrow. For the majority of your trip, you will remain on board the *Revolution* as you train your team. Once you are ready, you will take the *Cair Ilmun* and depart the Cruiser. Your ship has been outfitted with extra weaponry and the interior has been modified for extended living conditions." The Avalon unfurled her wings and leaned back in her chair. "If there is nothing else…"

"I have one more question," Keryn interrupted, staring defiantly at the screen. "Who takes over my Squadron?"

The Councilmembers turned to one another inquisitively. Keryn realized with a sudden heartache that a decision on her Squadron was of miniscule importance to the Council, regardless of how important it was to Keryn.

"You know the Squadron better than anyone," the Wyndgaart answered. "Therefore, it only makes sense that you get to decide who takes over your Squadron now. We trust in your decision."

But you don't trust me enough to lead the assault on Earth, Keryn thought sourly. Without the formal dismissal from the High Council, Keryn reached up and turned off the console. She didn't want to face any more of their questions, nor did she want to ask any more of her own. Whatever happened from this point on, Keryn was on her own.

Her mind full of chaotic thoughts, she exited the private transport and stood in the now empty causeway leading into the Farimas Space Station. Thoughts of her few nights within the station warmed Keryn's heart and left her with a longing for more. Instead of entering the city, however, she turned the opposite way and entered the elevator. Alone on the spacious lift, Keryn stared out the window as they exited the confines of the station and shot upward toward the orbiting ring and the dozens of awaiting Cruisers. The entire Fleet was docked above her, save the few ships still remaining in star systems throughout Alliance space, guarding key planets. The Alliance had invested everything they had to bringing this war to a swift and violent end. And, as her comrades in arms fought for their lives, Keryn would be wandering some arid, backwater planet, searching for Oterian filth among a planet of garbage. Her hatred renewed, she stormed off the lift as soon as it stopped, barely acknowledging the two guards posted outside the entryway to the *Revolution*.

There were a lot of decisions to be made, Keryn realized, and many tasks to be accomplished over the next few weeks. Aside from meeting her new team, she would have to do research to learn anything she could about Pteraxis. The last thing she wanted was to lead her team blindly onto an unknown planet. Thought of her brother Eza flashed through her mind. Had his leaders felt the same way before they were led to the slaughter? Or had they done their research and everyone died anyway? More importantly, she knew that she had to pick someone to be her replacement. It had to be someone she trusted explicitly; otherwise she wouldn't feel comfortable leaving her Squadron in their hands. In her mind, there was truly only one person she thought capable of the job.

So lost was she in her thoughts that she ran directly into Yen before realizing he was there. His broad smile distracted Keryn from her thoughts, but simultaneously pained her deeply. Confident in their mutual affection, Yen was oblivious to the fact that their time together had been cut painfully short. After a moment of staring at one another, Keryn noticed that there was a worry behind Yen's eyes.

"What's wrong?" she asked.

"Nothing," Yen said, suddenly distracted. "Did you hear? We're going to attack…"

"Earth," she interrupted. "Yes, I had heard."

"You have an uncanny knack for knowing everything before I do, and you're not even the psychic one in this relationship."

Keryn laughed softly. "Call it women's intuition."

"I call it unnerving," Yen replied with a smile. "Where have you been? I looked for you during the briefing, but I never saw you come in."

"That's because I never did. I had… another obligation to take care of."

"Want to talk about it?"

Keryn shook her head. "Maybe later. Right now, all I want to do is go back to your place and curl up in your arms. If I don't, I think I might scream."

Yen stepped aside and motioned for Keryn to lead. Because they were in uniform and supposed to act like professionals, they didn't hold hands while they walked. In truth, Keryn wasn't sure if she would have, even if given the opportunity. Right now she felt strangely alone, even when next to someone with whom she felt so comfortable. That loneliness extended outward like an aura, pushing away anyone trying to get close. There was a tension throughout her body that she yearned to release, and as they entered Yen's quarters, she was pretty sure she knew what she needed to from her whirling thoughts. As the door closed softly behind them, she turned and grabbed the front of his uniform, pulling his face down to hers. She lost herself in his passionate kisses. Her eyes closed, she didn't notice the small blue tendril extend from Yen's groping hands. As it brushed against her arm, chills of pleasure ran up and down her spine. She pulled away suddenly and placed a hand on his chest.

Keryn shook her head as she spoke. "Not tonight," she begged. "No powers, no enhanced emotions or sensations. Tonight I just want it to be you and me."

Nodding wordlessly, Yen led Keryn past the dinner table and into his bedroom.

Keryn buried her face in Yen's arm as they lay in bed together. He looked over, an obviously concerned look on his face, and caught her distant stare.

"Would you like to talk about it now?" he asked.

Keryn rolled onto her back and stared at the ceiling. "I'm going to be leaving soon," she muttered.

He rolled toward her, propping his head up on his elbow. Smiling, he ran his finger gently along her arm. "I know. We're all going to be leaving, just as soon as the Fleet is ready."

"That's not what I'm talking about."

"Then explain it to me."

Keryn rolled away so that only her back faced Yen. "The High Council tagged me for a special mission. I'm not going to Earth with you. In fact, I'll be gone in the next few weeks, once my team and I have completed our training."

240

Keryn could feel the bed move as Yen first sat up, then climbed completely out of bed. She could hear him pace as he ran through a myriad of questions. "Where are you going? Who is on this team of yours?"

She could hear a slight hint of jealousy in his voice; a hint of anger coating the corners of his words as though frustrated at not being included in her mission. "I'm supposed to capture a smuggler. Top secret mission and all that. I don't even know who's on my team yet, only that the High Council sent out reassignment orders to the people already."

"Then I'm coming with you," he said matter–of–factly.

Keryn sighed and sat upright in bed, catching Yen's irritated gaze. "You can't Yen. I know you want to protect me. It's a sweet gesture, but you have more important things to worry about than babysitting me."

"Keryn, there is nothing more important than you."

"Quit saying things like that!" she said angrily. "This isn't the time for mushy romance. We are at war and this war is about to get a lot more violent. You and I are really not that important in the grand scheme of things." She climbed out of bed and walked over to him. Sighing, feeling guilty for the surprise and hurt in his eyes, she reached out and took his hands. "And yes, there is something more important than taking care of me."

Leaning down, Keryn picked up her discarded uniform jacket. She pulled the shiny metal rank from the collar of her shirt and placed it in Yen's outstretched hands. "You're the squadron commander now. You have a lot more people to take care of than just me."

"Just like that?" he asked, dumbfounded.

"Just like that," Keryn reaffirmed. "The High Council granted me the responsibility of identifying my own replacement. I can't think of anyone better qualified or more

241

capable of taking care of the Squadron than you."

"But I gave up flying to be in the Infantry," he muttered.

"Maybe, but I saw how well you flew during the last battle. You're still a pilot at heart. And, luckily for you, you'll have plenty of time to realize your abilities before you reach Earth."

Yen reached out and pulled Keryn into a hug. She disappeared against his chest as he wrapped his arms around her. Her tears disappeared against his sweaty skin. As she pulled away from him, she noticed even his dark eyes were rimmed with red. Wordlessly, she began dressing as Yen absently tidied the bedroom. When she was done, he walked her to the door.

"Don't worry," she whispered. "We'll have plenty of time together before I leave."

"I know," Yen replied. "I love you, Keryn. Don't ever forget that."

"I know you do." Keryn leaned forward and kissed Yen before slipping through the door.

As the doors shut behind her, Yen walked immediately over to his console and initiated a room-to-room call. The screen flashed as the corresponding console chimed in another room. Slowly, the black screen faded to a pale face silhouetted against an inky black room. The Pilgrim ran his hand through his shaggy blonde hair, trying to groom it as he stared into the console's screen.

"What's up?" Adam asked groggily.

"I've got a huge favor to ask," Yen replied with a knowing smile.

CHAPTER 26

Keryn dreaded entering the training room. Opening the door meant that she had finally succumbed to the High Council's wishes and accepted that she would never lead her Squadron on the attack against Earth. Some unknown affront left her with a new team on a mission that seemed so incredibly secondary to that of the rest of the Fleet. Keryn struggled to find any way to describe her feelings other than that she felt like she had just been slapped across the face.

Looking down at her watch, she knew she was late. The rest of her team would already be assembled inside, waiting for their unseen leader. Keryn had intended to be a few minutes late, ensuring she was the last one to enter. Somehow, though, time had slipped away from her. By now, her team had been sitting for nearly thirty minutes in the room, either getting to know each other or at each other's throats. A part of her wished for the latter, so long as it meant that they would cancel her mission and reassign her as the Squadron Commander.

Frowning, Keryn realized she had stalled long enough. Entering her code, the door slid soundlessly open and she stepped inside. The interior of the training room was well lit from the few lights imbedded in the first half of the room. The ceiling in the second half, however, was covered with windows, presenting a phenomenal view of the star systems as they passed. The entire ceiling in that part of the room slopped gently downward, following the curve of the ship.

In the center of the room, in a mixture of sitting or standing, her team was gathered. Each wore an expression of impatience. Keryn scanned the crowd and frowned again. Her new team looked rugged, as though many had spent the night before in the brig and were only just released to attend this meeting. The large Oterian had yet to make eye contact with Keryn, though even viewing the profile of his face she could see that he was nursing a new scar running the length of his cheek. Keryn glanced around and saw a member of most of the major races represented: Oterian, Avalon, Uligart, and Pilgrim. Everyone on the team shared an open look of disgust, a feeling Keryn was all too familiar with. These were all soldiers who, like herself, had been pulled away from one of the most important missions of their lives to run errands for the High Council. And Keryn had now become the focal point for their combined frustrations. This was not a good start for her team.

As she finished her scan of the room, Keryn noticed another member of her team, detached from the others and standing near the large windows. His glossy black tail swishing back and forth in impatience, the Lithid had barely spared Keryn the recognition of her entrance. The other members of her team followed her gaze and turned to look at the ostracized Lithid.

"Don't worry about him, sweetie," a smug Uligart said, gesturing toward the Lithid. "He's been doing that ever since we got here. Guess he's just a loner."

Keryn closed her eyes and scowled. This was going to be harder than she thought. Turning slowly, she faced the Uligart. "First of all, I'm not your sweetie. I have a name, and it's Magistrate Keryn Riddell. For everyone else in the room, you can call me Keryn. For you, however, you can call me Magistrate Riddell or ma'am. Are we clear on that?"

The Uligart shrugged. "Crystal, ma'am," he replied lackadaisically.

"And secondly…" Keryn began.

"I'm not a loner," the Lithid replied in a familiar voice as he turned toward the rest of the group.

Keryn looked up and smiled. "Penchant. How wonderful it is to see a familiar face."

Penchant walked over and joined the rest of the group. "I appreciate the sentiment, but I know you're lying. I don't have a face."

"Aw," the Pilgrim male in the group replied as he leaned over a chair and threw his arm around the Avalon female sitting there. "I love a good group hug." With interest, Keryn noted that the Avalon didn't brush the Pilgrim's arm aside.

"Knock it off," the Oterian rumbled. The group seemed to respond to the Oterian's order, something else Keryn mentally noted. Hopefully, that would be something she could use later.

Keryn nodded toward the Oterian in thanks. "You all may already know one another, but I don't know you yet. Before we start introducing ourselves, let me explain something. Whether we want to be here or not, we've all been assigned to this mission. So long as I'm in charge, I don't need this turning into some strict military operation. We're going to be a team, stuck in close quarters for long periods of time." She turned toward the Uligart before continuing. "Against popular belief, I don't care about your rank or even what ship you came from. We're going to become real friendly with one another before this is done, so we might as well start getting comfortable with one another now. My name is Keryn. I'll be the team's leader and pilot."

She kept her gaze locked on the Uligart, who finally shrugged and took a step forward. "The name's Keeling. I'm a small arms expert."

The Oterian turned toward Keryn. She could better see the long scar that ran down the side of his face, reaching nearly from horn to jaw line. "Rombard. Heavy weapons."

The Avalon and the Pilgrim smiled simultaneously as Keryn looked toward them. Even before she noticed the rings on their fingers, their body language betrayed their familiarity. "I'm McLaughlin," the Pilgrim said as he ran a hand through his bright red hair. "I'm your demolitions man. This here is Cerise. She's going to be our over watch."

Keryn nodded and turned toward Penchant. "Penchant. Infiltration and espionage."

She nodded and took in her team. Though they were rugged and she was sure they would intentionally test her leadership over the next few months, each seemed very confident in their assigned tasks. "Alright," she said finally. "It looks like we have our team put together now."

"Not completely," a voice called from the doorway. Keryn turned to see Adam standing there, brushing his shaggy blonde hair from his forehead. "My name's Adam Decker. I'll be another heavy weapons specialist for the team."

Adam walked into the room, smiling broadly as he passed Keryn and took his place next to Penchant at the end of the line. He turned and looked at her inquisitively, as though awaiting his next order.

"Well, we…" she stammered. Taking a deep breath, she regained her composure before continuing again. "We have a lot to do, but I'd rather we all get to know each other a little bit better first. If we're going to be a team, we will need to be able to trust each other completely. Take a few minutes to get to know one another, and then we'll get back together and lay out our mission plan."

As the others separated, Keryn walked directly to Adam. Grabbing him by the arm, she pulled him away from the rest of the team. "What are you doing here?" she asked harshly in a low whisper.

"I'm on you team," Adam replied.

"No, you're not. You see, I had pretty clear orders. My orders say that I'm in charge of a six person team. Penchant, McLaughlin, Cerise, Rombard, Keeling, and me. That's six."

"I don't know what to tell you," Adam answered as he pulled a sheet of vellum from his jacket. "I have orders assigning me to this unit as well."

Keryn snatched the orders from his hand and reviewed the scrolling information. The orders were legitimate, but it was the date that struck her as odd. Everyone else had been assigned to the unit as soon as Keryn received her communication from the High Council. Adam's orders, however, were dated the day after, almost as though his assignment was an afterthought. Or a special request, she thought grimly. Looking over her shoulder, she made sure the rest of the team was still sufficiently engaged and not prying into their conversation.

"You want to be part of this team?" she asked.

"Yes, I really do."

"Then I have to be able to trust you. I'm going to ask you a question, and you're going to give me the honest answer. If I think you're lying, I'll make sure you're off this team."

Adam hesitated before responding. "Ask away."

"Did Yen put you up to this?"

Adam frowned, but his expression betrayed the answer. Keryn kept her stern gaze and watched as his resolve quickly melted. "Fine, yes. Yen put in a special request to get me reassigned. He thought you could use the help."

"No," she answered angrily. "He thought I needed a babysitter."

"Stop right there," Adam interrupted, his face suddenly flushed. "Do I look like a babysitter to you? Do I look like I have nothing better to do with my time and all my years of experience than to sit around with you, catering to your every need? I am a soldier, and have been one since before you entered the Academy. I'm good at what I do and I joined your group because you can use me, if you manage to pull your head out of your--"

"I'm sorry," Keryn said before he could finish his sentence. "I'm just frustrated with the assignment in general."

"Whether you appreciate it or not," Adam said as he placed a comforting hand on her shoulder, "this assignment is important. I've been around for a while and I've never heard of the High Council contacting someone directly about a mission. If they gave you this assignment, it's for a reason. Don't take it so lightly."

Looking over her shoulder once again, she saw a couple of the teammates laughing as they shared prior war stories. A level of camaraderie had already begun between the members, though she was still not included. Instead of spending time with them, like she should have been, she had let herself get distracted by Adam's arrival.

"We should go rejoin the others," Adam offered.

"Believe it or not, I'm glad you're here," she said as they began walking back to the rest of the team. "It's just nice to have both you and Penchant here."

"I'm glad I'm here too," Adam admitted. "Somehow, the thought of invading Earth scared the hell out of me."

The rest of the team settled down as Keryn and Adam rejoined them. They had pulled chairs together to better talk, and they now separated them so that everyone could see Keryn as she spoke. Though they still wore a skeptical look, the teammates still looked significantly more relaxed around one another.

"I guess we're going to be a team of seven after all," Keryn offered as Adam found a seat.

"So what's the plan, ma'am?" Keeling asked.

Keryn smiled. "Alright, you can drop the ma'am now. Our plan is simple. Out there, on a backwater little planet called Pteraxis, there is an Oterian smuggler. Not only did he make one of the most spectacular discoveries in recent science when he found the chemical that was used to destroy the *Vindicator*, he turned around and sold this wonderful new technology to the Terrans. Our mission is to find this bastard and make him tell us where this new weapon came from."

"And what if he will not tell us?" Cerise said condescendingly.

Keryn reached behind her and unclipped a pouch from her belt. "Well, I was given six of these little cases to make sure he would tell us." Opening the top of the pouch, she reached in and pulled out a glistening scalpel. Her gaze fell on the scalpel, which she spun lazily in her hand. When she spoke, her voice took on a distant edge, as though fantasizing about the scalpel's many uses. "Apparently, they're going to teach us how to use these to the best effect."

"You know," Keeling said, "I think I'm going to like this job after all."

Chapter 27

The briefing room filled quickly with the primary staff of the *Revolution*. Yen had already assumed his seat near the front of the room, the one traditionally reserved for the squadron commander. His assumption of the role had come as a surprise to most, since Keryn had only taken the job a couple months before. Everything about her departure remained veiled in secrecy, with rumors abounding about possible injury or mental illness. Yen didn't bother correcting them. Sometimes, it was good to have secrets. Secrets held their own power and power was what ensured Yen not getting removed from the job of squadron commander any time soon.

But Keryn's mission wasn't the only secret Yen had. Yen was eager to see the other secret he knew come to light during this meeting. The expressions of his peers and supervisors would be priceless indeed.

To Yen's left, Iana had claimed the seat reserved for the Squadron's second in command. Though Yen had a number of veteran pilots under his command following the last conflict, Iana was not only battle-hardened but someone he could trust. Yen knew the importance of having someone in whom you could confide when need be, and Iana had already proven herself trustworthy.

The room was filled with a multitude of conversations.

Many of the leadership positions throughout the ship were now held by people Yen didn't know. With so many wounded or killed during the last conflict, many officers and warrants had been cross-leveled from other vessels in the Fleet to fill voids in the chain of command. Yen didn't want to be anti-social, but he found little to talk about with the new personnel. Much like he and Iana sitting side by side, many old acquaintances gravitated to one another.

Yen closed his eyes, folded his hands in front of his face, and drowned out the dull roar of people talking over one another. Beneath his feet, Yen could feel the gentle vibrations of the massive engines propelling the *Revolution* forward. Inhibitors suppressed the pressure of flying at speeds beyond that of light; pressures that would crush a person's body were the inhibitors inactive. Even at such great speeds, it would be weeks longer before the Fleet even approached its target.

The entire Fleet had departed the Farimas Space Station a few days before, with the *Revolution* in the lead as its flagship. Over thirty Alliance Cruisers had joined the *Revolution*, comprising most of the Alliance's military might. If the assault on Earth were to be successful, it would require the entire might of the Alliance, save the few vessels left behind to protect key infrastructure throughout Alliance occupied space.

More than the might of the Fleet, however, was the timing of their assault. The remaining Terran Fleet, a force larger even than the Alliance Fleet, was on a mission elsewhere in known space, pursuing a false lead released through Alliance spies on Earth. The Terrans would never return in time to stop the assault on Earth, even if they did detect the Alliance Fleet. Moreover, the Terrans had no reason to suspect a secret weapon like the warp technology. The Fleet did not intend to get close enough to Earth to be openly detected by the Empire.

By the time the Terrans realized something was amiss, the Squadron would be appearing behind their defenses. At least, that was how it was supposed to work. In theory.

Theory didn't make Yen very comfortable with the plan. He had watched the successful presentation of the warp technology in the auditorium and was awed, just as everyone else had been. The possibilities for such a technology were virtually boundless. Except that every time Yen pondered the use of wormholes and event horizons, he remembered mutilated and dismembered animals, staring back at him from their jars of preserving chemicals. Those thoughts had ridden a hidden current of fear through the scientist's mind before he initiated the presentation. It was the stench of fear dominating his thoughts that made Yen uneasy. If the creator of the technology was fearful of its possible results, could Yen truly put himself and his men in danger by using the warp technology?

As Yen mulled over the troubling thoughts in his mind, Captain Hodge entered the room and took her place at the head table. Across from Yen, Eminent Merric took a seat on the captain's right. The left side of his face was still slightly swollen and red from his assault in the Frozen Nebula. To Yen's surprise, Merric had never made an official claim of assault against him. Though Yen kept awaiting the day security would come and place him in handcuffs while he worked, that day had yet to arrive. In a lot of ways, that made him even more nervous. Yen had certain expectations of people. When you stole, you were reprimanded. When you assaulted a senior officer, they filed a complaint and you were arrested. It was when people stopped being predictable that Yen began to worry. Though he would give anything to know what plots Merric was hatching, he didn't dare try to scan him. Merric would expect Yen to use his powers, and that might be the trigger he was waiting for to have Yen arrested. For now, Yen would have to be content wondering.

"We're already on our way to Earth," Captain Hodge said, officially calling the meeting to order. "But before we get there, there are far too many things that need to be accomplished. When we departed the Farimas Space Station, you were all told my expectations for each of your sections. I'd like to take this chance to go around the room and get a status update. Just give everyone a brief synopsis of what you've managed to accomplish and what still needs to be completed."

Yen's task had been daunting compared to some of the others. He only found out about his reassignment to squadron commander the day before the *Revolution* departed the space station. Since that time, he had to familiarize himself not just with the rebuilt ships in the Squadron but with the pilots themselves. Yen had no doubt that most rumors about Keryn's sudden departure as commander had stemmed from his own Squadron, since they were most vocal about the surprising change.

As Captain Hodge went around the room, addressing different officers, many of the new faces were introduced, though many of their names were forgotten as quickly as they were told. On occasion, Yen would look up to see how far around the table they had come, if only to gauge the time he had left before his own brief. He began paying attention as they reached a warrant seated on the far side of Iana. Knowing that Iana wouldn't brief, that meant that Yen would be next.

"Warrant Scyant," Captain Hodge said, gesturing toward a new Wyndgaart female. "Welcome aboard the *Revolution*."

"Thank you, ma'am," Scyant replied confidently. Yen looked up from his own fidgeting to examine the new warrant.

The Wyndgaart had dark grey hair that shimmered with a metallic hue. The blue and green tattoos framed her handsome face, which shone brightly with her broad smile. "I'm glad to be here."

"For those of you who have not yet met Warrant Scyant, she is taking over Weapons. She comes from the *Cavalier*, which was irreparably damaged during the latest Fleet battle. I understand that a number of other officers transferred over from the *Cavalier* while we were at Farimas, is that correct?"

"Yes, ma'am," Scyant replied. "A number of us did. I know we're all proud to be serving on the Alliance flagship for the upcoming battle."

"We're glad to have you as well," the Captain responded. "Tell us, what have you found during your inspections of the weapons bays?"

Scyant shrugged. Yen was very familiar with the motion. When used during meetings, it was a polite way of buying time as you figured out how to express your displeasure with the current system. "I think that my predecessor did an admirable job keeping the system functioning."

"But?" Captain Hodge probed, knowing Scyant was withholding the rest of her sentence intentionally.

Scyant laughed. "But I think we could do more. I have a few ideas that I'm implementing that should streamline the reloading process. My men are working on it now and, if everything works out, it should trim a few seconds off the downtime between volleys."

"Excellent work," the captain said appreciatively. Captain Hodge turned to Yen, who was next in line for briefing. "Squadron Commander Xiao. How goes the inspection of the new ships?"

Yen smiled. "The repair work was excellent. You'd

hardly know most of the ships were damaged. In light of our new battle tactics and the fact that we'll be using relatively untested technology, right now we're doing a reassessment of our strategies. Flying in rigid formations will not be as effective when each ship is carrying its own warp generator."

"And how are the pilots taking the changes you're implementing?"

Yen shrugged. "It's a different leader, with different ideas. I obviously have a much different style than did Commander Riddell, but I think the pilots are taking the changes in stride. There have been complaints, but nothing beyond what I would expect after a change in leadership."

Merric interrupted the conversation. "Have you had a chance to fully examine the warp generators that were installed? Are you confident that you and your Squadron will even be able to use them appropriately?"

Yen refused to take Merric's obvious bait. He remained calm as he continued. "As I stated, Eminent Merric, we are just getting used to a change in leadership. Over the next few days, we'll be taking a little more time to examine all the subtle nuances of the warp generator and how its system feeds into the *Cair* and *Duun* engines. The last thing anyone wants is a pilot accidentally warping himself into a star because he hit the wrong button."

His joked evoked a round of laughter from the officers and warrants. "Speaking of new ideas," Yen continued, "I would like to introduce my new second in command, Warrant Morven. She is a *Duun* pilot who served on board the *Vindicator*. As a battle tested pilot, I'm glad to have her expertise."

"I'm glad to have you here," Captain Hodge said, "even if just to keep your squadron commander in check." The captain let the laughter die before continuing with her brief. "As much as I am interested in updates on the ship, I know that's not the real reason you're all eagerly sitting around this table today. We've received the full telemetry from the High Council, explaining our mission in greater detail."

On cue, the lights dimmed around them and a trap door opened in the middle of the briefing table. A flicker of light erupted from within as the holographic projector created a blue and green world hovering a few feet above the table. Around the planet, spaced nearly an inch apart and encompassing the full expanse of the space above the planet, small triangles hovered menacingly. Yen knew as well as anyone at the table what those triangles represented.

"Our mission on Earth is truly three-fold, broken down into individual phases," the captain explained. "Phase one consists of disabling the satellite network around Earth. So long as that network is still operational, the Fleet does not stand a chance of gaining access to Earth. For that, we will lean on you, Commander, and your Squadron. The plan is that you and your Squadron will warp using the provided coordinates. That warp should place you between the planet's atmosphere and the satellite grid."

On the hologram, dozens of small blue dots appeared, hovering dangerously behind the triangles. Immediately, the dots began spreading over the Earth's surface.

"Once you arrive behind the satellites, you'll need to sufficiently disable their grid so that the Fleet can make its approach. Destroying a single satellite will not be enough to bring down the entire network. The satellites are interlaced in their signals, meaning that a single satellite being destroyed will only cause a brief delay as the system circumnavigates the destroyed nodule. If you want to take out the whole hemisphere of satellites, you'll need to take out a series of satellites, positioned seemingly randomly around Earth. These specific nodules," she gestured at the hologram as the blue dots destroyed twenty or more satellites, "contain the rerouting software that protects their whole grid. Bring those down and the entire system will suffer a catastrophic failure."

Yen furrowed his brow. "Excuse me, ma'am," he said softly. "Are we sure that this will work?"

"What do you mean, Commander?"

"It just seems odd to have so much information about the Terran defenses. I'm used to going into missions where I question how we'll escape, much less exactly where to strike to disable every possible defense they have."

"This is information directly from the High Council," Merric interceded. "Why would you assume their information to be wrong?"

"Excuse my skepticism," Yen replied angrily. "But it's not the High Council or you that will be warping into the heart of enemy territory!"

"Gentlemen," Captain Hodge said sternly before the conversation could get out of hand. "Commander, I understand your concerns, but Eminent Merric is correct. We have no reason to doubt the High Council's information. We must have faith in their ability to lead us to victory."

Yen frowned. It seemed easy for everyone to spout rhetoric about trusting the High Council, but none of them were placing their lives on the line. To his surprise, Yen felt a reassuring hand on his arm. He looked over and saw his concern vividly expressed on Iana's face as well.

"Phase two will commence once the satellite grid has been disabled," Captain Hodge continued as though the interruption had never occurred. "The Terran Empire relied heavily on its political infrastructure for guidance, both in the civilian and military sectors. If we can disable these political hubs throughout their world, we can cripple their ground forces before the battle even begins. Once the satellites are down, the Fleet will advance at top speed. Even accelerating like we will, it will still take us nearly two hours to reach Earth. During that time, it will be up to the *Duun* fighters to bomb these targets."

On the hologram, a series of red concentric circles appeared, spread evenly across the major continents. "These are not just political sites. These are also launching points for low orbit aircraft. We need these eliminated before we will be able to land a ground force."

"The final phase of this invasion will be the ground assault itself. Many of our ground forces will be on board the *Cair* transports that will warp in initially. The support teams will be on the Cruisers but, again, there will be a delay before their arrival. The immediate ground forces will be required to gain and hold key positions across the planet, many of which coincide with the initial bombing areas."

Overlapping green circles appeared, many of which mirrored the previous red concentric circles. "These will not be easy engagements. However, the Terrans have been lulled into a false sense of security over the past century. They have placed their major forces throughout known space and left only a small contingent to protect Earth itself. They rely too heavily on the satellites to protect them. We will exploit that weakness."

"Which brings me to my final point," Captain Hodge said, sighing. "I need a leader for the ground forces. This officer must be intelligent, cunning, and have years of combat experience. I actually have a number of officers that meet that criterion on board right now. However, there is only one that seems like a natural selection for the assignment. The ground force commander will be—"

Merric smiled broadly from across the table. Yen shrunk from that malicious smile. Merric outranked Yen and had nearly the same number of years in the Infantry, but the thought of spending an entire conflict fighting side by side with, and taking orders from, Merric turned Yen's stomach.

"—Commander Xiao," Captain Hodge concluded.

Yen sat in stupefied silence. His look of surprise hardly matched the combined look of horrific defeat and stunned disbelief that was painted across Merric's face. His confidents smile was gone, though he still bared his teeth in a feral snarl.

"Commander Xiao?" the captain prodded as the silence stretched on.

"I'm... I'm sorry, ma'am," Yen finally stammered. "Thank you for this..."

"This is ridiculous!" Merric yelled, interrupting Yen in mid sentence. "To hell with this! I am better qualified, I am senior in rank, and I deserve this, damn it!"

"Merric," Captain Hodge said sternly, "please calm yourself."

"Calm myself?" Merric demanded, pointing wildly in Yen's direction. "Are you serious? This poor excuse for a soldier gets promoted first to squadron commander and not even a week later is now in charge of the entire ground force! That is *my* job!"

"You forget yourself, Eminent Merric!" Hodge yelled as she quickly stood, her voice losing its melodic tone as it took on a screeching minor key. "And you will excuse yourself from this meeting before I find a reason to make you a Magistrate again!"

Merric scowled as he locked gazes with Captain Hodge. Growling softly, he turned back toward Yen, hate filling his eyes.

"This isn't over, Yen."

"Leave now, Merric!" the captain ordered.

Merric turned on his heel, stormed past the rest of the stunned crowd, and disappeared through the doorway. Breathing heavily, Captain Hodge sat back down and, reaching behind her, smoothed the ruffled feathers of her wings.

"I'm sorry about that," she said musically, her composure restored. "Believe me when I tell you all that every aspect of this mission has been examined in great detail. Eminent Merric was actually correct when he said that he had seniority and should have, by regulation, assumed command of the ground forces. Under different circumstances, I would have gladly obliged him. He is not only an intelligent officer, but he is well versed in combat. However, I am already putting Commander Xiao at great personal risk as he leads his Squadron against the Earth defenses. I will not put another of my senior officer's in harm's way just to satisfy one man's inflated sense of self-worth."

The captain's eyes darkened as she glared at everyone at the table before her. "That being said, let me also explain one other simple fact. I am not required, at any time, to justify my decisions to any of you at this table. I'll not abide someone second-guessing my decisions. If it happens again, I'll take it as an act of sedition. Do I make myself clear?"

She hardly waited for their responses before continuing. "Good. This concludes our meeting. You're all excused."

Everyone stood brusquely and saluted before filing out of the room. As the briefing room began to clear, Yen felt a cool hand on his arm. Turning, he found himself face to face with Captain Hodge.

"Please stay behind, Commander," she said. "There is something else we need to discuss."

Yen looked over his shoulder to where Iana waited. He

waved to her to get her attention, and then motioned toward the door. Understanding, Iana turned and left, leaving just Yen and Captain Hodge in the room alone. Yen swallowed hard, knowing what she wanted to discuss. Merric's outburst during the meeting, followed nearly immediately by the captain's desire to discuss a matter of importance, told Yen that Merric hadn't kept quiet about their episode during shore leave.

"Please be seated, Commander," Captain Hodge said politely as she returned to her own seat.

Hesitantly, Yen sat. "Ma'am, if this is about…"

Captain Hodge raised her hand, cutting him off. "I don't care about Merric right now. There is more to the mission than what I briefed. I didn't just select you to be the ground forces commander because of your previous experience in the Infantry. If that were my criteria, I would have selected any number of actual Infantry officers instead of picking a pilot who has been moonlighting as a soldier."

Yen nodded, taking the backhanded insult in stride.

"I selected you because of your unique talents. I hope I have not been misled about how far your powers have evolved since you first came aboard."

Yen closed his eyes and let the power coalesce in his hand. The blue serpent formed in his hand, weaving around his fingers and up his wrist.

"You have become quite talented with your powers, Commander," Captain Hodge said, smiling. "I also notice that you don't seem to suffer from the headaches you once had every time you used your abilities."

Yen's eyes opened slowly. Captain Hodge was right, though Yen hadn't noticed in some time. After surviving Purseus II with Adam, Yen had suffered terrible headaches every time he used his psychic powers for anything other than the most mundane uses. Without his realization, the headaches had slowly lessened before disappearing all together. During his shore leave, he had used his powers almost haphazardly without any side effects. And the uses of his powers when with Keryn…

"After you disable the satellite grid and ensure all your teams are dispersed to their correct locations," Captain Hodge began as she reactivated the hologram of Earth, "I want you to take your team here, to the Empire's capital." On the sphere hanging above the table, a large red dot appeared over a major city on the eastern coast of one of the continents.

"And once I get there?" Yen asked, intrigued.

"A team has already been prepared for you, with one of your former Infantry cohorts as your second in command."

Yen frowned. There were few "former cohorts" of Yen's still alive. "You mean Buren. I would prefer you sent someone else."

"I don't really care what you prefer," the Captain said coldly. "You and Magistrate Buren will lead your team into their capital. There will be other teams on the ground that will keep their main force occupied. Your objective is to find and capture a Terran scientist, Doctor Solomon."

"What did this guy do?" Yen asked.

"He was the lead researcher on two projects that you might find interesting. The first was a series of experiments using the newly discovered chemical, Deplitoxide. I think you remember its use during the last Fleet engagement."

"And the other," Yen asked, dreading her reply.

"He was also the lead scientist on a genetics project, working specifically with mutated genomes. Apparently, he found that it was possible to mutate a docile load bearing beast into a pathological killing machine."

Yen could feel his jaw muscles clenching and unclenching. "If this doctor really is to blame for what happened to my team on Purseus, then I'm going to tear him apart."

"No, you won't. Your orders are to capture him and bring him back alive. He has too much information in that head of his for you to remove it from his shoulders. Can you handle this mission, or should I give it solely to Magistrate Buren?"

Breathing heavily, Yen looked down at the blue tendril that squirmed in his hand in eager anticipation. He smiled sadistically and turned to Captain Hodge. "This is my mission. I'll find your good doctor. Earth doesn't have an army big enough to stop me."

CHAPTER 28

The room spun as Keryn was lifted from her feet and slammed hard onto the mat. As she stared up at the ceiling, she tried to get her bearings, but the room refused to quit turning. Sighing, she covered her eyes with her hands and tried to stop the disorienting sense of vertigo.

"Good," the rumbling Oterian voice commented from above her, "but you left yourself exposed for a grapple. Next time, strike and withdraw. Give the enemy nothing to grab a hold of."

Slowly opening her eyes, she stared into the massive face of her Oterian instructor. The Oterian, the latest in a long line of instructors, had been embarrassing Keryn in hand-to-hand combat for the better part of an hour. Having been trained for years in the Wyndgaart fighting styles, she quickly discovered how humiliating it felt to repeatedly find herself staring up at the ceiling.

Keryn groaned, rolled over onto her side, and propped herself up on an elbow. Tonight, she was sure that she would be spending a good portion of the evening with ice packs along her ribs and lower back, easing the pain of bruised muscles and aching joints. Looking through the one eye still not badly swollen, Keryn could see the rest of the team standing on the far edge of the padded mat. Half the group, Adam included, hadn't been in the ring yet. Adam, smiling as she caught his eye, still held onto his smug confidence. The other half of the team already knew better, as they sat on the side nursing new wounds.

"Did you hear what I said, Keryn?" the instructor asked.

Keryn reached up, took the Oterian's hand, and pulled herself to her feet. "Yes, I did. I'll go practice for a while on my own. However, I believe Adam is ready for a solid block of instruction."

Adam's stunned expression was perfect retribution for his earlier mocking. Keryn smiled as she moved to the side of the room and lay down on the floor. The cool metal floor felt wonderful on her sore back, but she kept enough awareness to be able to watch Adam during his sparing match with the Oterian.

To Adam's credit, his tall Pilgrim stature didn't look nearly as daunting against the eight-foot tall Oterian as it had seemed when Keryn had faced their instructor. Adam removed his shirt and stood ready. Keryn noted the strong muscles across his arms, shoulders and back, coupled with a rainbow of colored bruises covered most of his exposed torso. The older bruises had already faded to a sickly yellow, while the more recent ones were still an ugly purple. Dropping into a fighting crouch, Adam wisely waited for the instructor to approach him as opposed to the other way around. The reach of the Oterian left Adam at a disadvantage should he try to initiate the attack. Smiling, the instructor moved quickly forward in an attempt to smother Adam in his large, fur covered arms. Ducking and slipping agilely to the side, Adam maneuvered himself out of the path of the Oterian and struck out with a quick side kick. His foot landed roughly on the instructor's ribs, who flinched as he moved away. Smiling to himself, Adam slid back and readjusted his low fighter's stance.

"That was a good move, Adam," the Oterian rumbled. "You caught me by surprise, but I can guarantee it won't happen again."

"We'll see about that," Adam replied confidently.

The instructor moved forward, but with greater caution this time around. Keryn shook her head at Adam's brashness. She had watched three others before him approach their fights with much the same confidence, only to be decimated by the surprisingly fast Oterian. Watching the instructor's nostrils flare, Keryn knew that Adam was about to be exposed to the same punishment she had endured.

As the Oterian lashed out with one of his huge fists, Keryn watched Adam dart easily out of the way, shifting his stance as he stopped a few feet to the left of his previous position. From his new position, Adam had a clear view of the instructor's large ribcage from where the Oterian had overextended on his strike. Keryn frowned. Inadvertently, Adam had moved directly into a trap. The Oterian's strike had been much too slow for him to have been fully committed to the attack. Adam was in trouble and didn't even yet realize the world of pain to which he was about to be introduced.

Assuming he had an opening, Adam kicked straight ahead, aiming for the exposed ribs. Faster than Adam could track, the Oterian dropped his outstretched arm and swung his hand in a downward circle. As his now open hand came in contact with Adam's extended kick, the instructor clamped his meaty hand over Adam's ankle and jerked forward as he spun his weight. Ripped from his feet, Adam flew into the air, being spun in a circle by his ankle. Halfway through his spin, the Oterian released his grip and Adam went flying past the padded mat and landing heavily onto the hard metal ground beyond.

Groaning, Adam writhed on the floor, alternating his attention between his strained ankle and badly bruised shoulder.

Grunting as he stood upright, the Oterian stomped over to Adam's prostrate form. "You got cocky. You're not nearly as good as you think you are. If you're foolish enough to try something like that against a well–trained enemy, it *may* cost your friends their lives, but I can guarantee that it *will* cost you yours."

The instructor turned to the rest of the team, most of who unknowingly backed away from the intimidating Oterian. "I think we've done enough training this morning. Take a break, nurse your wounds, but come back to me in two hours. We have a lot more work ahead of us if you all are going to be ready for combat any time soon. Dismissed!"

Keryn glowered at Penchant, McLaughlin and Cerise, all of who had managed to somehow avoid participating in the training this morning. She knew their time would come soon enough and she smiled at that thought as she laid her head down on the cool ground. Reveling in the cold metal against her cheek and forehead, she didn't notice someone approach until a shadow fell over her.

"You want to grab something to eat or drink?" Adam asked, his voice strained as he spoke through clenched teeth.

Opening her violet eyes, she stared at the obviously miserable Pilgrim. "I figured you'd spend the next two hours soaking in an ice bath somewhere."

Adam smiled smugly and ran a hand through his shaggy blonde hair. "I thought about it, don't get me wrong. I just figured you'd be more prone to join me for a meal than you would for an ice bath."

Keryn shook her head. "You really just don't learn, do you?" The thought of a drink was appealing to her parched throat, but she was afraid that standing would cause too much pain in her already sore back. "I'll pass, but thanks."

Adam shrugged. "Your loss. I'll see you in a couple hours."

Though Keryn was tempted to follow him, she was far too comfortable to move from her spot. Aside from the physical damage from today's hand-to-hand combat, Keryn's body had been beaten repeatedly over the past few weeks of training. She and her team had endured nearly every conceivable type of training: from heavy and light weapons training to hand-to-hand combat to interrogation techniques. A shiver ran up Keryn's spine at the thought of interrogation training. Every member of the team had been given a surgical instrument set to be used for personal interrogation. Though they had practiced on cadavers, the feel of flesh splitting open at the easiest pressure from the razor-sharp scalpel made Keryn's stomach turn. The thought of doing that same thing to a living creature made her feel physically ill.

As if training for over twelve hours a day wasn't grueling enough, once she finished work she spent a good majority of her time with Yen. Both were completely engrossed in their work; her with her team and Yen planning both his Squadron and ground assaults on Earth. Neither spoke much of their missions, but when they were together they wanted to spend as little time as possible talking about work. Though the thought of all the time they spent wrapped in each other's arms did bring a smile to her face, it also contributed greatly to her continued exhaustion during each subsequent day's training. Her instructors had made a comment about her fatigue and lack of stamina and it was affecting her performance. The simplest distractions were resulting more and more often in her lying on her back, staring at the ceiling. If they didn't receive their deployment orders soon, Keryn wouldn't have to worry about Cardax or his smugglers killing her. She would be found one day soon standing on her feet or sitting in a chair, dead from exhaustion.

Keryn sighed deeply and pressed her cheek firmly against the floor, feeling the cool ground saturate her hot, bruised skin. Closing her eyes, she let the coolness soak into her body, relieving tension and washing away the tiring thoughts from her mind.

Keryn awoke sharply as the door to the room opened. A familiar shaggy blonde Pilgrim stood silhouetted against the outdoor light. Adam stepped inside and let the door slide shut behind him. She had no idea how long she'd been asleep, but the fact that Adam had now returned to the training room told her that it had been nearly the full two hours. Trying to push herself up, Keryn realized that all her muscles, which had previously just been sore, were now rigid and stiff. Without stretching beforehand, and simply falling asleep on a most uncomfortable location, her body had been allowed to heal as it had come to rest. Unfortunately for Keryn, it now caused pain to shoot through her joints as she tried to straighten both legs and arms that were permanently affixed in a crooked position.

Grimacing, she turned toward the frowning Adam as he walked in. "You don't look much better than I feel. Did your lunch not agree with you?"

Adam grunted as he walked past her, stopping finally at the curved window and staring out at the stars. Feeling slightly dejected, Keryn turned after him. He barely acknowledged her attention and chose, instead, to continue his musings at the back window.

"Adam," Keryn said, concerned. "Is something wrong?"

"Now why would you think anything would be wrong

with me?" Adam asked from behind her as she felt strong hands grab her around the waist.

Spinning, Keryn's eyes widened with confusion as she came face to face with Adam. Adam smiled broadly and winked at her before his gaze moved past her face to the stranger behind her. Turning back toward the first Adam, the one who had passed her and stood at the window, Keryn now found herself facing the featureless black oval of Penchant's visage. Though Adam laughed heartily, it took Keryn a couple passes of looking back and forth before she realized what had happened. Though Penchant had no expressions on his face, she could almost feel him smiling mischievously at her.

Joining Adam's laughter, Keryn shook her head in wonderment. "You're getting pretty good at that. You really had me going." She leaned forward until she was only a few inches away from Penchant's smooth face. "Of course, now you're going to make me wonder what else you can do with that body."

"It would never happen," Penchant said in his gravelly tone. "I hear you Wyndgaarts are a little too rough during your mating rituals."

"What's all this talk about mating rituals?" McLaughlin asked excitedly as he walked through the door, his arm thrown over Cerise's shoulder.

"Leave them be," Cerise said condescendingly. "You are only going to encourage them."

"Hell," Keeling commented as he walked in behind the couple. "If you're going to talk about mating, you might as well come to the expert."

"If I wanted relationship advice," Keryn retorted, "I'd be better off asking an Oterian rather than you. No offense, Rombard."

The massive Oterian ducked under the doorway as he entered, his horns still nearly brushing the sides of the doorframe. "None taken. Female Oterians are a lower intelligence life form. They're really only good for mating."

Adam blanched at the thought. "No romance? No seduction? Just 'get Bessie's head caught in the fence' and you're good to go?"

"I won't act as though I understand the reference," Rombard rumbled, "but romance is a waste. You mate to produce strong young for your clan, not for a lasting relationship. Why? How is mating done between Pilgrims?"

Adam shrugged. "Pretty much the same way."

"I just ate," Keeling interjected. "Is there any way we could not talk about Pilgrims mating? If you want to hear some good stories, you might as well…"

"If you children are done with story time," the Oterian instructor roared as he entered the room, "then I believe we are ready to pick back up with your training."

The entire team let out a simultaneous groan.

———

Keryn tried her best to stay on her feet at the end of their training, but wound up succumbing to her exhaustion and collapsing into a nearby chair. Her breath was labored as she tried to breathe through ribs that she was sure were broken. Though she had tried to ensure equal time with the instructor for everyone on her team, Keryn had the unfortunate pleasure of being selected to spar against the Oterian for a second round. She remembered a few tricks from their previous combat, but it had mattered little in the end. By the time they were through, Keryn was once again staring at a spinning ceiling from the flat of her back.

Now alone in the training room, she shifted positions

in her chair, trying to reach the bruise that she knew was spreading between her shoulder blades. If she remembered nothing else from her training, she would always remember that a stern punch between the shoulder blades was enough to stun nearly any race in the Alliance.

As she finished grimacing from the pain and opened her eyes, she was surprised to see a large fur-covered hand holding out a glass of water. Looking up, she met the gaze of her instructor. Keryn nodded her appreciation as she began to sip the water, savoring the burn in her raw throat.

"Thank you," she said hoarsely. She took another drink before continuing. "I'm surprised you stuck around."

"I made a promise that I would," the Oterian said quietly, his voice still carrying in the empty room.

Keryn looked up inquisitively. "Promise?"

"I'm your last instructor, Keryn. You've been trained on every major topic that we thought you might need. My job was to determine if you not only retained that previous knowledge, but that you were ready to face Cardax in battle when the time arose."

"So you were testing us?"

The Oterian turned away, though his voice was still clear. "Did you wonder why an Oterian was teaching you hand-to-hand combat? My race has vastly superior strength to the other races of the Alliance, but if you wanted the best combat instructors, you pick a Wyndgaart. So why me?"

Keryn nodded, realizing that this was yet another test. "Because Cardax is an Oterian."

"Exactly. It didn't make any sense to have you learn to fight against a Wyndgaart when your target is an Oterian. You needed to learn my race's weaknesses, few as they may be."

"But you beat us every single time we fought."

The instructor turned back to her. "You're right. Fighting isn't the only lesson I can teach you. I can also teach you humility. You don't like losing; I can see it in your face. But when you realize that you're not always going to be the best, you will learn to lean on others for support. All of you were able to hold your own against me by the end of today. Maybe not defeat me, but at least impress me. I have injuries that I'll be nursing tomorrow as well. But if I were attacked by all of you, not just in hand-to-hand combat but with you all carrying your pistols and rifles as well, I wouldn't stand a chance. You're a team now, regardless of your individual feelings for your teammates. Use their strengths and you'll be bringing Cardax back within no time."

Keryn smiled as she stood. "So we're leaving?"

"You'll be departing tomorrow," the Oterian replied. "Good luck."

CHAPTER 29

Yen sat in the cramped confines of the engine compartment on board one of the *Cair* transport ships. A series of tools lay strewn across the floor next to him, mostly forgotten. For over three hours, Yen had been tinkering with the new warp generators that the High Council had installed on all the ships in his Squadron. He couldn't shake the sense of distrust both toward the generators and the Council, but found solace sitting and analyzing the new machines. Even so, his interest in the generators had waned nearly an hour before and, since that time, he had remained in the engine compartment, lost in thought.

Focused on his own thoughts, Yen didn't hear the hatch door on the *Cair* open, nor did he notice the soft, quiet steps as someone approached the back of the ship where Yen sat huddled. He had left the engine compartment door open and was clearly visible to anyone inside the ship.

"Is this a private party or can anyone join?"

Yen looked over as Iana stooped lower, examining the engine and trying to deduce what caught Yen's attention so intently. Yen pushed the tools aside with a brush of his hand. Sliding over, Yen made room for Iana to squeeze into the engine compartment and take a confined seat beside him.

"You've been in here for hours with this thing," she said,

reaching out and running a finger along the top of the newly installed black cylinder. "Since it's still in one piece, I can only assume that you didn't find anything interesting. I mean, to keep your attention for all this time, I would expect the generator to be doing tricks."

"No, nothing interesting," Yen responded flatly.

Iana shrugged. "From that sour expression, I'm guessing you heard the news."

Yen picked up a wrench and turned it back and forth absently, letting it draw in his attention. Eventually, he sighed heavily. "I knew she'd be leaving soon, so I shouldn't be surprised. Somehow, I just thought we'd have more time together. After all this time, I feel like I'm finally connecting with Keryn in ways I didn't even know were possible. But instead of us getting the chance to explore our relationship and see where it could lead, she's going to be heading off on her mission."

"When I was young," Iana said softly, placing a hand on Yen's arm, "my father always told me that it is not the decisions we make, but rather the decisions that are made for us, that define who we become."

Yen looked up, confused. "I don't follow."

"Would you agree that you're at a pretty important crossroad in your life?"

Yen nodded.

"Well, right now you can choose one of two paths. Either you can pine away for Keryn and hope day after day that both you and she will survive your missions, find one another, and convince the High Council not to separate you for missions ever again..."

Yen frowned. "Or?"

"Or you accept that you don't get to make a decision this time. She's leaving, no matter what you choose to do about it.

But right now we need a squadron commander who is focused on the mission ahead instead of being focused on the girl he's leaving behind."

"When did you suddenly become full of sage wisdom?" Yen asked moodily.

"Didn't you know? Big surprises; little packages. I think the better question is: why do I get the feeling this is not the last time you and I are going to have this conversation?"

Yen smiled, but the mirth didn't erase the sadness in his eyes. Iana squeezed his arm gently, her own face filled with genuine concern.

"Are you sure you're okay?" she asked.

"Yeah," Yen said, nodding. "I guess I just didn't expect to be so affected by Keryn leaving." Sighing, he rubbed his face with his hands. "But you're right; I do need to focus on something else for a while."

At Yen's urging, Iana climbed out of the cramped engine compartment and left the *Cair* ship with Yen close behind. Finally in a more spacious area, Yen stretched and groaned as he tried to loosen stiff muscles.

"So what's the first bit of business we need to take care of?" he asked, glad to have Iana close by to change the subject.

"Well, you do have an entire ground assault team still waiting to find out exactly what they'll be doing once you land on the surface."

Yen frowned. He had been intentionally avoiding the ground assault team. Though he was perfectly aware of how important the mission was to their successful invasion, Yen also knew that he would have to face Buren. The idea of working so closely with a former teammate who so blatantly disliked Yen did not excite him.

"Later," Yen muttered. "What else do you have?"

Iana shrugged. "So long as we're on the topic of the invasion force, you still haven't picked a pilot who's going to take you down to the planet." She batted her eyes suggestively, to which Yen had no choice but laugh. "Laugh if you want, but I'm serious. You're not going to find a better pilot than me."

"I couldn't agree more. Unfortunately, that's the exact reason why I can't pick you to be my pilot. You're the best pilot I have, but you're also a *Duun* pilot. I need you in the air protecting my butt. Without you, I won't stand much of a chance of making it to the surface."

"Well," Iana conceded, "as long as we're clear that it's because I'm too good for you. So if you're not going to pick me to be your pilot, who are you going to pick?"

Yen began leading Iana away from the ship and toward the exit to the hangar bay. Whether he liked it or not, he needed to head down to the briefing room and start working on the ground assault mission. "I think I'm going to go with Warrant Pelasi."

Iana stopped in mid-step. "The Uligart? The pilot who just got here? You don't even know him."

"You're right, I don't know him. But his former squadron commander gave him some glowing recommendations. I have no doubt that he's going to be a capable pilot."

"A 'capable' pilot," Iana chided. "Remind me not to ask you for a letter of recommendation in the future."

"Joke if you want to, but I also picked him because if he turns out to be useless as a pilot, I'll always be there to take over. I'd rather have him under adult supervision than out there in a *Duun* by himself."

Iana nodded and rejoined him as they walked toward the doorway. When they passed through the hangar bay's exit doors, Iana reached out and put a comforting hand on Yen's shoulder.

"You know," she said, "I'm sure we can take care of the maintenance checks for the rest of today. Why don't you spend the rest of the day with your lady?"

"I still have a lot of work to do…"

"All of which will still be here tomorrow," Iana interjected. "We're just now at the Demilitarized Zone. We still have, what, almost a month until we reach our launch coordinates? We'll have everything done well before then. Take the time off now, while you still can."

"You really are a lifesaver, Iana," Yen said, smiling. "Thank you."

"Yeah, yeah," she muttered. "Do me a favor, won't you? Tell her bye. I'm going to be so busy here with the ships, I won't get a chance to be there when she leaves."

"I will," Yen agreed.

Iana smiled. "Good. Now get going."

Though he continued smiling as he walked away, Yen couldn't erase the sharp stab of regret in his chest, knowing that after tomorrow Keryn would be gone from his life.

———

The next morning, Yen carried Keryn's bags as they approached the airlock. The *Cair Ilmun* had already been launched from the hangar bay and was now docked to the exterior of the *Revolution*, ready for its departure. Though the night before had been filled with a myriad of passionate emotions, the morning felt stale. The pair walked in silence with an air of professionalism floating nearly palpably between them. Keryn had changed out of her Fleet uniform, instead donning a pair of sturdy hide pants, a loose blue shirt, and a thin brown jacket. Jutting from beneath the coat as she moved, Yen could see the pistol strapped to her hip. Even simply dressed and with her hair halfheartedly pinned up, Yen found her increasingly irresistible. His heart pounded painfully in his chest as he watched her walk calmly toward their inevitable separation.

As they exited the last lift that would bring them to the airlock, Yen found himself among a small group of soldiers, dressed in attire similar to that of Keryn's. A few other members of the *Revolution* were present as though saying farewell to the departing crew, but there were significantly less present than what Yen would have assumed. Frowning, Yen realized why. Most had other pressing tasks to accomplish with the pending assault on Earth only a month away. To everyone else on board, Keryn's mission was insignificant. Yen had to concede that her mission was pretty insignificant to him as well. It was the fact that she was leading the mission that drew him inexorably to the airlock.

The rest of Keryn's crew met her with warm smiles and friendly waves. A large Oterian with a dangerous scar running the length of his face took Keryn's bags from Yen and disappeared through the hatch, loading the bags onto the *Cair Ilmun*. The other members of her team went back to the minimalistic farewells that they were sharing with loved ones and friends. Even those were brief and, slowly, one by one, her team loaded onto the ship, ready to depart.

From the far side of the vestibule, Penchant walked through the thinning crowd. Not surprising to Yen, there wasn't anyone around sharing their goodbyes with the aloof Lithid. Adam, noticing Penchant walking past, broke away from the woman with whom he was saying intimate farewells and approached the pair as well. Reaching out, the Pilgrim shook Yen's hand before giving Keryn a hug.

"You ready for this?" Adam asked Keryn, his excitement

undisguised.

"I don't think we really have much of a choice," Keryn said. Yen could detect a hint of nervousness behind her words.

"How about you, Yen?" Adam asked, turning toward the psychic. "You've got way more responsibility than we do. How are you holding up?"

"You know," Yen replied. "The entire fate of the Alliance military is resting on my shoulders. What's there to be nervous about? You know, I really wish I had all three of you coming with me."

"Adam might have served you well on Earth," Penchant replied in his gravelly voice, "but I was never cut out for large scale assaults. I am better suited for the espionage mission."

Adam shrugged. "I don't think Earth's sun would have complimented my complexion."

Keryn cracked a smile for the first time that morning. "Why don't you two go load up the last of our gear and I'll meet you on board. We have a lot of flying ahead of us, so the sooner we depart the sooner we'll get there."

"Take care, Yen," Adam said, shaking his hand before turning away. Penchant nodded, his featureless face betraying none of his emotions.

When they had both passed through the airlock and the crowds had thinned to only a few crewmen working around the area, Yen turned to Keryn. A storm of emotions brewed behind her violet eyes.

"It's not too late for you to stay with me," Yen offered. "We could always find an excuse why you couldn't lead the mission."

"It became too late after I agreed to lead this mission. Now that I have so many people relying on me, there's no way I could possibly let them all down. I have to go."

"I don't want you to leave me," Yen admitted.

Keryn sighed and looked away. "I told you once before that this wasn't about you and me. This has always been about the mission and what's best for the Alliance. It doesn't matter what we feel for each other."

"And how do we feel about each other? You know I love you, but every time I say it you find a way to avoid saying it back."

"Please don't," Keryn pleaded, shaking her head.

"I love you, Keryn. I've loved you for a long time now. I am willing to wait for you, no matter how long it takes us to be reunited. We were meant to be together. If you feel the same way, then there's no reason why you can't look me in the eyes and tell me that we'll be together again someday."

"I can't promise that, Yen," Keryn replied sternly. "We are both getting ready to depart on long, dangerous missions. Even if, by some fluke, we both manage to survive, we are still going to be apart for months, even as long as a year. Who knows what's going to happen to us in that time. Just in the few months that we've been together, I've changed drastically. Things… happened in my life that will forever change who I am. I don't know what else might happen while I'm away. By the time we meet again, I may not even be the same person you remembered and loved."

"Keryn…"

"Please, let me finish," she interrupted. "If we had met at another time, in a different place, things might have been different between us. You truly do make me happy, Yen, and there is a part of me that loves you. But fate is conspiring against us. I'm not happy about leaving you, but you have to understand something about me."

"I sacrificed everything I knew in order to join the Fleet.

My parents and friends threatened to disown me if I joined. But I joined anyway, against their wishes, because of a sense of duty and honor. I still keenly feel that loyalty to the Alliance. My feelings for you are secondary to my mission. I look in your eyes and I know you're trying to understand that, but I can also see that you don't. You're an idealist. To you, it's as simple as 'we want to be together, so we will'. I'm a realist. I know that there's only a slim chance of us ever seeing each other again. Because of that, I know it's best if we part today as friends and nothing more."

Yen shook his head. "As long as there's a chance that we'll be together again, I won't give up that hope."

Keryn smiled warmly, her eyes watering with gentle emotion. She reached up and placed a hand on his cheek. "You're a dreamer, Yen. It's one of the things that drew me to you. But every dreamer eventually has to wake up."

She leaned in and kissed him firmly on the mouth. Yen could taste the sweetness of her lips mixing with the saltiness of her tears. Slowly, she pulled away, wiping her eyes on the back of her sleeve.

"Goodbye, Yen," she said quietly before turning and disappearing through the airlock. The door slid closed, sealing only moments before he heard the hiss of the area beyond depressurizing. Moving a little further down the wall, Yen found one of the viewports, through which he watched the *Cair Ilmun* pull free of the vestibule and, with its engines burning brightly, begin flying away from the *Revolution*.

Yen continued to watch until long after the *Cair Ilmun* carried away the woman he loved.

CHAPTER 30

Keryn stood up from the pilot's chair and stretched as best she could in the low-ceilinged cockpit of the *Cair Ilmun*. Everything ached in her body and she knew that the one-piece flight suit she was wearing was far from clean. Reaching up in mid-stretch, Keryn brushed some of her oily silver hair out of her face. Sighing in defeat, she pulled an elastic band free from one of the front pockets of her coveralls and used it to hold her thin hair back into a ponytail. During the month since their departure from the *Revolution*, she had worn her hair pulled back so many times that it was starting to form a natural crease from the tight elastic band. At this point in their trip, she would have gladly killed someone for a comfortable bed and a long, hot shower.

Setting the autopilot, Keryn turned away from the controls and opened the door that led into the modified crew quarters of the *Cair* transport ship. The normal interior for a *Cair* ship had been a long, open bay lined with trooper seats on either side, while still leaving plenty of space for excess equipment in the middle of the compartment. The *Cair Ilmun*, thanks to the foresight of the High Council, had been modified to appear almost like a civilian transport.

She stepped through the doorway and entered a wide room filled with plush couches and reclining chairs. A series of tables were strewn about, most covered with consoles that would allow the team to play an assortment of games to pass the time. Even now, Keeling and Rombard were engaged in an intense game of *Jach'tar*. Similar to the three dimensional simulations that Keryn had gone through at the Fleet Academy, *Jach'tar* was an Avalon strategy game that pitted two opposing fleets against one another. The victor was decided by a series of rules determined at the beginning of play, many of which Keryn quickly forgot. After repeated losses at the game, she had forgone any further challenges from the team.

The Uligart and Oterian looked relaxed while they played, but Keryn could see the strain behind their eyes. She had seen the same strain on all of them. For a month, they had been traveling at faster than light speed. Though the *Cair Ilmun* had been retrofitted with inhibitors much like those found on a Cruiser, the inhibitors were still unable to compensate for all the excessive gravities that were created from such high speed travel. The crew was being exposed to nearly one and a half gravities, but it was punishment on bodies not used to the increased pressure on their systems. Only Penchant seemed unaffected, though Keryn wasn't sure how much of that was due to his physiology and how much was just because she had no idea on how to read his different moods. She had never realized how much she relied on facial expressions to betray attitudes until she befriended someone without a face.

On top of the increased gravity, the *Cair Ilmun* just didn't offer enough alternative escapes from one another. Though they all considered one another as friends, it was still difficult to be in such close confines with each other for such extended periods of time. Keryn found her escape in the cockpit, though even that was unnecessary. They were traveling between star systems, covering such an expansive area of open space that she could have left the pilot's controls unattended for over a week and still not feared running into something. Still, it was time away from people, and she was coming to cherish her quiet time more and more.

As Keryn walked past the common room and entered the narrow hallway, a pair of doors split off to either side. To her right, Keryn looked into the medical bay. Sterilized instruments and state of the art treatment supplies lined the mirrored metallic shelves around the room. The room's soft light left Keryn feeling relaxed as, she was sure, was the desired effect of the quiet room. The single bed in the center, however, was not unoccupied. Smiling gently to herself, Keryn stepped out of the doorway and let the door slide silently shut behind her. Of all of the crew, there were only two teammates who she swore would never tire of one another's company. McLaughlin and Cerise, the Pilgrim and Avalon husband and wife, had grown withdrawn during the trip, choosing to spend the majority of their time searching out the private corners of the ship; at least searching out the minimal privacy that could exist with five other teammates on board.

Turning toward the left door, which would lead to the crew quarters, Keryn smiled to herself. She had never been opposed to interspecies mating, but the sight of it had never been commonplace on her home world. Now, being exposed to it in such great quantities, she couldn't help but try to suppress a childish glee at accidentally interrupting them time and time again.

The door opened to the crew quarters, exposing the brightly lit room. A series of bunk beds were stacked along the walls, with a number of wall lockers strewn intermittently between them. Most of the beds were unmade, a reflection on the relaxed attitude her team had toward their former military

285

expectations. Within the Infantry or Fleet, beds were always made before first formation, often with folded creases along the edges so sharp that they appeared ironed in place. Keryn, however, treated her team differently. After dismissing their ranks in lieu of first names and the approval of civilian clothes, she also allowed everyone a level of home front comfort. Even on their lengthy, draining mission, it had helped to bolster the morale of her team.

Sitting on their individual bunks, Penchant and Adam had dismantled their rifles in order to clean the smaller internal components. Across Adam's bed, dozens of small mechanisms were spread, each lying in a meticulously ordered series. Keryn had no doubt that, should he be required, Adam would be able to reassemble his weapon blindfolded. Adam noticed her at the doorway as he paused with rag in hand.

"Are we close?" Adam asked with a hopeful smile.

Keryn nodded. "A few more hours and we'll be in the system. Thirty minutes after that we'll be burning through Pteraxis' atmosphere."

Without looking down, Adam's hands began picking up and reconnecting the pieces of his rifle. "Not that I haven't enjoyed your company, but I'm ready to get off this ship."

"You don't have to convince me of that," Keryn said with a laugh. Though there was a palpable nervousness in the air, she was amazed at their ability to seem so relaxed. None of the team seemed concerned that they were so close to their objective, which set Keryn's mind quite a bit at ease.

Adam locked the last two parts of his rifle into place and pulled the bolt to the rear. He let it slide forward with a click before setting the completed weapon down on his bed. "I could use a break, if you have some time."

"I could give you another flying lesson," Keryn offered.

"Please do," Penchant muttered from his bunk. "Adam has been complaining incessantly for the past few hours."

Adam turned slowly and stared at the Lithid. "You know, I can never really tell when you're joking."

Penchant shrugged. "Neither can I."

"Come on," Keryn said, laughing again. "The cockpit awaits."

Adam stood and walked toward the doorway. "Somehow, you make that sound dirty."

For his humor, Keryn caught Adam in a surprisingly quick punch to his stomach. He coughed and doubled over, but continued following her into the hallway. Rombard and Keeling barely acknowledged the pair as they walked past and entered the cramped cockpit. Keryn stepped to the side and let Adam slide past her to take his place in the pilot's seat. Comparatively, Adam seemed greatly out of his element as the pilot. His muscular shoulders spilled over the sides of the chair and his thick fingers seemed nearly too large for the delicate controls. Still, his hands worked both quickly and efficiently as he ran through a series of checks. Adam had been learning quickly during their trip, spending an hour or more every day in the cockpit learning to fly. Though Keryn wasn't eager to lose Adam as an infantryman, she couldn't deny that Adam would make a good pilot if he was ever required. When he was satisfied that everything was working, Adam reached over to deactivate the autopilot.

"Are you going to let me fire a few rounds today?" he asked as he took manual control of the *Cair Ilmun*.

"I haven't yet," she replied. "Why ruin a good thing now?"

Though the normal *Cair* transport carried heavy machine guns and a minimal compliment of plasma rockets, the weapon system on the *Cair Ilmun* had been upgraded during the modifications to the ship's interior. An upgraded targeting array had been programmed into the computer system and a *Duun* class compliment of plasma rockets had been attached under the wing. Their ammunition stores had also been greatly increased, turning the simple transport ship into a small warship. Though Keryn was sure that they wouldn't be required to fire any of the shipboard weapons during their capture of Cardax, she wasn't eager to let Adam begin wasting their offensive weapons on a curious whim.

"So where to?" Adam asked, obviously dejected over her rejection.

Keryn leaned forward, her lips hovering only a few inches away from his ear. She pointed out the front of the cockpit window toward a bright red star that glowed brighter than those around it. "That's Pteraxis' star. Just keep us on that heading. If you want, you can stay in the pilot's seat all the way until we reach the system's borders."

"What else can we expect in the system? How many planets? Is there an asteroid belt?"

Keryn smiled at her eternal warrior. She reached out and pushed a series of buttons on the console. The screen in front of Adam shifted to show a representation of the star system ahead. The red sun glowed in the center of the picture, hanging bloated and swollen. Around it, only two planets rotated in their slightly erratic orbit.

"The system looks sickly," Adam remarked. "I'm surprised it's only got two planets."

"You really don't read the mission briefs, do you?" Keryn asked, surprised. She slid over and sat down in the co–pilot's chair. "The sun is dying. Even swollen, it's not putting off much more heat than the sun of Arcendor. The problem is that as the sun began to swell, it swallowed the closer planets. Apparently

Pteraxis used to be a rather lush planet. But as it became the closest planet to the sun through attrition, the temperature on the planet heated up leaving a desert world. Give it a few more centuries and the planet won't be inhabitable, if it's even still there at all."

"Oh boy," Adam said flatly. "You really know how to sell a vacation spot, don't you?"

"This isn't a vacation for you?" Keryn teased. "You seem like the type that always carries a rifle when he goes on a trip."

"Funny you should say that," Adam replied, laughing at distant memories. "I usually do carry a weapon, but it always ends badly for me. I remember this one time Yen and I took a trip to Dunbar to meet an informant…"

Adam let the sentence die as he saw Keryn's expression drop at the mention of Yen's name.

"I'm sorry, Keryn. I didn't mean…"

"Don't worry about it," Keryn interrupted.

Adam looked out the window, ensuring they were still on course. "Do you still miss him?"

Keryn shrugged. "A little bit. I haven't really thought a lot about him recently."

"That's a little surprising. You two were damn near inseparable when we were on Farimas. The way you two were heading, I wouldn't have felt off base if I had put money on the two of you having a surprise wedding just before we stepped through the airlock."

"A wedding?" Keryn asked, surprised. "Me?"

"You two seemed pretty happy together," Adam explained.

"We were," Keryn said softly, her eyes slipping out of focus. Less than a second later, she shook her head and went back to running a diagnostic on the *Cair Ilmun*'s engine. "I wouldn't have done something that rash, though. If we had more time together, things might have been different. If we weren't at war… well, who knows what would have happened. As it was, though, we were moving in two different directions with our lives. The military isn't conducive to long–term relationships."

Adam spun his chair so he was facing Keryn from across the center console. "So it's over, just like that? That seems a little harsh, don't you think?"

"It's not harsh, it's realistic," she replied, turning to face him. "Do you know how long it's going to take for us to get back to the *Revolution*? Do you know if the *Revolution* is even going to make it through the Earth invasion? Do you know if we are going to make it through our own mission?" When Adam shook his head, Keryn continued. "That's exactly my point. The future is too uncertain to lock myself into only one plan for my future. I don't know what's going to happen in the future… or who I'm going to meet."

She left her comment hanging as she turned around and began working on the console again. Adam, to her relief, didn't reply, but instead continued piloting the *Cair Ilmun* toward Pteraxis.

After the silence had stretched for a while, Keryn politely cleared her throat and spoke. "So what happened on Dunbar?"

"Excuse me?" Adam said, snapping out of his own daydream.

"What happened after you two found your informant on Dunbar?"

Adam laughed heartily into the cramped cabin. "Well, our informant's name was Darran. You can imagine my surprise when Darran wound up being a woman. That took both Yen and me by surprise. To make matters worse, she wasn't just any woman. She was a surgically augmented Uligart woman. And I don't think I need to tell you which parts of her had been surgically augmented." Adam sighed, but smiled mischievously. "She had a phenomenal set of..."

"How about we skip that part," Keryn urged.

For hours, the pair sat in the cockpit, telling stories and laughing at one another's growing list of misfortunes. By the time the warning light began blinking, warning the pair that they had entered into the star system, Keryn felt incredibly relaxed, regardless of the pending threat on Pteraxis. Adam stood and moved out of the way, letting Keryn slip into the pilot's chair. Compared to Adam, she was dwarfed by the high-backed chair. Keryn angled the *Cair Ilmun* toward the closest planet to the sun, a dirty brown planet accentuated with only a few meager splotches of blue water.

"We'll be hitting the atmosphere in less than ten minutes," Keryn said, her mirth replaced by driven focus. "Go let the others know to get everything ready and get strapped in."

Keryn didn't look behind her as Adam left, letting the door slide closed behind him. A few minutes later, she slammed into the atmosphere of Pteraxis. Dipping the nose of the *Cair Ilmun* and raising the darkening heat shields around the windows of the cockpit, Keryn flew using only the console's display as they passed quickly through the upper atmosphere and into the hot air of the desert planet. Within moments, the violent shaking of the ship subsided and she lessened the angle of their decent, directing the ship toward the coordinates they had been given for the Terran rendezvous with Cardax. The red sunlight flooded into the cockpit when she lowered the heat shields. Keryn squinted, surprised at how intense the sunlight appeared from the ship. Checking the gauges, she quickly noted that the external temperature was nearly one hundred and thirty degrees. Frowning, Keryn accelerated, eager to reach the coordinates.

Keryn's flight through the atmosphere was indicative of her attitude toward this entire mission. She intended to make a quick entrance, take Cardax into custody whether willingly or by force, and leave Pteraxis as quickly as possible. If all went well, they'd be off the desert planet and on their way home within the hour.

CHAPTER 31

"We are approaching the launch coordinates," Captain Hodge called over the intercom from the bridge of the *Revolution*. "All crews report to battle positions."

Having been contacted ahead of time by the captain, Yen was in the hangar bay well in advance of his pilots and ground assault teams' arrival. As they filtered in, he directed the ground teams to their specific *Cair* ships. Within moments, the sounds of whining plasma engines filled the bay. The acrid fumes filled the expansive room, burning Yen's nostrils. Regardless, he held his position near the door, letting his presence as the squadron commander be felt as his nervous pilots entered the hangar.

As the crowd passed by, many pausing to shake Yen's hand, the psychic finally spotted the man he had been waiting for. Yen caught the eye of the Uligart pilot and motioned him over. Pushing his way through the crowd, an Uligart wearing his full flight suit arrived at Yen's location. Snapping to the position of attention, he reported to his commander.

"Warrant Pelasi, reporting for duty, sir," Pelasi said before Yen gestured for him to relax. The pilot seemed surprised when Yen extended his hand and he paused before shaking.

"You need to relax, Warrant," Yen ordered. "You're my

293

pilot now, which means you need to feel comfortable around me. We'll be spending too much time together for you to constantly be snapping to attention every time I enter the cockpit of the *Cair Thewlis*."

"Permission to speak freely, sir?" Warrant Pelasi asked.

"Go ahead."

The Uligart sighed and his shoulders dropped from their previously rigid position. "It's just going to take some getting used to, sir. My last squadron commander was very strict and expected unwavering customs and courtesies whenever any of us were in his presence. It's just a little different to be around someone telling me just the opposite."

"Well, you have a lot to learn about how much respect you actually have to show this guy," a female voice chided from behind Pelasi. From the taller figures, Iana forced her way through the crowd. She stopped before the pair before nodding toward Yen. "Good to see you, sir."

"Glad to see you made it," Yen responded.

"It wouldn't have been a party without me," Iana joked, nudging Pelasi with her elbow.

Yen smiled. "Are you ready for this, Iana?"

Iana shrugged. "Let's see. We're going to use pretty much untested warp technology to appear, hopefully, behind the Terran satellite defense grid. Then we're going to blow up whatever fleet they manage to muster in defense while the rest of our invasion ground forces land on the home world of the Alliance's most hated enemies. What's there to worry about?"

"You know," Pelasi croaked, "you have a pretty unique way of putting things in perspective."

"Don't you worry, Gregario," she laughed. "I'll keep the Terrans off you. All you have to do is land on the planet."

Yen put a hand on her shoulder and gave her an

affectionate squeeze. "I know you're not all that worried, Iana, but be careful out there."

"I'm always safe," Iana said with a wink. "Speaking of being careful, I figured I had better give you a warning. Buren's waiting for you. He looks ready for a fight."

Yen stood up straight, his eyes scanning the crowd for the Uligart infantryman. "Where is he?"

Iana jabbed a thumb over her shoulder. "Back there, standing outside your ship. He doesn't look all that happy about being here."

"Isn't Magistrate Buren one of the people on your team, sir?" Pelasi asked, looking perplexed.

Yen frowned. "Yes, he is, though not by choice."

"Is there something I need to know about the team on board?" the Uligart pilot asked quietly. "There's not going to be trouble, is there?"

"No," Yen replied, shaking his head. "Buren and I pulled a mission together a year ago. It didn't go well and quite a few good men lost their lives as a result. He was put in a hospital. I thought they would have kicked him out of the service, but instead they apparently promoted him. I don't know what his problem is, but he obviously doesn't like me. And now, because someone higher up doesn't like me either, he and I will be serving together."

"It..." Pelasi began before stopping in mid–sentence.

"What is it?" Yen asked.

"Nothing, sir."

Yen frowned again. "Warrant Pelasi, if you're going to be my pilot, you're going to have to feel comfortable speaking your mind."

Pelasi seemed nervous. "I mean no disrespect, but it wasn't your fault, was it? The people dying, I mean."

"There was only one group responsible for those men dying: Terrans. And I intend to exact my revenge during our mission." Yen sighed and nodded to both the pilots. "Well, I probably need to go see what he wants. Get to your ships. Once the captain gives us the all clear, I'll order the launch. And, good luck to both of you."

"You too," Iana said before hurrying to her *Duun* fighter.

Though Pelasi and Yen were both heading to the same *Cair* ship, Pelasi intentionally distanced himself from the commander and entered the ship well in advance of Yen. Buren, Yen noted, hardly acknowledged the pilot as he passed. The boney protrusions along his cheeks, jawline, and brow twitched with irritation and impatience as he watched Yen approach.

"You're nearly late," Buren growled, his arms crossed defensively across his chest.

"Then I guess it's a good thing that I'm important enough that they won't leave without me."

Buren's hand shot out, grabbing a firm hold on Yen's upper arm. Yen paused in his steps and looked down at the offensive hand. Deep within him, he could feel the anger taking form, siphoning off his psychic energy and growing with a life of his own. It had been a while since Yen had felt that hatred, the anger having been suppressed when he was around Keryn. It frightened him to know that it was returning.

"You might want to take your hand off me," Yen warned.

"Let's get something straight," Buren said, though he did release Yen's arm. "I don't like you."

"What did I ever do to you?"

"What did you do to me?" Buren asked in shock. "Do you know what happened to me after our mission? I got admitted to a psychiatric hospital. Apparently, someone told them I was

296

having trouble adapting to the stresses of war."

Yen frowned, knowing that his own testimony had been damning toward Buren's mental state.

"I rotted in an institute for months before they decided I was fit to be released. The entire time I was there, I was left alone. No roommate. No friends. Just me, in a room full of objects so childishly secure that I couldn't have given myself a paper cut. Do you know what people do when they spend months inside their own head? They relive the horrors that put them there in the first place."

Yen wanted to feel sorry for the Uligart, but had trouble battling through his own dislike for the self-depravation.

"I know where this is going," Yen seethed. "What happened wasn't my fault."

"It wasn't..." Buren began, before pausing in disbelief. "It wasn't your fault? I was stuck in that outpost with you, while those *things* tried to tear their way in and eat us. I heard your teammates talking. I heard your boss talking about the captain. It didn't take a genius to put it all together. Something your team did led to us being slaughtered like animals on that planet. And, as far as I can tell, you're the only member of your team left. So like it or not, *everything* is your fault!"

Yen was done with the conversation, knowing that anything he said would lead down a dangerous path. Infuriated, he pushed past Buren and toward the rear of the *Cair* ship.

"This time around, let's try something different," Buren said as Yen walked away. "I figure that so long as you're willing to take orders from me, we might just make it out of this alive. That would be a pleasant change for you, wouldn't it? Actually leaving with your team alive?"

Yen stopped without turning toward the Uligart, anger seething just below the surface of his skin. He could feel the psychic energy crawling along his nerves, setting fire to his joints and muscles. Biting the inside of his lip, Yen bit back his anger and tried to respond tactfully. "You know, I think you and the *Revolution*'s tactical officer would be fast friends. However, he's not here, nor was he selected to lead this assault. *I* was. And whether you like it or not, I *am* your boss now. Whether or not you like *me*, when we are in front of the soldiers you will act as though you have never had a better friend than me."

Yen turned to face Buren, his anger unmasked. "The first time I hear even the least little bit of dissent or insubordination, I'll push you out of the first airlock I can find." Yen let his eyes flash a dangerous blue as he continued. "Is there anything you didn't understand about that?"

Buren glared, but said nothing. Turning sharply, the Uligart walked on board the *Cair Thewlis*. Yen watched him disappear into the dimly lit gloom of the ship's interior, his mind awhirl with Buren's words. Though he would have never believed it, Buren must have overheard Yen and Vance talking about the disk. Suddenly, the survivor's guilt Buren felt made significantly more sense. But it also left Yen in a delicate position. If Buren told others what he knew, there would be an inquiry. It could ruin Yen's reputation and career. Darkness spread its fingers across Yen's mind, finding root in the darker recesses of his mind. Yen frowned and stared at the interior of the ship, into which Buren had disappeared. Someone needed to teach the Uligart an important lesson, Yen thought. Knowledge is power, but it can also be a very dangerous thing in the wrong hands.

Shaking away the darker thoughts, Yen stepped on board the *Cair Thewlis*, closing the ship's rear hatch as he did. His eyes quickly adjusted to the interior, which was lit by ambient red light being cast from the warning lights positioned throughout the crew compartment. All of his team sat in their seats, their bodies appearing bulky under the thick body armor they all wore. Large caliber rifles and explosives were strewn in the spaces between the seats. Scanning the crowd, Yen made sure to make eye contact with each member of his strike force, stopping finally when his eyes fell upon Buren. Even seated across the compartment from Yen, the psychic could feel the Uligart's piercing glare. Yen ignored him and addressed his team.

"This will be your final brief before we get the go ahead for launch," he yelled into the spacious ship. From over his right shoulder, a display lowered from the ceiling and began glowing. Slowly, a representation of Earth appeared on the screen.

"As you are all aware, our team has been tasked with an important mission. Once we have warped behind Earth's defenses, the rest of the *Cair* ships will be dropping their teams in surgical strikes throughout the planet. Our mission, however, is a search and capture. There is a Terran scientist of great importance that the High Council wants alive."

The screen behind him changed, zooming in on the eastern coast of one of the large continents. The screen continued to enlarge until the team could make out specific city blocks. "Our intel has provided us the location of the scientist's laboratory. It is located here, on the outskirts of a large open park in the middle of the Terran capital city."

"Sir," one of the team members asked from Yen's right.

"You have a question?" Yen asked.

"Sir, what do we know about this park?" the Wyndgaart soldier asked, pointing at the odd architecture present throughout the park. "One of those items in the park looks quite a bit like a missile silo."

Yen nodded. "I saw the same thing when it was briefed to me. I have been promised, however, that everything in this park is harmless. The square lake, the silo, the dome… they're all artifacts of a former Terran government that ruled the continent before the Senate was created."

Turning his attention away from the soldier, Yen addressed the rest of the team again. "Our approach will not be easy. We'll be relying heavily on the *Duun* fighters to eliminate most of the anti-aircraft weapons along the coastline. Once we get past their batteries, we'll set down here, a few blocks from the park. We can expect a resistance from the Terran home guard, but they shouldn't cause us too much trouble."

"Our job is straightforward. Capture the scientist and return him to the High Council. Everything else is secondary. While we are performing our mission, everyone else will be occupying the Terran ground forces in order to buy the couple of hours it will take for the rest of the Fleet to arrive. In less than forty-eight hours, Earth will be ours."

The soldiers erupted in cheers. Yen felt their elation, knowing that he could lead the assault that puts an end to the Terran war, once and for all. Yet, for all his joy, he found his gaze falling back on Buren, who glowered from his seat, not sharing in the cheering of the others. Walking up the aisle, Yen passed Buren and paused at the cockpit door before turning back toward his men.

"Leaders, perform a pre-combat check on your men's gear. We'll be launching in less than ten minutes."

Yen stepped into the cockpit and let the door slide closed behind him, cutting off the chatter that seeped from the crew compartment. Feeling weary, Yen collapsed into the co-pilot's chair and leaned his head back against the headrest.

"That was a pretty good speech," Pelasi mentioned as

he ignited the engines. The *Cair Thewlis* rolled from its berth in the hangar bay and took its place among the other ships, which filled the center of the cavernous room.

Without responding, Yen stared at the closed doors at the far end of the room, the ones that, when open, would launch his entire Squadron into space. A myriad of worries weighed heavily on Yen's mind. His concerns over the warp technology collided with his pining for Keryn, which quickly intermingled with his new worries over Buren and the knowledge he possessed. Yen wracked his brain, searching for a simple answer that would solve all his problems. His powers crawled through his skin, offering Yen the answer he needed, if only he had the strength of will to use them. Instead, Yen closed his eyes, squeezing them tightly together. He remained in that position until the radio crackled to life.

"Commander Xiao," Captain Hodge called. "You are a go for launch." She paused, as though pondering whether or not it would be appropriate to continue. In the end, she cast aside her doubts. "May the Gods watch over and protect you."

Yen flipped a switch, activating his Squadron communications channel. As the Commander for the entire group of invading *Duun* and *Cair* ships, Yen's transmission was carried over multiple Cruisers. "All ships, we are a go for launch. Proceed with caution to the coordinates. Never forget that we are now past the Demilitarized Zone and well into Terran space. Expect anything."

At the end of the room, the door cracked open, revealing a sea of stars beyond the open bay of the *Revolution*. One by one, the fighters first, the ships poured from the *Revolution* and all the nearby Cruisers. Yen looked cautiously left and right as the *Cair Thewlis* launched into space, half expecting a Terran ambush to be waiting around every corner. To his amazement, the space as far as their scanners could reach appeared empty.

The Alliance had selected this launch point for many reasons; not the least of which was that, at full acceleration, a Cruiser could reach Earth in just over twenty–four hours. Were it not for the distractions that pulled the Terran Fleet away from Earth, the Alliance Fleet would have never been able to approach so close without being engaged. As it was, the Alliance had a clear approach to the Terran's greatest stronghold.

The Squadron spread out, filling the nearby space with its small ships. They seemed insignificant against the dark velvet of deep space, but carried a massive arsenal capable of leveling the major cities throughout the Terran home world. In these small ships, death for the enemies of the Alliance sat in each of the pilot's seats.

Yen could feel sweat beading on his brow and he clenched and unclenched his fist. The next step in their battle plan was obvious, but scared Yen badly. Try as he might, Yen was unable to shake the mental images that he had seen in the mind of the warp technology scientist: twisted animals and dismembered bodies. That damnation was only a push of a button away for his Squadron. As much as they stood a chance at raining death down upon the Terrans, Yen stood an equal chance of sending all his men to their deaths.

"Squadron Commander," Captain Hodge called over the radio. "Is there a problem?"

Yen ignored her call and, instead, switched his channel back to the internal Squadron net. "All ships, activate your warp generators."

Across Yen's field of vision, hundreds of small, red wormholes appeared, hovering only a few dozen feet in front of each ship. Yen gripped his chair tightly as Pelasi activated the *Cair Thewlis'* warp generator. A soft hum rolled through the ship, quickly followed by a pulse of energy. The pulse washed over Yen, leaving his body feeling alternately numb and charged with energy. In front of the ship, a red wormhole exploded to life, the event horizon open angrily like the hungry maw of a giant monster.

Yen took a deep breath and activated the radio once more. "All ships, move forward and enter the wormholes."

CHAPTER 32

Keryn skimmed the *Cair Ilmun* over the surface of the desert planet, watching intently toward the distant horizon and the small outpost town that marked their final destination. Below the ship, the exhaust from the engine kicked fine dust into the air and swayed the thick, resilient shrubbery that grew on the inhospitable surface of Pteraxis. Everything, from the clay–like dirt to the fine sand to the scraggly weeds, was cast in light tones of red, a result of the swollen red sun hanging bloated in the sky.

Even on board the ship, Keryn could sense the sweltering heat outside. Mirages rose from the desert's surface. Wavering images of distant lakes flickered near the horizon, only to disappear in the hot, shifting winds. A few rocky plateaus jutted from the desert floor in the distance and it was near the base of one of these that Keryn was heading. The unnamed town where Cardax had taken refuge sat in the spanning shadows of one of these plateaus, stealing whatever reprieve was offered from the oppressive heat of the afternoon sun.

With the engines burning hot, Keryn quickly covered the distance to the plateaus. The face of the planet changed as she grew closer. Within the shadow of the plateau, she saw more green grasses and small trees surviving in spite of the external temperatures. Living off the meager morning dew, the sturdy plants gleamed like a green oasis amidst the scrub brush and dirt that covered the rest of the planet. Flying closer, Keryn could see the shadow of the plateau shrinking as the bloated sun rolled toward the far horizon. Still in the crux of the shadow, buried into the base of the plateau's cliff face, a small town of two story clay buildings appeared, their upper floors overburdened with wooden railings and balconies overlooking the streets below. The town stretched only a short way, consisting of fewer than fifty buildings and bearing only a pair of parallel roads leading lengthwise along the cliff. As Keryn scanned higher up the cliff face, she could see a switchback trail leading up toward the top of the plateau, though the trail was well concealed when viewed from a distance. Along its route, Keryn could see small cavern openings, which she could only assume were the entrances to mine shafts.

Her curiosity getting the better of her, Keryn tilted the wings of the *Cair Ilmun* as she approached the settlement. With the ship tilted perpendicular to the ground, the underside of the ship facing away from the cliff face, she had a much clearer view of the mines as she passed over the town. Even from her vantage point, Keryn could see the sparkle of mineral veins running along the cliff walls, often disappearing into the shaft entrances. A few dirt-stained faces peered outward from the dark recesses, drawn toward the light by the roar of her transport's engines. They stepped out onto the switchback trail and out onto the scaffolding that supported the cliff walls. The scaffolding clung to the walls overlooking the town in a patchwork of timber and rope along the cliff face.

Keryn leveled out the ship and passed a few hundred feet above the town. It looked depressingly unexciting, with few people walking outdoors in the afternoon heat. As the sun crested over the protective shadow of the plateau, outdoor temperatures began rising to over one hundred and twenty degrees. Looking down at the one–piece flight suit, Keryn was glad that she had brought more sensible clothing. The clothing would also help her blend into the surroundings and not appear quite so much like a Fleet officer, since somewhere in the quiet little desert town was an Oterian smuggler with a death wish.

Quickly passing over the far side of town, Keryn followed the curve of the plateau until she came upon an open field, cleared of any shrubbery or rock outcroppings. There, spread along the desert floor, were cargo and transport ships, parked in the sand like a forgotten salvage yard. Keryn could recognize many of the ships. Some were former Wyndgaart transports or Oterian carriers, ships so old that they predated the creation of the Alliance. Though old, these sturdy ships were still flight worthy and capable of interstellar travel. Though their origins were different, they all shared a common bond: they had all been converted into merchant vessels. Their interiors had been gutted and opened to allow maximum cargo on each lift. The ships' former lives had been forgotten; their transformations from warship to cargo vessel were completed at the whim of the ships' new captains. Each captain had his or her preference on the specific vessels, some choosing an intimidating bulk while others chose the sleek forms and faster ships.

As Keryn found her spot to land, she scanned the crews that mingled in and around the parked crafts. Some showed a genuine concern for the vessel as they applied new plating or sealants to the external hull. Others, she noted, seemed to be doing little more than showing the façade of busy work. These crewmen were little more than glorified guards, told to remain behind with the ship while the captains and rest of the crew enjoyed the entertainment the town had to offer. Still others forewent the illusion of tidying their respective ships and stood by the external hatches, armed and wearing sour expressions. Keryn frowned as the landing gear extended on the bottom of the *Cair Ilmun* and they touched down on the surface of Pteraxis. She had hoped that there would have been some blatant identifying mark on one of the ships that would show her which of these belonged to Cardax. As it was, she would already have to waste time with her team searching through the city for one elusive Oterian. Finding his ship would have saved time.

Mentally altering her plans, Keryn shut down the engine and unbuckled from the seatbelt webbing. She activated the radio and called back to the rest of the crew, who she assumed was already busy preparing for their assault.

"We've landed," she said flatly. "Meet me in the common room in five minutes for the mission brief."

Turning off the radio, she opened the door to the crew compartment and passed into the dark, cool interior of the ship. As she had suspected, Keeling and Rombard were still enthralled in their game of *Jach'tar*, though both had already changed into civilian clothes for the mission. Keeling sat at an odd angle, as the rifle strapped to the Uligart's leg made it awkward to sit normally. Tilted at an angle, Keryn noticed that he struggled with the controls of the game and was quickly losing to the more proficient and comfortably seated Oterian. Rombard held no illusions about stealthy operations, having his large automatic rifle resting against the wall beside him. Though Keryn was sure that the Oterian stood no chance of hiding such a large rifle underneath his jacket, she also doubted that he would even if it were possible. The Oterian thrived on striking fear into his enemies, and few things would do so as effectively as his oversized rifle.

Keryn passed the common room, turned into the hall, and entered the living quarters. The narrow room was packed as the rest of the team changed out of filthy jumpsuits and into more comfortable clothing. Though the *Cair Ilmun* had a shower, it did little to wash away the permeating stench of so many sweaty bodies confined to so small a space. Changing quickly into her loose blouse, leather pants, and thin jacket, Keryn slid the magazine out of her pistol and checked ammunition before reloading the weapon and holstering it at her hip. With her jacket pulled around her, the bulge of the pistol virtually disappeared. By the time she was finished changing, she was alone in the room. Following the rest of the team, she found them all seated comfortably and impatiently near Keeling and Rombard, who were at the tail end of their game.

"Follow me," Keryn said matter-of-factly as she turned and opened the side door. A blast of hot, dry air struck her face, making her feel as though she stood near the open door of an oven. She coughed against the scorching breeze before stepping out into the harsh red sunlight. The rest of the team stepped out behind her. Turning, she faced her teammates and took in the sight of the imposing group.

Dressed in civilian clothes and heavily armed, they looked much the part of smugglers finding refuge on Pteraxis' uninviting surface. Even Penchant wore an Uligart face and loose fitting clothing, looking no more conspicuous than the rest of the group.

"This planet sucks," Keeling said as he squinted. He raised his hand and blocked the sunlight so he could look at the desolate surroundings. With the red light pouring down on the planet, all the parked ships took on a coppery hue, looking rusted and ancient.

"Well," Keryn replied, "hopefully we won't be here long.

We have about a half-mile walk back to the town. Penchant and McLaughlin, I need you here guarding the ship. Aside from the fact that I don't want the *Cair Ilmun* stolen while we're away, every other ship around here seems to have armed guards milling about. I don't want to look out of place. The rest of you are with me."

Under the glaring sun, the half-mile walk to the city was nearly unbearable. Far past its zenith, the shadows had receded from the swollen sun and it cast its harsh light down on the small group as they walked. Sweat made Keryn's thin shirt cling to her back and sent chills up her spine whenever one of the breezes blew across the featureless desert. She could feel her face flushing with warmth as the sun beat down on skin that, even naturally tanned as she was, had not seen direct sunlight during the past few months of space travel. Though she reveled in the sunlight as she walked, she could also feel the pinpricks of pain behind her eyes as she squinted against the glare. Being on a planet was a satisfying change of pace, but she wasn't eager to remain. More than anything, she wanted to finish her mission and be on her way.

Keryn frowned as the town came into view. From the ground, the collection of buildings looked even more depressing than it had from the air. The balconies hanging off the second floors of the clay buildings looked weatherworn and old, barely able to sustain weight should someone be standing upon them. A fine layer of dirt and dust covered every visible surface, giving everything the impression of having thrust directly from the soil below. It also gave all the buildings the same coloration, adding to the monotonous drone of the town.

Following the main trail from the landing field to the town, they found themselves entering the community on the road furthest from the cliff face. A second road butted nearly against the cliff and cut the only other swath through the unexciting buildings. From her vantage point, Keryn could see the switchback trail as well as the scaffolding that both enabled them to move ore and supplies to and from the mine, but also held back loose rocks that might fall on the town below. Though it appeared crude, the scaffolding also appeared sturdy and effective.

Keryn raised her hand and called the group to a halt.

"This is where we're going to split up," she said. "The town isn't very large, so it shouldn't be too difficult to find a massive Oterian among the short buildings. However, I expect every one of you to keep your eyes open. We don't know how many friends Cardax has in town or how many people he has in his pocket. He's dangerous, so be careful."

Keryn pointed toward the scaffolding that hung precariously about thirty feet above the town. "Cerise, I want you to start up there. It should give you a good position to watch the rooftops and make aerial passes if we need your help."

Nodding, the Avalon walked off toward the start of the switchback, choosing to walk up the path to her position rather than draw attention to herself by flying. Keryn appreciated her discretion.

"Rombard," she continued, turning back toward the Oterian, "you and Keeling are going to take the left road near the cliff. With it being a secondary path through the town, I'm hoping that you'll be able to keep any ambushers away from us. Adam and I will head down the main trail and see what we can find out. If you spot him or if you run into any trouble, call us immediately. Understand?"

"Absolutely," Rombard grumbled, throwing his large rifle over his muscular shoulder. "Let's go, little man."

The Oterian pushed Keeling toward the leftmost road. The Uligart knocked the large hand aside playfully while flashing Rombard an obscene gesture.

Keryn smiled as she turned toward Adam. The Pilgrim looked calm and relaxed, though she knew he carried a large caliber rifle concealed beneath his jacket. Reaching under her own coat, she fingered the holstered pistol at her hip.

"You ready for this?" Adam asked, arching an eyebrow.

Keryn turned back toward the town and stared down the deserted road. Nodding, she turned back toward Adam. "No problem," she lied, feeling the nervousness of walking into what appeared to be a ghost town. "Don't worry about me. Worry about Cardax. I'll feel a lot happier and more relaxed once we have him safely aboard."

"Then shall we?"

Keryn turned once more toward the town. She could feel the knot in her stomach, churning nervously at the thought of walking, though fully armed, into a hostile mining community. Swallowing hard, her mouth suddenly feeling dry, she nodded to Adam.

"Let's go."

CHAPTER 33

Yen felt as though he were being turned inside out. His mind felt crushed against the back of his skull while, simultaneously, his entrails tried to escape through his stomach. Nausea washed over him as colors, some hallucinated but an equal number real, danced before his vision.

As soon as the *Cair Thewlis* passed through the event horizon of the wormhole, Yen's world ceased making sense. The artificial gravity went haywire, changing the direction of the gravitational pull every three feet throughout the ship. He could hear some of the members of the strike force yelling from the crew compartment as they found themselves seated directly in the middle of where the gravity changed directions. Pulled in opposite directions by equal gravitational forces, their bodies threatened to revolt and split in two.

In the cockpit, Yen felt disoriented. The view from outside the ship made Yen feel as though he were sliding down a drain. A surreal fluid seemed to course down the walls of the tunnel around the ship, driving the *Cair Thewlis* forward at increasing speeds. Beams of light erupted from around the ship, passing insubstantially through both the hull and through their bodies. Whenever the light struck, Yen felt his nerves set ablaze as though he had been shot. As quickly as it came, the pain faded away, leaving him gasping for breath.

"How much... longer," Yen asked Warrant Pelasi as he gasped for air.

Yen could see the strain on Pelasi's face. The controls constantly threatened to leap from the Uligart's hands as he struggled to maintain a clear path through the wormhole. His expression showed Yen all he needed to know. A gravitational field had shifted behind the pilot, driving him painfully back into his seat. Looking down, Pelasi read one of the dials in front of him.

"Just a..." Pelasi groaned against the pressure. "A couple more seconds."

Those seconds felt like an eternity. Finally, as the shifting pressure on Yen's mind threatened to drive him insane, he saw a blue and green light shining ahead in the tunnel. Unlike the searing light that passed through the hull, this light seemed fixed and pure, an ending to their painful journey. Gritting his teeth, Pelasi drove the ship forward until they were launched from the end of the wormhole.

Reality immediately reasserted itself through the *Cair Thewlis*. Yen could hear the crashing of boxes and supplies in the crew compartment as regular gravity was restored. The pressure they all felt during their warp was gone, though a painful headache remained. Yen sighed heavily and leaned back in his chair.

Beside him, Pelasi coughed loudly, the cough sounding dangerously wet, as though the Uligart was dislodging blood. As Yen tried to look over at the pilot, he was distracted by the view out the front of the cockpit. Filling the front view, a massive blue and green planet hung in space. White clouds swirled across its surface as Yen watched, carried further around its equator by unseen winds. After the chaos of their warp, staring at Earth seemed serene. Shaking his head to wipe away any thoughts of tranquility, Yen glanced left and right. The *Cair Thewlis* hung in space between Earth and a series of massive satellites, which formed a comprehensive grid around the planet. Each nearly the size of a *Duun* fighter, the satellites hung quiet and deadly in space.

All around them, other Alliance ships were dropping out of warp. Many, like the *Cair Thewlis*, hovered at their exit point for moments afterward while the disorientation faded away. Not all ships appeared so lucky. From all around him, wormholes opened and dislodged metallic and organic debris. Ships turned inside out by the dangerous warp were spewed forth, cluttering the space around Earth with twisted metal and the bodies of Yen's fellow soldiers. Out of the corner of his eye, Yen saw an intense yellow glow light up the dark space around him. Yen turned and saw one of the satellites changing its trajectory and powering up. At the tip of its antenna array, a brilliant yellow glow began to build as the stored solar cells released all their energy into the weapon. Beyond the satellite, an unfortunate *Cair* ship had dropped out of warp on the far side of the satellite grid. Now targeted by the Empire's defensive network, there was little Yen or anyone could do but watch as it fired. A giant beam of yellow light leapt from the end of the satellite. The beam struck the side of the *Cair* ship, searing a hole directly through the hull. The satellite turned as it continued to fire, melting through the ship as it angled toward the cockpit. Soon, the entire ship was engulfed in solar flames as the few remaining pieces of debris floated further out into space. With the target destroyed, the satellite powered down before resuming its previous position.

Anger welled in Yen's chest as he watched so many Alliance soldiers and crewmen dying without ever having the opportunity to engage the enemy. To die in combat was to be expected, but to die just in transport to Earth was an embarrassment for the entire Alliance. Frowning, Yen remembered the scientist performing the warp presentation. Seeing what was happening to a full quarter of the Alliance invasion fleet, Yen realize the scientist had been right to be afraid of the possible results. More importantly, the scientist should be afraid of what Yen would do to him for this if he ever saw him again.

"Commander Xiao," a female voice called over the radio, "this is Alpha Leader."

Yen smiled at hearing Iana's voice. "Alpha Leader, this is Commander Xiao. I'm damn glad to hear you're still alive."

There was a pause before Iana replied. "I am, sir, but many of my pilots are not. I lost nearly a third of the *Duun* fighters during the warp. I have at least a dozen others with minor hull breaches from where bulkheads tore loose during the trip. They'll still be able to fight, but they won't be able to make any long flights in the near future. I don't think the smaller fighters were made to withstand that sort of a journey."

"Get your fighters together and provide what defense you can," Yen ordered. "We've caught the Terrans by surprise right now, but it won't be long until they start sending up their own fighters to meet us."

Yen waited until the *Duun* fighters began moving into protective positions around the *Cair* ships before he switched to the Squadron-wide channel. "All ships, this is Commander Xiao. *Duun* fighters will provide cover fire while the *Cair* ships move toward their pre-designated satellites. Eliminate your satellites quickly, and then begin your descent to the planet's surface."

The ships all split in different directions as the *Cair* ships, laden with plasma rockets, moved to destroy the integral satellites that interlocked the entire grid. If everyone were successful, destroying only a few satellites would disable the entire network, allowing the remainder of the Alliance Fleet to fly directly into orbit around Earth before starting the final invasion.

Warrant Pelasi turned the *Cair Thewlis* and accelerated toward a more distant satellite. According to the High Council's projections, the satellite they were ordered to destroy would be in orbit directly above the Empire's capital city. Once their satellite was destroyed, they would have only a short flight down to the planet's surface in order to apprehend the Terran scientist, Doctor Solomon.

Behind the *Cair Thewlis*, four *Duun* fighters fell into line, offering a more thorough protection for the strike force than they were for the rest of the *Cair* ships. Looking ahead, Yen could make out the targeted satellite, looking inconspicuous amongst all its brethren. Written across its side, as had been written along the sides of all the satellites, was the words Strategic Interlocking Nodule. There was nothing remarkable about the satellite, though Yen knew it held one of the relay stations within its computer that interconnected the rest of the grid for this section. Without this single satellite, a small portion of the network would be inoperable. Coupled with the rest of the targeted satellites, Earth would soon be unprotected from an invasion force the likes of which they had never seen.

As they grew closer to the satellite, his radio suddenly crackled to life.

"Here they come!" Iana cried out in warning.

Looking at the radar, Yen knew why she sounded concerned. The entire space around the planet was suddenly filled with small red dots, far more than they had expected as a defensive fleet around Earth. Nearly standing, Yen pressed his face against the window, trying to get a better view of the approaching ships. As they came into view, they were nothing like Yen expected. Anticipating an invasion, the Terrans had outfitted nearly every available ship on Earth with improvised armor and weapons. Many of the ships flying toward the Alliance strike force were little more than cargo vessels carrying bulky, outdated weaponry. Darting quickly between the hulking brutish ships, however, were smaller Terran fighters, the types that Yen had faced before. The Terran fighters were heavily armed and armored, and would pose a significant threat to the Fleet if not eliminated early.

"Keep them busy, Alpha Leader," Yen ordered. He switched over to the Squadron net as he continued. "All fighters, target the Terran fighters first. Keep them off the *Cair* ships until we can finish our mission!"

Switching off the radio, he turned toward Pelasi. "Get us in range as fast as you can."

Even with the inhibitors, Yen could feel the strain as the *Cair Thewlis* accelerated quickly, trying to put a distance between the Terran defensive fleet and themselves. Even accelerating, Yen could see a number of red dots breaking away in quick pursuit. Suddenly, the *Cair Thewlis* jerked as it was struck repeatedly by weapons fire.

Yen growled in anger. "What's our status?"

Pelasi checked the gauges. "No serious damage, sir. I don't think they were Terran fighters. It looks like they're firing older weapons that are having trouble puncturing our hull."

"I don't care what they're firing," Yen snarled. "Give them enough time and they'll find a way to blow us up." Angrily, he turned back on the radio. "Alpha Leader, where the hell is my cover fire?"

"I'm on my way, sir," Iana called back, the frustration

317

evident in her voice. On the radar, a blue dot broke away from the pack and hurtled toward the pursuing Terran ships. Though the *Cair Thewlis* continued to shake from weapons fire, Yen saw the missile launched from Iana's ship. Immediately, two of the red dots disappeared from radar. The gunfire eased as the *Cair Thewlis* closed the rest of the distance toward the satellite.

"Are we within range?" Yen asked to Pelasi.

The Uligart pilot checked his console before nodding.

"Then blow that bastard out of the sky."

Two plasma missiles leapt from the rocket tubes underneath each of the ship's wings. Streaking forward, thick smoke trailed behind them as the two missiles locked onto their target. The *Cair Thewlis* turned aside before the rockets found their mark, exploding violently in a spray of blue and purple plasma. The explosion tore through the outer plating on the satellite, showering the delicate inner wiring and computer processors with superheated flames. As though erupting from within, the satellite rocked from a series of explosions as the plates buckled and the nodule tore itself apart.

"Alpha Leader," Yen called over the radio. "Our mission is complete and we are heading for the surface. Think you can make a hole for us?"

"I think we might be able to manage that," Iana called back.

Three of the four *Duun* fighters dropped into a wedge formation in front of the *Cair Thewlis*, which turned and began diving for the planet. The Terran defenders bunched their ships in front of the four Alliance attackers, firing their meager weapons in hope of deflecting the diving ships. The outdated weapons of the Empire's modified transports had little effect on the Alliance fighters, which shattered through the defensive wall in a violent explosion of plasma and machine gun fire. The broken Terran ships fell away, opening a gap through which the *Cair Thewlis* passed on its way to Earth.

"We'll mop up the rest of these," Iana called, "and then join you on the surface. Be careful until then."

Yen didn't bother to respond. Instead, he turned toward Pelasi. "Take us into the atmosphere."

CHAPTER 34

Though the streets of the mining town on Pteraxis were empty, Keryn could feel the prying eyes of people watching her from the shuttered windows and storefronts as she and Adam entered the town. It was unnerving to feel so exposed. On the periphery of her senses, she could almost make out the inane gossip of their presence in town being spread from building to building. Their chatter was like that of mice, burrowing through a wall; scratching just beyond the realm of hearing.

"Where is everyone?" she muttered, as much to herself as to the Pilgrim who walked at her side.

Adam ran a sleeve across his brow, wiping away the dripping sweat. Even in the dry air, the warm breeze leeched the moisture out of his skin. Keryn suffered much the same, a sheen of sweat glistening across her tan skin and matting her silver hair, though she suffered in silence.

"If they were smart," Adam replied, "they'd be hiding inside, out of this heat. I've been outside for less than half an hour and I'm already sweating like a fat kid."

Keryn smiled, despite the situation. "Maybe we should follow their example. Do you see any buildings that look open for business?"

Adam shook his head. Since they'd entered the town,

they'd passed a number of signs advertising general stores and different forms of entertainment, yet no signs hung claiming that the stores were open. The doors on the fronts of the stores were closed tightly, as were the shutters. Though Keryn preferred to believe that they were closed due to the heat, that the residents of the town took a form of rest during the warmest parts of the day, she couldn't shake the feeling that they were just as much closed because of their presence. They had passed so many guards near the ships who stood openly in the heat to believe that everyone on Pteraxis took a break as soon as the sun began to set and crested over the protective shading of the plateau.

Involuntarily, Keryn's hand drifted under her coat to the pistol concealed beneath. Her nerves were on edge, both from the long flight and now from the suspicious reception on the planet. Like entering a den of predators, she felt like a prey set on the wrong path by the High Council.

"I want to get off the street," she said, her voice pleading as much as it was ordering. Luckily, Adam seemed eager to agree.

"There's got to be something open around here." He pointed to the nearest storefront. A faded wooden sign hung above the door, shaded by the awning that overlooked the street from the second floor. Though worn from wind and sand, the hand painted sign still clearly read *Yuchurio's Imports*. Watching the street as they walked, both turned sharply and headed toward the store.

Stepping onto the porch, Keryn kicked her boots against the wooden support beams, knocking off some of the clinging dust in a thick cloud. She could taste the dust from the back of her throat entering her nostrils, as though she was trying to breathe through a thin film of mud. Though she wanted to choke and spit the taste from the back of her throat, she refrained.

Adam raised his large hand and pounded loudly on the door. "Hello?" he called as he knocked again. "Is there anyone home?"

To their surprise, the door creaked open. The glint of metal chain told Keryn that the door wouldn't open much wider, it being held closed by a chain lock. From within the gloom, silhouetted by a much dimmer light pouring out of the building as compared to the bright red sun, a wind–worn face peered out.

"What can I do for you strangers?" a low voice asked the pair.

"We were wondering if you were open for business," Keryn said, her response not entirely a lie.

"No, I'm not," the Uligart store owner replied, his head moving back and forth as he took in the sight of the unusual pair. "We're closed down early today for... extenuating circumstances. Nor are you likely to find another store open around here."

Keryn frowned, the Uligart's words confirming her suspicions. The townsfolk, whether they knew Cardax or not, knew trouble was inevitable when they spotted Keryn and her team. As was often the case, the town went into hiding, hoping just to survive the pending storm.

"Listen," Adam interjected. "We're not here to cause trouble. All we want is to get out of this sun and ask you a few questions."

"You just want to ask a few questions?" the store owner asked suspiciously. "I've heard those words spoken before, every time a lawman comes to Pteraxis. Neither of you look much like the law, but you hardly look like merchants either."

"We're not the law, I promise," Keryn said. "Please, we just want to come inside for a second. We have money to make it worth your while."

The Uligart paused before nodding. "Show me."

Adam fumbled under his coat for the bills that they had been given before departing. The store owner hissed slightly as the red sun glinted off the metal barrel of Adam's rifle, which was exposed as he moved aside his long jacket.

"We're not here to cause you trouble," Adam reiterated, holding up a wad of money for the Uligart to see. "We just want some information."

Hesitating a moment longer, the store owner closed the door. From behind the thick wood, Keryn could hear a chain being moved aside. As quickly as it had closed, the Uligart opened the door once more and invited them both in. As Adam stepped into the blessedly cool interior of the store, Keryn keyed the throat microphone.

"Talon One, this is Talon Six."

"This is Talon One," Rombard called back, his thick voice rumbling even more in her earpiece than what it does in person. "Go ahead."

"We're heading inside a store to get some information. Keep your eyes peeled for Cardax but be careful. I think he already knows we're here."

"Roger that."

Taking one last glance up and down the main road, Keryn stepped into the darkness and let the Uligart close the door behind her.

Keryn's words were unnecessary as far as Rombard was concerned. He and Keeling had felt the same unease that she and Adam experienced as they walked down the parallel road. The Oterian could see his Uligart partner fidgeting, his eyes darting from side to side. Though Rombard's weapon was clearly visible, he was sure that Keeling would be the first to draw his pistols and fire should they run into trouble.

"Settle down, Keeling," Rombard grumbled, looking down on the significantly shorter man. "You're making me uneasy."

"I don't think it's me," Keeling quickly answered. "It's this damn town. It's this damn heat. It's… well, it's something I can't quite figure out."

Rombard nodded. His thick fur was soaked with sweat from the heat and each breath huffed loudly through his flared nostrils.

"It's like the town is alive," the Uligart continued. "The whole place is one living, breathing organism. And we're its prey, being led right into its maw before large teeth rise up from the sand and rock to close in around us."

"I don't think I'm going to let you read any more mission reports from the edges of known space," Rombard joked. "They're piquing your imagination a little too much."

Keeling stopped walking and turned to the Oterian, though he only came up to Rombard's muscular chest. "Laugh all you want to, but you feel it too. I know you do."

Rombard nodded. "I do. There is something wrong here."

Reaching under the thick fur of his neck, Rombard activated his microphone. "Talon Three, this is Talon One."

Cerise responded almost immediately, though her voice carried a musical discord of impatience. "Go ahead."

"Do you see anything from up there?"

Cerise peered over the lip of the wooden scaffolding on which she was lying. From her vantage point, she could look down on most of the town and, if need be, fly to either teams aid. She had been watching the town since both groups entered, but had yet to see any movement on the streets or roofs.

"Negative," she answered. "All is quiet."

"And that doesn't strike you as strange?" Rombard responded.

"No stranger than any of you."

"Keep your eyes open," the Oterian said. "Let me know the second you see something."

Frustrated, both with the situation and the Avalon, Rombard turned off his microphone. He turned to speak with Keeling, but saw the Uligart standing in a guarded stance. Following his gaze, Rombard looked into one of the heavily shadowed alleys that separated the dirty clay buildings. He saw nothing moving.

"What is it?"

Keeling shook his head slightly, his eyes never leaving the alley. "I saw something in the alley. Something big."

Rombard strained again to see anything in the alleyway. "I don't see..."

He was interrupted by a loud crack, like wood splintering or a box being torn open. The sound, he was certain, came from the alley.

The pair looked at one another.

"Shall we check it out?" Keeling asked, nervously.

Rombard nodded. "Let's go."

The store was blissfully cool, but it took some time for Keryn's eyes to fully adjust to the dimmer light. Blue lights danced in her eyes; artifacts from too much time outside under the imposing, setting sun. As her vision cleared, she took a look around the cluttered store. A multitude of items sat on shelves and on tables placed chaotically around the room. Many items she recognized, having seen similar craftsmanship in the stores in Farimas Space Station. Other items were foreign to her. Her fingers slid across a number of items as she walked around the room, her eyes moving to take in all the oddities within the store.

"We're a border planet," the store owner explained as Keryn looked at a strange electronic scanner. "We get traders in from both the Alliance side and the Empire side. You're looking at some of the very best in Terran biological research equipment."

Keryn dropped the scanner as though it had suddenly become hot, or that it suddenly carried an unseen contagion. She could hear the Uligart hiss in displeasure behind her as the object clattered loudly onto the wooden table.

"You said you came for information only," the store owner said impatiently. "So how about you leave my wares alone and ask your questions. I'd like to get this done quickly so that you can leave me in peace."

Though her back was too him, Keryn still frowned in displeasure. Something had the Uligart on edge. Whatever it was, she intended to get the information from the store owner, one way or another. Luckily for her, Adam's cooler head continued to intercede before she had the opportunity to play the damning inquisitor.

"Have you seen anyone unusual here in town?" Adam asked, leaning heavily on the wooden table behind which the Uligart stood.

"Everyone here in town is unusual," the store owner answered, while avoiding the question at hand.

"That's not what I meant, and you know it," Adam said,

his voice taking on a threatening edge.

"Then perhaps you should have started by asking the question you actually wanted answered," the store owner taunted.

Keryn snarled as she turned, drawing her pistol in one smooth motion. Pulling back the hammer on the pistol, she pointed it directly at the Uligart's face. "I don't have time for your games. We're here looking for an Oterian named Cardax. Do you know where he is or don't you?"

The Uligart's posture never changed; he still stood defiantly with his arms crossing his chest and an eyebrow raised in defiance. "First of all, girl, let me tell you that this is not the first time I've had a pistol pointed at my face, nor will it be the last. Do us all a favor and put that toy away." His cold eyes stared straight through her as he spoke. In the silence that ensued, Keryn realized that the Uligart had been serious. Realizing the pistol had little effect, she holstered her pistol under her jacket.

"Secondly," the store owner continued as soon as the pistol was away, "let me offer you a word of warning. You don't know what you're getting yourself into. You go around town, waving your guns like you have some authority here. But you don't. No one has authority in this town except for the miners and the people that work here. And we take care of our own. This Cardax you're looking for, he comes here often. He brings good money into town. If you go around thinking you can strong arm him into coming with you, you're going to be sadly, sadly mistaken. Do us all a favor and turn around. Take your friends, get back on your ship, and fly home. Leave Pteraxis and never think of it again."

"Sorry," Keryn snarled, "but I don't take advice from cowards who hide behind closed doors every time a stranger walks into town. If Cardax is here, we're going to find him, and the Gods can damn any man who stands in our way."

As they stared at one another, Keryn's transmitter in her ear crackled to life. "Talon Six, this is Talon One. We've spotted the target. He's moving through an alleyway, heading your direction."

Keryn keyed her microphone. "Talon Three, can you confirm?"

"Roger," Cerise replied. "Talon One is in pursuit."

"Any other movement?" Keryn asked, her eyes never leaving the Uligart.

"Negative, it is still a ghost town."

"Roger that. Talon One, stay in pursuit. We'll corner the target in the middle of the street, where he has the least chance of running."

Keryn turned off her microphone and sneered at the Uligart. "I guess we won't need your services after all. And you can take all your advice and shove it!"

Turning away, Keryn opened the front door to the store and she and Adam stepped out into the glaring Pteraxis sun.

CHAPTER 35

The *Cair Thewlis* fell through the sky like a comet, hurtling toward Earth's surface. Their escape from the Terran defensive fleet had bought them enough time to enter the atmosphere over one of the planet's many oceans.

Yen careened his head in an attempt to look at the world below as Pelasi angled the ship in a steep dive, but the world below was obscured. The innocuous clouds that Yen had seen from orbit had turned dark before his eyes. They boiled with an inner anger, punctuated by sharp flashes of lightning arcing from one swollen cloud to another. Thunder crashed loudly, jarring the ship as they grew closer to the storm clouds. Yen frowned at the sight. Earth was gone, replaced by a swirling mass of black clouds which roared out in challenge, daring the *Cair Thewlis* to pass into their bellies. The landing on Earth would be difficult with nature herself seeming to rise up in protest to the Alliance invasion.

Their ship seemed infinitesimally small as it was swallowed by the storm. Slipping beneath the clouds' surface, Yen could hear the gentle patter of rain start almost immediately, though it was hard to see anything beyond the windows of the ship. Droplets of water pelted the window before rolling toward the rear of the descending transport. The deeper they flew toward the heart of Earth, the denser the rain became until it was pouring in sheets that coated the front viewports.

Yen tried to block out the storm brewing outside the ship and, instead, focused on the storm brewing within him. The storm clouds were indicative of their entire mission. Innocent mechanisms, like the warp technology, became deathtraps when placed in the hands of the Alliance. Yen had lost so much during the conflicts, beginning with his time in covert operations and continuing as he took his position aboard the *Revolution*. It seemed that every fiber of the universe itself rallied against him and now that he had finally reached Earth, even the planet itself staged a violent protest. Sneering at the dark clouds around him, Yen knew that the planet would have to rupture and vaporize him where he sat before he would stop. He had the opportunity to lead the Alliance to the greatest victory ever recorded. More importantly, Yen was quickly becoming the figurehead who would be ushering in a new era of peace. Soon, Yen would be king among the Alliance. No, he corrected himself, he would be a God!

A brilliant flash of lightning wrenched Yen from his musings. He blinked away the spots of light that danced in his vision. The lightning strike had passed dangerously close to the ship and Yen was suddenly reminded of how much the *Cair Thewlis* was acting like a giant lightning rod, passing through the heart of a storm.

"Is that lightning going to be a problem?" Yen asked as he turned toward Warrant Pelasi.

The Uligart looked strained. His eyes darted back and forth between the controls and the radar, since Pelasi was flying completely on sensors as they passed through the blinding storm. "Gods, I hope not," he whispered.

"Anything I can do?"

Pelasi shook his head. "Not unless you can part the

clouds and give me a tunnel to fly through. We're pretty much running blind right now. I've got some sensor telemetry, but the ionized air is bouncing back a lot of false signals. I can't tell if we're one mile or a hundred above the surface. I'm just hoping I can figure it out before we hit the water."

Yen shivered at the thought of crashing into one of Earth's oceans. As much as he felt helpless, Pelasi had touched on something that Yen might just be able to help with. Yen shrugged and turned to his Uligart pilot. "I can't help with the sensors, but I might be able to do something about the weather."

Yen closed his eyes and began to concentrate. The air around him shimmered, causing the walls of the cockpit to appear as though they were malleable; the walls danced in the flickering mirage. Blue light emanated from his body and suffused the dancing waves of psychic energy. Ahead of the *Cair Thewlis*, the dark clouds ignited in blue flame, the wisps of the clouds burning away like fuses leading to a powder keg. The entire storm cloud began to unravel faster and faster until, through the darkness, they could see the dark, rolling ocean below.

Dropping below the bottom ceiling of the clouds, the *Cair Thewlis* was engulfed in a torrential downpour. Sheets of heavy rain washed over the ship as it began leveling out just above the churning ocean waves. Swollen by the sudden storm, the ocean swells grazed the bottom of the transport as it flew above the frothing waters. White crests sprayed the hull before dissolving into steam on the surface of the ship still heated from its entry through the atmosphere.

Once the ship was running parallel to the ocean surface and well on its way toward the Terran mainland, Pelasi pressed on the throttle. Plasma infused flames leapt from the back of the ship's engine, cutting a channel through the waves behind it as the superheated exhaust evaporated the ocean swells. Sea mists erupted from around the *Cair Thewlis* as it hurtled toward the shore.

Satisfied that Pelasi could handle the approach, Yen unbuckled from the copilot's chair and opened the hatch leading into the crew compartment. Throughout the compartment, boxes that had become unhooked during the warp were strewn around the open area between the seated team. Though knocked around, the team still seemed in high spirits, something Yen hoped they maintained as they finally touched down on Earth.

"Alright, gentlemen," Yen began as the stern faces turned toward him. "We're through the worst of it and are on our way to the capital. We're estimating a short five to ten minute flight until we reach the near shore and only a couple more minutes until we touch down on ground. Make sure you have everything you're going to need for this mission on hand. Once we touch down, we're going to hit the ground running. There won't be any time to sort through your gear when bullets are flying over your head."

Yen took a step into the room and reached up, using an overhead metal beam for support. "Get your heads on straight. Those of you who are too distracted or afraid probably won't be coming back alive. That's not cruel, that's honest."

Yen paused and caught Buren's angry look from the corner of his eye. Though he didn't justify his anger by even sparing the Uligart a glance in his direction, Yen felt infuriated that Buren would still judge him for what happened with the Seques. In the near future, he and Buren would have to reevaluate their relationship.

"Check your weapons and ammo. Cross–level if you're

short on any supplies. We'll be reaching their radar range…"

Before Yen could finish his sentence, a roaring explosion rocked the *Cair Thewlis*. Yen was tossed from his feet, his hand slipping from the metal bar he was using for support. Collapsing to the ground, Yen wound up unceremoniously intermingled amidst a pile of assault packs. Growling, he tossed the bags aside and climbed to his feet. No sooner had he spun on the doorway leading to the cockpit than a second explosion rocked the ship, dropping him back down into the packs.

Staggering forward, using the walls for support, Yen opened the door and stepped into the forward cabin. With the open viewports, he could now hear even more distant explosions, as though the entire stormy sky was filled with exploding ordinance.

"What the hell is going on?" Yen yelled, as he slid into the copilot's chair.

Warrant Pelasi's arms were taunt as he struggled to maintain control of the ship. "I don't know, sir. They just started opening up on us!"

Yen grimaced as the ship was rocked by another explosion. The right side of the window was filled with angry red flames as the round exploded nearby. As far as he could tell, though, the ship had yet to sustain any serious damage.

"Who?"

"Coastal guns, maybe?" Pelasi said, unsure. "They're packing some pretty serious explosives, whoever they are."

The force from another explosion drove the *Cair Thewlis* downward in a rapid descent. Yen could feel his last meal creeping higher into his throat and he suddenly felt very nauseas. As Yen braced himself against the forward console, Pelasi managed to regain control and pull the ship skyward moments before they would have crashed into the churning ocean below.

"Are you intentionally flying into every round they fire at us?" Yen yelled angrily, his heightened emotions overwhelming his sense of queasiness.

"Not intentionally, sir," Pelasi retorted.

"Then do you think it's even remotely possible for you to avoid one of the explosions?"

"I'm trying!" the Uligart yelled back. "If you're so concerned, you might call one of the other pilots and get some *Duun* support down here. You have them blast those guns to hell and maybe they won't do the same to us!"

Yen frowned at his pilot, knowing that though he was frustrated with Pelasi, the Uligart was also correct. Reaching to his throat, Yen activated the Squadron channel.

"Alpha Leader, this is Commander Xiao. If you're not too busy up there, we could really use some of that air superiority we've heard so much about!"

Iana's voice called back over the radio, though the background noise was filled with the sound of alerts and sirens sounding from within her cockpit. "This is Alpha Leader. No, sir, of course we have nothing important going on up here. Just relaxing and having the time of our lives. Hell, when you boys get done down there, feel free to come join us. We're getting ready to fire up the blender and make some cocktails."

"Can the chatter, Alpha Leader, and get me some air support!"

"Roger, sir," Iana called back. "I'm breaking away two *Duun* fighters to your position now."

Yen closed the channel and turned back to his pilot. "Buy us time. Dodge, weave, do whatever you have to do. Just keep us in the air long enough for the *Duun* pilots to get here."

Warrant Pelasi turned on the internal ship's

communications. "Everyone hold tight. This is about to be a bumpy ride."

The *Cair Thewlis* dropped nearly to the ocean's surface before climbing steeply toward the overhead cloud cover. Pelasi continued a random flight pattern as they moved ever forward toward the Earth shoreline. He rain began to lessen as they grew closer to the shore. In the far distance, Yen could see the faint silhouette of mighty skyscrapers, the tops of which were lost in the clouds above. Closer, however, the flash of fire alerted him that while the lightening rain allowed him to see the shore, it also allowed the large caliber coastal guns to see him as well.

"Incoming!" he yelled before another barrage of explosions rocked the ship. Gritting his teeth, Yen hoped that the *Duun* ships would reach them before they were blown out of the sky.

In response to his prayers, two small ships streaked overhead, rocketing toward the coast. The small *Duun* fighters were nearly impossible to track by the massive guns that jutted out over the water. Firing in a defensive pattern, the coastal guns tried to keep the two darting fighters at bay, but to no avail. From the cockpit of the *Cair Thewlis*, Yen watched as smoky trails leapt from the missile racks under the wings of the *Duun* fighters. The plasma rockets streaked toward the shore, the missiles separating until they were each targeted on one of the large caliber cannons. The guns continued to fire, but Yen knew that their fate was sealed as soon as the missiles were launched. Onboard the missiles, the computer system tracked the inbound rounds from the coastal guns and easily avoided the barrages. They drew close to the large cannons before launching skyward, flying over a hundred feet above the massive cannons before turning in midair. Hurtling downward, the plasma rockets slammed into the coastal guns one after another.

When the plasma missiles struck the cannons, the gloomy sky between Yen and the rest of the Terran capital city lit up in a solid wall of burning plasma. The purples and blues of the plasma danced through the center of the flames as subsequent explosions erupted. Fuel cells, ammunition depots, and coastal guns exploded in steady progression, wreaking more and more havoc to the nearby Terran communities.

The *Duun* fighters disappeared through the flames, oblivious to the potential hazard as another series of explosion erupted from around the gun ports. Beyond the closest set of flames, Yen could see further explosions from within the city as the *Duun* fighters launched volley after volley into the city itself. Though hardly carrying the destructive capacity of the plasma bombs on board the Cruisers, the rockets bore enough explosives to bring down some of the heavenly skyscrapers, which collapsed into the city below.

By the time the *Cair Thewlis* broke through the wall of flames along the coast, the Terran capital city lay in ruins. Metal and stone lay twisted around one another in a macabre dance. Terran civilians nearby the multiple rocket strikes were lucky, having been instantly obliterated by the explosions. Others on the outskirts of the blasts, however, were now buried beneath tons of rubble and, in many cases, burning debris.

Yen stared out the window and struggled to fathom the depth of destruction and loss of life caused by a single pass of the *Duun* fighters. Suppressing a sadistic smile, Yen imagined the sheer volume of destruction that would be waged once the rest of the Fleet finally arrived on Earth.

"Sir," Pelasi said, the Uligart angling the *Cair Thewlis* further into the heart of the capital city, "I've got something on radar."

Yen broke his attention away from the rain–streaked window and examined the radar. Overlaid on the radar, a satellite image showed the terrain of the city. Ahead, blinking red on the overlay, a section of the city was illuminated. Tracking his gaze outside the window toward the area marked on the map, Yen noticed a sudden downturn in the height of the buildings, as though the closer they got to the heart of the city, the more the buildings bowed in solemn reverence to the area contained within.

As the buildings grew ever shorter, they eventually leveled out at a series of two and three story structures. Beyond the low buildings, however, the structures stopped altogether in an architectural cliff face. In the valley created by the lack of buildings, lush green grass spread over multiple city blocks. There, towering over the green grass and flowering trees, Yen could see the large tower, jutting toward the sky. The odd, square–sided structure reached over a hundred feet high before ending in an elongated point. As to the purpose of the building, Yen couldn't fathom, nor could he understand the rectangular lake that sat at the base of the tower and stretched away like a long, reflective shadow.

Breaking his attention away from the grassy park, Yen gestured toward an open square a few city blocks away. "Put us down over there." As Pelasi complied, Yen continued. "Once we hit ground and download the equipment, I want you airborne again."

"Sir?" Pelasi asked, confused.

"You're our way out of this hellhole. If you stay on the ground and this ship gets damaged, then we've not only walked right into the lair of the enemy, but we took away our only way out. I've been in that situation before and I have no intention of repeating a bad mistake. Land, download us, and then get the hell out of here. Understand?"

Pelasi nodded. "Yes, sir."

The *Cair Thewlis* set down heavily on the paved Terran square, its heavy alloy body crushing the flimsy vehicles beneath it. Before Yen could climb out of his chair, he could hear the back door to the ship dropping and a scurry of booted feet. He opened the door and was proud to see that most of his men had already hurried off the ship.

"I'll be manning the radio, sir," Warrant Pelasi called from behind him. "The second you all get into trouble, call me and I'll be back here."

"I know you will," Yen replied as he hurried to catch up to his men.

Yen stepped outside and wrinkled his nose in displeasure. The city smelled at though far too many Terran bodies had been living on top of one another for far too many years. It permeated the buildings and floated along the air like wisps of smoke.

Looking around, Yen smiled at his men. They had already moved into defensive positions around the square, ensuring that no counterattacking Terran forces could gain an upper hand while approaching down any of the main thoroughfares. Catching Buren's eye, Yen motioned for the officer to join him.

Approaching, the Uligart looked eternally unhappy. "Sir?"

"Take your men and sweep around the outskirts of the park," Yen ordered. "I'll take my team and make a more direct approach. Our forces should be able to meet near the eastern side of the park, which was the last known location of the doctor we've been sent to retrieve."

Yen could see the obvious disagreement cast on Buren's

face. Both the men knew that the outskirts mission was one that relegated the subordinate commander to little more than a supporting role while the primary commander, in this case Yen, claimed all the honors for the victory after making his direct attack. Though Yen had little time for the rivalry that Buren perceived, he couldn't resist a small barbed attack to the man's ego.

Buren sneered as he replied. "Yes, sir."

"And Buren," Yen said, his voice sickly sweet with false concern, "do be careful."

"Like you care," Buren snarled as he turned and walked away.

Yes, Yen realized, they would have to reevaluate their relationship very soon indeed. That, however, would have to wait for the time being. Motioning toward his team, Yen's men took up positions on both sides of the road as they began their approach on the park.

CHAPTER 36

The street was cast in harsh shadows as the brilliant red sun began setting on the distant horizon. Half the town was swallowed by the darkness; the edges of buildings and darkened alleyways disappeared into nondescript lines that defined the separation between the structure and the ground on which it sat. A hot breeze blew across Pteraxis, carrying clouds of sand through the streets of the small mining town. The fine particles of sand settled over Keryn as she and Adam stepped into the street.

The town took on an eerie look in the failing light. Shadows lengthened as they watched, giving them the impression of constant movement out of the corners of their eyes. They glanced from side to side, but they found only longer shadows and darkened corners. Where before the mining community looked like a ghost town, now it appeared as though the dead had awoken and sought revenge on the living. Just the thought of it made the hairs on Keryn's neck stand on edge.

When a gruff voice suddenly whispered in Keryn's ear, she nearly screamed in surprise before she realized that it was only her radio.

"Talon Six, this is Talon One," Rombard called over the radio, his voice more subdued than Keryn remembered ever hearing it.

"This is Talon Six," Keryn replied, her heart pounding in her chest.

"We've reached the corner of the alley and are ready to move in."

Keryn shook her head, though she knew Rombard wouldn't see the movement. "Negative, Talon One. Hold your position on the secondary street. Wait for my command." Without speaking it aloud, she finished her thought: if we need you, you'll know right away.

Having been inside when Rombard began pursuing Cardax, Keryn could only make assumptions on which alleyway the Oterian was cutting through. She had assumed that they would have plenty of sunlight left to find the smuggler before the red orb disappeared over the horizon, but the rapidly setting sun caught her off guard. At the rate the sun was disappearing, it would only be another twenty minutes or less before they lost the meager light they had remaining.

Motioning ahead, Keryn drew her pistol as she and Adam moved cautiously forward. Cardax was hiding from her, toying with her while they quickly lost their sunlight. In spite of the heat of the Pteraxis afternoon, Keryn felt a chill at the thought of getting stuck on the planet after dark. A knot formed in her stomach, as though her body was reacting to the unseen danger. The planet itself seemed to want them gone, and Keryn was all too willing to oblige once they'd captured the smuggler.

Though there seemed to be movement from every shadow, Keryn was still surprised when one of the shadows detached itself from the side of a building. Still a block away, the towering figure moved slowly and deliberately until he slipped out of the shadows and into the dim, red light. Even from a distance, the Oterian smuggler towered over both the Pilgrim and the Wyndgaart. Standing over eight feet tall, he was swathed in dark fur. His long horns bent forward like spears. Though the Oterian appeared to smile, it came across significantly more like a sneer of displeasure.

"Cardax," Keryn growled at the smuggler.

"You reek of it, you know?" Cardax yelled across the distance. "You and all the rest of your little group. You all carry the disgusting scent of the Alliance. I smelled you the second you entered this town."

"Spare me," Keryn yelled back, raising her pistol. "One way or another, you're coming with us!"

"Such dangerous threats from such a little girl," Cardax said, raising his arms to the side as he started stepping forward. "There's really no need for all that. In fact, if you were smart, you'd go ahead and put that toy gun down before someone gets hurt."

"Are you threatening me?" Keryn asked indignantly. "You turn your back on your race and the entire Alliance, and you still have the audacity to threaten me?" The anger built within her and she ground her teeth together while she spoke.

In response, Cardax laughed heartily. "Betray the Alliance? That's rich. This is the same Alliance that hunted me like a dog from one end of known space to another. I spend just as much time now fleeing bounty hunters as I do conducting my business."

"You betrayed us!" Keryn screamed. Try as she might, she couldn't understand how Cardax was so blinded by his own arrogance. Though she kept her eyes on the Oterian, she also scanned the buildings around her. Their conversation was far from quiet; the townsfolk had to have heard them. Yet no faces peered from closed windows to see the disturbance. Keryn longed to have the Voice once again. Its consult would have been useful in a situation like the one she now found herself, and it was always capable of watching the periphery while she focused on the task at hand. Realizing how lost she felt without the Voice, Keryn felt a pit grow in her chest, filled only with a dull ache of loss.

Cardax, blissfully unaware of Keryn's inner turmoil, continued talking. "I never betrayed them. They betrayed me. I made one of the greatest discoveries in history when I found Deplitoxide. I was a businessman and only wanted to profit from my discovery. And what did I get for my troubles? The High Council sent Alliance Warships after me; chased me all the way into the Demilitarized Zone. I was captured by the Terrans because I was trying to save my own life! You have no idea the tortures I endured at the hands of the Terrans. A weaker man would have died, but I persevered."

"Enough talking," Adam interrupted, pulling his rifle free from under his jacket. "Get on the ground."

Cardax continued walking forward and talking, as though he hadn't heard Adam speak. "But I learned an invaluable lesson as a result of being the Terran's captive. I learned that loyalty has nothing to do with oaths of allegiance to one side or another. Loyalty, just like everything else in this universe, has a price. You find how much someone charges for their undying loyalty, and even the most devoted soldier will willingly die for your cause. Don't believe me? Next time you're with all your friends, ask them how many would continue to serve the Alliance if they no longer received a paycheck. None of you are doing your job because you have some unfailing sense of loyalty to the Alliance. Take away the money, and every one of you would find a new line of work."

"What's your point?" Keryn yelled, though Cardax was

now only a few dozen feet away.

"My point is that this entire town had a price, and I had a lot of money to spend. My point is that these people appreciate the money I give them and aren't eager to lose it. My point is that they're willing to do anything to protect my donations…"

Cardax smiled wickedly, his dark eyes glistening in the dying light. "…even kill your friends guarding your ship."

"Is someone there?" Penchant called out in a coarse voice. His Lithid eyes, covered by his Uligart disguise, worked like a solar panel, absorbing the dim light and amplifying it, allowing him to see well in darkness. Even with his enhancements, however, he didn't see anyone nearby. In a normal situation, that would be a blessing. Just moments before, though, the entire landing zone had been teeming with life. Now, as though whisked away on the warm Pteraxis breeze, the place was dangerously quiet.

"No one's there," McLaughlin said in his thick accent. Sitting on the ground with his back against the *Cair Ilmun*, the Pilgrim tilted back his hat so he could see the Lithid. "You're hearing things."

"Lithids don't have an active imagination," Penchant said. The Uligart face he wore wrinkled its forehead as he strained to hear another sound.

"You don't say?" McLaughlin said sarcastically. Pushing off from the ship, he stood and dusted off the back of his pants. "You're just on edge, and there's no reason to be. We're on guard duty, the absolutely most boring job they could find for the two of us."

"Something's wrong," the Lithid said, turning to stare at McLaughlin with a stern glare. "We should contact the others."

As Penchant reached toward his throat, the Pilgrim

reached out and grabbed his wrist. Though Penchant looked angry, McLaughlin simply shook his head. "If there was trouble, don't you think we would have heard something by now? We're close enough that we would have heard gunfire or explosions. Since we didn't hear anything, then I think you probably need to relax a little more."

Penchant pulled his wrist free of McLaughlin's grip and turned the opposite direction. McLaughlin shrugged before rolling his eyes. "Listen, if you're that's worried about them, let's just ask someone if they've heard anything from town. That way, we don't have to bother Keryn with radio chatter if nothing is really going on." Glancing toward town, McLaughlin smiled. "We'll just ask one of these people."

Turning quickly, the Lithid saw figures materializing from the dark shadows cast between the ships. From the angry expressions on their faces, Penchant knew they came with deadly intent. Though the smile never faded from McLaughlin's face, Penchant noticed that the Pilgrim slid his hand beneath his coat in an innocent gesture, but one that put his pistols easily within reach. A noise behind him alerted Penchant that other crewmen from the various ships had circled around and now had the pair trapped.

"How's it going, gentlemen?" McLaughlin asked, stepping toward the approaching group. "How about this weather?"

Penchant eyed movement from his right as well, meaning that they were now completely encircled. To his left, the Lithid noted the narrow clearance between the belly of the *Cair Ilmun* and the ground. Though the space would be an incredibly tight fit for the other races, Penchant's malleability would enable him to slide easily under the ship. McLaughlin, however, would never be so lucky.

"Anything I can help you with?" McLaughlin asked generally to the crowd as the pair searched for an escape route. "You all don't seem very talkative. What's wrong? Seque got your tongue?" The Pilgrim's voice took on a nervous tone as he continued to speak rapidly. "Whatever your problem, I'm sure we can come to an arrangement, but only if we're able to talk about it."

"I'll talk," a gruff Terran said as he stepped forward and reached to the pouches clipped to his belt. From within one of the pouches, he pulled a small blue orb. "The Empire sends you a gift!"

As the Terran pulled back his arm to throw, McLaughlin drew his pistols blindingly fast. His first round caught the Terran in the wrist, blasting through both the bones and completely severing the hand. The severed extremity, along with the sphere still clutched in its grasp, disappeared into the darkness as it was flung away from the Terran. Firing his second pistol, the Terran was struck in the chest. The bullet shattered ribs, sending both metal and bone fragments into the soft tissue of the Terran's heart and lungs. Wordlessly, the would-be assassin clutched at his chest before falling to the ground.

McLaughlin began firing wildly into the crowd, all the while laughing excitedly as he pulled the triggers on his pistols. Penchant, falling into place at his back, drew his own rarely used pistol and began firing as well, trying to keep McLaughlin from being flanked. Caught entirely by surprise by the ferocity of McLaughlin's attacks, the crowd began to fall back, scrambling to find cover as round after round cut through their ranks. Soon, however, the mob mentality reasserted itself and they surged forward toward the gunmen.

McLaughlin fell back toward the safety of the *Cair Ilmun,*

346

as he alternated firing into the advancing crowd and reloading his weapons. Blinded as he was with keeping his enemies at bay, he never noticed the second blue orb rolling across the dirt toward his feet. Penchant, noticing the grenade, yelled a warning before diving under the ship. His Uligart façade melted away as his body elongated and thinned enough that he could fit into the cramped crawl space. McLaughlin, entirely focused on keeping the approaching crewmen at bay, never heard the warning from Penchant and only looked down as a loud pulse of noise that preceded the explosion caught his attention.

As the shockwave lifted him from the ground, the shell of the explosive broke apart and filled the air with deadly metal projectiles. McLaughlin's head snapped backward from the blast as metal fragments bit into his exposed flesh. Smaller fragments cut into his legs and set his pants and shirt ablaze. His body hair burned away and filled the air around him with an acrid smell. As his body was flung wide, larger fragments of the grenade tore into his right arm. Cutting through the muscle and sinews, the jagged shrapnel ripped free fragments of flesh and bone as it passed through his muscular arm. The bone shattered under the assault as all but a small strip of flesh was obliterated in the blast.

McLaughlin fell to the ground nearly ten feet away from where he had been standing before the explosion. To the amazement of all who were nearby, he let out a scream of pain as his ruined arm landed beneath the weight of his body, the limb held on by little more than strips of worn and burned flesh. Blood gushed from his numerous wounds, soaking immediately into the dry and thirsty ground.

The crewmen close to the incapacitated Pilgrim raised their weapons and stepped toward McLaughlin, ready to end his pain.

On the far side of the *Cair Ilmun*, unnoticed by the enemies that had surrounded them on the other of the ship, Penchant slid from underneath its belly and growled in anger.

———————

Keryn turned with a start at the loud explosion and jets of flame that lit up the sky from the direction of the flattened landing zone. Turning back furiously toward Cardax, Keryn pulled back the hammer on her pistol as tears stung her eyes. Though she already knew the answer, she asked the question anyway.

"What was that? What have you done?"

"That," Cardax growled sinisterly, "was the beginning of the end for you and your team, little whore. Say goodbye to me now, because mine is the last face you're ever going to see in this universe."

"Ambush!" Cerise yelled over the radio as the town seemed to explode to life.

All around Keryn and Adam, doorways opened and shuttered windows flew out wide as armed townsfolk stepped out into the near darkness, their weapons trained on the team members and murderous looks in their eyes.

CHAPTER 37

Iana turned sharply aside as another rocket went streaking past her right wing. The Terran fighters had been chasing her for the better part of half an hour and Iana had not, as of yet, found a way to lose them. She felt the sweat beading on her brow and soaking through her fine, blonde hair. She angrily wiped the sweat away and focused on the radar once again. Behind her, ever present, were the three fighters pursuing her in a lazy orbit over the northern continent.

Somewhere far below her battle, Yen and the *Cair Thewlis* were heading directly for the Terran capital. The plan had been for Iana and her three fighters in Alpha team to provide direct air cover for his ship. Upon arrival, however, even Iana had been surprised by the scope of the Terran space defenses. Improvised Terran warships offered little more than a dangerous distraction while the true Terran fighters provided the deadly firepower about which Iana was worried. Destroying the fighters before they had a chance to engage the *Cair* transports became her overarching concern, meaning that Yen was now flying solo as he skimmed the ocean's surface.

Warning sirens roared through the confines of the cockpit as the Terran fighters launched another salvo of plasma rockets. Tilting to the right, Iana dropped her ship into a roll and sighed in relief as she watched the smoky trails of the missiles pass dangerously close. Her relaxation, however, was short lived as her radio began to chime.

Reaching forward, she answered the radio just in time to hear Yen's angry voice. "Alpha Leader, this is Commander Xiao. If you're not too busy up there, we could really use some of that air superiority we've heard so much about!"

Iana sighed in frustration. "This is Alpha Leader. No, sir, of course we have nothing important going on up here. Just relaxing and having the time of our lives. Hell, when you boys get done down there, feel free to come join us. We're getting ready to fire up the blender to make some cocktails."

"Can the chatter, Alpha Leader, and get me some air support!"

Knowing Yen couldn't see her, she still shook her head in irritation. Though her mission priority was still to protect the *Cair Thewlis*, she hardly had the resources to defend against the pressing Terran assault, much less split her assets to assist Yen. In the end, however she knew that only one priority truly mattered.

"Roger, sir," Iana called back. "I'm breaking away two *Duun* fighters to your position now."

Switching channels, she called out to her other pilots. "Alpha Three and Alpha Four. Break formation and provide cover fire for the *Cair* force. Once you've done sufficient damage on the surface, get back up here and give us a hand."

"Roger that, ma'am," Alpha Three replied.

Iana watched with regret as two of her four *Duun* fighters disengaged from their battle and dipped into the atmosphere, their hulls glowing hot as they passed through the friction–heavy upper layer. Sighing, she knew that she and Alpha Two were now entirely on their own.

Glancing through her forward window, Iana located

Alpha Two from amidst the combination of wreckage, debris, and still flying craft. The space above Earth seemed like a long-forgotten graveyard, a place where old ships went to die. Iana frowned at the reference, realizing that this area was now also a place where old pilots went to die as well. Alpha Two seemed engaged with a small Squadron of the makeshift Terran ships and, though she was holding her own, Iana could use her help.

"Alpha Two, this is Alpha Leader."

"Go ahead, ma'am," Alpha Two's musical Avalon voice replied.

Iana smiled to herself in the cockpit. "How familiar are you with a criss–cross?"

After a brief pause, Alpha Two responded. "I'm not familiar with the name, but I'm pretty sure I know what you have in mind."

"Good," Iana replied. "Then on my mark. Three…two… one… mark!"

Iana pressed forward on the controls, dropping her *Duun* fighter into a steep dive directly toward Earth's surface. Simultaneously, her Avalon counterpart pitched upward, the two ships on a collision course. Iana felt her heart pound in her chest as she checked the radar. As she had assumed, the Terran fighters had maneuvered to match her new trajectory. Still firing, they were only slightly further behind now than they had been moments before. Iana watched through the forward window as the improvised fighters chased Alpha Two, their weapons ports now facing Iana front-on. Gritting her teeth, she accelerated. Even with the inhibitors lessening the pressure on her body, Iana still felt the gravitational forces began pressing on her limbs. Her chest feeling like a weight pressing on her lungs, she managed a few hitched breaths as she tried to open a gap between her *Duun* fighter and the Terrans in pursuit.

Flicking the controls, Iana caused the nose of her fighter to tilt slightly upward. Though it was hard to tell from her current position, she hoped that the Avalon noticed the gesture. If not, their cross was going to end in a bloody mess. As the miles disappeared between the ships, Iana eased up on the accelerator. Her slowing ship became a prime target for the Terran fighters in pursuit and they pounced, eager for the kill. Blinded by their desire for the kill, they failed to notice Alpha Two close the rest of the gap. At the last moment, Iana turned her controls upward just as the other *Duun* fighter dipped low. Iana could feel the buffet as the other ship passed within a few feet from the bottom of her *Duun*, the blast from her engine rocking Iana in the cockpit.

Behind her, the Terrans were completely surprised when a second *Duun* fighter launched toward them, missiles already leaping from their launchers under the ship's wings. Trying to dodge, only one of the Terran fighters was able to avoid the plasma barrage. The other two were struck in the cockpits, their glass shattering as the rocket penetrated the windows and exploded on top of the pilots. The blue and purple flames consumed the two ships as they silently exploded in the void of space. Wasting no time admiring the explosion, Alpha Two turned sharply in pursuit of the third fighter.

Iana smashed through the center of the improvised fighters, sending the weaker ships scattering in all directions. Firing her machine guns haphazardly, bright tracer rounds filled the dark space as the bullets slammed into the reinforced hulls of the ships. Finding the cracks in between the hastily armored ships, Iana's bullets bit deep into the crafts, tearing open their bellies and spewing forth their precious oxygen.

Though she had only destroyed three of the ten improvised fighters, Iana barely slowed as she turned in a wide arc, angling back toward the powerless satellite grid. Pushing forward on the accelerator, she quickly distanced herself from the slower moving improvised aircraft the Terrans had created as a defense for Earth. Though still capable of destroying her *Duun* fighter with their plasma rockets, they lacked the sophistication and advanced computer-targeting systems that were standard on the Terran fighters. As a result, Iana found herself merely avoiding the improvised ships; brushing them off as though they were little more than an insect while she bought herself time. Her salvation came moments later when Alpha Two cut a swath through their formation, destroying another pair of their ships. Turning sharply, Iana rejoined the battle, leaving the remaining five ships decimated from a combination of gunfire and rocket explosions.

With their sector temporarily cleared, Iana leaned back heavily in the pilot's chair and, reaching up, rubbed her eyes feverishly with the back of her hand. She could feel the dull ache growing behind her eyes as the tension built in her body. It had only been an hour since they warped into Earth's orbit and still an hour until the rest of the Fleet arrived, but they had been fighting the entire time. The current break in combat was the first reprieve she had truly earned since their initial invasion.

With her eyes still closed, she brushed her hair aside and activated the microphone at her throat. "Alpha Three, this is Alpha Leader. Give me a status report."

The response was filled with static as the transmission passed through Earth's thick atmosphere. "The *Cair Thewlis* has safely landed at the capital. We are on our way back to your location."

"Roger that," Iana said wearily. "You have temporarily clear skies."

Sighing, Iana ran her own words through her mind: *temporarily clear skies*. Somehow, the Terrans continued to send ships out to intercept the invasion Squadron. Every time her pilots decimated the latest wave of enemy vessels, another launched from a different position on the planet's surface and the battle began anew. So far, they had been lucky. Iana didn't believe it was anything more than luck that had kept her and the majority of her pilots alive over the past hour. However, she was losing more and more fighters each time the Terrans counterattacked. At the rate they were going, the Terrans would win a war of attrition after simply waiting for all the Alliance ships to make a mistake and be destroyed. Honestly, Iana had no reason to assume the results would be any different than just that. A small Squadron of Alliance *Duun* fighters and *Cair* transports had invaded the Terran home world. Even without their Fleet, the Terrans had vastly superior military numbers at their disposal. Iana frowned, having trouble believing that she ever thought this attack was a good idea.

"Alpha Leader, this is Bravo Three," a rushed, gruff Oterian voice called over the radio. "The Terrans have launched another wave of ships from the southern pole. They destroyed the *Cair Bailun* before we even knew they were there!"

"Get back into formation and eliminate the Terran fighters before they get to any of the other *Cair* ships," Iana ordered. "We still have…"

"The *Cair Noumlik* has been hit!" a worried, effeminate voice interrupted. "They're targeting the *Cair*s."

Iana scowled. She should have guessed that it would only be a matter of time before the Terrans figured out the Alliance strategy. They'd now be targeting all the *Cair* ships, both still in space and on the planet.

"Alpha Three, this is Alpha Leader. The Terrans are

doing a search and destroy on the *Cair*s. Is the *Cair Thewlis* still alright?"

"Yes, ma'am," Alpha Three called back, his voice clearer as he passed through the upper atmosphere. "It's still in one piece in the middle of…"

The radio suddenly went dead. Iana cocked her head to the side as she awaited the rest of the sentence that just wasn't coming. "Alpha Three, say again."

Again, silence stretched over the radio.

"Alpha Three, respond!" she ordered.

"Twelve o'clock low," Alpha Two called out. "Terran fighters!"

Iana tilted the nose of her ship so that she was facing Earth's surface. Far below her, skimming the surface of the atmosphere, three small Terran fighters were silhouetted against the vibrant blues and greens of the planet. Scanning in front of the fast craft, Iana could see the rapidly cooling blue and purple vapors, a signal that plasma missiles had exploded nearby. A knot grew in Iana's stomach at the sight. She had to assume that the plasma bursts were what remained of both Alpha Three and Four. If that were the case, then the Terran fighters had nothing standing between them and the *Cair Thewlis*. Yen and his entire team could be in grave danger.

Without giving orders, Alpha Two fell into position beside Iana as she dove toward the Terran ships. She pressed heavily on the accelerator, speeding forward until the growing pressure on her chest threatened to break her ribs. Her hands and feet grew cold as her heart struggled to pump blood to her extremities. Even under the intense pressure of the dive, however, she still knew that she would never catch the Terran fighters before they reached Yen and his men. In her ambivalence, she had very possibly caused the tide of battle to turn against the Alliance Fleet.

Her eyes watering from the gravitational forces, she saw a faint red glow from the corner of her eye. Glancing over, her heart skipped a beat, both in excitement and fear. She did have a solution, if she was brave enough to try. Yen was counting on her to do the right thing, even if it meant endangering her own life. Realizing how much hung in the balance, Iana quickly realized that she didn't truly have a choice in the matter. Sliding her hand over to the button, she took a deep breath.

"I'm really going to regret this," she muttered just before activating the warp generator.

CHAPTER 38

Yen leaned back heavily against the rubble behind which he had taken cover. Heat from still burning fires radiated against his yellowed skin, a stark contrast to the cool rain that still poured from above. Rivulets of water cascaded down the debris strewn across the road and followed the course between the larger pieces of concrete like newly formed urban rivers.

Yen reached up and brushed his dark hair out of his face before refocusing on the weapons check he was performing on his pistol. Satisfied that his pistol would still function in the heavy rain, he proceeded to check the belt of grenades strung around his waist. Though the grenades seemed like a coarse approach, especially for Yen's preferred psychic subtlety, they were effective against entrenched Terran forces.

To Yen's left and right, he could see the rest of his team spreading out, finding cover behind the other debris that littered the road, as well as moving quietly into the husks of demolished buildings nearby. The passing *Duun* fighters had done considerable damage to this part of the city, reducing many of the buildings to little more than heaps of rubble, charred black from the persistent plasma fires.

In the distance, gunfire filled the gloomy air. Buren's force had encountered significantly heavier resistance than had Yen's team. Then again, Yen realized, he wasn't sending his own men headlong into danger. Preferring a slower but more tactical approach, Yen's team had been methodically moving forward, finding cover wherever possible. At the same time, he had dispatched scouts to examine the enemy line and report back any weaknesses. Even entrenched as they were, the Terrans had to be pulled thin with the Alliance striking so many targets on Earth simultaneously. Once Yen found the opening he was looking for, he would exploit it and find a way into the park beyond.

A scurrying sound alerted Yen to the return of one of his scouts. The Lithid slipped around the corner of the rubble behind which Yen was sitting and crouched beside the commander.

"I don't know who this scientist is," the Lithid began, his gravelly voice hissing the words, "but the Terrans are doing all they can to protect him. They have a pretty solid perimeter established all around the park."

"I know what the good Doctor Solomon is capable of," Yen replied. "And believe me when I tell you that the Terrans didn't bring enough soldiers to keep me out."

"I was hoping that would be your answer," the scout's voice called from behind the featureless mask. Pointing a clawed hand to the north and west, the Lithid continued. "There is a point approximately two blocks from here where the Terrans have established a roadblock. It's well defended, but their position leaves them cut off from immediate reinforcements. It would be a difficult fight, but if we can attack quickly and decisively, the Terrans will be demolished before additional soldiers can arrive."

Yen nodded thoughtfully. Behind his dark eyes, a seething hatred burned. Destroying the Terran defenses would only be the first step in a more significant act of retribution against the Terran doctor. "If we break through their lines, can the rest of the team then hold that position against the Terran reinforcements?"

"We can hold that position for as long as you need us to," came the Lithid's flat reply.

Smiling wickedly, Yen stood and flashed a series of hand and arm signals. His group leaders stood and began directing their men forward, toward the weakness in the Terran lines.

Yen had no illusions that breaking through the Terran line would be easy, but he also knew the rage that grew inside of him. Only a few city blocks beyond the roadblock, the Terran scientist responsible for the destruction of nearly all his friends and former teammates sat in his laboratory, working on twisted experiments and new weapons. There wasn't a force in the universe strong enough to keep Yen from his goal.

Moving quietly forward, Yen led his men to a corner where a side street intersected the one they had been following. According to his scout, this road led directly to the park, in front of which sat a roadblock that gave the Terrans plenty of cover from which to engage Yen's approaching team. Sliding slightly forward, Yen peered around the corner. Halfway down the street, a series of vehicles were piled on top of one another. The ten-foot high wall blocked the street from one end to the other. From the gaps between the compressed vehicles, however, gun barrels jutted forward, all trained toward the end of the street where Yen stood. The quantity of firepower, coupled with the cover the Terrans had, left little doubt in Yen's mind that a frontal assault would be suicidal.

"What are you thinking, sir?" one of Yen's group leaders whispered from behind him.

"If we're going this way, we're going to have to do

something about that wall," Yen muttered. "They've got vehicles piled up on top of one another, making it nearly impossible to get any clean shots on the Terran guards behind it. And judging from the looks of them, those vehicles can take quite a beating."

Yen paused as his last words rattled around his mind. Taking another quick look around the corner, Yen marked the strewn debris littering the road, leading up to the wall. Though some of the buildings on the road had collapsed during the *Duun* assault, the debris was minimal, consisting of little more than fist sized rocks and small slabs no more than a couple feet across.

Moving quickly, Yen's team hurried back the way they had come until they were able to locate a vehicle that had hardly been damaged during the assault. Though blackened by soot, the body of the vehicle seemed in solid condition. Without starting the engine, Yen reached inside and threw the transmission into neutral as he released the parking break. Joining the rest of his team behind the vehicle, they pushed it forward, at first rolling it slowly over the rocks that littered the road until finally, picking up momentum, they were able to move it near the corner around which the barricade had been erected.

"Search your packs for any explosives," Yen ordered in a hushed tone. "Pile everything you have in the backseat." Turning toward his demolitions expert, he continued. "Rig everything we have to a single detonator. Give me the trigger when you're finished."

His team worked quickly and efficiently, loading the backseat with a surprisingly large amount of explosives. Demolitions were never Yen's specialty and he struggled to fathom the amount of damage that quantity of explosives could do. In the end, Yen realized that he just didn't care. His men would make a hole through that wall, even if he had to level half the city to do it. With that in mind, he motioned for his men to hurry and load the rest of the bombs.

With the explosives loaded, Yen closed his eyes and focused on the vehicle. Without a driver, Yen used his power to ignite the spark plugs and start the engine, which roared loudly to life. Reaching out his hand, Yen assumed the position of a driver. Pressing down on the ground with his right food, the engine revved as the car sped around the corner, the tires screeching loudly as it first turned, and then accelerated, down the street toward the roadblock. Gunfire erupted from behind the wall as the Terrans opened fire on the advancing vehicle. Between the bullets shredding the body of the car and the jostling of driving over the debris in the road, the vehicle shook violently as it surged forward.

Yen watched, detached, as the vehicle sped toward its target. The amount of fire left little doubt that any real driver would have been long dead behind the wheel. Having no driver, however, Yen looked out of the front windshield like a specter, driving the vehicle unwaveringly toward the wall. The mobile bomb slammed into the wall head on, crushing the front of the engine block and sending rods tearing through the dashboard and into the front seats. The impact fused the front of the vehicle to the wall, interlocking twisted pieces of metal. Releasing control of the car, whose tired still spun from the jammed accelerator, Yen pressed the button on the detonator and lunged for cover.

The shockwave rocked the ground, throwing asphalt up to meet Yen as he fell to the ground. Flames leapt a hundred feet into the air, scorching the buildings as far as half a block down the street. The buildings closest to the wall cracked and shattered from the explosion and the heat, sending further debris cascading onto the road.

The roadblock itself melted from the assault. Shredded metal, glowing a vibrant red from the heat, were launched into the horrified Terrans who had been hiding behind the wall. Shards of metal bit into flesh and ripped through body armor only moments before a sheet of flames rolled over the injured soldiers. Bleeding and burning alive, the Terrans cried out in pain and terror as they lay writhing on the street.

Yen clung to the ground, amazed at his excessive use of explosives. Expecting to just destroy the wall, he never expected so much collateral damage. When the buckling of the asphalt finally subsided, he climbed to his feet and yelled for his men to follow.

Leading the charge, Yen hurried around the corner and rushed toward the decimated blockade. When he got closer to the roadblock, he noticed movement from the corner of his eye. Drawing his pistol, he dropped into a defensive crouch and turned. From within the rubble of a recently collapsed building, a Terran staggered out into the street. Torn and bloodied, the Terran walked unsteadily toward the Alliance soldiers. Above his right elbow, the Terran's arm had been torn away, leaving only a ragged stump from which blood poured onto the street. Long gashes lined the man's face and his attempts to speak were thwarted as he coughed up a fine mist of blood.

Yen saw the pleading look in his eyes, but felt no sympathy in his heart. Reaching out, a small rock lifted off the ground a few feet away. Feeling his power reaching out and caressing the rock, Yen tilted his head to the side as he examined the Terran. Having lost significant amounts of blood, the Terran didn't even recognize the danger until it was too late. Yen sent the rock hurtling toward the injured Terran with a flick of his wrist. Spinning like a drill, the rock tore through the man's chest, shattering ribs and grinding the organs beneath to a pulp. Ripping free of the man's back, the rock flew into the collapsed building, trailing behind it a gushing river of blood. A look of surprise spread across the Terran's face moments before he crumpled into the street.

Attuned now to the sounds of survivors, Yen could hear other movement throughout the area. Focusing, the air whipping wildly around him, dozens of rocks began to lift from the ground. Swirling around him, the rocks moved with him as he paced forward. The largest, a stone slab nearly three feet long, hovered in front of him like a shield, protecting Yen from any enemy fire.

Slowly, wounded Terrans began crawling out from beneath sheets of metal and slabs of concrete. One by one, Yen sent his deadly projectiles launching toward them, cutting through flesh and finishing off those unfortunate enough to have survived the car bomb. Yen passed through the decimated wall and strode forward like a conquering general, oblivious to the sea of death that surrounded him.

Before him, Yen could see the crisp, green trees that wavered in the gentle rain. A soft scent of nature filled his nostrils, replacing the smell of death that had permeated the rest of the city. The park beyond seemed unscathed, as though it remained blissfully unaware of the destruction that waited like a predator on its outskirts. Through the shifting trees, Yen could make out the rain infused surface of a pond and, towering above the trees, the tall, square monument that filled the center of the park. Beyond the monument, Yen knew, was the laboratory of Doctor Solomon.

"Please..." a soft voice called out from Yen's side. "Please... help me..."

Yen turned slowly until he could see the Terran soldier. His leg obviously broken and blood caking his shoulder and face, the Terran sat awkwardly on his knees. Reaching out with empty hands, the Terran pleaded for sympathy and compassion. Yen smiled, but it was not a warm smile. The Terran had come to a man searching for sympathy and compassion, two of the things Yen found lacking in his heart. With an absent gesture, the large stone shield spun toward the Terran. Striking him in the chin, the stone obliterated the Terran's head, decapitating the man. Blood poured like a geyser from the man's torn neck before the body collapsed to the street.

Yen closed his eyes and reveled in the power. The psychic energy filled him with a sadistic bliss and Yen felt both alive and invincible. Revenge was at his fingertips, regardless of the High Council's orders to bring Doctor Solomon back alive. He couldn't wait to close his fingers around the Terran scientist's neck.

Motioning toward the Lithid scout, Yen gave the man his orders. "Hold this ground, no matter what. I won't need long to do what I need to do."

Gesturing to a team of four, Yen set out with his small group and entered the park. Though he could still hear the distant gunfire, it seemed surreally detached from his walk through greenery. Even the rain, which had lessened to a minor drizzle, seemed somehow comforting as he walked through the lush grass.

Ducking low, Yen passed below the hanging branches of the trees and entered the open mall of the park, dominated by the rectangular lake. Though obviously shallow, the lake was an impressive manmade structure. Stretching far to his right, and ending at the foot of the square tower, the surface of the water was broken only by the fine misting of rain. Motioning to his men, they spread out and began moving around the lake, toward the far side.

As Yen stepped onto the slabs of stone that formed the edge of the pond, his soldiers were lifted from their feet by an unseen explosion and tossed violently into the far trees. Yen could hear the crashing branches and the cries of pain as his men disappeared from view. Turning back toward the stretching lake and the monument beyond, Yen drew his pistol.

Pain lanced up his arm as the pistol was wrenched from his grasp and tossed harmlessly aside. Looking left and right, Yen felt panic build in his chest. He was being assaulted by someone he couldn't see. As he turned, he felt a force clench around his waist and lift him from his feet. With incredible power, he was hurtled backward toward the trees beyond. Though surprised, Yen was able to create a psychic shield around him seconds before his spine struck the tree. His body shattered through the thick trunk of the tree and he collapsed onto the soft ground. Though his shield absorbed much of the impact, he still groaned loudly as pain lanced up his back.

From beyond the ruined tree, Yen watched in amazement as a Terran stepped out from the far side of the pond. Walking across the water, Yen noted that the man hovered inches above the lake, never touching the surface. Waves of psychic energy emanated from the Terran and rolled around his form.

The dark haired Terran drifted downward until he stepped lightly onto the ground on the far side of the lake. Smiling maliciously, he looked to the prone form of Yen.

"Come out, Yen Xiao. I have waited for this day for a long, long time!"

CHAPTER 39

Keryn and Adam broke for the nearest doorway as gunfire erupted around them. Packed clay from the road erupted in sprays of shrapnel, biting into the backs of the pair's arms and legs as they ran. From behind them, Keryn could hear Cardax's rumbling laughter over the din of weapon fire. Snarling, Keryn turned and fired a couple rounds in his direction, causing the Oterian to dodge for cover. Adam grabbed her around the waist as he passed, pulling her toward the unmarked, two-story wooden building.

"Not now!" he yelled as he dragged her away. Though lifted from her feet by his powerful arms, Keryn continued to fire wild shots at the retreating smuggler.

Setting her back on her feet without breaking stride, Keryn and Adam bounded up the two wooden stairs that led onto the building's porch. Keryn, taking the lead, counted her blessings that the townsfolk seemed poorly trained with their weapons. Though they had filled the area around them with bullets, not a single one had, as of yet, found its mark. As they neared the doorway, it was suddenly flung wide. A stout Pilgrim blocked the entrance, a double-barreled shotgun held in the crook of his arm. Surprised, the man hesitated as Keryn bounded up the stairs. Lowering her shoulder, she caught the Pilgrim in the stomach. Together, they tumbled into the room, their bodies regressing into a mass of swinging limbs.

As they rolled across the floor, Keryn immediately regretted her decision to grapple with the much larger man. Though stocky and overweight, the Pilgrim held a surprising storehouse of strength, one that he levered to his advantage. Thrown onto her back, the air was forced from Keryn's lungs as the man threw himself on top of her. One hand closed over her throat as another settled over her mouth, blocking her attempts to cry out in pain. The Pilgrim's hand felt crushing on her throat as she struggled for air. Realizing her dangerous predicament, Keryn bit down hard on the fleshy skin between the man's thumb and forefinger. Shaking from side to side, she held her grip even as the man howled in pain and a coppery taste filled her mouth.

Easing his grip on both Keryn's mouth and throat, she brought her knees up tight to her chest and launched her hips skyward. The force of her double-footed kick caught the Pilgrim under the chin, rocking him to his feet as he reeled backward. A room-shaking explosion jarred Keryn as the first round of Adam's large caliber rifle shattered through the man's shoulder. Staggering backward toward the door, Adam stepped protectively over Keryn and fired again. His second shot lifted the man from his feet and flung his body onto the front porch. Adam slammed the door and pushed a nearby dresser behind it, barring the entrance to the building.

Turning, he hurried to Keryn's side. Kneeling down, Adam reached out and gently wiped the side of her face. As he pulled away his hand, Keryn could see the rich, red blood on his fingertips.

Keryn shook her head. "It's not mine," she said hoarsely. She wiped away more of the blood as Adam helped her to her feet.

With her assistance, Adam turned over a heavy wooden table in the center of the room and they took cover behind it. From the street, the townsfolk, with Cardax in the lead, shifted and began firing heavily into the building. The thin glass window shattered, littering the ground with broken shards. Though behind cover, they could hear slivers of wood breaking free and flying across the room.

She rubbed her throat, feeling the bruises where her throat microphone had bit into the flesh as the Pilgrim tried to strangle her. Her knees felt weak and unsteady. Keryn wearily leaned against the cool wood of the table and slowly began filtering out the overwhelming sounds of devastation from all around her.

A cursory glance around the room told Keryn what she needed to know. There were no other exits from the building in which they were trapped. Dozens of townspeople, if not more, filled the street outside, advancing quickly on their position. The insignificant amount of furniture they had hastily thrown in front of the door wouldn't last. The already decimated window would offer easy access into the room for Cardax's minions. In addition, as far as Keryn could tell, they had no exit from the building, aside from going through the middle of an angry, armed mob.

"Keryn," Adam asked as he peered around the corner of the table, "what do we do?"

Keryn didn't reply and, instead, closed her eyes and tried to disappear within the grain of the wooden table. She had never felt so unsure of herself. It was her fault that her team was now trapped and facing their deaths. Clenching her eyes shut, she felt anger well in her chest. She had always had the Voice to fall back on; a pinprick of wisdom that cut through the chaos of her life. But now, a bitter silence prevailed in her head. No advice was shared, though she yearned for help. She was on her own. Alone. And it scared Keryn to death.

"What do you want us to do?" Adam asked sternly.

"I don't know," Keryn whispered.

———

A roar from Rombard's heavy rifle split the air, the massive round striking the support beam beneath one of the nearby balconies. The wooden balcony buckled and collapsed, spilling the Uligart gunner onto the hard ground. As he tried to stand, Keeling shot him twice, dropping him dead to the ground. Groaning, Keeling slid back behind the crates they were using for cover, holding his abdomen. Dark blood soaked his shirt and ran between his fingers.

"Keeling's been hit," Rombard rumbled into the microphone, foregoing any pretenses of call signs. "They've got us pinned. What are your orders?"

The radio was strangely silent; he heard no traffic from either Keryn or Adam. Rombard ducked as a round splintered the crate near his head. Looking toward the rooftops, the Oterian spotted not just the shooter who just nearly shot him, but also a number of others taking up positions on the tops of nearby buildings.

"Cerise, this is Rombard. I could use some help with those guys on the roofs."

"I see them," came her haughty reply.

A dark shadow passed over Rombard and Keeling as Cerise glided down from her high perch. Her machine gun was firing before she touched down on the roof, spraying the crouching rifleman. Turning, she fired again, catching a surprised Oterian in the chest. The fur covered sniper staggered backwards before falling over the side of the building. He caught the railing of the balcony under his chin before flipping and collapsing onto the hard–packed ground below, bloodied and broken. She continued firing into the other rooftop townsfolk, covering Rombard and Keeling below.

"Talon Six, what do you want us to do?" Rombard asked as he looked down at his Uligart counterpart. Keeling winced at the pain as he alternated stretching first one leg, then the other in an attempt to alleviate some of the burning sensation in his abdomen.

It wasn't Keryn who answered. Instead, a thick, gravelly voice cut into the radio traffic. "This is Penchant. We had some trouble at the port. McLaughlin is hurt pretty bad."

Rombard frowned and shook his head. Without waiting for a reply from anyone in the town, the Oterian preemptively responded. "Penchant, I can't raise Keryn on the radio. Secure the *Cair Ilmun* and get ready for an immediate evacuation." Turning his attention to the rooftops, he continued. "Cerise, I know you're worried, but don't you dare leave us right now."

Confirming his fears, he watched the Avalon launch from the roof and fly toward the port on the far side of town. With both Keeling and McLaughlin injured and Cerise gone, the Oterian knew he was on his own. His fears were even more reinforced by the fact that neither Keryn nor Adam had responded during any of the dialogue between the rest of the team. Rombard cursed loudly into the radio before reaching down and scooping up Keeling in one of his enormous arms. The Uligart curled into a ball and groaned at the sudden movement. Breaking their cover, Rombard sprinted down the street; Keeling's screams growing increasingly louder as the Uligart tried to stop the shaking in his intestines.

The town's blocks flew by in a blur as Rombard's massive legs picked up momentum and he charged toward the rear of the town. Around him, muted only by Keeling's yells of pain, the gunfire increased. He felt the sting of rounds grazing his muscular legs and arms and felt the bite of a round connecting with his left shoulder. Through it all, he continued moving, knowing that to stay in one place was certain death.

Though the air was full of the sound of gunfire, Rombard heard a single round echo through the air louder than any other. The town seemed to grow suddenly quieter as blood splashed across the Oterian's face. Staggering to a slow walk, Rombard looked down at the now silent body cradled in his arms. Keeling's head lolled forward, drooping limply and rolling from side to side. The entire back of his head was split open; his dark blood splashed across the Uligart's clothing and staining Rombard's fur.

Snarling, Rombard dropped the body and swung back toward the approaching townsfolk. Clutching his heavy rifle, the Oterian switched the selector switch to fully automatic as he braced himself for the impending recoil. As he squeezed the trigger, his ears rang from the sound of cannons exploding near his head. The bullets leapt from the end of the rifle in rapid succession, shredding the people who stood unprotected in the street. Shifting his aim, Rombard fired into a balcony laden with shooters. The torn bodies of townsfolk were visible only briefly before the entire area was consumed by a cloud of dust, as the rounds decimated the wood and plaster building behind them.

Though still outnumbered, the Oterian made great headway toward getting himself free of the town. Attaching another drum of ammunition to the bottom of the rifle, Rombard smiled at the red glowing barrel as he squeezed the trigger once more. He howled in anger at the townsfolk as he continued firing. Turning his aim once more, a bullet tore into the top of his right shoulder as another caught him in the side of the face. Staggering, he looked up and saw a pair of riflemen standing on top of a nearby roof. With Cerise gone, no one had stopped the militant members of the community from regaining the high ground. Though his shoulder ached from the gunshot, Rombard tried to raise his rifle toward the new threat. Both riflemen opened fire, the bullets tearing into the Oterian's body. His knees buckling, he slumped to the ground and stared up toward the dark cliff face. With a curse to the Avalon still on his lips, the Oterian's last breath slipped from his body.

They were dead. She knew it in her heart without even having to ask over the radio. The rest of the team was already dead and she and Adam would soon be following suit.

Keryn huddled behind the overturned table, feeling lost and alone. The townsfolk had yet been able to get into the building, but they were growing closer. Every time she had ever entered combat, the Voice had always been there to support her. Subconsciously, it guided her decision–making and military tactics. Though often unwanted, the Voice gave Keryn comfort when times were rough. Now, facing a staggeringly superior force, she realized just how alone she truly was.

The concerned calls on the radio had gone unanswered. Keryn yearned to reply, but simply didn't know the answer of what to do next. Her lack of confidence bled over her frustration, the two feeding one another until she felt unable to move; frozen in spot even as enemies grew even closer.

Adam continued to fight as though he hadn't noticed her pressed tightly against the protective table. His rifle fired time and again, sending assaulting townsfolk flying from the broken window. The street beyond was littered with bodies of those foolish enough to get within range of Adam's barrage.

Adam slid back down behind the table and reloaded his rifle. He glanced over at her huddled form, but Keryn barely acknowledged his presence. She pulled her knees tighter to her chest and wrapped her arms protectively around her legs, as she bit back the tears that stung her eyes.

Adam, to his credit, didn't belittle Keryn. He barely spent more than a second looking in her direction before continuing his reloading. When he spoke, his voice was barely over a husky mutter, barely audible in Keryn's ringing ears.

"I don't know what's going on in your head, but you need to get over it and fast. I know you're scared. I know this is new to you. But you only have one of two options. Either you fight with me, or we both die. I don't know about you, but I'm not a big fan of the latter."

Keryn opened her mouth to reply, but the words never came. She closed her mouth again and stared off at the wall.

"I got it," Adam continued. "You're not an infantryman. You're much better off behind the controls of a ship. You're good at fighting, but this really isn't your style. I understand all that. But I also don't give a damn about any of that. You don't get to choose your situations. You just adapt and overcome any adversity thrown at you. Believe me, I'm not happy being in this situation. But I sure as hell won't lie down and let these bastards kill me!"

Keryn whispered something softly, beyond Adam's ability to comprehend.

Adam looked around the corner, ensuring that no more townsfolk were approaching the open window. "What was that?" he asked over his shoulder.

"They're dead and it's my fault," Keryn said pathetically. "I led you all into a trap."

Adam turned sharply toward her. "Yes, you did."

Keryn looked at him in disbelief. She had expected a myriad of responses, but not that. Adam had always been her biggest advocate, and yet he was now just as quick to turn his back on her when she needed him.

He shook his head when he saw her stunned expression. "You led us into a trap. There's no denying that. But you didn't do it on purpose. You couldn't have known that the entire town was going to turn on us. So you led us into a trap. So what? That act alone doesn't make you a poor soldier or a poor leader. My last commander walked us right into a trap too. It cost a lot of people their lives. But to this day, I have nothing but the utmost respect for him."

"My point is, either you can sit here and feel sorry for yourself or you can accept that you made a mistake. You may have led us here, but you didn't kill us. Cardax did that. He turned these people into a bunch of bloodthirsty monsters. And right now, while we're discussing your shortcomings, he's making his way toward the port so he can escape this planet. I don't know about you, but I'd like to see him dead for what he did here."

Keryn nodded and took a deep breath. Having Adam as her voice of wisdom somehow filled the lonely void she had been feeling in her chest. The Voice was gone, but a new voice was quickly taking its place.

"Alright," she said, though her voice still quivered slightly. "What do we do now?"

Adam nodded in affirmation. "The first thing you do is get on the radio and let them know that you're still our leader. Get everyone back to the *Cair Ilmun* and let's make sure Cardax doesn't get away."

"We're surrounded. How are we going to get out of here?"

"You leave that to me," Adam said as he stood and moved

toward the back wall. He continued speaking as he worked, his actions hidden from Keryn's view. "People kept telling me that chivalry was dead. I don't believe that. I still firmly believe that chivalry is alive and well in some men. And a chivalrous man," he continued as he hurried away from the wall, "always opens the door for a lady."

As Adam hurried back toward the table, Keryn could see the metallic object affixed to the wooden wall. Adam gestured toward the object as he covered his head with his hands. "You may want to cover your face."

No sooner had Keryn protected her face between her knees than a concussive blast ripped through the room. Though the blast was focused into the wall, Keryn could still feel her ears pop from the sudden change in pressure. Coughing away the thick dust that now filled the room, she squinted in order to notice the large hole shorn through the back wall. Beyond, Keryn could see the scrub brush and the long, flat desert that marked the outside border of the town.

"Ladies first," Adam motioned as he shook plaster and wood slivers from his hair.

Together, they rushed through the hole and turned toward the space port.

CHAPTER 40

Iana wanted to vomit.

Her stomach was being pulled inside out as she tumbled through the wormhole, her *Duun* fighter rebounding off the flowing walls of the distorted tunnel. Being able to see the exit to the tunnel so close ahead did little to alleviate the incredible disassociated feeling she experienced throughout her body. Her limbs barely felt like her own as gravitational distortions appeared throughout the cockpit, pulling blood flow in multiple directions throughout her body. Though she maintained her grip on the ship's controls, her knuckles were sickly white.

Sirens filled the cockpit as the internal sensors warned of microscopic hull breaches forming throughout the ship. Iana had been lucky to survive the first warp when the Squadron appeared behind the satellite grid. Had she another choice, she would have never put herself through such torture a second time. Unfortunately, Iana found herself with little other choice. Terran fighters had skimmed the atmosphere, remaining under her radar as she tried to keep Yen and his team safe. By the time she had noticed the fighters, they were too far away to catch before they would reach the *Cair Thewlis*. Left with no other option, Iana had risked her own life to warp closer to Earth. Though only a few hundred miles, the trip through the wormhole felt like an eternity.

Gritting her teeth, Iana gritted her teeth and accelerated toward the end of the tunnel. Smoke was now starting to trail from one of her machine guns under her left wing. It boded ill, since the machine gun carried a large complement of ammunition. Iana hoped it wasn't a fire. If the ammunition belts ignited, she wouldn't have to worry about seeing Yen and his team killed. She'd be dead long before that happened.

Finally, much to Iana's relief, the blue and green planet at the end of the tunnel came fully into view as she was launched out of the end of the wormhole. Disoriented and sickened, it took a moment to gain her bearings. Earth was now significantly closer than it had been before, but that didn't mean that Iana had warped to the right location. Scanning her radar, she let out a sigh of relief as the three Terran fighters appeared directly below her. Aside from the structural damage to her ship, Iana's warp had been perfect. Angling downward, Iana dove toward the three unassuming fighters.

Her rockets were launched before the Terrans were able to register that an Alliance ship had inexplicably appeared on their radars. Splitting their formation, one of the fighters climbed to intercept Iana while the other two continued skimming the atmosphere. Her plasma rockets streaked downward toward the darting fighters. The first two missiles struck the atmosphere and exploded prematurely, the tension causing the warheads to detonate. Sparks of plasma soared across the sloping atmosphere, filling the sky below with a dancing spectacle of lights. The third rocket, however, found its target, detonating near the engine well of one of the fighters. Consumed in flame, the Terran ship broke apart.

Instead of taking evasive maneuvers, Iana charged headlong toward the advancing Terran fighter. The one closing the distance with her was not her main concern. She knew that he was only a distraction; a tool to keep her preoccupied while the other fighter began its strafing runs against the *Cair Thewlis* and Yen's team. Whether or not she destroyed the closer ship, she would have to bypass it eventually to reach the skimmer, the one she considered to be the much larger threat.

Fire leapt from the front of the Terran fighter as it climbed toward Iana. Turning into a barrel roll, Iana watched as tracer rounds flashed by the cockpit. Her *Duun* fighter jerked as bullets pierced her right wing. She glanced nervously out the window, but saw that the damage was minimal. Armored plating had been stripped away and shredded, exposing the wing's mechanical inner workings. But, as far as she could tell, the wing was still fully operational.

Pressing down on her console, Iana returned fire. The forward machine gun, the one located under the nose of the *Duun*, fired first, filling the space between them with hundreds of rounds of hot metal. As the Terran turned to dodge the barrage, she opened fire with both the machine guns located under the wings of her ship. Not surprisingly, the machine gun under the left wing refused to fire. Pounding on the controls, she saw more smoke starting to billow from the weapon that had been damaged during her second warp.

Even without the second machine gun, her damage was done. The Terran fighter was struck repeatedly along the back half of the ship and small spouts of flame jutted from the punctures. The damaged fighter still continued forward, though its movements were now significantly more jerky and unsteady. Cutting her controls to the side at the last possible moment, Iana flew harmlessly past as the fighter continued its flight out further into space.

With the path now clear to the Terran fighter below,

Iana accelerated into a steep dive, intent on attacking the ship from an angle that exposed the most surface to her assault. With the entire top of the ship open to her, Iana smiled broadly as she began firing her full complement of working machine guns. Round after round struck the atmosphere below the Terran fighter as he dodged and weaved in an attempt to shake her relentless attack.

Furrowing her brow in frustration, Iana dove closer, ensuring that her next volley would be fired from a much closer range. Her *Duun* fighter shook angrily as she pushed the controls forward, the damaged wing responding with trepidation as Iana approached the friction–filled atmosphere. The tones from her targeting array sounded wildly as her computer searched for a lock on the shifting Terran ship. Falling into place behind him, she stayed in stoic pursuit until she heard a solid tone, a satisfying notification that the Terran was now firmly in her sights.

Squeezing on the trigger, flames leapt forward as tracer rounds coated the hull of the Terran fighter. Smoking, the fighter pitched forward, its tail end flipping up above the cockpit. Angling downward, the fighter struck the atmosphere at an awkward angle. The friction from the atmosphere shredded the Terran ship as it pitched and rolled into a glowing ball of flame. Debris from the ship was cast far and wide, spreading like sand over the surface of the planet.

Satisfied and exhausted, Iana pulled up and began her flight back toward Alpha Two, who was still flying through the large open space between the satellite nodules and Earth below. Though weary, Iana knew that she had bought Yen all the time he should need to complete his mission. She hoped, however, that she had also bought herself some time to unwind. The Terran counterattacks, rightfully so, had been constant. Though she didn't expect that to change now, she reveled in the momentary silence.

The silence, as she already knew it would be, was short lived.

"Alpha Leader, this is Charlie Four!" a harried voice called over the radio. "I have multiple launches!"

"From where, Charlie Four?" Iana asked, the exhaustion evident in her voice.

"From everywhere!"

Iana sat up in the pilot's chair and checked her radar as other calls began filtering through.

"…entire southern hemisphere has launched ships…"

"…got multiple launches from previously unrecorded space ports…"

"…hundreds of ships heading our way. It looks like everything the Terrans have left has just been launched…"

The radar was filling with red dots. Though nervous, her pilots were right in their assessment. This was the final push for a determined and desperate Terran defensive fleet. Feverishly typing on the console, Iana tried to calculate just how many ships they were now facing, but quickly lost count. If she had to guess, she would say that her remaining Squadron was now outnumbered twenty to one. Even if over half of those ships were the improvised fighters, she still doubted that they really stood a chance, especially not in the closer confines of the orbit around Earth.

Flipping a switch, Iana killed all the traffic from the Squadron. Pilots continued to yell in frustration, but their ships were no longer transmitting to the rest of the fighters. It was a rarely used kill switch that suadron commanders and, in Iana's case, close subordinates, had installed in their ships. When Iana spoke, her voice cut over all the other traffic and was clearly heard by ever remaining pilot in the Squadron.

"Have all the *Cair*s safely made it to the surface?" she asked, her voice calm and confident.

Though the replies were hesitant at first, they all quickly realized the necessity for answering quickly. "Roger, ma'am," a gravelly voice replied as Iana let off the silencing switch on her console. "All remaining *Cair* transports have made their drops on the surface."

Iana grimaced. She was glad that the transports were safely on the planet but if the Terran ships regained air superiority, then the ground forces were still very much in danger. As far as Iana was concerned, that really only left her one option.

"All Squadron elements," she ordered over the radio. "We need to buy the ground forces some more time. Break orbit immediately. Let's see if we can pull as many of the Terran ships away from Earth as possible."

She turned off her radio and sped past Alpha Two, who fell into position beside her, and the pair launched past the dormant satellites and into the open space beyond. Behind her, filling the radar, dozens of Terran ships pursued.

"You want me?" she muttered. "Then come get me."

CHAPTER 41

"Iexpected more out of you," the Terran called, clicking his tongue in disappointment. "I thought you were going to be a real challenge. You've turned out to be just another toy that I'll break much too soon to fully enjoy."

Yen wiped the spittle from his mouth with the back of his hand. The Terran psychic had attacked thus far with frightening power, tossing Yen aside as though he were little more than a ragdoll. Standing, Yen brushed the dirt and grass from his uniform and faced the Terran. "Who are you? What do you want?"

The Terran shook his head. "It's not that easy, Yen. If you want to know who I am," the psychic explained as he pressed a finger against the side of his head, "you'll just have to come find out for yourself."

Anger brewed beneath the surface as Yen faced the psychic. The Terran was full of an unfounded arrogance, an arrogance that would only end when Yen humiliated the man. Though the Terran spoke with surprising confidence, he had yet to see what acts of retribution Yen was capable of committing.

If the psychic was foolish enough to mock him, Yen would show the Terran what he could do. Smiling, Yen rose to the challenge. The air around him shimmered and danced as he concentrated, building up the psychic energy within him. In a furious blast, Yen launched the psychic power forward, eager to drive it into the Terran's mind. He would not only tear away the information he sought piece by piece from the Terran's brain, he would leave the Terran's mind shattered and broken.

Yen's eyes glowed blue as the underlying psychic energy all around him emerged like pockets of light amidst a drab and grey world. The plants and grasses remained unchanged, though they looked lackluster and bland; none of their vibrancy and life remained. The water turned dark and bottomless, stretching like a starless night. In stark contrast, however, the Terran stood like a funeral pyre. A rainbow of colors swirled around him like a blaze, burning far brighter than Yen had ever seen before. Concentrating further, Yen was consumed by a similar fire as he stood and stepped toward the psychic.

As he approached the Terran, the earth beneath his feet shook violently. Bursting from the ground, a perfectly smooth, dark grey wall sprang up between them, reaching higher than Yen was able to see. The Terran's smiling face was the last thing Yen could see before being completely confronted by the impassable wall. Resting his hand against the wall tentatively, Yen could feel only a single word whispered as though from a thousand mouths:

Achilles.

Yen knew that this was just a trick of the Terran. It was a mental block, creating an impasse between Yen's mind and that of the other psychic. The wall was meant to block Yen's intrusion into the other's thoughts. And, try as Yen might to break through the wall, he found it an effective defense. Slamming his fist angrily against the wall, Yen felt the physical projection firmly beneath his hand. A small sliver of dark grey material broke free of the wall and fell to the ground, where it evaporated into a fine mist. Sheathing his hands in blue energy, Yen slammed his fist repeatedly against the wall, slowly chipping away at its impressive might. Beyond the wall, radiating like a lighthouse in the drab, grey world, Yen could sense that his persistence was an annoyance to the Terran.

As his fist connected once again with the wall, Yen felt a terrible psychic backlash. Lifted from his feet, he was hurtled backward, where he fell to the ground. As his eyes focused once more, he found the wall gone. Lively greens had once again infused the trees and grass, and the fine, misting rain once again fell on his face. Glancing left and right, he realized that he was on the ground exactly where he had been before approaching the psychic. Everything that had happened – the wall, his attacks, and the backlash – was all a projection from the Terran's mind. He had shown Yen exactly what he wanted him to see. The Terran had toyed with Yen as though he were insignificant. Anger raced through Yen's veins at the thought of someone so passively ignoring him.

"Achilles, is it?" Yen asked acidly.

"That is the name my father gave me," Achilles replied coolly. He showed none of the frustration and anger that saturated Yen's body.

Yen rubbed his temple as he tried to wash away the dull ache behind his eyes. He had never heard of a Terran psychic wielding as much power as Achilles did. It was unusual, unnatural. A sudden realization washed over Yen. Achilles was, indeed, unnatural. He was an abomination.

"Your father? You mean Doctor Solomon," Yen replied. "Growing a science experiment in a test tube hardly makes him a father."

For the first time, Yen noticed anger on Achilles' face. "I was born of flesh and blood, old man! And Doctor Solomon *is* my father. He did more for me than my biological father ever could!"

Yen brought his knees up underneath himself. Behind him, he let a blue tendril begin to manifest in his hand. "You're a genetic freak, Achilles. How much do you want to bet that you weren't the first psychic the good doctor tried to create? And what do you think he did with all the others?"

To Yen's surprise, Achilles laughed. The Terran's emotions rolled unabated from one end of the spectrum to the other, the man hardly in control of his own bizarre mood swings. Yen stared at Achilles with a hint of fear creeping up his spine. Mental instability was a dangerous trait for a psychic. If he wanted to defeat the Terran, Yen would have to strike quickly.

"Of course there were others," Achilles replied. "And every one of them was found to be unworthy of my father's praise. Only I was powerful enough to survive!"

Yen wrapped his fingers around the tendril as it grew in length. "And let me guess: if I want to get to your father, I'll have to go through you?"

"Close, but wrong. Whether or not you want to get to my father, you'll never get through me alive!"

"We'll see about that," Yen replied coldly as he brought his hand around from his back. The blue tendril elongated as it flashed outward, striking out like a whip. The air cracked as though from a lightning strike, as the whip struck the hard stone slabs near the pond. Achilles, however, was no longer standing on the stones. Looking quickly left and right, he found the Terran standing a dozen feet away, laughing maniacally.

"Your thoughts are imprinted in the front of your mind for all to see. I knew you were going to attack even before you did!"

Growling, Yen lashed out again and again with the

psychic whip, its glowing blue length lighting up the area around the two warriors. Every time Yen struck, Achilles had already moved out of the way, his body little more than a blur as he constantly shifted his position just out of the way of the assault.

Retracting the whip, Yen made the tendril rigid like a spear. Leaping to his feet, he charged Achilles. Lunging forward, he drove the spear directly at Achilles' heart. This time, the Terran didn't dodge. Instead, quicker than Yen could follow, he reached out and grabbed the end of the tendril before it reached its mark.

"You are going to have to do much better than that," Achilles mocked. A wave of psychic energy rolled down the length of the spear and passed into Yen's arm. His entire body felt on fire as the energy rolled through his nervous system. His head rocked back in pain and a scream passed his lips. For the second time, Yen was lifted from his feet and thrown backwards. Soaring through the air, Yen collapsed into the shallow, rectangular pool. The frigid waters enveloped him and Yen quickly sat upright and coughed up the cold water. Wiping his dripping hair from his eyes, Yen looked to the confident Achilles.

Infuriated, Yen felt his blood burn with hatred as he looked at the Terran. Caught unaware once again, Yen had been tossed aside; humiliated by this Terran freak. Coughing, Yen's gaze boiled with a deep seeded rage. "What are you?" he yelled in disbelief. "What do you want of me?"

"What I am is not important," Achilles chuckled softly. "You're asking all the wrong questions. If you want to know about me, you should know who I *was*, not who I *am*." Achilles' eyes flared with emotion as dormant memories rolled through his mind. "I was not always my father's son. Once, long ago, I was the son of another man, a merchant on a planet near the Demilitarized Zone."

Achilles jaw tightened as he remembered painful memories. "I had a mother once, too. She was kind and beautiful. But she died. They both died. They were killed by your people: mercenaries and soldiers with nothing better to do than annihilate an innocent merchant town. My biological parents did nothing wrong, but they were slaughtered by your kind."

"You want me to feel sympathy for you?" Yen retorted. His goal, Doctor Solomon, was only a few hundred feet away. Yet instead of extracting his revenge, he was busy being thwarted time and time again by the doctor's science experiment. "How many innocent civilians have been killed on the Alliance worlds? How about the millions that died during the Empire's Manifest Destiny Directive? Who gives a damn if your parents died? The best thing that could have happened is if you had died with them. And if you stay in my way, I'll make that a reality!"

"With what?" Achilles replied, his calm demeanor reasserting itself. The emotion was now vacant in his voice. He spoke as though the conversation about his parents never happened seconds before. "Will you make another whip for me? Your biggest failure, Yen Xiao, is that you are too stuck in the physical world. You have vast, untapped potential, but you waste it on these pathetic whips and spears. People like you and me could rule the universe, if only you had the mind to master your powers. Instead, you find yourself rooted in what you can see and touch."

"You have no idea what I'm capable of," Yen growled.

"Oh, but I do," Achilles replied. "Your mind is an open book to me. I can see the recesses of your subconscious where you push your true powers out of fear. You don't believe me?

Then think about all the times you have been a dominant power in battle. How many times have you defeated an enemy because of your psychic strength? And yet you are so easily defeated by me. It's pathetic. I thought you would be a much better challenge, especially after my father mentioned you by name. But if this is all you can do, I hardly see a reason to keep you alive."

As Achilles walked forward, mirror images of him began to separate from the original. First ten, then twenty duplicates of Achilles strode forward, each moving independently of the others. Glancing back and forth, Yen felt a stab of fear in his chest. He knew that this was only happening in his mind, but try as he might he was unable to break free of the illusion. Standing in the water, Yen formed a pair of psychic whips, one in each hand, and began striking the closest of the images.

One by one, the false images faded from view under Yen's assault. Disrupted by the new psychic power, they wavered and disappeared. For every one destroyed, however, another seemed to materialize before him. Staggering backward, Yen sloshed through the pond as he moved closer to the monument at the far end. The images closed in, growing progressively closer despite Yen's fevered attempts to destroy them. He had no idea what these images would be capable of should they reach him, but he had no intention of finding out.

"Old fool," a voice whispered from behind him, alerting Yen to the danger moments before a pair of open palms struck him in his lower back.

An explosion of pain rocked Yen's body as he was lifted effortlessly into the air. Suspended and paralyzed, Yen was turned slowly around until he faced the darkly smiling Achilles, who stood hovering above the lake's surface, his hand upraised as he lazily spun Yen in circles.

"I had thought to keep you around, so that we might learn from one another," Achilles said angrily. "But I realize now that there is nothing that I could possibly learn from you that I do not already know. You have no intrinsic value to me. You're nothing more than my puppet. But like all toys, I've grown weary of playing with you. I'm no longer a child, so I must discard my childish things. Goodbye, Yen Xiao."

Achilles' outstretched hand closed into a fist and Yen felt his throat constrict. Though he struggled for air, Yen was helpless to stop the Terran from choking the life from his body. Instead, Yen could only glare in rage as he struggled to draw breath.

CHAPTER 42

Through the hole in the wall, Keryn and Adam slipped into the cool desert night. They slid along the buildings, trying to leave as little a silhouette as possible in the bright moonlight. Aside from the occasional gunfire, the town had taken on an eerie silence. Keryn took a deep breath and hoped that the tentative ceasefire that had existed when Adam was guarding the window to their building would hold for a while longer. As long as the townsfolk continued to believe that a deadly gunman was waiting just inside the room, they would be hesitant to approach the building. Keryn hoped that the diversion would buy them enough time to make it out of the town's limits before they realized the dupe. The thought of running like a madwoman toward the landing field with an entire armed town in pursuit did not appeal to her.

Staying low, the pair moved from box to barrel, constantly scanning the area ahead as they moved from one cover to another. Passing alleyways that led back to the main thoroughfare through town, they paused and peered toward the lamp lit main street. Unlike the shadowy darkness through which they moved, the setting sun had automatically activated the flickering lanterns that illuminated the two main roads through town. As Keryn's eyes moved up the cliff face behind town, she could see similar lanterns lighting the length of the switchback trail. Craning her neck, the pinpricks of lantern light stretched the entire height of the plateau's face before disappearing at the crest of the plateau's top.

From within the glowing pools of light, Keryn could see townsfolk moving. They moved with an air of caution, though their awkward graces as they tried to slip stealthily within the shadows made it apparent that they learned their techniques more from console videos and less from actual soldier training. Frowning, Keryn felt pity for the simple citizens of the town. Their vision clouded by the large sums of money that Cardax had poured into their meager lives; they were willing to toss aside their morals and self-respect just to protect their new way of life. They were willing to die for a smuggler about which they knew next to nothing. Would they be so willing to die for him if they knew that Cardax had sold out the Alliance? Keryn wondered if they would so willingly accept the Oterian's money if they knew just how much he had soaked it in blood beforehand.

With a nudge from Adam, she slipped from behind her crate and passed the exposed alleyway. Though the town was relatively long, the end quickly approached. From the end of town, the desert opened up, leaving little protective concealment. The pair would have to move quickly but carefully to avoid detection. Looking up, Keryn both admired the myriad of stars while simultaneously feeling disappointed that there weren't any clouds hanging in the sky. The large disk of the moon stole away many of the shadows that they could have used to move undetected. Instead, the silvery illumination would leave them exposed while they ran away. Still, she had seen the unimpressive marksmanship of the townsfolk. Once they made their break from the town, she doubted any of the pursuing gunfire would even come close to them.

Lost in her bemusing, Keryn nearly ran into a figure as he detached himself from an upcoming alleyway. She started bringing her pistol to bear on the new target before she caught the moonlight glistening off the cool metal of the figure's pistol, trained on her chest. Deep in thought, she had let a civilian get the drop on her. Keryn scowled at her own ineptitude. Her frown deepened as she realized that she knew the figure.

A confident smile spread across the Uligart's face as he looked back and forth between Keryn and Adam. "I warned you that you should have just left town. We don't like when people threaten our source of income."

"The storekeeper," Adam grumbled. "From Yako…"

"*Yuchurio's Imports*," the Uligart hastily corrected. "You two just couldn't leave well enough alone, could you? You had to stick your nose where it didn't belong. Now your friends are dead and you're about to be turned over to the person that killed them. I'd be surprised if you saw tomorrow's sunrise!"

"You don't have to turn us in," Keryn offered.

The Uligart turned sharply on her. "Of course I do!" he hissed. "Do you have any idea how much money Cardax will pay me for capturing you both?"

"It seems like you've got your mind set on it," Adam interrupted, his voice getting a little louder than the whisper they had all been using. "You might as well call out and let the rest of the town know where we are."

"Keep it down!" the Uligart ordered. "You think I'm going to get other people involved and share my fortune? No, you're mine and mine alone."

Keryn looked down and noticed the gun wavering slightly in his hand. His grip was awkward, as though he didn't usually carry a pistol. She didn't notice the traditional calluses that would mark a steady gunman. The Uligart's hands seemed smooth, the hands of a storeowner and not a gunfighter.

She took a step forward, smiling broadly. "First of all," Keryn said condescendingly, "this isn't the first time I've had a pistol pointed at me, nor will it be the last. Go ahead and put that thing away before someone gets hurt."

The Uligart took a step back, his eyes locking intently on the Wyndgaart woman. "Stay back," he stuttered.

"And secondly…" Adam rumbled as he stepped forward. His hand shot out in a blur, catching the pistol near the trigger well and smashing the Uligart's fingers between Adam's fist and the pistol's grip. With a grunt of pain, the pistol went flying from the storekeeper's hand and was lost in the desert beyond.

"…you really should have called for help," Keryn finished as she stepped forward.

The Uligart's eyes opened in surprise as Keryn's knife slid smoothly into his abdomen. The sharp blade slashed through organs as she turned the knife upward until the tip of the blade entered the Uligart's right lung. He opened his mouth to scream, but only a gurgle escaped. He leaned forward, his weight falling on Keryn's shoulder. Slowly, as she supported his weight, she lowered the storekeeper down to the hard, desert clay as his blood soaked his shirt and pants. Once he was firmly on the ground, Keryn leaned back and looked at the Uligart, who looked surprised but peaceful on the ground. With a sharp twist, she pulled her knife free, splashing her own arms with the Uligart's dark blood. She angrily realized how much she wanted to do the same thing to Cardax. Looking up with a renewed determination, Keryn led Adam out of the town and into the desert separating the mining community from their landing field.

The gunfire Keryn expected never came. Whether their distraction worked better than she had anticipated or the townsfolk had lost their heart once Cardax was gone, she didn't know. However, she counted her blessings as she and Adam sprinted through the tough shrubs that littered the desert floor. As they rounded the edge of the plateau and the landing field came into view, flames leapt from the bottoms of two of the ships as they ignited their burners and began lifting off from the planet's surface. The two ships seemed fairly nondescript, but Keryn knew that one of the two carried the traitorous Cardax. Increasing her speed, she sprinted the rest of the distance to the cleared landing zone. By the time she arrived, however, the air was thick with traces of burning plasma exhaust. The smell burned her lungs and caused her eyes to water. More importantly to her, though, was the fact that both ships were little more than distant specks on the horizon by the time she reached the nearest of the still parked ships. Cardax was getting away and she had yet to even reach the *Cair Ilmun*.

As they hurried through the smoky haze, the exhaust from the departing ships became thicker. The once distinct figures of parked ships became nondescript, amorphous shapes all around Keryn. She staggered forward, supported only by Adam's comforting touch on her back. Keryn's eyes burned and she coughed roughly as she searched for the telltale lines of the *Cair Ilmun*. With tears streaking from her eyes, she didn't notice the limp shape lying on the ground before her. Keryn's foot caught on the figure and she fell to her knees before the body.

"Stop!" Keryn yelled moments before Adam would have tripped over the body as well.

Adam stopped and pulled his rifle free. His soldier instincts took control as he turned, scanning for any nearby threat. "Is it one of ours or one of theirs?"

The body was face down before her and, in the darkness, it was hard to make out any details. Frowning, she slipped her hands underneath the body in order to roll it over. As her hands slid between the body and the sand, she felt them sink into a thick, tacky fluid. In surprise, she immediately pulled her hands away. Dripping from her fingers, a mixture of sand and blood fell from her fingers in congealed droplets.

Though she felt her stomach turn, she slid her hands back beneath the body and rolled it over. The face was badly torn and bloodied, but evidently Uligart. Keryn let out a sigh of relief and sat down heavily in the sand.

"It's not one of ours."

"There are more over here," Adam said coldly.

Keryn didn't bother looking at the other torn figures that were strewn around them. She already knew how they would appear. The Uligart's stomach had been torn open and the exposed entrails were coated in sand. The man's throat had also been torn away, leaving a ragged wound from ear to ear. Keryn felt bile rise in her throat at the sight. While she hoped that this was the work of one of her teammates, she feared that they had met a similar fate.

From behind her, sand crunched beneath a heavily booted foot. Keryn leapt to her feet and pulled her pistol free as Adam turned toward the sound as well, his rifle at the ready. From out of the smoke, a humanoid shape emerged. The pink, fleshy skin and straw-like hair showed predominantly Pilgrim features, though most of his skin was covered in blood. His arms were held defensively before him, his palms outward, in a sign of peace. Despite the reassurances that the Pilgrim was unarmed, Keryn and Adam didn't lower their weapons.

As they watched, the fleshy skin began to peel away from the Pilgrim's hands and face. It sank beneath the surface, revealing the cold, smooth Lithid exterior. The clothes themselves melted as well, all part of the illusion created by Penchant as he walked unnoticed through the landing field.

With a sigh of relief, Keryn lowered her weapon. "Penchant. Where is Cardax?"

The featureless face motioned toward the stars above. "He left on one of the two ships."

"Which one?" Keryn asked impatiently.

Penchant looked toward the distant horizon for a moment before turning back and shrugging. "I don't know."

"You don't know?" Keryn asked indignantly. "How can you not know? This was your one responsibility!"

"I was a little busy!" Penchant yelled back, his voice sounding like boulders crashing together. The Lithid motioned toward the bodies strewn about. "Cardax left us a present while you were gone."

"McLaughlin," Adam interrupted. Keryn, too, remembered the radio transmission saying that the Pilgrim had been injured. "Where is he?"

"Cerise already took him into the *Cair Ilmun*, but he has been hurt pretty bad. He was standing close to a grenade when it exploded."

"Rombard and Keeling?" Adam asked, though he lacked the conviction in his voice.

Penchant shook his head. Keryn felt her heart sink. She had no doubt that Rombard and Keeling were already dead. Now, with McLaughlin injured as well, that nearly reduced her team in half, and they were no closer to capturing Cardax. Grimacing, Keryn realized that she no longer wanted to capture Cardax. To hell with the High Council and their directives. Keryn had every intention of making the Oterian pay for what he did to her team on Pteraxis.

"Get in the ship," Keryn said sternly. "We have a smuggler to kill."

"You mean catch?" Adam asked.

"I didn't say catch."

Without another word, the trio, led by Penchant, found the *Cair Ilmun* and climbed aboard. A part of Keryn wanted to go to the medical bay and check on McLaughlin. The more sensible side, however, knew that the more she delayed, the better the chance that Cardax would escape. Instead, she turned toward the cockpit and strapped herself into the pilot's chair. Bypassing the majority of ignition protocols, Keryn cold started the engine and, within moments, the *Cair Ilmun* was lifting off the planet's surface.

She didn't give a warning when she began a heavy acceleration within the planet's atmosphere. The conflicting gravities between the planet and the inhibitors on the ship made her feel even queasier then before, but she knew that Cardax had a head start. She no longer had the luxury of patience. When they hit the atmosphere, Keryn was nearly tossed from her seat by the impact. At first, the *Cair Ilmun* skipped like a stone against the protective layer around the planet. Finally, the ship eased through and rocketed into space.

As telemetries came online, the console before her showed two distinct engine signatures. Though they passed through the atmosphere at the same time, they immediately branched off. One began a slow arc away, heading toward the back side of the sun. The second hurtled away from the planet on a trajectory that would take it far outside the system. Keryn immediately read through Cardax's strategy. The smuggler would burn at a high acceleration out of the system in order to save himself, while his support craft would hide behind the sun and launch a surprise attack once she began pursuit. In a normal scenario, Keryn would have been impressed by his tactics. In fact, she would intentionally destroy the guarding craft first before pursuing Cardax. This, unfortunately, was a far from normal situation. Aside from her desire to kill Cardax, the *Cair Ilmun* had been heavily outfitted with state of the art armor and weapons. Even if Cardax's support craft ambushed them, Keryn stood a strong chance of destroying both ships with minimal damage to the *Cair Ilmun*. Confident that she was making the right choice, Keryn accelerated toward Cardax's ship.

Though she watched the radar to ensure the guardian ship was still traveling toward the sun, Keryn's focus was on the plasma engine burning brightly before her. With the modified engines, the *Cair Ilmun* was quickly catching the fleeing craft. Reaching forward, she entered a series of commands into the console and brought her weapons online. A compliment of plasma rockets activated in the launch tubes beneath each wing. Machine guns whirred in preparation for the pending assault. Within the cockpit, Keryn's violet eyes burned with rage and revenge. Though Cardax was fleeing at maximum speed, he would soon be within targeting range.

On the console, the targeting array turned from green to red, indicating that she was finally within range to fire her first volley. Keryn snarled as her hands fell to the console and she uploaded the final data to her missile launchers. With all preparations completed and Cardax's ship within her sights, Keryn's finger hovered over the firing mechanism.

With a pang of remorse, Keryn remembered the training her team had gone through together on the Revolution. Rombard's stern leadership, McLaughlin's carefree attitude, and even Keeling's overbearing confidence; all the memories burned in Keryn's chest and brought stinging tears to her eyes.

"This is for all of them," she whispered into the quiet cockpit. "Burn in hell, you bastard!"

Pushing the firing button, four plasma rockets launched from underneath the wings of the *Cair Ilmun*. Streaking through the empty space, the smoky trails locked on to the fleeing ship. Though it tried to dodge the missiles, it was futile. The rockets struck the back of the ship nearly in unison. The small transport, laden with extra fuel cells, erupted into flames that consumed the entire ship. As the flames died away, scorched sections of the ship drifted free, filling the view before the *Cair Ilmun* with a sea of debris. Sobbing with relief, Keryn sagged in the pilot's chair.

The silence in the cockpit seemed stifling as Keryn laid back in her chair. Aches that she had ignored all day suddenly assaulted her senses. Her neck tightened to where she wasn't sure she would be able to turn her it from side to side. Along her shoulders and arms, Keryn felt a tight burning from overuse. Exhaustion seemed to infuse every cell of her body. At the same time, she began to feel immediate regret. Their team had been sent on a specific mission: to capture Cardax and learn anything they could about Deplitoxide. Instead, she had let her emotions overwhelm her common sense. In an act of retribution, she had destroyed the one lead the Alliance had on stopping the latest threat. Resolved to her fate, Keryn reminded herself that with Cardax gone, there was a slim chance that the Terran Empire would ever find a resupply of the dangerous chemical. Though Deplitoxide would be a threat in the immediate future, the Terran stores would eventually run dry. Satisfied in her attempt at justification, Keryn allowed herself a thin smile.

Opening her eyes, she noticed a blinking light on the console. She had an incoming transmission, though the source was unknown. Could the High Council already know that she had failed her mission? Keryn had heard of the seemingly omnipotent power of the Council, but doubted that even they could have learned that she killed the smuggler instead of capturing him as she had been ordered. Still, her hand shook as she reached out and pressed the blinking button.

"And I was starting to worry that you weren't going to answer," a familiar Oterian mocked as his full visage appeared in the console's monitor.

Keryn's anger surged back to the surface. Cardax was still alive. She scrambled to read the radar and noted the second ship rapidly approaching the outer gravitational pull of the sun. As it grew closer, its speed increased exponentially. The second ship was never trying to hide on the back side of the sun. All along, Cardax intended to use the sun's gravity as a slingshot in order to escape. And Keryn, blinded by emotion, had fallen right into his trap.

"Oh, don't look surprised, little girl. You won't catch me now; I can save you the trouble of trying to do the math. But you did great; better than I would have ever expected. But like I guessed, your best just wasn't good enough."

"You bastard!" Keryn yelled into the monitor. "I'm going to find you! I don't care how long it takes, I will find you and I will kill you!"

"Such attitude," Cardax said condescendingly. "I have no doubt that you'll chase me. In fact, I'm counting on it. But last time I underestimated you. It won't happen again. Next time we meet, I'll make sure you're good and dead before I leave the planet."

"I swear that you will never get away from me."

Cardax looked at something below the monitor screen. "I'm sorry, little girl. It seems that I'm losing the transmission.

Apparently I was too busy escaping to keep you within range."
The Oterian shrugged. "Oh well, until next time. Bye now."

With his parting words, the screen went black. Keryn howled in rage as she slammed her fist into the console until her hand was raw and bloodied. Collapsing in emotional turmoil, Keryn fell back into her chair and cried loudly into the lonely cockpit.

Chapter 43

"There are so many of them!" Alpha Two bemoaned over the radio.

"Forget about them and just keep flying," Iana ordered as she sped away from Earth. "If we don't draw them away, the ground forces won't stand a chance."

Though Iana sounded confident on the radio, she felt the same fear that was evident in her Avalon counterpart's voice. The radar showed hundreds of Terran launches, as wave after wave of fighters and impromptu vessels joined in the chase of the fleeing Squadron. What she originally assumed was twenty to one odds was quickly growing, and not in her favor. She had heard the cries of her fellow pilots as they were struck by machine gun fire and plasma rocket explosions; the Alliance ships being destroyed in the dead of space and left as little more than obstacles for the rest of the Terran ships to bypass as they hunted down the rest of the Squadron.

Pressing her accelerator to the maximum, Iana's *Duun* fighter launched from Earth's orbit and sped through the dark void of space. Her fighter fought against her, and the controls threatened to be pulled from her grip, as she sped through the darkness. The damaged wing, the one that had been pierced repeatedly by Terran machine gun fire, wobbled unsteadily under the increased gravitational pressures. Closing her eyes momentarily, Iana prayed to whatever God would listen that her fighter would stay together just a while longer.

Iana wished she had a better plan than she did. She had left orbit around Earth under the assumption that she could lure the Terrans away, but once she was free of the satellite ring, she realized that she was flying blindly in a solar system that she didn't know. Leading the rest of the ships, Iana dove into an asteroid belt. Weaving through the chaotically drifting boulders, Iana tried to buy both her and her team time to devise a plan. Typing hastily on her console, she brought up a display of the planets, hoping to find another inhabitable planet nearby. The reports she scanned were incomplete and unhelpful. The Empire had settled on a nearby red planet, but the current orbit took it to the far side of their sun. The Terran sun was too hot to fly to the closer planets and beyond the inhabited red planet, it became little more than gas giants. Still, seeing little other option, she turned and sped at full speed toward the closest of the gas giants and the largest planet in the system.

Sweat beaded on Iana's brow. The gas giant was still some ways off, though she could make out the distinct white and brown strata of the planet's gaseous exterior. A number of small moons orbited the planet, but offered little assistance or escape for the fleeing Alliance force. For now, Iana was forced to fly through unobstructed empty space while hundreds of enemy ships pursued and continued a steady rate of fire on her small *Duun* ships. Flying at top speed, the improvised ships were lagging behind but the Terran fighters were still keeping pace. Their haphazardly fired plasma missiles streaked by, filling the space in front of Iana's ship with choking grey smoke. It obscured her view of the planet but, simultaneously, gave her cover as the Terrans were now unable to lock onto her position.

Dipping her wings, she spun lazily lower, hoping the change in position would further complicate the enemies' weapons fire.

Concealed within the smoke, Iana turned back to her console, eager to search for any hint that might give her the edge she needed to survive this battle. The gas giant's moons offered little reprieve, being little more than empty rocks. The planet itself, however, offered quite a few more possibilities. It seemed to be radiating a significant amount of both heat and radiation. Though they were far from the amounts present near the sun, the levels of radiation were still high enough that they might be used as a blanket that would scatter radar signals. If that were the case, the Terrans would have to fire manually without computer-aided targeting arrays. Since most pilots were unused to that style of fighting, it gave yet another boost to the Alliance forces.

Aside from the radiation, Iana also intended to use the intense gravitational forces being emitted by the gas giant. Much like the Alliance Cruisers had done before in order to hurry from one destination to another, a fighter could sling shot around the planet and open a significant gap between itself and any pursuing enemy.

Iana switched on her radio and spoke over the Squadron-wide channel. "All Squadron elements, head toward the gas giant. Getting close to the planet should diffuse the Terran radars and buy us some more time."

"I think I'm already ahead of you on that, ma'am," Alpha Two called back.

Iana checked her radar and was surprised to find that the Avalon was right. While Iana was diving in order to avoid the Terran rockets, Alpha Two had passed her by and was now on her way toward the gas giant, quite a few miles ahead of Iana's *Duun* fighter.

"Roger, I've got you on radar," Iana confirmed. "Stay on course and I will catch up to you shortly."

Another vibration rolled through Iana's ship. Glancing out the window, she could see scraps of metal, peeled back by the Terran machine gun fire, flickering as though threatening to tear free. Beneath, she could see ice crystals forming on the intricate network of wires and cables within the wing's core. The *Duun* fighter wasn't made to sustain long, exceptionally fast flights like she was now experiencing, much less two wormhole jumps and exposure to repeated enemy fire. Her *Duun* fighter was reaching the end of its life expectancy and was quickly dropping Iana's life expectancy with it.

"Hold together, you piece of crap," Iana growled as she tried to compensate for the damaged wing. In her cockpit window, the smoke cleared from the rockets and the gas giant came into view. Though still some ways off, Iana now dared to hope that she would reach it before the Terrans caught her. As to what she intended to do once she was there, that still remained to be seen.

"Alpha Leader, I've got a problem," Alpha Two called to her. "I'm getting some pretty serious fluctuations on my command console."

Iana furrowed her brow in concern. She wondered if this wasn't another Terran trap. "What sort of fluctuations?"

"I..." the Avalon began before pausing. "I don't know. My radar is going haywire. Controls are jerky and growing unresponsive!"

"Get yourself out of there," Iana said nervously, sensing that there was something going on that she couldn't understand. "Alpha Two, do you copy? Alpha Two?"

Other ships began calling over the radio, experiencing similar issues. Iana ignored them, instead angling her ship toward her wingman's position. In the distance, she could see the *Duun* fighter, its engines still burning brightly as it sped forward. Its path, however, was erratic, taking Alpha Two first toward one of the faint rings of small stone debris before launching her back in the other direction. From the chaotic flight pattern, Iana was sure that the Avalon was no longer in control of her ship. Her new trajectory, Iana noticed, now had Alpha Two flying into danger. One of the planet's moons had passed into view and was moving in an intercept course with the small *Duun* ship. Dwarfed by the moon, her counterpart wouldn't stand a chance in a collision.

"Alpha Two, get out of there!"

She didn't reply and Iana watched in horror as the *Duun* fighter slammed into the moon, creating little more than a minor explosion on the moon's surface. Iana cringed, and then shook her head slowly. The anguish of losing yet another pilot pained Iana. The loss also caused a deeper confusion within her. She knew that flying straight ahead was a death trap. Whatever had disabled Alpha Two was doing the same to a number of the Squadron fighters that passed too close to the gas giant. Behind her, however, hundreds of Terran ships were still gaining on her. If she slowed down, even for a second, they would catch her and destroy her ship. From her current position, there wasn't even time to adjust her angle and fly away from the gas giant. Gritting her teeth in frustration, Iana realized that she didn't truly have much of an option. Iana continued forward and charged toward the planet. If she were going to die, she wasn't going to give the Terrans the satisfaction of pulling the trigger.

Almost immediately, Iana's consoles began to flicker as something interfered with her electronic systems. Her *Duun* fighter tilted slightly, changing its flight path. She pulled hard against the controls and managed to realign her trajectory. No sooner had she regained control of her ship, however, that it was pulled violently in the other direction. The screen flickered wildly before fading to black. She tugged on the controls, but they moved limply in her hand without having any effect on the ship. The engines still burned at full speed, unaffected by whatever had taken control of her ship, but she had lost the ability to maneuver. The memory of Alpha Two flying uncontrollably into one of the gas giant's moons ran through her mind and Iana frowned at the thought.

Suddenly, Iana was jerked to the right, nearly pulling her from her seat. Her shoulder slammed into the cockpit's glass window, bruising the skin, as the seat restraints bit into her flesh. Awkwardly, Iana pushed back against the alien force and slid back into the seat. She slowly felt the tugging sensation building again, threatening to pull her in another direction. Along her waist and boots, the sleeves of her one-piece flight suit, and the buckles of the restraints, Iana felt the tug growing. She realized, in horror, that it wasn't a Terran weapon that had disabled her ship. It was the planet itself. On top of the radiation, the gas giant was emitting an incredible magnetic field, one that was strong enough to short out her controls while leaving the ship itself intact. Alpha Two's erratic flight pattern suddenly made perfect sense as she passed from one part of the field to another. And Iana, foolishly, had flown right into the field without a second thought.

Realizing that her fate was now in the hands of chaotically overlapping magnetic fields, she slumped in her chair and stared out the front window. Though she had been jerked from side to side repeatedly upon entering the field, it seemed that her pattern had now stabilized. Growing closer to the planet, the nose of her *Duun* fighter angled away from the gas giant's core. Instead of flying headlong into the atmosphere, it appeared that the magnetic fields would keep her skimming along its surface.

A knot grew in her stomach at the thought. The planet was creating intense gravitational fields as well as the magnetic fields. She would be slung around the edge of the planet; much like the Fleet had done when advancing on Earth. The difference was that she would not be in control. Instead of being able to slow or control her rapid acceleration, she would simply be along for the ride. Iana found herself wondering if either she or her ship would be able to survive such an intense trip.

The forces began pulling on her fighter and it sped up rapidly, quickly outstripping the normal capabilities of her engine. The inhibitors did little to lessen the pressure that began to build on her chest and limbs. The skin on her face grew taunt and strained as the speed increased; Iana found her arms pinned to the sides of the pilot's chair.

Speeding around the planet, Iana covered half the circumference of the gas giant in mere minutes. Air was stolen from her lungs and she strained to find replacement breaths. Pain lanced through her joints as the acceleration increased beyond the realm of what was safe for a pilot. The vibrations she had felt before returned with such ferocity that it jarred her in her seat, despite the gravity holding her in place. Rolling her head to the left, she stared out the window at the already damaged wing. It shook in opposition to the bouncing the rest of the ship was experiencing. Sheets of metal peeled away as piping within the wing's interior collapsed from the force. With a loud screeching, the wing tore down its center, half of the wing ripping free and tumbling out of sight.

The loss of the wing unbalanced her *Duun* fighter and

catapulted Iana free from the decaying orbit she had been in around the gas giant. Weight slammed into her skull as her fighter tumbled away from the intense gravity; sparks of light danced in her vision briefly before fading, replaced instead by a hazy darkness that crept along the edges of her sight. The world seemed to close in tightly around her as unconsciousness found root in the recesses of her mind.

Angrily, Iana bit her lip to stave off the weariness that she felt. Struggling, she reached out for the controls, fighting against the pressure on her limbs. As her fingers closed around the controls, she battled with the ship, slowly stopping the spinning and haphazard flight until, eventually, she regained a small semblance of control.

Alone, gasping for breath and moaning against the pain she felt throughout her body, Iana fell heavily into the pilot's chair. Her controls were still sporadic at best and the radar was not functioning. Her trip had taken her most of the way around the gas giant, meaning that she had been expelled somewhere close to where the Terran forces now lay in wait. Shaking her head slowly, Iana wondered why she had bothered. Her ship was now severely damaged and she had no idea the scope of her own injuries. And, throughout all of her pain and suffering, she had wound up almost directly back where she had started, staring down a Terran assault group.

Through the cockpit window, Iana could see some of the Terran fighters breaking away from the main pack and moving in her direction. Judging from their movements, she assumed that they knew where the danger areas were around the gas giant and were quick to avoid them. The fighters moved to intercept her, leading Iana to believe that she had been tossed completely clear of the magnetic interference. A small smile spread across her face, a mirth that didn't reach her eyes. Though she appreciated the irony, she didn't find the humor in realizing that the gas giant had only thrown her free of its grasp after completely disabling her ship. In essence, it had left her debilitated but left the dirty work of killing her to the Terran pilots.

Letting go of the controls, she crossed her arms across her chest and stared at the approaching pilots. Stoic to the end, Iana refused to look away from her executioners. Rapidly, the Terran fighters closed the distance until she was sure that they were within range of their deadly missiles. Frowning, she stared straight ahead, a sense of dread filling her chest and making it hard to swallow.

To her surprise, the closest fighters erupted in flames; obliterated within seconds from an unseen enemy. The rest of the Terran fighters turned quickly and tried to speed away from Iana's *Duun*. As they fled, dark projectiles shot through the air from somewhere beyond Iana's view, striking the Terran ships and tearing unceremoniously through their thick hulls.

In the distance, the swarm of Terran ships scattered and tried to flee. Blue and purple plasma filled Iana's vision as the entire universe in front of her erupted into flames. Small fighters, silhouetted in the explosion, sped away only to be consumed by the rolling shockwave as rocket after rocket exploded in the empty space.

As Iana stared in awe at the devastating firepower, a dark shadow passed over her ship. Looking upward, Iana stared into the dark underbelly of an Alliance Cruiser as it passed overhead, still raining down its rail gun slugs and large yield plasma rockets on the surprised Terran forces. In its wake, another Cruiser passed, followed by yet another. From around the far side of the gas giant, dozens more Cruisers entered the solar system and destroyed the fleeing fighters.

All around her, walls of metal appeared as her *Duun* fighter was swallowed by an open Cruiser hangar bay. In front of her, the large hangar doors slid shut and her *Duun* set down heavily on the metallic floor. Alliance soldiers hurried to her ship to render aid. Iana smiled as they cut away on the cockpit, trying to free the trapped pilot within. Her salvation had come not in some carefully devised plan by her and the other members of the Squadron. It had come instead from an Alliance Fleet who was willing to fly at such incredible speeds that they arrived ahead of schedule.

Finally, after all she had been through, Iana allowed tears to stream down her face. The Fleet had arrived. In her heart, she knew the fall of the Empire was now inevitable.

CHAPTER 44

Yen's lungs screamed for air as he was suspended in the air above the rectangular, manmade pond. Achilles' psychic, vice-like grip tightened around his throat, choking out what little oxygen remained in his body. Though Yen struggled against the Terran's power, he was helplessly trapped. There was no physical hand crushing the life from his body against which he could break free. And with a lack of air clouding his mind, Yen couldn't find the mental clarity to concentrate on severing Achilles' psychic control. Instead, Yen felt his limbs growing heavy as darkness crept into the corners of his vision. His legs slowly stopped kicking in the cool, damp breeze. His arms clawed weakly at his throat before flopping, limply to his side. The muscles on the sides of his neck tightened until it caused Yen physical pain, but he was unable to find the smallest iota of breathable air.

Through the haze of his vision, Yen could see the mocking smile of Achilles, staring up from his place on top of the water. Though Yen could see the Terran's lips move first as if forming words and then laughing heartily, the sounds never penetrated Yen's ears. All he heard was the pounding of his fading pulse rushing through his head, sounding like the beating drums of a war party on the march, moving off toward a distant kill. Yen hated Achilles; he hated everything the Terran was. An abomination, a scientific experiment, unnatural. To a pure born psychic, the fact that Yen would soon be killed at the hands of a freak of nature was abysmal. Even though he neared death, a furious rage still burned through Yen's body. If he could only find a way to break free, Yen would exact a most painful and permanent revenge on his Terran counterpart.

Even as Yen's consciousness faded away and the beating in his ears retreated even further, a single gunshot split through the rain-soaked air. Achilles staggered as blood sprayed from his shoulder. The shot had only been glancing, barely grazing Achilles; a much less impressive shot than Yen had hoped for. Achilles' reaction to the gunshot, however, was remarkable. His concentration broken, the Terran sank into the water, finally coming to rest with the pond lapping above his knees. Turning, Achilles was able to raise his psychic shield before a volley of gunfire erupted from the tree line to Yen's left. The rounds ricocheted off the wavering red shield in front of the Terran as Achilles threw his arms up protectively in front of his face.

To Yen's surprise, the pressure on his chest and neck began to lessen. Cold air slipped down his throat and burned his lungs, which cried out for more. In hitched breaths, Yen drew the moist air into his lungs and coughed painfully, feeling each breath burn agonizingly in his throat. As the psychic grip slackened on his body, so did the height at which Yen was being held. Slowly, Yen drifted back down into the frigid waters of the pond.

Yen, gripping his chest tightly, turned and watched as Achilles regained his composure. Stepping toward the Alliance gunmen, Yen's own soldiers who had accompanied him into the park, Achilles rose out of the water until once again he glided across the surface. The Alliance bullets continued to ricochet harmlessly away, none able to find a weakness in Achilles' defenses. Reaching out with both hands, Achilles closed his eyes as his outstretched fingers angled toward the trees behind which the soldiers hid. Quickly closing his hands into tight fists, the trees exploded one by one, the bark and splintered wood becoming deadly projectiles that flew into the faces and exposed flesh of the Alliance soldiers. Skin shredded under the assault, spraying the grass behind each of the men with gore. Only the soldiers' torsos, protected by the dense body armor, escaped the great punishment that the rest of their bodies endured. Collapsing to the ground, hardly recognizable as the once distinct soldiers they had been, Yen could only hear the weak mewling of the dying men from where he sat in the water.

Despite Achilles' ferocious assault, Yen managed a confident smile. In a moment, Achilles had annihilated four of Yen's best soldiers. But, simultaneously, he had shown something Yen had waited a long time to see: Achilles had a weakness.

Turning back toward his prey, Achilles frowned at seeing Yen pushing himself to his feet in the cold water. "I would have guessed that by now you would have had the common sense to die."

Yen coughed, his chest still aching from Achilles' last attack. "I never was a very quick learner."

Achilles strode forward dangerously, a predatory look in his eyes. "I'll just have to do a better job of teaching you this time." The air around Achilles began to flicker as he let the psychic energy build.

Yen backed away until he was near the short end of the rectangular lake. Behind the stalking Terran, silhouetted in the darkening sky, Yen could still see the large stone monument

414

watching like a sentient judge of the day's battle. Surprising Achilles, Yen didn't show a level of fear that the Terran would have expected. Instead, Yen smiled broadly. When he had been suspended in the air, Yen had wanted nothing more than another opportunity at revenge against the Terran. Given that opportunity, he wasn't about to let it pass.

"I think it's about time I taught you a lesson instead," Yen replied.

Yen quickly unclipped one of the grenades hanging on his belt. In a swift motion, he pressed the grenades activation button as he tossed it forward, its trajectory taking it straight toward the Terran's chest. Red lights flared to life around the equator of the grenade as the short fuse counted down toward detonation.

Opening his hand, his palm facing the grenade and Yen, Achilles laughed as the grenade came to a stop in midair, hovering only a couple feet in front of the Terran. The circling red light stopped flickering around the explosive as Achilles let out a hearty, crazed laugh.

"A grenade?" he said in disbelief. "The two greatest psychics in the universe face each other and you insult me by attacking with a grenade? What's wrong with you?"

Yen heard the faint cracking as the shell of the grenade broke apart along its seams. The individual outer plates floated away from the grenade's core, floating in an orbit around the rest of the explosive. From where Yen stood, he could clearly see the rest of the grenade's inner workings. Hovering, encased in red psychic energy, the detonator was separated from the rest of the explosive, pulled apart by Achilles' will.

"I had such high hopes for you, Yen," Achilles mocked as he began dismantling the core of the grenade. First, the explosive components fell harmlessly into the cool water at Achilles' feet. Then, he pulled apart the more volatile detonator and explosive caps. "I thought that you would show up on Earth like Death riding his pale horse. You would stream through the cities, leaving piles of Terran soldiers in your wake, piled like lost souls caught in eddies on the River Styx." Achilles let the last of the components drop into the water before returning his gaze to Yen, his eyes flaring angrily with inner red light. "But instead, you come to me with little control over your vast power. You are easily defeated without even so much as a strain on my part. Then…then when you finally show some inner strength, the best you can do is throw a meager grenade at me! You don't deserve to exist in my universe!"

"I'm not done yet," Yen growled. In rapid succession, Yen unclipped the other three grenades from his belt and launched them at the infuriated Terran. All three flew through the air in perfect arcs, guided by Yen's psychic power. And each of the three, much as the single grenade had done previously, were stopped before coming in contact with Achilles.

One by one, the lights went out around the circumferences of the grenades as Achilles deactivated their detonators. Howling in frustration, Achilles waved his hand and the shell around the first grenade exploded outward, exposing the core within. Yen didn't flinch as the shell rebounded off his psychic shield, glanced away, and disappeared into the surrounding darkness. Above the pair, as if in response to their own brewing anger, lightning split the dark sky.

"You're not even listening to me!" Achilles yelled as the rain grew heavier, splashing across the surface of the pond. "You have incredible untapped potential, yet you struggle to think of anything except the most mundane of attacks. I can't believe you would even waste my time with these… things."

"One of your…" Yen began before the words faded away.

He could feel his power building inside of him, rising like an unchecked tide coursing through his body. Swallowing hard, he continued. "One of your... biggest faults... is that you... underestimate people too much."

Blue tendrils of power arced across Yen's body, rolling as though his body were a lightning rod, conducting unseen sources of psychic energy. In front of Achilles, the grenades inched forward and the one on the far right flickered back to life. Snarling, Achilles focused deeper, shutting down the grenade once more.

"Here you are, nearly killing yourself, and for what? To inch a grenade just a little closer to me? In the end, I'm still more powerful than you will ever be. You're just delaying the inevitable!"

"Nothing... is inevitable," Yen gasped. His eyes watered as pressure built in his temple and the strain began to cause physical pain in his spine. Yen's cornea was consumed with blue as the energy saturated his body. From within his mind, Yen could hear the joyful chorus of the psychic power crying out at its freedom. Shivering from far more than the cold, Yen concentrated harder.

The metal casings that had been blown free from the first grenade launched across the surface of the pond, reforming around the grenade's core. With a flash of brilliant blue light, the shell reformed and fused together.

"Stop that!" Achilles yelled as the casing blew apart once more. This time, Achilles didn't bother angling the shards of metal toward Yen. Instead, the shell flew away and splashed into the water, joining the remains of its previously dismantled brother. "You're wasting both our time! You're a fossil, Yen Xiao! You're a has-been. You're little more than a footnote in this war! When I'm done with you, history books won't even remember you! Just lie down and die like a good puppy!"

Psychic power roared through Yen's core. His head whipped backward in surprise as the energy shattered through Yen's controls and countermeasures. Never before had Yen pushed himself so far or so hard. The anger which he struggled to contain merged with the psychic power and fed it, letting it grow like a sentient leech, feeding off Yen's own essence in order to defeat so strong an opponent. Blue tendrils broke free of the yellowed skin on Yen's back, reaching out like the legs of a spider. They reached around his body, snapping out toward Achilles like chained animals. At their tips, they elongated into razor–sharp spines and blades while still others formed hungry maws filled with row after row of saw–like teeth. Yen's power was free of his control and was eager for retribution against Achilles.

Even the Terran seemed startled by Yen's sudden transformation. He stepped backward in surprise, his feet skimming the water. The grenades before him gave chase, remaining only just beyond a foot away. Yen's lips pulled back into a malicious snarl as blue light poured from his eyes.

"Impressive," Achilles said breathlessly. "It looks like you're finally accepting who you are and who you have the potential to be." The Terran's eyes narrowed as he continued. "But it still won't be enough. You're wasting all this energy and you're still no closer to detonating these grenades!"

"I noticed... a weakness about you... Achilles," Yen said, his voice little more than a rumbling growl. "Science may have... given you the power... but your abilities... are limited. You don't seem... to be able to use your powers... to multitask."

Achilles seemed taken aback by Yen's accusation. Frowning, his nostrils flaring in anger, the Terran glowered at his enemy. "What makes you think I can't? I've focused on all three grenades simultaneously. And what about you? You've been straining all this time on these grenades and you're still not strong enough to get them to me! I'm still stronger than you!"

Yen smiled wickedly. When he spoke, gone was the breathy, weary tone he had taken before. "And what makes you think that I've been concentrating on the grenades?"

Lightning split the sky, revealing a massive shadow that blanketed the area around Achilles. In horror, Achilles looked skyward. Above him, held aloft by Yen's power, the giant stone monument hovered, its pointed tip turned downward like the point of an enormous spear. His body shaking, the Terran turned his gaze back toward Yen. Though Yen could feel the coppery taste in the back of his throat and could feel blood oozing from his nostril, he still smiled.

"You wouldn't," Achilles hissed in disbelief.

Releasing his psychic control over the monument, tons of stone came crashing down on top of Achilles and the grenades. The ground beneath Yen's feet shook violently, throwing him into the water, as the giant stones fell one by one on top of the Terran psychic. Sprays of water filled the air as the monument crushed the outer walls of the pond, sloshing its shallow waters into the soft, grassy earth beyond its borders. Clouds of dust billowed outward, stinging Yen's eyes and burning his already raw throat.

As the last of the stones fell to the ground, Yen pushed himself to his feet, brushing off what debris and dust he could. His hair was matted with water and grey dust and his face was pale white. Only his eyes still burned with the intense blue inner light, glowing brightly in the dark night air. Stepping out of the water, Yen shook himself free. Almost as an afterthought, he released the last bit of his psychic control. From beneath the piles of rubble, Yen smiled as he heard three muffled explosions; the final nail in Achilles' coffin.

Pain roared through Yen's brain as he staggered forward. Yen leaned heavily on one of the nearby trees and closed his eyes as tears cut tracks down his dust–covered face. His eyes closed, Yen didn't notice the blue tendrils that reached out from his body on their own volition. As he pushed away from the tree and tried to regain his bearings, the tendrils lashed out at the tree behind him, scoring long tears across its bark.

Yen's nerves felt like they were on fire, but a single thought was able to cut through his pain and distraction. Somewhere, close by, Doctor Solomon was hiding in his laboratory. The doctor had already suffered strike one when he mutated the Seques and killed so many of Yen's friends. Strike two was modifying Deplitoxide to disable the engines on Alliance Cruisers. And now, as though adding insult to injury, Doctor Solomon had created the abomination Yen had just faced. There would be no other opportunities for the doctor to become a God.

Anger boiled beneath the surface of Yen's skin as the tendrils whipped in anticipation. Not only would Solomon no longer play God, Yen would do one better. It was time to send the doctor to meet his maker.

CHAPTER 45

Cardax had escaped.

The words rolled through Keryn's mind like a poison, burning away her reason and leaving only a vacant, aching hole in her chest. The reality of her situation washed over her in crashing waves that threatened to drown her. Choking back sobs, Keryn lowered her head to her hands and let the hot, salty tears spill from her eyes.

Keryn had failed not just her mission, but she had failed her team as well. Regardless of Adam's comforting words on Pteraxis, she had led her team into a trap from which two of her teammates didn't survive. A third now lay in the medical bay, his blood smearing the floor beneath the operating table. With a sigh of resignation, Keryn realized that she couldn't even bring herself to go check on McLaughlin. Though she hadn't seen him since they climbed aboard the *Cair Ilmun*, she knew she couldn't face the accusing looks in the eyes of the surviving team.

Sitting in the cockpit, Keryn felt abandoned. Her hands drifted aimlessly toward the console and brought up the radar. The small red dot marking Cardax's ship was beginning to fade from the screen as he sped out of the galaxy. Soon, he would be beyond the *Cair Ilmun*'s radar range and would be unreachable. She knew that they should begin pursuit, but depression weighed heavily on her shoulders. She couldn't bring herself to activate the engines and begin the chase. Even if she did, Keryn wondered what the result would be. Would they catch Cardax on another of his bribed planets? Would she lead them into another trap? Would she have to watch the rest of her team die before she finally died herself?

The responsibility of leadership was a burden to Keryn, one that she had to bear alone. Except, she realized, she never should have had to bear it alone. There should have been someone supporting her, keeping her from trouble, and protecting her every step of the way. Had it been there for her, she might have been able to avoid the trap on Pteraxis, and Rombard and Keeling would still be alive. McLaughlin wouldn't be in the medical bay, fighting for his life. Keryn might have cut herself off from the rest of the team, but she was abandoned long before they ever reached Pteraxis.

Her pity quickly turned to anger as she yelled out into the empty cockpit. "Where are you? I know you're here! Answer me, damn you!"

I'm here, the Voice replied coolly. *I've always been here.*

Keryn bared her teeth in a snarl of frustration. "Don't you give me that condescending tone! Where have you been? I needed you and you abandoned me!"

I can't abandon you any easier than I can create my own body and walk away. I'm a part of you, whether we like it or not.

"My team was ambushed," she replied, feeling her anger grow at the Voice's blasé attitude. "Some of them died. *I* could have died! You don't care about that, do you?"

But you didn't die, the Voice hastily answered. *You are still alive, aren't you?*

"That's not the point, and you know it! My team needed you and you weren't there for us."

Let us clarify some things, the Voice said angrily. Keryn could feel its irritation in her mind. *You wanted me gone. You cast me out of your mind when you severed the merger between us. I may be a part of you, but I am also a sentient entity with the memories of hundreds of your ancestors in my consciousness. And I have* never *been as insulted by a Wyndgaart as I was by you. You used me for your own gain when you were in danger, but once that danger had passed, you cast me out. Banished me to a hell you can't begin to comprehend. So I'm sorry if I'm not overly sympathetic to your plight.*

Secondly, I'm not here to support your team. I don't give a damn if every member of your team dies. I only care if you die, and you didn't. If you had been in any real danger, I would have been there to save you. You don't have the prerogative to call on me whenever it suits you and then belittle me when I'm not needed. I have helped generations of your family and never have I been treated with such blatant disrespect.

If you want me to be there for you, we need to reevaluate our relationship.

"I don't want you here," Keryn said softly, much of her fire burned out.

Yes, you do, the Voice replied. *You forget, I can see everything you think. You're going after Cardax, which means you're intentionally going to try to get yourself killed. You're going to need me.*

There was a pause before Keryn replied as she tried to gather her thoughts. "What makes you think I'm going after Cardax?"

Because I know you better than you know you. Because you've never failed at anything you've ever done. You've stumbled along the way, but you've always overcome every challenge. Because no matter how insulted you felt about the assignment

423

when the High Council gave it to you, it is still your mission to complete. And, even if it kills you, you will get the information out of Cardax.

"So just like that, we're friends again?" Keryn chided.

We're not friends. We're more of a… symbiotic relationship. What I need from you, I take. What you need from me, I give.

Keryn felt the flare of anger again. "You make it sound like you have all the power, dispersing your well wishes whenever it suits you."

I told you we would have to reevaluate our relationship.

Keryn stood quickly up from the pilot's chair and turned toward the doorway leading into the rest of the ship. Though she couldn't escape the Voice, she knew the Voice was aware of the metaphorical turning of her back. "You may have to be in my head, but that doesn't mean I ever have to listen to you."

You are correct about that, the Voice calmly replied. *You don't have to listen to me. In fact, I'll do my best to stay quiet. But I'm never going away again, no matter how much you want me gone. I'm going to become more a part of you than you could have ever fathomed before.*

Keryn angrily stormed out of the cockpit and made her way back to the medical bay. As the door slid open, the faces of the surviving team members turned toward her. After their fight against Cardax's second ship, the entire team had been in the medical bay, checking on McLaughlin. Grimacing, Keryn looked each of the teammates in the face. She expected to see their condescension. And there was a look in their eyes, but it wasn't accusatory. It was concern, both for McLaughlin and, unless she mistook their intent, for her as well.

"How is he?" she asked, her voice barely more than a whisper.

Cerise slid out of the way, her body no longer protecting

the Pilgrim on the table. Keryn's stomach twisted at the sight. The mechanical surgery arms that extended from the medical bed were patching a number of smaller shrapnel holes. His right arm had already been amputated, leaving a smoothly sheered stump where the strong arm had once been. She could see the strata of the bones and muscles, exposed to the ship's recycled air. The burns on his face marred his once handsome looks. Much of his hair was burned away, leaving scarred and twisted flesh beneath. Though sedated, Keryn could still see the pained expression on his torn face.

"Is he..." she began, before the words caught in her throat. "Is he going to make it?"

Adam shrugged. "I don't know. The wounds aren't too severe. Though he won't be the same man when the surgeries are done, none of his wounds alone should be enough to kill him."

"However?" Keryn asked, sensing there was something Adam wasn't telling her. Judging from the saddened expression on Cerise's face, Keryn guessed that everyone else already knew what Adam was going to say.

"However, there's more to his injuries than just the damage from the grenade. Look at this."

Adam turned the medical console toward Keryn so she could see the screen. The blue tinted screen showed a series of near transparent cells, tightly packed against one another and elongated. Muscle tissue, Keryn realized. She turned toward Adam inquisitively.

"Just watch," he said.

As she turned back toward the screen, Keryn noticed invasive black cells, only a tenth the size of the muscle cells, sliding between the membranes. Almost as one, the black cells turned and punctured the outer membranes of the muscle cells. Keryn watched a fluid transfer occur between the cells as the black viruses deflated and died. The fluid, however, immediately began breaking down the structural integrity of the muscle cells. Within seconds, the majority of the muscle cells had ruptured, genetically degrading into a primordial soup.

Keryn turned sharply toward Adam, her surprise evident on her face. "Were those…"

"McLaughlin's cells," Adam finished. "They were a sample taken just minutes ago from his damaged arm. The grenade was laced with something; a biological agent that I can't identify. Once it gets into a person's system, it breaks down the body on a cellular level."

"You said this was from his arm," Keryn replied hopefully. "Maybe we stopped its spread when we amputated his arm."

Cerise sobbed loudly from the other side of the room as Adam shook his head. "We did scans at random points throughout his body. Whatever this is, it's aggressive. We've already found signs of it in his liver and kidneys." Grabbing Keryn by the arm, Adam pulled her close so they wouldn't be overheard. "Listen, I can give him a regenerative cocktail of chemicals that will greatly slow the break down in his cells, but I am way out of my league with this. This is Terran biological technology. I wouldn't even know where to start searching for a cure."

Keryn closed her eyes and frowned. "We may not know where to find a cure, but I know someone who might."

Without an explanation, Keryn left the medical bay and walked back to the cockpit. She closed the door behind her, typed furiously on the console, and entered a code that only she had been given. After only a moment's hesitation, the screen turned from blue to a dark black with a bright red

426

symbol emblazoned in its center. As the High Council's emblem faded, it was replaced by a dimly lit council chamber. Around the semicircular table, six high-backed chairs rested, the seats for the six members of the shadowy Council. To her surprise, only a single robed figure was present.

"Magistrate Riddell," the Wyndgaart Councilmember stated flatly. "You have failed to capture Cardax. Why is it you call us now?"

"I may not have captured Cardax yet, but I'm not giving up," Keryn retorted. "But I need your help right now. A Terran biological weapon injured one of my men. It's destabilizing his organs. There's nothing I can do for him here, but I hoped that you might be able to provide us with a cure."

The Councilmember crossed his hands thoughtfully before him. "Were we in a different situation, I would gladly provide you with a cure for his disease." Keryn grimaced at his tone and waited for the rest of his statement. "However, Pteraxis is not near any of our medical treatment facilities. It would be a long journey to get him the care he requires."

"That's fine," Keryn said, her heart pounding in her chest. "We can make a detour and drop him off, then get back on the trail of Cardax."

Keryn didn't have to look at the screen to see the Wyndgaart shake his head. "I'm sorry, but if you made such a detour, you would lose Cardax's trail forever. Your mission is too important to sacrifice for the well-being of a single soldier. Capture Cardax, and then bring us your teammate for treatment. Not before."

Slamming her fist angrily on the console, Keryn replied defiantly. "To hell with my mission! We're talking about the life of one of my men!"

"Do you defy the will of the Council?" the Councilmember

replied, his voice rising in irritation, if not anger. "You would do well to remember your place, Magistrate. Bring us the information we seek from Cardax, then we will provide the best care possible for your man. Not before!"

With a finality in his voice, the Councilmember ended the transmission, leaving Keryn staring at the bright red High Council symbol, which also soon faded from the screen. Clenching and unclenching her jaw, Keryn leaned back in the pilot's chair. Though she may not agree with the High Council, she had no options remaining other than to follow their directive. Whether to the Voice or now the High Council, once again she felt like the pawn of a higher power.

Inputting new directives into the console, a faint vapor trail appeared on the radar. Though Cardax had a sizeable lead on the *Cair Ilmun*, his plasma exhaust trail was still visible and easy to follow. Keryn typed in a new course and set off in pursuit before putting the system on autopilot and moving back toward the medical bay.

In the common room, she ran into Adam, who was coming up to see her. "What did your friends say?" he asked.

Keryn shook her head. "They said that we had better find Cardax, and fast."

Adam shrugged. "So, what do we do?"

Last time Adam had asked her that, she had hesitated. Her indecision had lost good men their lives and had irrevocably changed Keryn forever. This time, however, there was no hesitation in her response.

"We're going to find Cardax and I'm going to personally carve every bit of information we need out of his body."

CHAPTER 46

Yen was completely consumed by the power. Lifting the stone monument from the ground had pushed him way beyond what even he had thought possible. The result had been like opening the Pandora's Box of psychic energy and unleashing a hellish beast that opened its maw and swallowed him whole. Taking on a life of its own, Yen's power roared through his veins and set his brain alight. The pain was nearly unbearable and brought tears to his eyes. Yet he didn't fear his newfound power. Instead, he reveled in the freedom he felt, especially the freedom of knowing that he had evolved beyond that of his previous mortal limitations. The psychic power whispered to him, enticing Yen's mind with thoughts of domination over all that would oppose him. Smiling malevolently, Yen knew that the whispers were less of a new sentient voice and more an outlet to his own subconscious. Despite the physical pain, he had never felt more alive... or more powerful.

The power saturated his essence. Yen could feel it cascading like a waterfall through his body, igniting his nerves. His psychic energy filled him like a clay vessel until he was overflowing, yet the power still didn't abate. Blue tendrils of power rolled over his body like bolts of lightning, emerging from his back before submerging into the skin of his shoulder.

His eyes had taken on a dark, stormy color until nothing remained but the deep, flawless blue, like perfect orbs stolen from the heart of a storm cloud.

Though the power was invigorating, it was also taxing. Yen's breaths came in labored gasps and exhaustion spread through his limbs. Despite the weariness, he was driven forward by his own rage and anger, emotions from which the psychic power seemed to feed. And all his anger had a single target: the Terran doctor.

Standing before the columned exterior of the Terran scientific headquarters, Yen tilted his head back so that he could see the broad, metal letters printed above the large doors. The words were a jumbled mess to Yen; the universal translator implanted behind his ear did little to translate the written Terran language. Still, he didn't need to read the words to know what they meant. He had found what he was looking for. Behind those doors, Doctor Solomon hid in his laboratory. Yen could feel the Terran's mind and taste his palpable fear in the air as though the doctor were standing directly before him.

Alone, Yen strode to the doors. Pressing his palm against the cool wood, Yen could sense not only that the doors were firmly locked, but could also feel the presence of Terran soldiers hiding beyond. They thought themselves well protected behind their barricades and locked doors, but Yen knew better. There wasn't a place on the entire planet where they would be able to hide from Yen, should he choose to chase them.

Streams of blue energy flowed from his hand in all directions, some seeping through the narrow crack between the doors while others stretched outward, coating the edges of the wooden portal. Inside the building, the lock began to rattle as Yen's power wrapped its tendrils around the metal bar they had thrown over both doors as a locking mechanism. Despite the metal bar's incredible weight, Yen easily lifted it from its crook and dropped it onto the stone floor with a clatter. The measly deadbolt lock was also thrown aside, completely unlocking the door before the possessed psychic warrior.

Instead of simply opening the door, Yen's blue streams of power blew apart the metal hinges holding the massive doors in place. With a psychic thrust, the doors were lifted from the ground and launched into the room beyond. Their weight slammed into the defensive bunkers the Terran soldiers had erected, crushing many of the soldiers beneath their bulk. Stepping confidently into the room, Yen scanned the broken defenses of the Terran forces. A few members of the guard still survived, having dove to safety only seconds before the doors came crashing down on their positions.

Still climbing to their feet, the Terrans were helpless as Yen strode forward, piercing blue tendrils of energy whipping around his body. Lashing out, the tendrils elongated into razor fine points. Bypassing the body armor as though it didn't exist, the tendrils passed into the Terrans' bodies before becoming corporeal. Trapped within their bodies, the tendrils slashed back and forth like caged animals, eviscerating the Terrans from within. Gurgling on their own blood, the soldiers were helpless as the psychic energy shredded lungs, perforated stomach lining, and pierced hearts. Within mere moments, the remaining Terran defenses were strewn dead on the floor.

Yen closed his eyes and drank in the power that filled the room. The pungent scent of blood and death filled his nostrils and he took a deep breath. A sadistic smile passed across his lips as he stretched his arms outward, calling back his psychic pets. One by one, they withdrew from the Terran bodies and, snaking around, drove into Yen's. Each tendril that passed back into him filled him with a greater sense of calm. But Yen could feel an uneasiness on the edge of his consciousness. The power reveled in its own might, but Yen wondered just how much control he truly had. Much of what it had done thus far was a result of his own broken psyche. Eventually, Yen feared that the power might deviate from his desires and begin pursuing its own course.

Pushing such thoughts aside, Yen climbed the broad stairs that led to the building's second floor. His booted feet clicked on the hard marble floors and behind him bloody footprints marked his path through the science hall. Ahead, drawing him forward like a moth to a fire, brain waves of Doctor Solomon called out to Yen from down the darkened corridors.

"I'm coming," Yen whispered into the darkness.

Yen crested the stairs and found himself in a long hall. Closed doors confronted him on both sides of the hall, but Yen ignored them. They were little more than distractions, set there to lure Yen away from his true purpose. Fearlessly walking down the hall, Yen stepped between the narrow pools of light that were cast by the emergency lights set along his path. Casting only small circles of light, the rest of the hall remained enveloped in a cool and comforting darkness.

Ahead, Yen could sense his prey hiding within a room at the end of the hall. Undaunted by the gloomy darkness around him, Yen walked purposefully forward. So intent was he on the room at the end of the hall that he noticed little else. Yen was caught completely off guard when he heard the safety being switched off on the machine gun to his left.

"Move and I'll kill you where you stand," the Terran soldier said.

From his periphery, Yen could see the green glow of the soldier's night vision goggles. Focused as he was on Doctor

Solomon, Yen hadn't given a second thought to further Terran defenses around the doctor. Freezing in place, Yen sensed another Terran emerging from a doorway behind him.

"Get down on your knees," the first Terran ordered.

The power bristled beneath the surface. The Terrans were making a huge mistake by ordering Yen around. No one had that power anymore.

"Get down now!" the Terran reiterated, pushing the barrel of his machine gun against Yen's shoulder. A round fired from that range would kill Yen instantly. Yen had no intention of allowing the Terran to take that shot.

"I don't think so," Yen replied coldly. The energy welled inside of him and slithered from his skin like oil. The tendrils struck both Terrans before they knew what had happened. The tendrils passed through the soldiers' legs and wound up their spines before taking root within their brains. "In fact, I don't like either of your tones. When speaking to a God, it would do well to remember your manners. So why don't the two of you bow before me?"

From the corner of his eyes, Yen could see the closest Terran's body tense as he tried to fight the command. But with Yen's tendril rooted within the soldier's mind, he could do little other than obey. Turning around finally, Yen looked at both the Terrans, kneeling in protested reverence. Feeling their overwhelming hatred, Yen frowned. Before he realized what he was saying, Yen felt his lips moving of their own volition.

"Neither of you are worthy to worship me. You'd both be a much better sacrifice in my honor. Go ahead and kill yourselves."

Their hands shaking, both Terrans turned their weapons upward before cramming them under their chins, the barrels pointing toward their brains. Yen watched as their fingers hesitated on the triggers.

"I don't have all day," he said coolly.

The echoing gunshots followed Yen as he turned and walked down the hall. A few feet beyond the two Terran bodies, the reality of his actions slammed into Yen. Doubling over, he felt hot bile spill from his throat as he vomited onto the floor. The pain behind his eyes grew unbearable as it felt like he was burning from within. Hot, salty tears spilled down his face as he dry heaved onto the ground.

Fear finally gripped Yen's heart. Lifting the monument had been too much for his body to withstand. Now, having pushed his power beyond its limit, he no longer had control. Unwittingly, he had ordered a pair of Terrans to take their own life and, more importantly, they had so willingly obeyed. The thought sickened Yen as it frightened him. If he could so dispassionately order the deaths of the Terran soldiers, what else was he capable of?

Standing weakly, Yen stumbled down the hall. Though Doctor Solomon's signal was still clearly ahead of him, Yen took a moment to search the rest of the hall. To his amazement, he realized that there was no one else around. No more Terrans waiting in ambush. Finally, it would truly be a private conversation between Yen and the good doctor.

Yen reached out and pressed the button that should have opened the door. He didn't expect it to work. He expected Doctor Solomon to have locked himself inside, behind walls of protection. Yet, to his surprise, the door slid quietly open.

In stark contrast to the hallway, the interior of the laboratory was well lit. The bright light only aggravated Yen's headache, making him squint to make out the details of the room. Rows of tables covered with beakers and vials full of unidentifiable fluids filled the center of the room. View screens, some showing the exterior of the building while many more showed samples of specimens, lined the walls around the room. A single, massive monitor covered the entire far wall, though it stood black and silent.

Standing in the center of the room, an older Terran pulled his white lab coat tighter around his thin frame. Thinning white hair covered his head, though his face carried few of the lines Yen would have expected from a man of his age; another example of the extents of genetic and biological research that were being conducted within this facility. Yen had no doubt that Doctor Solomon had experimented on himself, granting himself extended youth and virility.

"Yen Xiao," the man said, his voice strong despite his age. "I have been waiting for you."

The doctor stood supremely confident, though Yen could still sense the man's deep fear. Though Yen had yet to say a word, a single thought dominated Solomon's mind: he knew that he was going to die today.

"Doctor Solomon. We have much to discuss, you and I."

Solomon shook his head and frowned. "No, we really don't."

Yen was taken aback by the doctor's audacity. He couldn't help but feel as though he was being led into a trap. But every time he tried to focus on that train of thought, his headache flared anew and drove all thoughts from his head.

Taking advantage of Yen's hesitation, Doctor Solomon continued. "You were ordered to take me in alive, but you and I both know that you won't do that. You want me dead, so I don't see that we really have much to discuss at all. Kill me, and let's get it done with."

"That's not the way this works," Yen replied, infuriated as the doctor raised his arms in order to expose himself to attack. "You die when and how I say you die! After all you've done, there is no way in hell that I'm going to make this quick and painless."

"Come on and do it already," Solomon mocked. "You know that if you let me live or, by some miracle I escape, I'll never stop my research. All the men you've lost along the way fighting against the Terrans will be multiplied tenfold if I survive. I will find every biological weapon at my disposal and unleash them on every Alliance planet. I will sit back and laugh as you all die horrible, plague–ridden deaths."

"Do you have a death wish, old man?" Yen replied, as much confused as he was angry. Whether Solomon had come to terms with his God, he was now fully prepared to die.

"I can't abide by cowardice," Solomon said with a grimace. "Either you kill me, or get out of my lab." Lowering his hands, the doctor leaned forward as though examining Yen for the first time. "You know, I think I was mistaken. You don't have the guts to kill me. Go ahead. Get out! Come back when you have the balls to do what needs to be done!"

Furiously, Yen sprinted across the room, grabbing Solomon by the front of his jacket. His head spun as the psychic power yearned to be unleashed. It reached out hungrily, nipping playfully at Solomon's hair and clothes. Try as he might, Yen found himself unable to reel in the probing tendrils. He felt as though his brain were swelling, soon to split his skull apart and spill onto the floor.

"Shut up, you bastard!" Yen growled.

"And if I don't," Solomon whispered, inches from his face. He seemed oblivious to the biting tendrils around him. "What are you going to do about it?"

"I'll tear you limb from limb." Again, Yen knew that the words weren't his, but the power bubbled dangerously close to the surface, consuming him from within.

"Then do it already and quit wasting both our time."

Yen felt his own energy drain from his body as the tendrils grew thicker and sharp fangs protruded from each of their ends. Serpentine, the tendrils whipped back and forth, ready to strike.

"Let him go, Yen," a familiar voice ordered from the doorway behind where Yen stood holding the doctor.

The tendrils turned and looked behind him, saving Yen the trouble of turning around. From the eyes of the tendrils, Yen could see Buren entering the room, the rest of his team in tow.

"This isn't your affair, Buren," Yen snarled in response.

"This *is* my business," the Uligart quickly retorted. "I know what your orders were. They were to bring Doctor Solomon back alive. And if you can't complete your mission, then you need to walk away before someone gets hurt."

Buren's thinly veiled threat did not go unnoticed by either Yen or Solomon.

"Don't listen to him, Yen," Solomon whispered. "Do what you want to. Kill me!"

"Shut up," Yen muttered to the doctor. As Buren's team spread out into the room, Yen felt his attention drawn in too many directions at once. Each tendril sent back the image of what it saw, unfiltered, directly into Yen's mind. He saw a dozen different images of the room like a kaleidoscope spinning in his vision. The nausea brewed once again in his stomach as he felt his control slipping away.

"Put down the doctor," Buren ordered.

"Don't listen to him," the doctor prodded. "You're in control here, not him."

"Both of you, shut up!" Yen said a little sterner. He shook

his head, trying to dislodge the confusion that festered in his mind.

"Kill me, you gutless coward," Solomon hissed.

Yen bared his teeth as the power surged in his body. The power was slipping quickly out of his grasp and there was little he could do to stop it.

"Drop him," Buren threatened, "or I'll drop you!"

Yen's head felt ready to explode, the pressure growing so great that Yen struggled to maintain consciousness. His organs felt like they were being turned inside out as the psychic energy filled every cell of his body. The power was bubbling quickly to the surface and there was nothing Yen could do to stop it.

"Do it now!" Solomon yelled in Yen's face. "Kill me!"

"I *will* kill you, Yen!"

Throwing his head back, Yen screamed as the psychic power erupted from his body. Waves of blue, pulsing energy rolled from him, filling the room. Doctor Solomon threw up his hand defensively, but they did little to protect him. The waves licked the Terran's body like hungry fire, feeding off a new fuel. The flesh on Solomon's arms and legs blistered and cooked, charring before flaking away in long strips. The softer flesh of his eyes, lips, and tongue boiled and melted under the assault, running in rivulets down his face. Choking on his own gore, the doctor collapsed to the ground as his body continued to cook away.

The expanding wave tossed tables haphazardly throughout the room, pushing them far away from Yen, who stood at the epicenter of the explosion. Hissing filled the air as bubbling chemicals mixed and scored long streaks in the stone floor. The Alliance soldiers caught in the wave were thrown against the wall, their bodies crushed from the force of the blast. Broken and bloodied, they fell unmoving to the floor.

Buren squeezed the trigger on his rifle as the wave rolled toward him. The round was caught by the psychic power before it could leave the barrel. Instead of firing toward Yen, the bullet exploded in the chamber, causing a chain reaction that ignited the other bullets in the magazine. The rifle exploded in Buren's face, shredding the Uligart's face with jagged strips of metal. Screaming in pain, Buren was thrown into the corner, where he clawed at his ruined flesh. A reptilian tendril of blue flame emerged from Yen's body and rushed across the floor toward the howling Uligart, consuming his body. Buren shook uncontrollably as he tried to break free of the scorching energy. Like the doctor before him, Buren's flesh was cooked away and his dark blood boiled and evaporated into the air.

As suddenly as it began, the serpentine tendrils and rolling flames roared back into Yen's body, leaving the laboratory quiet and dark. Coughing in pain and feeling both emotionally and physically drained, Yen staggered in the now eerily quiet room. Sparks fell from the shattered lights above his head, providing the only meager lighting in the otherwise dark room. No furniture or bodies, aside from that of Doctor Solomon, rested anywhere near Yen's standing form, which stood on the only patch of unburned ground in the entire laboratory.

Sighing, Yen felt the psychic power within him dwindling, as though the core of its might was spent. It left him feeling hollow, as he tried his best to regain control over the power that remained. Opening his watering eyes, Yen looked around him at the devastation he had caused. Barely discernable Alliance bodies were cast, forgotten, into the corners of the room, their bodies intermixed with twisted furniture and broken glass. All the monitors around the room were shattered, save the massive wall-sized monitor that had been protected by a thick screen.

Exhausted, Yen turned toward the exit of the room. He didn't know how he would explain what happened to either his remaining teammates or the High Council. At the moment, however, he couldn't concentrate on anything other than the horror of what he had just done. He was only vaguely conscious of Alliance soldiers at the doorway.

Yen was startled as bright blue light suddenly illuminated the room. Turning slowly, he faced the large monitor on the wall, which had since turned itself on. Entranced, he took a step closer as an image began to emerge. Slowly, the screen came into focus and Yen found himself staring at a familiar face.

From the monitor, the larger-than-life image of Doctor Solomon smiled back.

EPILOGUE

"My name is Doctor David Solomon. If you are watching this video, it means that I am already dead. Five years ago, I inherited the Terran Mutation Project that was created nearly one hundred years ago as a safeguard against invasion by the Interstellar Alliance. However, in all that time, the Alliance and the Empire have both stoically remained fastidious about the terms of the Taisa Accord. Both sides remained loyal to the non-invasion agreement and obeyed a no-fly zone through the approved Demilitarized Zone."

"Though both sides strictly obeyed the precepts of the Accord publicly, our spies sent back information to the Lords' Senate that the Alliance planned military operations against Terran outposts. I was approached, following this discovery, to turn the Terran Mutation Project from a defensive to offensive weapon. My results were spectacular! My shining accomplishment with the Project came with the modification of the Seque, a domicile load-bearing creature native to Alliance occupied space."

"My work with the Seque was highly successful. My experiment cost thousands of Alliance citizens their lives. For my part, I was lavished with praise by the Lords' Senate. It was truly the highlight of my career. At least it was, until a chance encounter with an Oterian smuggler flying through the Demilitarized Zone. After being taken captive, the Oterian revealed his cargo, a strange substance that was later designated as Deplitoxide. The disenfranchised smuggler agreed to provide more of the chemical to us, which we weaponized for rocket attacks against Alliance ships. Armed with the new weapons, I ordered the fleet into Alliance space."

"Initial tests were very promising, until the small fleet was destroyed by an Alliance counterattack. The rest, as they say, is history."

"It would have been the end of my story, except that I wasn't done with my research. Deplitoxide had too many uses outside of ship-to-ship engagements to be content with our results. The chemical's ability to transmute heat and energy had far reaching implications, many of which the universe will experience now that I'm dead."

"The Lords' Senate had approved one last bit of research, knowing that a strike by the Alliance was highly probable after we invaded their space. The research was as intriguing as it was revealing. The hypothesis of our research was simple: if the Deplitoxide had the ability to transform the engine fuel of ships into a black tar, then the effects on a burning sun would be catastrophic."

"To that end, the Terran Empire pre-positioned canisters of Deplitoxide in orbit around forty-three different suns in thirty-two galaxies. As this message is playing, signals are being sent to these canisters. If we can't defeat the Alliance by force, then we'll simply have to kill them where they live."

"While I know I will always be remembered for this brazen scientific gambit, I can only hope my research is continued by those who would not live under the yoke of Alliance domination. I was known in life; let me be immortalized in death."

YEN (MUIR'RATHI)

The Muir'Rathi were once a dominant race throughout the Known Universe. Born with exceptional psychic abilities, the Muir'Rathi served as aristocracy on their conquered worlds. While they lived in palatial estates, the Oterians labored in their factories and fields until an upstart Oterian led a revolution that overthrew the ruling class. Over the next hundred years, the Muir'Rathi were hunted virtually to extinction.

Three hundred years after the revolution, there are only a few Muir'Rathi remaining in the Known Universe and virtually none that serve in any capacity within the Alliance military.

Though their miniscule number is enough for easy recognition, their physical appearance is also unique among the Alliance races. Their yellow skin and dark hair are matched by a series of flexible spines that protrude down the length of their back.

Yen Xiao knew of his psychic heritage when he was recruited to a special operations team, assigned to defend the

Demilitarized Zone from Terran Empire incursions. Following the destruction of his team, he began realizing the expanded potential of his psychic powers and now utilizes his skills as a Squadron Commander onboard the *Revolution*.

ULIGART

The most numerous race in the Alliance, the Uligart have colonized hundreds of worlds throughout the Known Universe. This great diversity allows the Uligart to appear in nearly every level of Alliance leadership, both within the Fleet and the Infantry.

The Uligart's vast colonization enabled them to be the first race encountered by the Terran Empire, as it began its space exploration program. Despite the initial camaraderie the two races felt toward one another, their friendship fell apart following the destruction of a Terran colony ship at the hands of the Lithid. Terran declarations of martial law on planets originally claimed by the Uligart led to open hostilities, which also led to the Uligart leading the push for an Alliance against the aggressive Empire.

Although Uligart share many similarities with Terrans, to include general body shape and reproductive gestation periods, the Uligart are easily recognizable by their protruding bone structure. Along all major ridgelines on their body, the Uligart bones are visible as boney extensions. Most noticeable are the bones that protrude from the Uligart's face, specifically along the brow, hairline, jaw, and cheekbones.

ABOUT THE AUTHOR

J on Messenger, born 1979 in London, England, serves as a United States Army Major in the Medical Service Corps. Since graduating from the University of Southern California in 2002, writing Science Fiction has remained his passion, a passion that has continued through two deployments to Iraq and a humanitarian relief mission to Haiti. Jon wrote the "Brink of Distinction" trilogy, of which "Burden of Sisyphus" is the first book, while serving a 16–month deployment in Baghdad, Iraq. Visit Jon on his website at www.JonMessengerAuthor.com.

CPSIA information can be obtained at www.ICGtesting.com
Printed in the USA
LVOW08s0214141014

408468LV00002BB/7/P